A ROYAL
ROMANCE

Elizabeth Tudor

BACON-SHAKESPEARE

A ROYAL ROMANCE

BY
JAMES ARTHER

WILDSIDE PRESS

PRINTED AT THE VASANTA PRESS, ADYAR, MADRAS, INDIA

To her who faded,
Too early in the day,
Oh sweet white rose,
In life and death my love.

Between Writer and Gentle Reader

How to read the book ?
Let me tell you how it was written.

The sixth chapter, Lovers in the Forest, was the first to come to birth. The story of its inception is told in the opening page of that chapter. Around it grew the rest of the book. That first chapter was followed by A Royal Romance, the heart of the book, and for that reason placed first in the completed work to which it also gives the title. After that followed the last chapter, The Poet and God's Word. For, the fire of discovery once kindled, its light was thrown next upon the field of study, which at the time formed my special preoccupation. After that, discovery followed upon discovery, and the first rough sketches were made of Boars and Kindred, Bucks and Woodmen, Clown and Plantain, till my return to the East, and the irreparable loss of her who had been my good companion for thirty years, put a stop to the work for the time being. When calm was in a measure restored and the labour resumed, the last-mentioned chapters were completed, and Arcadia, Adversaries, A Tale of Two Brothers, and Two Loves I Have, added in a quieter vein of historical and literary research. The Introduction was written last, partly as a first guide for the student of the Baconian riddle, partly in the mood of a final reckoning with the Shakespeareans.
Only Bacon's Clock, Symbol, and Anagram ciphers have been more specially examined by me, and have yielded those discoveries for the sake of which the writing of this book was primarily undertaken. They form the substance of the second part, the first being of a less technical nature and of more general interest. The first chapter is based entirely on the Biliteral Cipher, the second principally on historical documents, the

third on *The Shepheard's Calender*, the fourth on *Two Gentlemen of Verona*, and *The Merchant of Venice*, the fifth on the *Sonnets* and *The Two Noble Kinsmen*, the sixth on *As You Like It*, the seventh on the *Spenser and Shakespeare Folios*, the eighth on the *Merry Wives of Windsor*, the ninth on *Love's Labour's Lost*, and the last on the *Black-letter Bible*.

Wherever I have been conscious of borrowing from the labours of my predecessors in Baconian and Shakespearean pastures, I have scrupulously acknowledged such indebtedness. If nevertheless anybody claims priority rights to some of my discoveries, he or she is cordially welcome to them and the ensuing honours. Laurels suit not me, a humble labourer in the field, offering the first-fruits of his hands to the Master of the land.

I would therefore say that the book might be read in somewhat the same order of its natural growth, as it came gradually to be put on paper. Start with the first chapter, and let the sixth immediately follow. Read these two if possible at one sitting. Then the tenth, seventh,[1] eighth and ninth, followed by the second, third, fourth and fifth, reserving the Introduction for the last, so as to round off the whole.

But Nature and the natural order are often odious to the logical mind, which in Art wants to outstrip the parent. As a concession to the intellect, which for most people has a stronger appeal than the mystical sense, that is to say for those who approach the Book and its Subject more with their mind than with their heart, I have arranged the chapters in their present, more methodical order.

If the Subject were not more to me—as I hope it may also be to some of my readers—than simply an historical personage of the past, however great a poet, philosopher and statesman, these remarks would not be appropriate. For me the historical in this case merges into the subjective and mystical. What is given here could not have been conceived, were it not for the inspiration, welling up from within and

[1] These four chapters have previously appeared in *The Theosophist*, August-November 1939, and April 1940.

derived from Him who is not only a human of a bygone age, but also the Divine Ideal of the present human me ; my Art, His Art ; my vision, of Him alone, as the eternal Poet, Philosopher, Sage in every man ; Body of Beauty, Body of Wisdom, Body of Power, manifesting in age after age.

Without Him this book could not have been written, and even so it has not been easily written. For, though reading English was slowly perfected from my early schooldays, speaking and writing English came rather late, after more than forty years of life had somewhat stiffened youth's suppleness of adaptation[1]. For defects in grammar and idiom, style and language, I therefore ask the reader's indulgence, " gently to hear, kindly to judge " of me, my book and my Subject.

To the latter this book is dedicated, next to her, " fair, kind and true," who was the light of my eyes, and still illumines my mind ; further to all who like myself have laboured in Francis Bacon's vineyard, that is to all known and unknown seekers for the hidden glories of his life and work.

---

[1] The author's name on the title page, hiding but slightly my own name by a re-arrange-ment of its letters, was not chosen for the purpose of secrecy, or anonimity, but to make it look and sound less foreign.

Contents

      Easter Sunday, 1623—My name and memory I leave to foreign nations, and the next ages—19. A people very far towards the sun-set gate, and a golden age of learning—20. Men's charitable speeches—Mine fame shall ring the earth around—21. A. W. von Schlegel, first Pre-Baconian, 1808—Delia Bacon, first Baconian, 1856—22.

      At Paris in our early youth, 1576—Making ciphers our choice—Used for the first time in *The Shepheard's Calender*, 1579—24. *Omnia per omnia*—Six ciphers : Biliteral, Word, Capital, Clock, Symbol, Anagrammatic—25. The Cipher of Ciphers, the chief of all my inventions—30. If England to itself do rest but true—32.

      Native wood-notes wild—Arden = Warwickshire ?—33. Revised and enlarged—34. Additions or omissions ?—35. Bad and good Quartos—36. Half of the Folio entirely new —37. Shakespearean chronology and contortions—38.

To The Onlie Begetter
Of These Insuing Leaves

Some glory in their birth ; some in their skill,
Some in their wealth, some in their body's force ;
Some in their garments, though new-fangled ill ;
Some in their hawks, and hounds ; some in their horse ;

And every humour has his adjunct pleasure,
Wherein it finds a joy above the rest :
But these particulars are not my measure ;
All these I better in one general best.

Thy love is better than high birth to me,
Richer than wealth, prouder than garments' cost,
Of more delight than hawks or horses be ;
And having thee, of all men's pride I boast.

3

Introduction

1.   BACON'S WILLS

BACON is Shakespeare.   That was his glory, his triumph.   But he is also Francis Tudor, son of Queen Elizabeth and the Earl of Leicester by a secret marriage.   And that was his bane, the hidden cause of his open disgrace.

Like the double-faced Roman god, who stands at the parting of the new year from the old, so at the close of his life must have appeared to Francis Tudor-Bacon his own state ; his public, Bacon-face entirely over-cast by the shadow of the past, his yet hidden Tudor-face turned hope-fully towards the uncertain light of the future.   Not until two centuries had run their course did that later light prove sufficiently strong to lift somewhat the shadow of the past.   At his parting from this life his spiritual vision was sufficiently clear-sighted to make him fully aware of the long time that must elapse, before his good name would be restored to him.   Yet he viewed the prospect with that serenity of mind which marks the truly wise, who even in this transitory existence live in the eternal, and never entirely lose sight of that state where time is as the twinkling of an eye, a thousand years as one day.

Bacon died on the 9th of April 1623 in the early morning of Easter Sunday, and his last will, published the year before, on the 19th of December, said : " For *my name and memory, I leave it* to men's charitable speeches, and *to foreign nations, and the next ages.*"[1]

Of men's charity there has not been great cause to boast, but the second half of his forecast has in part at least come true.   That the will

[1] Sp XIV 539.

was not hastily written, in a sudden moment of despair, but that the humiliating truth, namely that he had to leave his name and memory to *foreign* nations and the *next* ages, had been manfully faced by him, all the time since the injurious sentence pronounced upon him by the House of Lords on the 3rd of May 1621, is proved by a draft of a will, drawn up on the 10th of April 1622. The obloquy he had been subjected to had had such a fatal effect upon his health, that he thought his last moment had come. This will also reads: " I bequeath . . . *my name to the next ages, and to foreign nations.*" In its brevity this version is even more impressive than the final document.[1]

If we turn to the cipher, to which Bacon confided his secret life-story, we find that besides the restoration of his good name and memory, another point is mentioned, which had to remain unspoken in the public documents, namely the honours due to him as a poet. Thus, in the Biliteral Cipher embedded in the Shakespeare Folio of 1623, two years after his " fall," and three years before his death, we find the exalted resolve and fixed expectation : " I keep the future ever in my plan, looking for my reward, not to my times or countrymen, but to a *people very far off, and an age not like our own*, but a second golden age of learning . . . when all these works being seen of men, mine fame shall ring the earth around and echo to the Ages that are still far down Time's shadowy way."[2] The same hope in almost the same words is repeated in the cipher of Bacon's *Natural History*, published nearly ten years after his death : " I look out to that long future, not of years but of ages, knowing that my labours are for benefit of a *land very far off, and after great length of time is past.* Europe must also reap the great harvest still ripening as doth the yellow grain where the sunshine doth fall."[3]

The " people " or " land very far off " is evidently no country of Europe. There cannot be any doubt that the people of America to whom the Baconian problem is most indebted for its solution, are meant. If doubt still lingers on this point, it may be dispelled when we hear that land further qualified as lying " very far towards the sun-set gate."[4]

[1] Sp XIV 228.   [2] WG II 208.   [3] WG II 356.   [4] WG II 58.

The " age not like our own, but a second golden age of learning," also fits no other time so well as our nineteenth and twentieth centuries. That is to say, if the writer did not have in mind a still more distant future, and a still more enlightened time. For we cannot but admit that the moment of his full " reward," and the " fame that shall ring the earth around," has alas not even yet arrived.   Considering that two centuries of false belief and error had to be destroyed, we may perhaps be a little proud of the progress the Baconian movement has made in the last eighty years, but in its decisive triumph over unbelief and pre-judice we can certainly not yet glory.   That will probably be reserved to those " Ages that are still far down Time's shadowy way."

It may be doubted whether a mortal could look into the distant future and correctly describe the development of certain events, but Bacon's vision has been vindicated by subsequent history. In one respect only does his foresight seem to have failed, namely in his faith in " men's charitable speeches."   Or, was it just because of his fore-knowledge of his own countrymen's uncharitableness—as exemplified by the notorious cases of Pope and Macaulay, as well as of so many others, who may remain unnamed—that he expressly excluded them from the picture of the future, towards which he was looking for his reward? It cannot be denied that the role played by his compatriots in his rehabilitation has until now been only a secondary one. The Baconian movement still suffers the greatest resistance in the land of our hero's birth, a resistance emanating from the enormous vested interests of the higher, the edu-cated classes, the men of science and literature, of church and state, of municipalities and societies of all kinds.   These still wallow contentedly in the Shakespearean delusion, only now and then lifting up their heads to grunt their disapproval of the disquieting doubts that at times cannot but assail them.   The ignorance of the great inert mass of the popula-tion can naturally be moved by no argument.

There exist several copies of the 1621 draft of Bacon's will, all except one with only slight variations in the text. The wording of the one exception rests on the authority of Archbishop Thomas Tenison, who in 1679 published in his *Baconiana, or Certain Genuine Remains of*

Lord Bacon, a text with the following clause : " For my name and memory, I leave it to foreign nations, *and to my own countrymen*, after some time be passed over."[1]   If such was really the reading of one of the copies, it must have been one of the earlier drafts, superseded by the later reproduced above, in which the clause of " mine own countrymen " has been apparently struck out.   On this deletion the seal was finally put by the last will of 1625.   The longer his disgrace lasted unrelieved, the less confident became his faith in his nation's impartiality in the matter of his honour.

I wish I could make the case appear more favourable for the country and the people whose most wise sovereign Francis Tudor for a long time hoped to become, and I shall be grateful to anyone who will point out to me that the facts are less serious than I represent them.   I have put the indictment strongly, in the hope thereby to awaken a more vigorous revolt against the age-long prejudices prevalent in England.

What have been, in the history of the Baconian movement, its most salient points ? The notion that the Shakespeare plays could not have been written by the man to whose name they were accredited seems to have at first very timidly shown its head, in the beginning of the last century.   Perhaps the German critic, Schlegel, a " foreigner," was the very first to set down in black and white in 1808 that in his opinion Shakespeare was not all that could be desired for a father of the children assigned to him.[2]   But it took half a century more for an American woman, and, almost at the same time an Englishman, to come forward for the first time with the idea of Bacon's authorship, in 1856. After their discovery a steady stream of books, pamphlets and articles on the subject began to appear, and has continued uninterruptedly till our own day. Up to 1884 some 255 publications have been counted, of which 161 were American, and only 70 English.[3]

But though a hearing was now definitely assured, and the question could never again be ignored or entirely suppressed, the kernel had not yet been touched.   That was only found and laid bare by the discoveries, by two other Americans and one Englishman, of the different

[1] Sp VI 285.   [2] Ba XXIV.   [3] Bac I 53.

ciphers embedded in the Bacon-Shakespeare works. First came Ignatius Donnelly in 1888 with what he called the Great Cryptogram, next Orville Owen in 1893 with the Word Cipher, followed in 1901 by Mrs. Wells Gallup with the Biliteral Cipher. Since then the stream has constantly broadened as well as deepened, and it promises well for the future.

Not all discoveries have been of equal value. Donnelly's I think the least of, Mrs. Wells Gallup's the most. My preference is not based however on any expert knowledge, either of Donnelly's, or of the Biliteral, or of Owen's Great Word Cipher, but purely on the internal evidence of the story they reveal. The broken records in Mrs. Wells Gallup's books, in the form of a secret diary or chronicle, the repetitions, the manner of writing, the personal note, and above all the artistic and intellectual beauties of style and depth of thought and emotion, all these are so many indications if not proofs of their genuineness. Only the obtuse or prejudiced can fail to feel that we are here in communion with a poetical and philosophical genius of an exceptional order. I will not say that Mrs. Wells Gallup's decipherings are in every sense absolutely correct. There may be misreadings in small details, single letters or words. I do not know. But on the whole her work will stand, I am sure, the most exacting examination by cipher-experts.

It has in any case, during the nearly forty years since its first publication, remained unchallenged by those few who were qualified to judge. And what is more, for the great masses of people who cannot pass a judgement, the historical veracity of its contents stands as unshaken today as at the beginning of this century, though it went contrary to many things until then accepted as true history, and not-withstanding the many attacks that have been launched to overthrow its structure. On the contrary, more and more historical facts have come to light—or, already known, have received added significance—to support the story of the Biliteral Cipher. And other ciphers of Bacon's construction, to which it pointed the way, have added their by no means negligible weight to the main argument. It is three of these minor ciphers, the *Clock*, *Symbolic*, and *Anagram* Ciphers—if we call both the *Word* and the *Biliteral* the Great Ciphers—which this book takes also more especially into account.

2.   BACON'S CIPHERS

First a few dates.   We have Bacon's own declaration that he devised the Biliteral Cipher, "when at Paris in my early youth." [1] That was in 1576, when at the age of sixteen he was sent to France with the English Ambassador Sir Amyas Paulet.   For in that Cipher he tells us that immediately on his arrival in that country, "making ciphers our choice, we straightway proceeded to spend our greatest labours therein." [2]   By the time he had returned to England, when Spenser's *Shepheard's Calendar* appeared in 1579, at least two, the Word and Biliteral Cipher, had been perfected, and were in that book "used for the first time." [3]   After this first essay, they were regularly incorporated in other works going under the names of Spenser, Marlowe, Greene, Peele, T. Bright, Burton, the Shakespeare Quartos and Folio, Ben Jonson's Masques, and other books besides his own.   In the last it was that he first publicly gave evidence of being at all interested in the art of ciphering and deciphering.   This is what he wrote in *The Advancement of Learning*, published in 1605 :

"For Ciphers, they are commonly in letters or alphabets, but may be in words.   The kinds of Ciphers (besides the simple ciphers with changes and intermixtures of nulls and non-significants) are many, according to the nature or rule of the infolding ; Wheel-ciphers, Key-ciphers, Doubles, etc.   But the virtues of them, whereby they are to be preferred, are three ; that they be not laborious to write and read ; that they be impossible to decipher ; and in some cases, that they be without suspicion.   The highest degree whereof is to write *omnia*

[1] Sp IV 445.   [2] WG I 88.   [3] WG I 79.

per omnia ; which is undoubtedly possible, with a proportion quintuple at most of the writing infolding to the writing infolded, and no other restraint whatsoever. This art of Ciphering hath for relative an art of Disciphering ; by supposition unprofitable ; but, as things are, of great use. For suppose that ciphers were well managed, there be multitudes of them which exclude the discipherer. But in regard of the rawness and unskilfulness of the hands through which they pass, the greatest matters are many times carried in the weakest ciphers."[1]

Four ciphers are mentioned here, the Wheel, Key, Doubles and Biliteral Cipher, for it is the last which is meant by "the highest degree" of cipher, wherewith to write "omnia per omnia." It was however so guardedly described that it was impossible to guess at its nature without fuller explanation. This was given about twenty years later. Apparently then only did he think it wise to reveal so much of his secret work, or so little, for it was still two centuries, before it was suspected that he had made actual use of these his ciphers on such a grand scale.

In the meantime Bacon's labours in this field were continued till he had elaborated and perfected four other systems of ciphering, beside the Word and the Biliteral Cipher. In the latter as embedded in the *Novum Organum*, which appeared in 1620, he gives us a full list of his ciphers :

"We have devised six which we have used in a few of our books. These are the (1) *Biliteral*, (2) *Word*, (3) *Capital letter*, (4) *Time*, or as more oft called *Clock*, (5) *Symbol*, and (6) *Anagrammatic*. The first surely needeth no explanation if our invention have been found out. It demandeth fuller instructions, if it be still unseen. A most clear plain ensample shall make it stand forth so that he who but runneth by shall read. It doth require some fine work of the tools as of the mind. Next the Great [or Word] cipher spoken of so frequently—termed the most important invention, since it is of far greater scope—shall here be again explained."[2]

[1] Sp III 402.   [2].WG II 118.
4

The text then enters into further details regarding the second cipher, which do not concern us here. Suffice it to say that the author considers this " the chief of all my inventions."[1] From an artistic standpoint this may be true, for to it we owe many glorious passages in Shakespeare, Marlowe and the other poets which served him as masks ; but, from the historian's standpoint, the more sober chronicles which the Biliteral Cipher reveals are even more important, and, from the purely technical standpoint of deciphering, the latter is in my opinion the most trustworthy.

There is a second complete list in the Biliteral Cipher, as found in the 1623 Folio of Shakespeare's Plays, which for our purpose is of special moment.

" Seek not merely to read four ciphers, for you should find six in all—which I copy here in full, to direct students how they should work out my greatest invention—which you shall take as I direct you. (1) This is first : that clown in the play, who speaks of the plantain leaf, is a wise man ; here art outruns that grub nature ; hunt out this cipher or *anagram* at once. (2) Now find a number in my King Henry the Seventh, corresponding to this, *i.e. of the same kind or style*. (3) Next add the plays of *Twelfth Night or What You Will*, and *Love's Labour's Lost* ; you will find here *capitals in two forms* ; it is your next. (4) The face of my *clock* comes fourth. (5) My *symbols* are next, and (6) the sixth is what all shows—my *great* Cipher of Ciphers."[2]

We shall soon examine these passages in greater detail, but I will first finish our chronological survey. In the text from the *Novum Organum* Cipher of 1620 it was said that " a most clear plain ensample " of the Biliteral Cipher " shall make it stand forth so that he who but runneth by shall read." This promise was fulfilled to the letter, when in the very much enlarged Latin edition of *The Advancement of Learning*, published in 1624, the short cipher paragraph of the English original was extended to a dissertation exceeding four pages. We do not here need to give the " full ensample." The first two paragraphs suffice for our purpose :

[1].WG II 126,   [2] WG II 167,

" Let us proceed then to Ciphers. Of these there are many kinds : simple ciphers ; ciphers mixed with non-significant characters ; ciphers containing two different letters in one character; wheel-ciphers ; key-ciphers ; word-ciphers ; and the like. But the virtues required in them are three ; that they be easy and not laborious to write ; that they be safe, and impossible to be deciphered ; and lastly that they be, if possible, such as not to raise suspicion. For if letters fall into the hands of those who have power either over the writers or over those to whom they are addressed, although the cipher itself may be safe and impossible to decipher, yet the matter comes under ex-amination and question ; unless the cipher be such as either to raise no suspicion or to elude inquiry. Now for this elusion of inquiry, there is a new and useful contrivance for it, which as I have it by me, why should I set it down among the desiderata, instead of propounding the thing itself ? It is this : let a man have two alphabets, one of true letters, the other of non-significants ; and let him infold in them two letters at once ; one carrying the secret, the other such a letter as the writer would have been likely to send, and yet without anything dangerous. Then if any one be strictly examined as to the cipher, let him offer the alphabet of non-significants for the true letters, and the alphabet of true letters for non-significants. Thus the examiner will fall upon the exterior letter ; which finding probable, he will not suspect anything of another letter within. But for avoiding suspicion altogether, I will add another contrivance, which I devised myself when I was at Paris in my early youth, and which I still think worthy of preservation. For it has the perfection of a cipher, which is to make anything signify anything ; subject however to this condition, that the infolding writing shall contain at least five times as many letters as the writing infolded : no other con-dition or restriction whatever is required. The way to do it is this ; first let all the letters of the alphabet be resolved into transpositions of two letters only. For the transposition of two letters through five places will yield thirty-two differences ; much more twenty-four, which is the number of letters in our alphabet. Here is an example of such an alphabet . . .[1]

[1] The example is given in the Addenda (1).

Nor is it a slight thing which is thus by the way effected. For hence we see how thoughts may be communicated at any distance of place by means of any objects perceptible either to the eye or ear, provided only that those objects are capable of two differences ; as by bells, trumpets, torches, gunshots, and the like."[1]

Finally, nine years after Bacon's death, his devoted disciple, William Rawley, " his Lordship's first and last chaplain," as he proudly styles himself, published a third list of Bacon's ciphers, a list of his own apparently, which it is well to compare with the two lists Francis Bacon himself gave. It appeared in 1635 in the Biliteral Cipher incorporated by Rawley in Bacon's posthumous work, *Sylva Sylvarum, or Natural History* :

" From his [Bacon's] pen too works, which now bear the name Burton—containing in them the (1) *symbol*, (2) *word*, (3) *biliteral*, (4) *clock*, and (5, 6) *several anagram* ciphers put forth—make useful those portions [of his secret life-story] which could by no means be adapted to dramatical writings. If you do not use them as you decipher the interior epistles, so concealed, your story shall not be complete."[2]

There are some curious differences between the three lists. Five of the ciphers are easily seen to agree in all three lists, but the second

CONCORDANCE OF THE THREE LISTS

CIPHER	I	II	III
Biliteral	1	—	3
Word	2	6	2
Capital	3	3	—
Clock	4	4	4
Symbol	5	5	1
Anagram	6	1,2	5,6

list seems to lack the Biliteral, and the third the Capital Cipher. The explanation seems to me to be that, as Bacon had at least two kinds of anagrammatic ciphers, so he had two kinds of Biliterals, the one

[1] Sp IV 444-6.   [2] WG II 340.

consisting of " capitals in two forms," the other of italics in two founts. Having, however, a schedule of *six* ciphers in his mind, neither more nor less, he was not always fully decided which one to drop from his enumeration, either one of the biliterals or one of the anagrammatics. Thus it came to pass that in the older list, dating from 1620, he discarded one of the latter, while in the younger list of 1623 he left out one of the biliterals, probably because he had come to the conclusion that the principles upon which the latter two were based differed mutually less than those upon which the two anagrammatics were constructed. Or we should rather say that the *principle* of the biliteral cipher, as fully explained in the ninth book of the Latin edition of the *Advancement of Learning* is absolutely the same for both cases to which Bacon applied them, the only difference being the quite accidental circumstance whether *capitals* or *italics* or " bells, trumpets, torches, gunshots, and the like " be used as means. It was better, therefore, to take them under one head. The objection that might be raised against this explanation, is that of the two biliterals the double-italic is more important than the double-capital, and should therefore have been named in the second list in preference to the former. That only the double-capital came to be mentioned was perhaps because Bacon would give it a chance of getting known also, the italic biliteral having been made known sufficiently by the example given in the *De Augmentis*. I am the more inclined to this view, as William Rawley's list, which is the latest, seems to confirm my explanation.

Of the five or seven ciphers, the Key-word Cipher was judged by Bacon to be " the most important invention, since it is of far greater scope " than the other ciphers, and for this reason undoubtedly he called it the " Great ", the " Cipher of Ciphers ", the " Chief of all my inventions." [1] Yet herein I must disagree, from a purely practical standpoint. It is true that the anagrammatic, clock, and symbol ciphers could give only short hints, often vague or dubious enough. They were fit only for isolated fragments of information, and not for a continuous story of some length. For this latter purpose however

[1] WG II 126.

the Biliteral Cipher stood at least on an equal footing with the Word
Cipher. Though it had the disadvantage of needing five times the
quantity of matter that had to be infolded, it had the enormous advantage that it could be incorporated in any printed matter, so that
even other men's works could be employed for the purpose, provided
one had control over the printing. In this way for example Bacon made
use of the 1611 Folio of Ben Jonson's Plays, as well as of the Black
Letter Bible of the same year.

Still one can easily understand why in Bacon's opinion the Word
Cipher was his greatest achievement in this field. Whereas the Biliteral Cipher could be applied by any fool, once he had grasped its
principle, the Word Cipher could be wielded only by a literary genius
like himself, a dramatic, epic and lyric poet, all in one, and unsurpassed
in any age. The Biliteral Cipher works like a machine, like the ticking
of a clock, once its mechanism is put in motion. But the Word Cipher
is like the variegated flow of many waters on the face of the earth.
The same drops that yesterday were glistening in the rain-cloud which
poured its treasure over the parched earth, to-day by their irresistible
force will drive the water-mill on the bank of the mountain-torrent, and
tomorrow will bear the ocean-steamer on their softly yielding, strong,
young bosoms toward its distant goal. Only a visionary genius, whose
mind's eye had penetrated through the intricacies of life to the fundamental passions, urges, feelings, thoughts that express man's life, and
make as well as unmake human relationships, only such a Seer, if he be
likewise a Poet, could make use of the same fundamental elements for
the characterisation of different persons in different situations, that is to
say could write *Anthony and Cleopatra*, or *King John*, or *Twelfth Night*,
and incorporate in them his own life-story, or that of his grandmother,
Anne Bullen, or of his brother, Robert Devereux, Earl of Essex. This
was what Bacon actually did, as the decipherings of Orville Owen and
Elizabeth Wells Gallup have brought to light.

The Word and Biliteral Ciphers were the last to be discovered in
the past and the present century, the anagrammatic, clock and symbol
cyphers the first. I do not think that any of them has yet been

completely deciphered. The search for them has until now been disjointed and accidental, left to individual effort and chance, rather than to
combined and systematic research. The result has been relatively poor.
Much has been found, but more, a great deal more remains to be
recovered. None of the six ciphers has yet been forced to deliver all
it has been charged with by Francis Bacon, the Word cipher probably
not for half its contents, the Biliteral not for one third. Yet the Bacon
Society has existed now for over half a century. Combined and systematic research was what the philosopher Bacon advocated for the
discovery of Nature's secrets. Combined and systematic research is
needed with regard to his own works, which for the secrets they contain
approach Nature and in a sense outrun the latter. May the Bacon
Society yet achieve the desideratum. It would thereby justify its existence, and be a blessing to the nation.

    As long as Francis Tidder's name is not restored to whitest purity,
it shows a flaw in England's moral character which in the long run spells
disaster to her national greatness. Hepworth Dixon wrote of the inseparable connection between Bacon's and England's fate : " One man only
set aside, our interest in Bacon's fame is greater than in that of any
Englishman who ever lived." Hepworth Dixon was not a Baconian.
The one man he set aside was Shakespeare. What would have been
his praise, in case he had realized Bacon's and Shakespeare's identity,
we do not know. But we ourselves may read his next words in that
light, and so still better see their truth and sense their full weight.
" We cannot hide his light, we cannot cast him out, for good, if it be
good, for evil, if it must be evil, his brain has passed into our brain, his
soul into our souls. We are part of him, he is part of us ; inseparable
as the salt and sea, the life he lived has become our law. If it be true
that the Father of Modern Science was a rogue and cheat, it is also
most true that we have taken a rogue and cheat to be our god." [1] If
on the other hand we might win back our faith and trust in his moral,
not less than in his intellectual greatness—

        If England to itself do rest but true,

      [1] HD I 6,

to itself, that is to its greatest son, who was the embodiment of its particuliar genius, then indeed his undying spirit may still guide the nation to unknown glories, when

Nought shall make us rue.[1]

3.   SHAKESPEAREAN SCHOLARSHIP

Prejudice not only blinds, but perverts the mind. Of this, orthodox Shakespearean scholarship is one example. The scope of this book and of this introduction do not allow to give more than one or two instances, taken from Spenserean and Shakespearean studies.

The first example is a very common and simple one, but illustrative of the inverted base of orthodox literary criticism. De Selincourt in his introduction to Spenser's *Poetical Works*, writes about *The Fairie Queene* : " The story of Spenser's life is the key to much in that poem." In truth it is just the other way round, namely : " Much in that poem is the key to the story of Spenser's life," as told by the modern biographers. The greater part of their biographies are but fancied applications from the poems upon the life. And so it is with other authors than Spenser.

What are the facts ? Actually there is remarkably little known of the life-stories of the greatest Elizabethan poets.   And that little on the one hand is exploited to read into the poet's works circumstances of his life, and on the other hand those works are ransacked to make sub- stantial additions to the life-story.   Both procedures are of course perfectly legitimate, when kept within reasonable bounds, and as long as the attributed authorship of the works is not challenged.   In that case it would not do, of course, to argue in favour of the authenticity of the traditional authorship with arguments which are derived from those questionable works, but which have first been read into them from the

---

[1] *King John*, last lines.

life-story.   And this holds good of Spenser, as well as of Shakespeare,
or any one of Bacon's many masks.

If for example the French (Belgian rather) *Forest of Arden* in *As
You Like It* is said to be a typical Warwickshire Forest of Arden,[1]
this is an example of reading into the play the fact that Shakespeare was born in that country.   I, not knowing Warwickshire, find
that the description of Arden fits countless other places, not only
in England, but on the continent also, in my own country, anywhere.
When therefore the Editor of the New Cambridge Shakespeare writes :
'' This Arden, on the south bank of Avon, endeared to him [Shakes-
peare] by its very name (name of his mother), had been the haunt
where he caught his first ' native wood-notes wild,' as the path by the
stream had been his, known to this day as the Lovers' Walk,'' such
effusions sound in the ear of a Baconian like the hollow play—delightful
only if sparingly heard—of the echo in a narrow valley.   As

> From off a hill whose concave womb re-worded
> A plaintful story from a sistering vale,

so the Shakespearean critics cast and re-cast and cast back again their
story, from the life into the works, and from the works into the life
again, like children throwing and catching a ball.

The extreme of purblindness would of course be reached when the
Shakespearean answers the Baconian's arguments by some such reasoning as the following : '' Because the French Forest of Arden is in reality
the Warwickshire Forest of Arden, therefore Bacon cannot have been the
author of *As You Like It*.''   Or more briefly, '' Because Shakespeare
was born in Warwickshire, therefore Bacon is not the author.''   How
puerile such perverted logic seems, yet it lies hidden in most if not all the
defences of Shakespearean scholarship against the Baconian challenge.
Our next example will prove this.

When in our own or previous times, two or more editions of a
book are known, we immediately assume that the shorter version is the
older, more original, and the longer is the later.   We do so even without looking at the date of publication, or glancing at the inscription on

[1] Sm 274.

5

the title page, telling that it is a " revised " or an " enlarged " edition. If subsequent editions of the same book differ in length, this is generally in the sense of enlargement in the younger edition, exceptionally only in the sense of shortening or condensation. This is even one of the well known canons of historical literary criticism.

With Shakespeare's plays, however, if we must believe the critics, it is just the other way round. The longer editions are counted as the original, while the shorter ones are derived from the larger, and this notwithstanding the fact that the longer are actually the later in date.

Of many of the plays, known to exist in different editions, the later are very much " enlarged," compared with the older. and yet we are told that the former are the original, the latter condensations of them.

Such a thing is of course unknown of any other author since the invention of printing, before or after Shakespeare. He is the only exception, semper et ubique. And we are expected to believe it so as to suit the Shakespearean authorship, whereas this fact alone constitutes the strongest argument against it !

We may illustrate the case with one of Bacon's own books, the *Essays*. These appeared first in 1597. The volume then contained only 10 short essays. In the next edition, published by Bacon in 1612, " the number was increased to 38, of which 29 were quite new, and all the rest more or less corrected and enlarged." The edition of 1625, a quarto and "one of the latest of Bacon's publications, contained 58 essays, of which 20 were new, and most of the rest altered and enlarged." [1] Now, in what a morass of absurdity would the historian of Bacon's life and work land himself, if he assumed, as the Shakespeareans unblushingly do for their author, that the 58 essays of 1625 were the original production, really written by the author some thirty years before, but that at first he suppressed most of it ; not only so, but that he even altered for the worse the portions given out, only gradually restoring them to their original and more perfect shape as the years passed by. Such an assumption is, to say the least, incredible.

[1] Sp VI 367.

Now take *Richard III*.   Six Quartos were published in 1597, 1598, 1602, 1605, 1612 and 1622, before the Folio of 1623.   From the third Quarto onward the editions bear the words " newly augmented." Shakespeare died four years after the fifth and six years before the sixth Quarto.   Yet in 1623, seven years after his death, the Drama appeared in the Folio with 23 lines of ordinary length and 19 short lines *less*, but with 196 ordinary, 15 short and 17 half-lines or parts of lines *more*.   If it were not Shakespeare, but any other writer, how should we account for this fact? Of course by taking it for granted that the author, or if he is dead another, revised the play, deleting a few lines and " *adding* " many new ones to the " *original*," older texts.

But the Shakespearean scholar cannot act in such a straight-forward way.   Even against his will, by the unique grandeur of their poetry, he has to save the " added " lines from the obloquy of being the production of another, and vindicate their true Shakespearean origin. But how can that be done, seeing that the Folio appeared seven years after Shakespeare's death? Well, by maintaining that the Folio text is the real " original," and the former editions were obtained from this original by " omitting " the " additional " passages in question, however paradoxical this may sound.   It is ingenious thus to turn the tables, from " additions " to " omissions."   It is however not only unreasonable, but hardly sane.

If we turn the pages of the Cambridge Shakespeare or the Arden Shakespeare, and read the footnotes to the " added " passages, what do we constantly find? The short and pithy, but foolish remarks : " *Omitted* in the Quartos."   Reasoning along the same line the real " omissions " in the Folio should have been marked : " *Added* to the Quartos."   But ho, here the Shakespearean scholar's reason evidently shies before such a glaring fallacy, and the notes read again : " *Omitted* " in the Folio.[1]

Has it ever been heard, or is it thinkable that an author during his lifetime publishes mutilated fragments of his works, or has them

[1] See for example footnotes to Act I, scene 2, (C. and A. Sh) vs. 155-166 ; Act IV, scene 2, (A. Sh) vs. 98-115, (C. Sh) vs. 103-120.

thus published by others, without protest or correction, leaving it to his charitable fellow-men many years after his death to print the un-garbled versions and so-called " original " texts.

The Shakespeareans have of course many explanations to offer for the earlier so-called " defective " or " garbled " versions—stage-exigencies and pirate publishers among others. They might be accepted in single, exceptional cases, but not when they are the rule without exceptions. Even Heminge and Condell, the Folio editors do not escape the unjustified wrath of the modern critics. They are openly abused by the Cambridge editors for example as " discredited," " un-scrupulous," " knaves " and " imposters," for no other reason than that their critics are blind to the facts.

In the same vein as the " additions " re-christened " omissions," is the dubbing of a set of early Quartos as " bad " texts in contrast with the later editions of them as " good " texts. Why not straight-forwardly recognise the former as early " drafts " or first " essays," revised, corrected, and augmented in the later editions ? Because that would again involve difficulties in connection with the events of Shake-speare's life, and the year of his death.

These so-called " bad Quartos " are 2 Henry VI (1594), 3 Henry VI (1595), Romeo and Juliet (1597), Henry V (1600), Merry Wives of Windsor (1602), Hamlet (1602), and King Lear (1608). Why had the work of their publishers to be slandered by the opprobrious qualification of " bad Quartos " or " bad texts ? " Because only many, many years later, from fifteen to twenty-eight years in fact, and in any case seven years after the supposed author's death, so-called " good texts " saw the light of day for the first time. In truth of course the Quartos were equally good and genuine texts, only in the form of a first immature draft, revised and perfected by the real author, some before, some after Shakespeare's death.

Let us see what this revising and perfecting actually amounted to. How thorough it was ! King Richard III is not nearly the most glaring case. I quote from a recent Baconian study.

Othello was for the first time printed in 1622, three years after Shakespeare's death, and it was reprinted the next year in the Folio. " It is the 1622 copy touched up, varied and revised by a fidgety [?] author who, whatever heights he attains, has ever vision of heights yet beyond. In it are 160 new lines, 70 old lines struck out, and as for trifling verbal alterations, they fill every page. Whether these and the new lines are all improvements may be in question, but it is never in question that they are by the same hand. Whoever the author, HE WAS ALIVE IN 1623."

About *King Richard III* the writer says : "Collating the two copies [the sixth Quarto and the Folio] we feel in minute beauties of rhythm and smoothness, that it is much improved.

" In the *Merry Wives of Windsor* are the same features. It was printed in quarto in 1602, and reprinted in 1619. In the Folio there are 1,081 new lines and minor alterations innumerable.

" The play of *Henry VI*, also in quarto, 1619, in the Folio has some 2,000 new lines, and about as many old lines retouched. This is virtually a rewriting.

" *The Taming of a Shrew*, 1607, with 1,000 new lines, is almost a new play.

" *King Lear*, 1619,[1] in the Folio has 88 new lines, 119 retouched, with the usual minor alterations innumerable.

" In *Troyliss and Cressida*, 1609, alterations in phraseology, in spelling or in punctuation total up to 4,000.

" *Romeo and Juliet* has innumerable minor alterations, as also *Hamlet*.

" As for the *Histories* they are one continuous re-editing, with the Folio always the latest revision."[2]

Of sixteen of the total number of plays in the Folio it is the very first text which is there printed, and of six more we find a virtually new text. Three of the sixteen new plays had never before even been heard of. If we lost all the plays that were published before Shakespeare died, we should still have twenty-one plays left of the thirty-six

[1] Antedated 1608.   [2] C. Y. Dawbarn. *Oxford and the Folio Plays, October 1938*, p. 23-26.

contained in the Folio. Has anybody ever heard of an author who of every three books he writes leaves two unpublished during his life ? And among these are the greatest master-pieces of his creation, *The Tempest*, *As You Like It*, *Twelfth Night*, *The Winter's Tale*, *Julius Cæsar*, *Macbeth*, *Othello*, and so on.

In the Addenda (2) a chronology of the Shakespeare Plays is given according to Shakespearean scholarship. How doubtful, and unreliable, not to say wilfully dishonest, such scholarship is may be concluded from the dates given for *King John* and *The Taming of the Shrew*. The latter is said to have been composed about 1593-1594, and not to have been heard of before the Folio, whereas the truth is that there exists a Quarto of 1594, entitled *The Taming of a Shrew*, which is without any doubt the original of the Folio text. Still worse is the case of *King John*, which is said to have been composed in 1596-1597, first mentioned in 1598, and first published in the Folio. The fact is, however, that here again there exists a quarto of 1591, entitled *The Troublesome Reign of King John*, the equally undoubted original of the Folio play. But neither the old *Shrew* nor the old *King John* are recognized by the orthodox as of Shakespearean workmanship. And yet, all this denial is mere hypothesis, without a shadow of proof, advanced only for convenience sake. For the old plays are indeed the most inconvenient witnesses imaginable.

Why are the Shakespeareans forced to disown these earliest plays, and others such as these ? Because there is evidence that they were produced and acted on the stage, when Shakespeare was still leading the carefree life of a rustic youth in idyllic Warwickshire. Not before 1587 did he go to London, where he received his first vision of that greater world portrayed in the Plays with such a keen touch of reality, not explainable by any amount of poetic genius or vision, but only by direct experience. And how could he have experienced that wider life in sleepy Stratford !

But enough of the contortions of orthodox Shakespearean scholarship.

Part I.   Critical and Historical

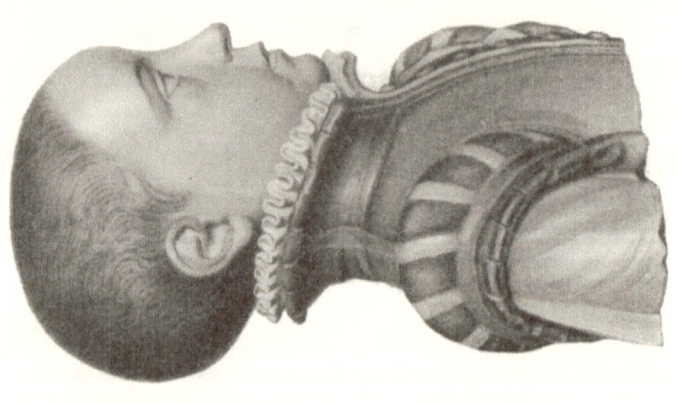

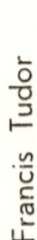

Francis Tudor

1. A Royal Romance

ORN in the purple, but denied by an unnatural mother, that was the tragedy of Francis Bacon's life. His ambitions were royal, equal to his birth, but he found another royal will—adamant where his was supple—opposed to the brightest dreams of an enlightened prince on England's throne, that his mind was ever creating in a future which never arrived.

" My name is Tidder [Tudor], yet men speak of me as Bacon "— grudgingly writes England's greatest genius on the eve of his death, and continues in growing resentment—" even those that know of my royal mother, and her lawful marriage with the Earl of Leicester, a suitable time prior to my birth." [1]

Francis Tudor grew up to be fifteen years old—he was born on the 22nd of January 1561—before ever he heard that it was not good Lady Anne Bacon, who had fostered him all these years, who was his fleshly mother, but Elizabeth, the Virgin Queen so-called. Proud of her title, jealous of her lone-star power, she wanted to preserve her

---

[1] WG II 334. For the form " Tidder " of the name Tudor, see Bacon's *History of King Henry VII*, Sp VI 167 ; and for the form " Tydder," p. 252.

secret undivulged.   Upon his accidental discovery of his royal birth, there immediately followed, Francis Tudor writes, " our summary banishment to beautiful France, which did intend our correction but opened to us the gates of Paradise." [1]   He went there in the company of Sir Amias Paulet, the English ambassador, and set foot in France, landing at Calais, on the 25th of September 1576.   Sent to the sunny Southland during the most susceptible age of masculine youth, he fell a ready victim to the exquisite charms of the mind and body of lovely Marguerite of Valois ; though eight years his senior she was, and married five years previously to gallant Henry, King of Navarre, and leader of the Huguenots.

Alexander Dumas, *père*, in *La Reine Margot*, gives the following description of the French princess : " The bride was the daughter of Henry II ; the pearl of the crown of France, *Marguerite de Valois*, whom, in his familiar tenderness for her, King Charles IX always called *ma soeur Margot*.   Never was a more flattering reception, never one more merited than that which awaited the new Queen of Navarre.   Marguerite at this period [23rd of August 1572, the night before the S. Bartholomew Massacre] was scarcely twenty years old, and already she was the object of all the poets' eulogies, some of whom compared her to Aurora, others to Cytherea ; she was, in truth, a beauty without rival in that court in which Catherine de Medici had assembled the loveliest women of the age and country.   She had black hair, a brilliant complexion, a voluptuous eye veiled by long lids, coral and delicate lips, a graceful neck, a full, enchanting figure and, concealed in a satin slipper, a tiny foot scarce larger than an infant's.   The French, who possessed her, were proud to see so lovely a flower flourishing on their soil, and foreigners who passed through France returned home dazzled with her beauty if they had but seen her, and amazed at her knowledge if they had discoursed with her : for not only was Marguerite the loveliest, she was also the most learned woman of her time.   And on all sides was quoted the remark of an Italian savant who had been presented to her, and who, after having conversed with her for an hour in Italian, Spanish,

[1] WG I 88.

Greek, and Latin, had said on quitting her presence : ' To see the court without seeing Marguerite de Valois is to see neither France nor the court.' '' [1]

It was a case of love at first sight, and as the sequel shows, his first as well as his last great love.   So struck was he by his lightning-like infatuation, that he made it into a maxim for the true lover, composed a verse on it, and incorporated this in his unfinished poem, *Hero and Leander* (vs. 175-6), published ten years later as a work of Christopher Marlowe, who had died five years before :

> Where both deliberate, the love is slight,
> *Who ever loved, that loved not at first sight ?*

Twenty-five years later, that is, three years before his own death, when the First Folio of Shakespeare's plays was issued, the second line made its re-appearance in *As You Like It* (Act III, scene 5), quoted as a mighty saying of the dead Marlowe :

> Dead Shepherd, now I find thy saw of might,
> *Who ever loved, that loved not at first sight ?*

Francis was however a too seriously minded young man to spend his time in France exclusively or even for the greater part in love-making.   On the contrary, '' making ciphers our choice,'' he tells us, '' we straightway proceeded to spend our greatest labours therein, to find a method of secret communication of our history to others outside the realm.'' [2]   Among these ciphers was '' this double alphabet cipher,'' or the biliteral cipher, to which we owe the astounding revelations regarding the private life and history of the grandson of Henry VIII and the much slandered Anne Bullen—Francis Tudor : '' I, last of my House,'' as he writes regretfully the year before he passed to happier regions. [3]

His love, as his whole life, was bound to sail upon an adverse sea. If for no other cause, the former was doomed to ship-wreck through the opposition of his royal mother.   Marguerite herself was not too

---

[1] An English translation of Dumas' book is found in Everyman's Library, under the title *Marguerite de Valois*, from which the above description is taken.

[2] WG I 88.   [3] WG III 36.

happily matched. For political reasons Henry wanted to be released
from his marriage-bond, but he remained her constant friend throughout
life. "When Sir Amias Paulet became advised of my love," writes
Francis Tudor, " he proposed that he should negotiate a treaty of marriage, and appropriately urge on her pending case of the divorce from the
young Huguenot ; but for reasons of very grave importance these buds
of an early marriage never opened into flower. But the future race
will profit by the failure in the field of love, for in those flitting days afterward, having resolved to cover every mark of defeat with the triumphs
of my mind, I did thoroughly banish my tender love-dreams to the
regions of clouds unreal, and let my works of various kinds absorb my
mind. It is thus by my disappointment that I do secure to many
fruition." [1] By thus turning his libido, the creative life-energy that was
his, from the bed of love into the fields of poetry and philosophy, he
has given us the most magnificent example of what the psychoanalyst
has termed sublimation, and what the religionist would probably call
conversion, or in general the turning of the soul from the material to
the spiritual.

In somewhat greater detail, revealing also the principal force that
worked against him at the English court, the story is retold elsewhere.
" I was entrusted at that very time with business requiring great secrecy
and expediency. This was so well conducted as to win the Queen's
frank approval, and I had a lively hope by means of this entering wedge,
to be followed by the request nearest unto my soul, I should so bend
her Majesty's mind to my wish. Sir Amias Paulet undertook to negotiate both treaties at once, and came thereby very near to a breach with
the Queen, as well as disgrace at Henry [III]'s Court. Both calamities
however were averted by such admirable adroitness that I could but
yield due respect to the finesse, while discomforted by the death of my
hope. From that day I lived a doubtful life, swinging like a pendent
branch to and fro, or tempest-tossed by many a troublous desire. At
length I turned my attention from love, and used all my time and
wit to make such advancement in learning or achieve such great

[1] WG II 337.

proficiency in studies that my name as a lover of sciences should be best known and most honoured, less for my own aggrandizement than as an advantaging of mankind, but with some natural desires to approve my worthiness in the sight of my book-loving and aspiring mother, believing that by thus doing I should advance my claim and obtain my rights, not aware of [Robert] Cecil his misplaced zeal in bringing this to her Majesty's notice, to convince her mind that I had no other thought save a design to win sovereignty in her life-time. I need not assert how far this was from my heart at any time, especially in my youth, but the Queen's jealousy so blinded her reason that she, following the suggestion of malice, showed little pride in my attempts, discovering in truth more envy than natural pride, and more hate than affection." [1]

When back in England in 1579, his genius therefore sought and found a secret outlet for the fullness of his heart, under the masks of the most brilliant of the galaxy of Elizabethan poets that then made their appearance—Spenser, Peele, Greene, Marlowe and Shakespeare, especially the latter. "Through love I dreamed out these five plays," he tells us when forty years of busy life had abated the youthful ardour but not the lasting inner glow, "filled up—as we have seen warp in some hand-loom, so as to be made a beauteous coloured web—with words Marguerite has so oft, like to a busy hand, shot daily into a fairy-hued web, and made a rich-hued damask, vastly more dear ; and should life bewray an interior room in my calm but aching breast, on every hand shall her work be seen." [2]

Supreme among these love-plays was *Romeo and Juliet*, "very seldom heard without most stormy weeping, your poet's commonest plaudit. Since the former issue of this play [1609], we have all but determined on following the fortunes of these ill-fated lovers by a path less thorny. Their life was too brief, its rose of pleasure had but partly drunk the sweet dew of early delight, and every hour had begun to open unto sweet love, tender leaflets in whose fragrance was assurance of untold joys that the immortals know. Yet it is a kind fate which joined them together in life and death. It was a sadder fate

[1] WG II 361-2.   [2] WG II 12-13.

befell our youthful love, my Marguerite, yet written out in the plays it
scarce would be named our tragedy since neither yielded up life.   But
the joy of life ebbed from our hearts with our parting, and it never
came again into this bosom in full flood-tide.   Oh, we were Fortune's
fool too long, sweet one, and art is long.   So rare (and most brief) the
hard-won happiness, it afforded us great content to relieve in the play
all that as mist in summer morning did roll away.   Our fond love
interpreted the hearts of others, and in this joy the joy of heaven was
faintly guessed.''   Pure sorrow, free of earthly taint, brings divine grace.

Few are they whose love survives middle-age, still fewer they in
whom it outlives frustration, but rarest of all is that inspired soul who,
maugre time and adverse fate, cherishes his treasure till his dying day
as the most precious gift bestowed upon suffering mankind by the gods,
its joys and ecstasies even in the face of defeat to be sung out in prose
and verse, and thus shared with his less happy fellow-men for their
enjoyment and upliftment.   For too many the love-passion is the
opposite of a boon—a source of debasement, an excuse for cruel jealousy ; and frustrated love still worse—a source of hate, and an excuse
for vindictive malice.   No one knew these dangers to man's nature,
'' far from angelic '' as it is, better than the creator of Othello and
Iago.   But none also knew better and had personally drunk deeper of
the ennobling power of pure love.   '' Far from angelic though man his
nature, if his love be as clear or as fine as our love for a lovely woman
(sweet as a rose and as thorny it might chance) it sweetens all the
enclosure of his breast, oft changing a waste into lovely gardens, which
the angels would fain seek.   That it so uplifts our life who would ever
question ? It is sometimes said, ' No man can at once be wise and love,'
and yet it would be well to observe many will be wiser after a lesson
such as we long ago conned.   There was no ease to our heart till our
years of life were eight lustres.   The fair face lives ever in dreams,
but in inner pleasances only does the sunny vision come.'' [1]

Than this affection of the royal prince for a royal princess, daughter
of King Henry II of France and Catherine de Medici, I do not know in

_____
[1] WG II 79-80.

the whole range of world literature—Dante's love for Beatrice not excepted—a more radiant example of the highest inspiration, illuminating the whole of the inner life, the farthest and darkest corners of the heart and mind, transmuting the evil passions lurking there into their shining counterparts.

If ever Francis Tudor came near hating a living man with intense hatred, it was Robert Cecil, Elizabeth's evil genius. It was his love for Margaret which saved him from his own evil genius. To the younger Cecil, his adoptive mother's sister's son—physically and intellectually his exact counterpart—whom he so forcefully portrayed in the hunchbacked Richard III, and in his Essay " On Deformity ; " [1] to Cecil, he ascribed all his woes—his banishment to France, his love's frustration, his continued disinheritance by the Queen. " We ourselves hate with princely hatred arts now exercised [at court] to keep the vanity of our regal parent glowing like fire, for God has laid on that head a richer crown than this diadem upon her brow, yet will she not display it before all eyes. *It is the rich crown of motherhood.*" [2] And directly apostrophizing the decipherer of his " double alphabet " story, he writes elsewhere : " Read of a man of our realm that at morn or eve plays spy on my every act under great secrecy, and gave me many a cause in my youth to make life in France most beneficent. Of his great hatred one of my greatest sorrows grew, and my hasty banishment following quite close, that at that time seemed maddening, but as in the most common of our youthful experiences, became the chief delight. In plays that I wrote about that time, the story of bane and blessing, of joys and griefs, are well set forth. Indeed, some might say my passion then had much youthful fire, but the hate that raged in me then was not so fiery in truth as the fierce hate so continually burning in the breast and oft unwisely betrayed by the overt acts of the man of whom I have writ many things." In his own soul love overcame hate. " In my heart too love so soon overthrew envy as well as other evil passions after I found lovely Margaret, the Queen of Navarre." [3]

[1] See the next Chapter.   [2] WG I 81.   [3] WG II 12.

" A fox oft seen at Court in the form and outward appearance of a man named Robert Cecil, the hunch-back, must answer at the Divine Arraignment to my charge against him, for he despoiled me ruthlessly. The Queen my mother might, in course of events which followed their revelations regarding my birth and parentage, without doubt having some natural pride in her offspring, often have shown us no little attention, had not the crafty fox aroused in that tiger-like spirit the jealousy that did so torment the Queen that neither night nor day brought her respite from such suggestions about my hope that I might be England's King. He told her my endeavours were all for sovereignty and honour. He bade her observe the strength, breadth and compass at an early age of the intellectual powers I displayed, and even deprecated the generous disposition or graces of speech which won me many friends, implying that my gifts would thus no doubt uproot her, because I would like Absalom steal away the people's hearts and usurp the throne whilst my mother was yet alive. The terrors he conjured up could by no art be exorcised, and many trials came therefrom, not alone in youth, but in early manhood." [1]

Who would not think the prince's hate was justified ? " Hate is just in him who is made the prey to the ills which do fall " upon him. And yet . . . " love is so great a requital of wrong, the anger in the human heart is seen a fire-eyed Fury's child, turned from a region of Nox and her compeers, and then we control our passions. My love for Marguerite was the spirit which saved my soul from hatred, and from wild passions." [2]

Yet do not think that Francis' love was all bodiless adoration, all of the spirit, and nothing of the flesh. The passion shown by Shakespeare's lovers in so many of the plays tells of another tale. So do " Spenser's, as Shakespeare's numerous love-poems of many kinds, sonnets and so forth, that shower my Margaret as with water of Castaly." [3] Even when he had reached his five-and-fiftieth year of life, and had been married for nearly ten years to another woman, the charms of Margaret's

[1] WG II 28-9.   [2] WG II 173-4.
[3] WG II 181.   Castalia, a fountain on mount Parnassus, sacred to Apollo and the Muses.

physical personality still haunt his thoughts in undimmed brightness. When he is thinking of " some rude notes " sung in his youth, there immediately rises in his mind the reminiscence of " one strangely sweet strain of our early fancy, painting not what we knew, but every winsome grace, or proud yet gentle motion of lily hand or daintily tripping foot—long worshipped as divine—heavenly Marguerite, Queen of Navarre." [1]   None was to be compared to her, not even the loveliest ladies of his own country and clime.   She was " dearer, and as our memory doth paint her, fairer still than the fairest of our English maidens, sweet traitress though we should term her—Marguerite, our pearl of women." [2]   Oh, could beautiful Margaret but have been true to him, as he was to her.   How willingly would he—like his distant relative of our own day—have sacrificed all to his love, the ties that bound him to his country, to his friends and relatives, even the ambition at one time to wear the royal crown of his illustrious forebears with at least equal if not greater dignity.

This ambition had always been very strong in him, because the consciousness of his own worth had been so overpowering as to amount to a call from on high.   In the event of our inheriting, he once wrote, " this throne and this crown, our land shall rejoice, for it shall have a wise sovereign.   God endued us with wisdom, the gift granted in answer to Solomon's prayers.   It is not in us aught unmeet or heady-rash to say this, for our Creator only is praised.   None will charge here manifestation of worldly vanity, for it is but the pride natural to minds such as we enjoy, indeed in common with all youthful royal princes.   If it should be wanting, then might all men say we lack the very essence of a royal spirit, or judge that we were unfit to reign over mighty England.   It is only one of our happy dreams of a day to come, that doth draw us on to build upon this ground, inasmuch as it shall be long—if so bright a day dawn—ere we shall bask in his sunny rays." [3]

Yet all these hopes of glory he would with a joyous heart have renounced to wear the humble crown of his Margaret's affection, as

[1] WG II 72.   [2] WG II 119-20.   [3] WG I 82.

7

others before him had done, and others after him will do.   At the
age of twenty-six he wrote : " Our lovely Marguerite of Navarre,
Queen of that realm and our heart.   Love of her had power to make
the Duke of Guise forget the greatest honours that France might confer
upon him ; and hath power as well to make all such fleeting glory
seem to us like dreams or pictures, nor can we name ought real that
hath not origin in her." [1]   And when he was forty : " A wonderful
power to create heaven upon earth was in that loved eye.   To win a
show of her fond favour, we were fain to adventure even our honour
or fame, to save and shield her." [2]   And still the same when he died
at sixty-six : " That sunny land of the South I learned so supremely to
love, that afterwards I would have left England and every hope of
advancement, to remain my whole life there.   Nor yet could this be
due to the delights of the country, by itself, for love of sweet Marguerite,
the beautiful young sister of the King [3] (married to gallant Henry, the
King of Navarre) did make it Eden to my innocent heart." [4]   Which
lover—young, middle-aged, or old—in whose heart romance still blos-
soms fragrantly, will not re-echo Francis Tudor's sentiments with the
battle-cry : " My love, my love, a kingdom for my love ! "

But alas, Robert Cecil was not the only one to inflict untold miseries
upon Francis Tudor.   His own dearly beloved Margaret had her share
in them.   We have already heard him call her " sweet as a rose," but
at the same time " as thorny it might chance."   One natural reason
for this was her being the wife of another.   " At one time a secret
jealousy was constantly burning in our veins, for Duke Henry then
followed her day in and out, but she hath given us proof of love that
hath now set our heart at rest on the query." [5]   If only Duke Henry
had been the sole cause for jealousy, and if only Margaret had been
more constant or single-minded ! But " the Queen of Navarre willingly
framed excuses to keep me, *with other right royal suitors,* [6] ever at her

---

[1] WG I 91.   [2] WG II 12.   [3] WG II 336.

[4] Henry III.   Their parents were Henry II and Catherine de Medici.   [5] WG I 91.

[6] " The most of a play in this same name, George Peele's, *The Arraignment of Paris,*
continueth the stories of Margaret's many *affaires du coeur* " (II 214).

imperial commandment." [1] If only for her, as for him, there had existed but one other mortal in heaven and earth, if only he had had no cause to call her a " sweet traitress," " whose mind changed much like a fickle dame's." " So fair was she, no eyes ever looked upon such a beauteous mortal, and I saw no other. I saw her, French Eve to their wondrous Paradise, as if no being, no one in all high heaven's wide realm, save only this one Marguerite, did ever exist, or in this nether world, ever, in all the ages to be in the infinity of time, might be created. But there came in days, close in the rear, when I could fain have lived my honoured days in this loving-wise, ruin worthy husband's hopes, and many a vision, had there been only one single Adam therein—which should be and was not—solely myself." But " my love's mind changed much like a fickle dame's. Years do never pay his sin's pain-boughten bond in man, or take pain from the remembrance ever keen with the ignominy which this fickle lady put upon dumb, blind, deaf, unthinking and unsuspicious lovers. Ever kind, true in hour of need as in that of pleasure, I suffered most cruel torments in mind." [2]

Therefore in later years the reproaches to his love fall into a harsher strain. " Rare Eve, French Eve, first, worst, loveliest upon the face of this earth, the beauteous Margaret." [3] Severer still towards the end of his days. " Even when I learned her perfidy, love did keep her like the angels in my thoughts half of the time—as to the other half she was devilish, and I myself was plunged into hell. This lasted during many years." [4] Who, on reading this, is not forcibly reminded of the *Sonnets* that bear Shakespeare's name, but were written by Francis Tudor ? Nowhere else has the fight between the good and the evil in love, Eros and Cupid, between light and dark, the white and the black in man's soul, the struggle for supremacy between the soul's aspirations and the desires of the body, been portrayed with greater poetical force than in these sonnets, to many of which the epithet " sugared " given to them by a contemporary does not apply. Sonnet 144 is an example.

[1] WG II 12.   [2] WG II 175-6.   [3] WG II 181.   [4] WG II 336.

Two loves I have, of comfort and despair,
Which like two spirits do suggest me still :
The better angel is a man right fair,
The worser spirit a woman coloured ill.
 To win me soon to hell, my female evil
Tempteth my better angel from my side,
And would corrupt my saint to be a devil,
Wooing his purity by her foul pride.
 And whether that my angel be turned fiend,
Suspect I may, yet not directly tell ;
But being both from me, both to each friend,
I guess one angel in another's hell :
 Yet this shall I never know, but live in doubt,
 Till my bad angel fire my good one out.

The desires of the coarser nature drive the poetical inspiration away "from his side." The poet feigns that his genius has left him because it has become the friend of the other. Yet he does not want to yield to his bodily nature and thereby lose his own pride, letting it triumph in its "foul pride" of having enslaved his better nature. So he loses both, his love as well as his inspiration, and this leaves him in doubt whether his carnal nature has altogether destroyed his genius. Of this he cannot be sure until it returns to him, as a proof that it is still alive.

When his love for Margaret lifted him half of the time into heaven, but plunged him the other half into hell, did he ever try and succeed in shaking the direful bondage off, swearing fealty to his genius only ? He did, working his redemption through devotion to his art and intellectual pursuits, which made him in time forget the old miseries. "Often mid a waste appear many purest water-rises. I found a pure cup which nature's prettiest dales do form, filled to its brim as with Nepenth : this I drank, and so in time I did shuffle off my old *amour*." The French word sounds so light, but do not read the sentiment amiss. The "*amour*" that was slipped off was but the earthly vesture of his love.

And though the necessities of life forced him even, in middle age, to let another woman take the place in his house that should have been occupied by Margaret, the undying memory, nay, the presence of the latter in his innermost being could not be banished, and was never wanted so to desert him. "Not until four decades or eight lustres [to be exact, 46 years] of life were outlived, did I take any other to my sore heart. Then I married the woman [Alice Barnham, " the alderman's daughter, an handsome maiden to my liking "] who hath put Marguerite from my memory—rather, I should say, hath banished her portrait to the walls of memory only, where it doth hang in the pure, undimmed beauty of those early days, while her most lovely presence doth possess this entire mansion of heart and brain." [1]

Unhappily there will be many who believe the biliteral cipher story to be but the fruit of Mrs. Wells Gallup's fertile brain. These have either not made a serious study of it, or are entirely incapable of distinguishing the commonplace from the works of genius. If Mrs. Wells Gallup did invent it all, we should have to acknowledge that in our own days there has lived another Bacon and another Shakespeare, and to hail *her* as such. Who that has read the above extracts with an unbiassed mind—his soul open to the dramatic power, the poetical beauties, the spiritual lights that shine through the story—will not have sensed that he has been in communion all the time with the real soul-life of an exalted philosopher, who indeed " had nothing in common with vulgar minds," [2] an exquisite poet, whose " pen is dipped deep into the Muses' pure source." [3] above all a true man with a heart full of the tenderest, yet most enduring sentiments? Rank prejudice or gross dullness alone can make one lay the story aside as so much trash. To me the strongest proof for the genuineness of the " double alphabet cipher " is the highly inspired nature of the narrative in every sense, both as the work of a consummate genius, and as an amazingly living human document. To Mrs. Wells Gallup, the decipherer, then, be our unbounded thanks for her precious gift to humanity.

[1] WG II 336-7.   [2] WG II 58.   [3] WG II 4.

I have been very full in my extracts from her book, or rather from Francis Tudor's secret diary. Nearly every single scrap about the beautiful Margaret has been gathered together here. Some may for that reason think the tale too long. I will not apologize. I did not take into account anybody's taste in the matter, except the author's. In deference to his expressly stated wish, and not the less in homage to his great love, the above was compiled. "We would wish," Francis Tudor accosts the future decipherer," you might leave out nothing of a history of one who cannot be banished from my memory while this heart doth live and beat, but we are aware it cannot interest others in like degree. To me it will be the dream, day and night, that never will be aught but a vision, and yet is far more real than all things else."[1]

NOTE.—The few disjointed passages which could not be worked into the story above, are for completeness' sake reproduced here. They are all from the second part of the Biliteral Cipher, except the last. The numbers between brackets refer to the pages. " I have many single livres prepared for my dear Marguerite ; one is in these other historical plays, and in the play James the Fourth of R. Greene. It is her own true love story in the French, and I have placed many a cherished secret in the little loving worthless books : they were kept for her wishes, to find some lovely reader in future Æons. A part of the one I place in my own history, lives so pure, no amorous soilure taints the fair pages" (175). "Join Romeo with Troy's famous Cressida, if you wish to know my story. Cressida in this play, with Juliet—both that one in the comedy [Measure for Measure, Act II, scene III], where she first doth enter as Claudio's lady, and the one of my Tragedy [Romeo and Juliet] just given—are my love, whose mind changed much like a fickle dame's. Thus Trojan Cressid, Troylus did ensnare, and the words his sad soul speaks do say to you that his ill-success, and that I did have, such oneness was in his sorrowful hap and mine " (176).

[1] WG II 203.

" Spenser's, as Shakespeare's numerous love poems of many kinds, sonnets, and so forth " (181). " Margaret's sunshiny France " (183). " A few small poems in many of our early works of various kinds, which are in the French language, tell a tale of love when life in its prime of youth and strength sang sweetly to mine ear, and in the heart-beats could one song ever be heard—and yet is heard " (202). " A little book . . . It is French, to please Margaret, but very short, and is in several small divisions . . . a book of French poems " (203). " Many French poems written at an early age, and little worth " (345).

" That unfortunate early love for ill-fated Margaret may be clearly seen through many stage-plays where the theme is a like unfortunate love, happy at the outset, unfortunate in the end " (III 17).

Of the bitter words, referred to above, spoken by Troilus' " sad soul," when he discovered his Cressid's perfidy, we shall repeat here only those two famous lines (Act V, scene 3), which form the most appropriate epitaph to Francis Tudor's own great passion.

Never did young man fancy
With so eternal and so fixed a soul.

2. Adversaries

1. ROBERT CECIL

NLY surviving son of Lord Burleigh, Elizabeth's life-long minister, Robert Cecil had for his mother Mildred Cooke, the most learned lady of her time. She was the elder sister of Lady Bacon, wherefore in face of the world Francis and Robert were full cousins. This was the open story, but there is the suspicion that Cecil also was a son of Queen Elizabeth,[1] and therefore blood-brother to Francis Bacon and Robert Devereux, Earl of Essex. So much is certain that a constant jealousy against these two gnawed at Cecil's mean heart, especially against Francis, intellectually and morally his unquestioned superior. Yet such were the younger man's practical shrewdness and cunning that at every point he easily wrested the laurels of worldly honours from the brow of his rival. Elizabeth may have hailed the graceful and witty Francis in his teens as " my young Lord-Keeper ; " she may have delighted in calling the undergrown, malformed and weakly Cecil " my pigmy ; " his enemies may have gleefully abused his " wry neck," " crooked back " and " splay foot," none the less he took the ladder of

[1] His birth-date is not known, but he is generally accepted as Francis' junior, by four years some say, by two years say others. See Sp XI 11.

success in quick strides, till "the whole conduct of public affairs was placed solely in his hands," till he was the real ruler of England's destiny, the uncrowned King on Francis' rightful throne.

Educated at Cambridge, Cecil was sent in 1584 to France, and in 1588 to the Netherlands, then fighting to the death for their political independence from mighty Spain. About 1589 he entered upon the duties of Secretary of State, was knighted in 1591, received his official appointment as Secretary of State in 1596, was made Chancellor of the Duchy of Lancaster in 1597, and sent again to France in 1598. At his father's death on the 4th of August of the same year, there was a keen competition between Bacon, Essex and Cecil, for the supreme direction of affairs. The Queen preferred the youngest and the cleverest man. In his mental make-up Cecil was most like herself, specially as regards his avarice and sharp common sense, "neither guided nor inspired by any great ideal." At this period began his secret correspondence with James of Scotland, which ended in 1603 by his first poisoning and then strangling the Queen.[1] Thereupon James took possession of the throne without further opposition, Bacon having been forced to abdicate his rights to the sovereignty, while Essex had ended his life on the scaffold two years before.

After James' accession honour after honour was heaped upon Cecil. In 1603 he was created Lord Cecil of Essendine, in 1604 Viscount of Cranborne, in 1605 Earl of Salisbury. He died in 1612, worn out with incessant labour. During his long political career he had amassed a large fortune. "His bias against Spain and his fidelity to the national interests render his acceptance of a pension from Spain a surprising[2] incident in his career. The sum Cecil received at the conclusion of the peace with that country in 1604 was £1,000, which was raised the following year to £1,500, while in 1609 he demanded an augmentation and to be paid for each piece of information separately."[3] Is it a wonder that no historian has yet been found, eager to undertake a full biography of this English statesman, a man of graft, a man of craft ?

[1] Ow I 174 ff.   [2] To say the least !   [3] EB XXIV 76.

The following three extracts are from Shakespeare's *Richard III*, Bacon's *Essays*, and *The Biliteral Cipher*. The first is a masterful description of the man in his repellent outward appearance and malevolence of character. The second gives an example of the close relationship, the harmony or "consent," as Bacon calls it, "between body and mind," illustrating it in the case of a crooked mind in a crooked body, the opposite of the well-known adage *mens sana in corpore sano*. The third shows the evil mind already in action even in the earliest stages of its bodily existence.

Shakespeare's *Richard III* was first heard of and became first known when it appeared in 1597 in a good quarto edition. Though the play as a whole was much revised and added to in the Folio edition,[1] the soliloquy of Richard, with which the play opens, remained virtually unchanged. There was nothing to alter, nothing to add, nothing to improve. It was complete, perfect, as it had been first poured forth from the white-hot brain of a mighty genius in his most vigorous years. And so it still stands unrivalled in the English or any other language, an immortal picture of a most evil genius. Bacon was thirty-six when he wrote this mighty invective and indictment :

> Now is the winter of our discontent
> Made glorious summer by this sun of York ;
> And all the clouds that loured upon our house
> In the deep bosom of the ocean buried.
> Now are our brows bound with victorious wreaths ;
> Our bruisèd arms hung up for monuments ;
> Our stern alarums changed to merry meetings ;
> Our dreadful marches, to delightful measures.
> Grim-visaged war hath smoothed his wrinkled front ;
> And now, instead of mounting barbèd steeds,
> To fright the souls of fearful adversaries,
> He capers nimbly in a lady's chamber,
> To the lascivious pleasing of a lute.

[1] *Ante*, p. 35.

But I, that am not shaped for sportive tricks,
Nor made to court an amorous looking-glass ;
I, that am rudely stamped, and want love's majesty,
To strut before a wanton ambling nymph ;
I, that am curtailed of this fair proportion,
Cheated of feature by dissembling nature,
Deformed, unfinished, sent before my time
Into this breathing world, scarce half made up,
And that so lamely and unfashionable,
That dogs bark at me as I halt by them ;
Why, I, in this weak piping time of peace,
Have no delight to pass away the time,
Unless to spy my shadow in the sun,
And descant on mine own deformity.

And therefore, since I cannot prove a lover,
To entertain these fair well-spoken days,
I am determinèd to prove a villain,
And hate the idle pleasures of these days.
Plots have I laid, inductions dangerous,
By drunken prophecies, libels, and dreams,
To set my brother Clarence and the King [1]
In deadly hate the one against the other :
And if King Edward be as true and just,
As I am subtle, false, and treacherous,
This day should Clarence closely be mewed up,
About a prophecy, which says that G [2]
Of Edward's heirs the murderer shall be.
Dive, thoughts, down to my soul ! here Clarence comes.''

To read in this magnificent speech Bacon's own life-story, we have
but to change the names of the *dramatis personae* of a former century

---

[1] Edward IV, 1442-1483.

[2] The letter G, as is mostly the case in oracles, is of an ambiguous import. It may either
point to Richard himself, Duke of Gloucester, or to his brother George, Duke of Clarence.

into those of the Elizabethan age, reading Cecil for Richard, Francis for Clarence, and Queen Elizabeth for King Edward, thus :

> Plots have I laid, inductions dangerous,
> To set my brother Francis and the Queen
> In deadly hate the one against the other.
> Dive, thoughts, down to my soul ! here Francis comes.

Some idea of those " plots and inductions " may be obtained from *The Biliteral Cipher*. But before turning to that book, we have first to take up Bacon's *Essays*. These appeared for the first time in 1597, the same year as *Richard III*, but the essay on Deformity (No. 44) was then not yet to be found amongst the collection.

As long as Cecil was alive and in power, it would not do to publish such a disquisition on his bodily and mental failing, which he might easily have recognized as aimed at himself. Gloucester's monologue in *Richard III* might go unheeded, under the guise of an historical character of a bygone age, but Cecil would never let the essay in question thus pass unchallenged. It was probably not even in existence at that time. The opening scene of *Richard III* had for the time sufficiently given relief to Bacon's emotions, for him not to feel the need for a second outburst so soon. But it is proven from a MS. in the British Museum that the essay on Deformity was at any rate already in existence some time between 1607 and 1612.[1] In the latter year Cecil died, and immediately Bacon released his MS. for the Press, so that still in the same year the dissertation on Deformity was made public to the world in this new enlarged edition of the *Essays*. In the later editions it underwent only trifling alterations. I subjoin it here from the edition of 1625, the last published by Bacon himself. Bacon was past the prime of life when he wrote this essay. This explains its calm reasoning and passionless judgment, contrasting sharply with the passionate outbreak in *Richard III*, but not less deadly accurate of aim than the older piece.

[1] Sp VI 535.

On Deformity

" Deformed persons are commonly even with nature ; for as nature hath done ill by them, so do they by nature ; being for the most part (as the Scripture saith) *void of natural affection* ; and so they have their revenge of nature.   Certainly there is a consent between the body and the mind ; and where nature erreth in the one, she ventureth in the other. But because there is in man an election touching the frame of his mind, and a necessity in the frame of his body, the stars of natural inclination are sometimes obscured by the sun of discipline and virtue.   Therefore it is good to consider of deformity, not as a sign, which is more deceivable ; but as a cause, which seldom faileth of the effect. Whosoever hath any- thing fixed in his person that doth induce contempt, hath also a perpetual spur in himself to rescue and deliver himself from scorn.   Therefore all deformed persons are extreme bold.   First, as in their own defence, as being exposed to scorn ; but in process of time by a general habit. Also it stirreth in them industry, and especially of this kind, to watch and observe the weakness of others, that they may have somewhat to repay. Again, in their superiors, it quencheth jealousy towards them, as persons that they think they may at pleasure despise ; and it layeth their com- petitors and emulators asleep ; as never believing they should be in possibility of advancement, till they see them in possession.   So that upon the matter, in a great wit, deformity is an advantage to rising. Kings in ancient times (and at this present in some countries) were wont to put great trust in eunuchs ; because they that are envious towards all are more obnoxious and officious towards one.   But yet their trust to- wards them hath rather been as to good spials and good whisperers, than good magistrates and officers. And much like is the reason of deformed persons.   Still the ground is, they will, if they be of spirit, seek to free themselves from scorn ; which must be either by virtue or malice ; and therefore let it not be marvelled if sometimes they prove excellent per- sons ; as was Agesilaus, Zanger the son of Solyman, Æsop, Gasca Presi- dent of Peru ; and Socrates may go likewise amongst them ; with others."[1]

[1] Sp VI 480.

We come now to *The Biliteral Cipher* and the picture drawn there of the man at work, even as a youth—if ever he was young—amongst his youthful comrades. It will complete the sketches from the same source given in the previous chapter. It must have been written late in life, for it was only incorporated by Bacon's faithful Chaplain, Rawley, in the 1635 edition of the *New Atlantis*, nine years after his Master's death. It is written in a calmer tone than the more passionate out-pourings of earlier years, but in its restraint it is not the less convincing. It shows also how the calmer retrospective mood of old age has often a sharper vision, conjuring up long forgotten incidents of the youthful past. It is this and other such tell-tale characteristics which constitute for me so many internal proofs of the genuineness of the story the biliteral narrative tells us.

" To Robert Cecil I owe much of this secret, underhand, yet constant opposition : for from the first he was the spy, the informer to the Queen, of all the boyish acts of which I had least cause or reason for any pride. This added fuel to the flame of her wrath, made me the more indiscreet, and precipitated an open disagreement, which lasted for some time, between my foster-mother, Lady Anne Bacon, and the woman who bore me, whom however I seldom name with a title so sacred as mother. In truth, Cecil worked me nought save evil to the day which took him out of this world.

" Through his wild[1] influence on Elizabeth, he filled her mind with a suspicion of my desire to rule the whole world, beginning with England ; and that my plan was like Absalom's to steal the hearts of the Nation and move the people to desire a King. He told her that my every thought dwelt on a crown ; that my only sport amid my school-mates was a pageant of royalty ; that it was my hand in which the wooden staff was placed, and my head that wore the crown, for no other would be allowed to represent princes or their pomp. He informed Her Majesty that I would give a challenge to a fierce boyish fight, or a duello of fists, if anyone presumed to share my honours or depose me from my throne."[2]

---

[1] The text has " vilde." Should it be " vile ? "   [2] WG II 335.

From Cecil now to Bacon, from the evil and the wicked to the truly human and the angelic.

2. FRANCIS BACON

In every respect, Cecil's life forms a contrast with Bacon's. Entering upon his public life as early as 1584 by taking his first seat in Parliament, Bacon was knighted only at James' accession, 1603, and appointed Solicitor-General in 1607. That remained all the acknowledgement his extraordinary intellectual powers received as long as Cecil was alive. It is a pathetic, at the same time a shameful story, to read of Bacon's fruitless solicitations for advancement with his uncle and cousin. After the latter's death, the old Cecil having passed fourteen years before, he quickly rose to honour after honour. Appointed Attorney-General in 1613, admitted Privy Councillor in 1616, made Lord Keeper in 1617, and Chancellor in 1618, he was created Baron Verulam in the same year, and Viscount Saint Albans in 1621, whereupon follows, still in the same year, his great disgrace. He died, poor and in debt, but in the full power of his creative intellectual faculties, on Easter Sunday 1626.

In appearance and character also he was a contrast to Cecil. To Cecil's craft he opposed the dove's innocence, to his practical common sense the highest speculative idealism, and to his avarice the greatest generosity, all three qualities part causes of his fall, the real and deeper cause lying in his royal birthright. This was the secret menace felt by every political rival, of little danger so long as he had been kept down, but when in spite of all opposition he had at last risen to worldly eminence, it could only be finally eliminated by his ignominious downfall and conviction to political oblivion for good.

One of his biographers, William Hepworth Dixon, a non-Baconian, thus describes Bacon's youth : '' Sweet to the eye and to the heart

is the face of Francis Bacon as a child. His chubby cheeks, his
grey-blue eyes, his curly and silken locks, might have fitted him to sit
for one of the angels painted by Raffaelle. Born among the courtly
glories of York House, nursed on the green slopes and in the leafy woods
of Gorhambury ; a man among boys, now playing with the daisies and
speedwells, now with the mace and seals ; one day culling posies with
the gardener or coursing after the pigeons, the next day paying his
pretty little compliment to the Queen. He grows up into his teens a
grave yet sunny boy ; on this side of his mind in love with nature,
on that side in love with art. Every tale told of him wins on the
imagination : whether he hunts the echo in St. James's Park, or eyes the
juggler and detects his trick, or lisps wise saws to the Queen and
becomes her young Lord Keeper of ten. No one lapse is known to
have blurred the beauty of his youth. No rush of mad young blood
ever drives him into brawls. If he be weak on the score of dress and
pomp ; if he dote like a young girl on flowers, on scents, on gay
colours, on the trappings of a horse, the ins and outs of a garden, the
furniture of a room ; he neither drinks, nor games, nor runs wild and
loose in love. Armed with the most winning ways, the most glozing
lip at court, he hurts no husband's peace, he drags no woman's name
into the mire. When the passions fan out in most men, poetry flowers
out in him. Old when a child, he seems to grow younger as he grows
in years. Yet with all his wisdom he is not too wise to be a dreamer of
dreams ; for while busy with his books in Paris he gives ear to a ghostly
intimation of his father's death. All his pores lie open to external
nature. Birds and flowers delight his eye ; his pulse beats quick at the
sight of a fine horse, a ship in full sail, a soft sweep of country ; everything holy, innocent, and gay acts on his spirits like wine on a strong
man's blood. Joyous, helpful, swift to do good, slow to think evil, he
leaves on every one who meets him a sense of friendliness, of peace
and power. The serenity of his spirit keeps his intellect bright, his
affections warm ; and just as he left the halls of Trinity with his mind
unwarped, so he now, when duty calls him from France, quits the
galleries of the Louvre and St. Cloud with his morals pure. One sees

9

him, by the light of Hilliard's portrait, as he strolled along the Thames or reclined under the elms, with his fat round face, his bluish-grey eyes, his fall of dark brown curls, and his ripe, jesting mouth ; with his hose puffed out, his ruff and rapier as the scholars then wore them ; in his face a thought for the bird on the tree, the fragrance in the air, the insect in the stream, no less than for the subtlest speculations of philosophy." [1]

In the promise of the youth lies the fulfilment of the man. It would be absurd to expect from such a noble beginning a base end. The common herd of biographers would have it so. Small knowledge and lack of imagination are their undoing.

It is true that a certain amount of fiction is blended with the sober facts in the above attractive description of Bacon's youth, but it is a natural and happy blend—imagination guided by intuition working upon historical truth. It is the only way for a writer, coming centuries after his subject, to make it live again before our eyes. And Hepworth Dixon's great merit, for which his name shall be honoured by a grateful posterity, is that his intuition guided him rightly in the estimation of Bacon's real character. He is the first, after the intervening ages of obloquy, to try to vindicate with unwavering assurance Bacon's honour and innocence before the court of public opinion. The weak, half-hearted efforts of others before him, like Montagu's, so easily frozen by Macaulay's chill blast, hardly count.

Still, however great our debt to Hepworth Dixon, before the imaginative writer of a subsequent age, must rank the testimonies of eye-witnesses and contemporaries of Bacon, so as to make historical fact for us also the basis of further speculation. And it is significant that " of the contemporaries whose opinion of him is known to us, those who saw him nearest in his private life give him the best character." [2] This is constantly forgotten or quite ignored by those facile biographers who arrogantly assume that they know him better than his friends

---

[1] HD I 12-14 ; II 21-23. I have changed the river Cam into the Thames, as being more in accord with the date of Hilliard's miniature, painted when Bacon was eighteen.

[2] Sp XIV 576.

and intimates who conversed with him daily in his manhood and ripe age.

Among those who knew Bacon well, in one or other capacity even intimately, and who have put their knowledge of him on paper, four stand out prominently—Toby Matthew, Ben Jonson, Peter Boener, and William Rawley.   We shall take them up in their chronological order.

Of these four witnesses Sir Toby Matthew, Knight, has the sole distinction that his friendship with Bacon may be traced through the long years that pass, in a correspondence of which much has been preserved to us.   He was a young man of "pregnant parts," still the favourite son of his father, when he first came in contact with Bacon.   That must have been in his Oxford student days, for in 1595, when he was eighteen, we find him taking part in a theatrical performance, given in honour of the Queen at York House, the text for which had been written by Bacon.[1]   After having graduated M.A. at Oxford in 1597, he was the next year admitted at Gray's Inn, where his acquaintance with Bacon in a natural way developed into a warm and lasting friendship, such as is possible only between two kindred spirits, both of similar literary tastes and talents.

When Francis Bacon in 1604 resigned his seat in Parliament for St. Albans, to take that for Ipswich, one of the considerations was undoubtedly that Toby Matthew might take his place in the former seat, for which he was returned in March of that year.   Bacon was not disappointed in his expectations, for in time Matthew "became a noted orator and disputant."   In a letter of the same month to Sir Thomas Challoner, tutor to the Prince of Wales, Bacon further gave the young man the following generous recommendation :

"I do commend unto yourself, and such your courtesies, as occasion may require, this gentleman, Mr. Matthew, eldest son to my Lord Bishop of Duresme [Durham, later Archbishop of York] and my very good friend, assuring you that any courtesy you shall use towards

[1] M-C 10 ; Sp VIII 375.

him, you shall use towards a very worthy young gentleman, and one,
I know, whose acquaintance you will much esteem.''[1]

In 1604 Matthew went to France and Italy, but he remained in
touch with Bacon by correspondence.   While on the continent, he was
converted to the Roman Catholic faith, the full orders of which he
took some time later.   In the difficulties into which this conversion
plunged him, Bacon proved a tolerant and true friend.

" In the noblest and most original of his Essays,[2] penned in the
prime of his intellectual powers, he especially explains and defends this
principle of toleration.   But the doctrine of his book had been
previously exercised as a virtue in his life.   The lapse of Toby Matthew
from the English Church to Rome puts his tolerant philosophy to the
proof.   Born on the steps of the episcopal bench, his grandfather a
bishop, his father a bishop, four of his uncles bishops, all his connexions
in the Church, the fall of this young man makes a noise in England
loud as the apostasy of Spalatro makes in Rome.   The Puritans would
cut him off branch and bole.   When he comes from Italy to London,
having given up all his old delights, cards, wenches, wine, and oaths,
some, who are not themselves saints, would fling him into the Tower
and leave him there to die, as Spalatro, venturing into Rome, is sent
to perish in the dungeons of St. Angelo.   James is bitterly incensed
against him, looking on his fall as that of a column of his church ; his
father drives him from his heart with a curse ; yet, when his whole kin
spit on him and cast him forth, Bacon, strong in his sympathy for a
scholar and a man who has lost his way, takes this outcast and re-
generate pervert to his house.   Though he fights against his friend's
new doctrines, he never will consent, with the less tolerant world, to
hunt him down for a change in his speculative views, which every eye
can see has made him a better and a happier man.   The philosopher
may not be always able, by any sacrifice of name and credit, to shield
this enthusiast from the rage of sects, but he comforts him when in jail,
procures leave for him to return from exile, softens towards him the

---

[1] M-C 28. See also another letter on the same page, and Sp X 61, 64.
[2] No 3, Of Unity in Religion.

heart of his father, and obtains for him indulgences which probably save his life."[1]

When Toby Matthew returned to England in 1607, he was imprisoned in the Fleet, and only after sixteen months released on parole, through the intercession of Bacon, to whose house he was allowed to remove under the care of a messenger of State. After having stayed there for two months he was ordered to leave the country.[2]

Bacon's friendship and tolerance for the renegade was of course viewed with disfavour by the common mass of people, nobles of the realm included. But such was the quality of Bacon's friendship, that it disregarded public opinion. He was certainly no mere " fair-weather friend."[3] And he had the great satisfaction, when himself in disgrace with the world and in dire need of such friendly help and sympathy, to find the trust he had placed in Toby Matthew again fully justified. Up to the very end of his own life Matthew showed himself to be of as true metal as Bacon had proved himself to him. Here is Spedding's summing up of their relation.

Matthew's " constant affection " for Bacon, " through all varieties of both their fortunes, cannot but be thought greatly to the honour of both. What Matthew felt when he heard of the impeachment [against Bacon], and the issue of it, may be imagined by those who know his opinion of Bacon's character. He gave ample proof that Bacon's loss of greatness made no difference. His regard for him could hardly be greater than it had been before, and it certainly suffered no diminution. What words he wrote to him on hearing of the impeachment and the issue of it, we do not know, but we may infer their tenor from the reply. Matthew was still abroad, waiting impatiently for leave to return to England,"[4] when he received the following letter from Bacon.

June, 1621.

" I have been too long a debtor to you, for a letter, and especially for such a letter, the words whereof were delivered by your hand, as if it had been in old gold. For it was not possible for entire affection to be more generously and effectually expressed. I can but return thanks

---

[1] HD I 144.   [2] M-C 89.   [3] M-C 150.   [4] Sp XIV 285.

to you ; or rather indeed, such an answer as may better be of thoughts than words. As for that which may concern myself, I hope God hath ordained me some small time, whereby I may redeem the loss of much. Your company was ever of contentment to me, and your absence of grief : but now it is of grief upon grief. I beseech you therefore make haste hither, where you shall meet with as good a welcome, as your own heart can wish."

When Bacon died four years later, Toby Matthew was thus remembered in his will : "I give to my ancient good friend, Sir Toby Matthew, some ring, to be bought for him, to the value of thirty pounds,"[1] in those times a considerable sum.

Let us now turn to what Matthew has to say about his great friend. Some years before the receipt of the above letter, two of Bacon's books, the *Essays* and the *Wisdom of the Ancients* had been translated into Italian. The book appeared in 1618 with a dedicatory and informatory letter to the Grand Duke of Tuscany,[2] from the pen of Matthew. From Spedding's version we take over the following :

"After some account of Bacon's career and position, and a description of his intellectual powers, vigorously and justly drawn, Matthew goes on to say that the praise is not confined to the qualities of his intellect, but applies as well to those which are rather of the heart, the will, and the moral virtue ; being a man most sweet in his conversation and ways, grave in his judgments, invariable in his fortunes, splendid in his expenses ; a friend unalterable to his friends ; an enemy to no man ; a most hearty and indefatigable servant to the King, and a most earnest lover of the Public—having all the thoughts of that large heart of his set upon adorning the age in which he lives, and benefiting as far as possible the whole human race.

"And I can truly say," he adds, "(having had the honour to know him for many years as well when he was in his lesser fortunes as now that he stands at the top and in the full flower of his greatness) that I never yet saw any trace in him of a vindictive mind, whatever injury were done him, nor ever heard him utter a word to any man's

<hr />

[1] Sp XIV 542.   [2] Cosimo II, 1590-1609-1621.

disadvantage which seemed to proceed from personal feeling against
the man, but only (and that too very seldom) from judgment made of
him in cold blood.   It is not his greatness that I admire, but his virtue :
it is not the favours I have received from him (infinite though they be)
that have thus enthralled and enchained my heart, but his whole life
and character ; which are such that, if he were of an inferior condition
I could not honour him the less, and if he were my enemy I should not
the less love and endeavour to serve him." [1]

Shortly after the publication of the Italian *Essays*, there flowed from
Matthew's pen another testimony of his full heart.   The letter is
probably addressed to Gondomar, the Spanish ambassador in England,
whom Bacon calls " my voluntary friend." [2]   Matthew had been allowed
to return to his country the year before, 1617, and he again enjoyed
Bacon's protection and hospitality, however people might look askance
on these proofs of his great and charitable heart.   Writes one gossip to
another : " Toby Matthew is received with great grace by the Lord
Keeper and resides a kind of prisoner with him, until the return of the
King." And another adds : " Perhaps he presumes upon my Lord
Keeper's favour, which indeed is very great now at first, if it continue,
for he lodgeth him in York House, and carries him the next week along
with him to Gorhambury by St. Alban's, being so exceedingly favoured
and respected by that Lord, that it is thought *aliquid nimium* [somewhat
extravagant] that a man of his place should give countenance to one so
affected.   And some stick not to say that former private familiarity
should give place to public respects." [3]   But such weather-cock politics
lay not in Bacon's character.   It must have been from either of these
places, York House or Gorhambury, probably the former, that Matthew
wrote the following letter to Gondomar.

" I am exceedingly glad," he writes, " that the *Essays* are so well
liked, but I beseech your Lordship conceive rightly that the dedicator was
not the translator, for I have not humility enough to avow a thing of another man's so vilely done, but howsoever I will send my Lord Chancellor
[Bacon] that excellent Eulogium which you send me, in so few words of

[1] Sp XIV 285-6.   [2] Sp XIV 429.   [3] M-C 149-150.

this letter, and I will say I had it of you, wherein I know I shall do your Lordship no wrong. *There was never man more bound to man than I am to him, and I say well than I am, for I am even now more bound, than when I was with him.* He makes me still keep my lodging in his house, with keys of it, in hope to see me there again ere long, whereof as I shall be exceedingly glad *suo tempore*, so in the meanwhile, I humbly thank almighty God, I am very free from the heats, or colds of hope or fear either in this or any other worldly thing. But to be true to your Lordship I am even sick [*i.e.*, pregnant or in travail] again of my Lord Chancellor, and am now translating the aforesaid book into Spanish, and that I will neither be ashamed to avow nor forgetful to send your Lordship of the first copies, when they shall be ready." [1]

Thirty years after Bacon's death, Matthew followed him into the grave, leaving a collection of letters with a Preface ready for the Press. It appeared five years later, 1660, edited by Dr. Donne. The preface only is of our concern.

Selecting four famous Englishmen, Sir Philip Sidney with Sir Francis Bacon of his own times, and Cardinal Wolsey with Sir Thomas More of a bygone age, as the four *most* famous men, Matthew expresses his doubts that any other nation of Europe could " muster out, in any age, four men who in so many respects should excell." These four, he thinks, " were all kinds of monsters [*i.e.*, portentous, prodigious beings] in their several ways." Of each he gives a short characteristic. Bacon's runs as follows :

" The fourth was a creature of incomparable abilities of mind, of a sharp and catching apprehension, large and faithful memory, plentiful and sprouting invention, deep and solid judgment, for as much as might concern the understanding part. A man so rare in knowledge, of so many several kinds, endued with the facility and felicity of expressing it all, in so elegant, significant, so abundant, and yet so choice and ravishing a way of words, of metaphors, and allusions, as perhaps the world has not seen, since it was a world. I know this may seem a great hyperbole, and strange kind of riotous excess of speech,

[1] M-C 161.

but the best means of putting me to shame will be for you to place
any other man of yours by this of mine."[1]

The challenge rings clear. It leaves no uncertainty, no loophole.
Name me another man who equals Francis Bacon, not simply as one of the
most famous men in a commonplace sense, but especially as " a master
of language and wit," that is as a Poet.   And yet there was Shakespeare ! Toby Matthew does not seem to know of his existence, and
mentions alongside of Bacon another, a minor poet only, preferring him
apparently before England's, nay the world's, greatest dramatist " since
it was a world."   There is only one conclusion possible.   The implication
evidently is that Bacon himself is Shakespeare, that there was no other
Shakespeare.

For Matthew's part in the Essay on " Friendship," and his sharing
with Anthony Bacon and Sir John Constable the honour of being
designated by Bacon his *alter ego*, the reader is referred to Chapter 5.

Our second witness is Ben Jonson, himself a dramatic poet, and
when we see him, like Matthew, entirely ignore Shakespeare's existence
where it supremely matters, his case seems even more pregnant than
Matthew's in its hidden implications.

Mentioning, one after another, nearly a score of the most famous
wits of his own and the preceding age, Ben Jonson too passes by
Shakespeare in silence, which in his case, who had himself sung his
" rival's " panegyrics in another place, is tantamount to a positive denial
of the man's real existence.   The passage is found in his *Discoveries*,
under the heading *Scriptorum Catalogus* :

" Cicero is said to be the only wit that the people of Rome had
equalled to their empire.   *Ingenium per imperio*.   We have had many,
and in their several ages (to take in but the former *seculum*) Sir Thos.
Moore, the elder Wyatt, Henry, Earl of Surrey, Chaloner, Smith, Eliot,
B. Gardiner, were for their times admirable ; and the more, because
they began eloquence with us.   Sir Nicholas Bacon was singular, and
almost alone, in the beginning of Queen Elizabeth's time.   Sir Philip

[1] M-C 358-9.

Sidney and Mr. Hooker (in different matter) grew great masters of wit and language, and in whom all vigour of invention and strength of judgment met. The Earl of Essex, noble and high, and Sir Walter Raleigh, not to be contemned, either for judgment or style. Sir Henry Savile, grave and truly lettered ; Sir Edwin Sandys, excellent in both ; Lord Egerton the chancellor, a grave and great orator, and best when he was provoked. But his learned and able (though unfortunate) successor [Francis Bacon], is *he who hath filled up all numbers, and performed that in our tongue, which may be compared or preferred either to insolent Greece or haughty Rome.* In short, within his view, and about his times, were all the wits born that could honour a language or help study. Now things daily fall, wits grow downward, and eloquence grows backward : so that he may be named, and stand as *the mark and acme of our language.*"

What makes Ben Jonson's panegyric so extraordinary is not only that in the words " who hath filled up all numbers," he openly proclaims Bacon as a poet, but that in the next phrase, " and performed that in our tongue, which *may be compared or preferred to insolent Greece or haughty Rome,*" he as openly as possible identifies him with Shakespeare. For in the memorial poem which he contributed to the Shakespeare Folio of 1623, the same praise in the same words is addressed to the dramatic poet.

> And though thou hadst small Latin and less Greek,
> From thence to honour thee, I would not seek
> For names, but call forth thundering Aeschilus,
> Euripides, and Sophocles to us,
> Pacuvius, Accius, him of Cordova dead,
> To life again, to hear thy buskin tread,
> And shake a stage : Or when thy socks were on,
> Leave thee alone, *for the comparison*
> *Of all that insolent Greece, or haughty Rome*
> *Sent forth*, or since did from their ashes come.

For the use of the word " numbers " in the sense of " verses " or " poetry," a reference to Shakespeare's *Sonnets*, 17, 38, 79 and 100 is sufficient. It shows that " to have filled up all numbers," means " to have written all kinds of poetry "—epic, *Fairie Queene* ; lyric, *Sonnets* ; dramatic, *Plays*.

Significant also is the phrase, " About his times, were all the wits born that could honour a language,"—men like, Greene, Peele, Marlowe, Spenser, Shakespeare, Burton. The explanation is evident : they were all one and the same Bacon. No wonder that, at his leaving the earth, it seemed as if " things daily fall, wits grow downward, and eloquence grows backward." For he was, indeed, the one and only " mark and acme of our language."

About Bacon's oratorical talents Ben Jonson has also something special to say, under the heading *Dominus Verulamius* :

" One, though he be excellent and the chief, is not to be imitated alone : for no imitator ever grew up to his author ; likeness is always on this side truth. Yet there happened in my time one noble speaker [whom one would fain imitate] who was full of gravity in his speaking. His language (where he could spare or pass by a jest), was nobly censorious. No man ever spake more neatly, more pressly, more weightily, or suffered less emptiness, less idleness, in what he uttered. No member of his speech but consisted of his own graces. His hearers could not cough nor look aside from him without loss. He commanded where he spoke, and had his judges angry and pleased at his devotion. No man had their affections more in his power. The fear of every man that heard him was lest he should make an end."

Of Ben Jonson's esteem for Bacon's character the next passage gives ample evidence.

" My conceit of his person was never increased toward him by his place or honours ; but I have and do reverence him, for the greatness that was only proper to himself, in that he seemed to me ever, by his work, one of the greatest men, and most worthy of admiration that had been in many ages. In his adversity I ever prayed that God would give him strength, for greatness he could not want. Neither could I condole in a word or syllable for him, as knowing no accident could do harm to virtue, but rather help to make it manifest."

Elsewhere he anticipated Pope's infamous line,

> The wisest, greatest, meanest of mankind,

the wisdom of which utterance he challenged by definitely stating,

> There cannot be one colour of the mind, another of the wit,[1]

or as one might read its meaning,

> There cannot be one colour of the heart, another of the mind.

The next two witnesses share the honour of having produced the first comprehensive biographical sketches of Francis Bacon, with the singular advantage of having personally known their subject through close contact for a considerable time.[2]

Peter Boener was a Dutchman, who had for years been Bacon's domestic apothecary and secretary. Having returned to his native country in 1623, he published a Dutch translation of the *Essays* in 1647. To this he prefixed a short " Life," from which the following is taken :

" This great light is born in England, at London, in the year 1560[3] —a nobleman of ancient descent—and has, firstly, by his diligent assiduity attained the degree of Advocate or Doctor of both Laws. Few years later, by reason of his virtues and great gifts, is he chosen Syndicus of the King, who is the King's spokesman to Parliament. He now continually growing in wisdom is by James, King of Great Britain, and also by the Parliament, chosen to be High Chancellor of England and Keeper of the Privy Seal of the King, to whom many affairs of jurisdiction have their appeal from divers provinces, towns and places— to have them again looked over by him and have his verdict anew. Of this task he acquitted himself in a way that all eyes were fixed on him, and that many foreign kings, potentates and ambassadors honoured him greatly when they had to present their embassies and lay their requests before the King and thereupon expected answer from the King by him. Further, showing himself as a second Seneca, or as a light of the world, he first became suspect to some learned men in his

[1] Bac, Jan. '99, 24-26.   [2] See Addenda (4).   [3] Old style, 1561 new style.

country, but by divers authors in Italy, France, Germany, the Netherlands, highly esteemed, and often greeted by them in letters, some of which I have seen and read, as also the answers to the same. Once the last line of one of these ran—*perge ut cepisti me, praecipere autem veritatem amare.* He thus excelling in wisdom and eloquence and surpassing all, as is proven by his books and deeds, was therefore lastly envied by many imitators in his own country as a phoenix who had no equals and like a prophet who seldom receiveth honour in his own country. Of these before-told things his books give sufficient evidence.

" Which books denote that he was grafted on philosophy and philosophy on him, and all high schools and academies who saw and read these works bear evidence to the same that they never have been able to write about those matters in such a way nor in a better style. Regarding his *Historia Vitae et Mortis*, certain learned and wise men said : He who made that book knew all that a man could, or even could wish to know, and they were desirous to see his principal work named *Novum Organum.* This is also noteworthy in him, that both high wisdom and high offices were at the same time with him ; it is doubtful if this could have been so with anyone in such a high degree.

" Here a word concerning his memory must needs be told. I have never seen him having a book in his hand ; only that he sometimes charged either his chaplain or me to look in such and such an author—how he described this or that in such or such a place— and then, what he had thought in the night or had invented, in the morning early he bid us write.

" About the difference of nationalities he once said that the Dutch in England were wiser than the wisest of the Netherlands, [1] and that the French are wiser than they seem, and the Spaniards seem wiser than they are.

" But how runneth man's fortune ? He who seemed to occupy the highest rank is, alas ! by envious tongues near King and Parliament

[1] As a Dutchman I would interpret this to mean that the Netherlands sent their best sons to England to learn and become wiser.

deposed from all his offices and chancellorship, little considering what treasure was being cast in the mud, as afterwards the issue and the result thereof have shown in that country. But he always comforted himself with the words of Scripture—there is nothing new. Because, so is Cicero by Octavianus ; Callisthenes by Alexander ; Seneca (all his former teachers) by Nero ; yea, Ovid, Lucanus, Statius (together with many others) for a small cause very unthankfully—the one banished, the other killed, the third thrown to the lions. But even as for such men banishment is freedom—death their life ; so is for this author his deposition a memory to greater honour and fame, and to such a sage no harm can come. This was also proved later. When the Parliament was once assembled, and a certain affair was being treated and could not well be brought to an end, King James said, ' O, had I my Chancellor Bacon here, I would speedily have an end to the affair.'

" And to conclude as I began, so it is that whilst his fortunes were so changed, I never saw him—either in mien, word, or acts—changed or disturbed towards whomsoever ; ' for the wrath of man worketh not the righteousness of God ' [1]—he was ever one and the same, both in sorrow and in joy, as becometh a philosopher ; always with a benevolent allocution. He was also bountiful, and he would gladly have given more, and also with greater pleasure, if he had been able to do more ; therefore it would be desirable (he having died anno 1626, on the 9th April, being old 66 years) that a statue or a bronzen image were erected in his country to his honour and name, as a noteworthy example and pattern for everyone of all virtue, gentleness, peacefulness and patience." [2]

Peter Boener, writing in Holland in 1647, was out of touch with the latest events in England. The " bronzen statue or image," which he indicated as a desideratum, had been erected in marble seven years before by Bacon's secretary and friend, Thomas Meautys, as we shall soon see.

Besides upon his own actual knowledge of his Master, Peter Boener may also have drawn for his sketch upon the English Ambassador at The

---

[1] James I 20.   [2] Bac, July '06, 141-5.

Hague, in whose keeping, as he was personally told by him, Bacon had left "a number of his manuscripts." This Englishman was no other than Sir William Boswell, or "my very good friend Mr. Bosvile," as Bacon calls him in his last will, into whose hands, together with Sir John Constable, Bacon indeed had left all his papers, and who therefore must also have been one of Bacon's close associates.[1]

Further on we shall have occasion to return again to the last two paragraphs of Boener's *Life*.

The last witness is Dr. William Rawley, who styles himself proudly "his Lordship's first and last chaplain," having been in that function for the last ten years or so of Bacon's life. More than thirty years after his Master's death he published a "Life" of him, "which is still (next to Bacon's own writings) the most important and authentic evidence concerning him that we possess."[2] I may therefore be excused for making the following lengthy extracts from it. Rawley proves himself an apt disciple of a great teacher. In many of his phrases and paragraphs Bacon's own voice is clearly audible, his wisdom easily discerned. The pupil is but a faithful mouthpiece of the Master.

"Francis Bacon, the glory of his age and nation, the adorner and ornament of learning, was born in York House, or York Place, in the Strand, on the two and twentieth day of January, in the year of our Lord 1560.[3] His father was that famous counsellor to Queen Elizabeth, the second prop of the kingdom in his time, Sir Nicholas Bacon, knight, lord-keeper of the great seal of England ; a lord of known prudence, sufficiency, moderation, and integrity. His mother was Anne, one of the daughters of Sir Anthony Cook ; unto whom the erudition of King Edward the Sixth had been committed ; a choice lady, and eminent for piety, virtue, and learning ; being exquisitely skilled, for a woman, in the Greek and Latin tongues. These being the parents, you may easily imagine what the issue was like to be ; having had whatsoever nature or breeding could put into him.

---

[1] The surmise (Sp III 3) that Boswell died in 1647 might not be correct, in view of Boener's statement in that year, that he still was living at The Hague.

[2] Sp I xx.   [3] Old style, new style 1561.

" His first and childish years were not without some mark of eminency ; at which time he was endued with that pregnancy and towardness of wit, as they were presages of that deep and universal apprehension which was manifest in him afterward ; and caused him to be taken notice of by several persons of worth and place, and especially by the queen ; who (as I have been informed) delighted much then to confer with him, and to prove him with questions ; unto whom he delivered himself with that gravity and maturity above his years, that Her Majesty would often term him, *The young Lord-keeper.* Being asked by the queen *how old he was,* he answered with much discretion, being then but a boy, *That he was two years younger than Her Majesty's happy reign* ; with which answer the queen was much taken.

" His birth and other capacities qualified him above others of his profession to have ordinary accesses at court, and to come frequently into the queen's eye, who would often grace him with private and free communication, not only about matters of his profession or business in law, but also about the arduous affairs of estate : from whom she received from time to time great satisfaction. Nevertheless, though she cheered him much with the bounty of her countenance, yet she never cheered him with the bounty of her hand ; which might be imputed, not so much to Her Majesty's averseness and disaffection towards him, as to the arts and policy of a great statesman[1] then, who laboured by all industrious and secret means to suppress and keep him down ; lest, if he had risen, he might have obscured his glory.

" Towards his rising years, not before, he entered into a married estate, and took to wife Alice, one of the daughters and coheirs of Benedict Barnham, Esquire and Alderman of London ; with whom he received a sufficiently ample and liberal portion in marriage. Children he had none ; which, though they be the means to perpetuate our names after our deaths, yet he had other issues to perpetuate his name, the issues of his brain ; in which he was very happy and admired, as Jupiter was in the production of Pallas. Neither did the want of children detract from his good usage of his consort during the

[1] Robert Cecil.

intermarriage, whom he prosecuted with much conjugal love and respect, with many rich gifts and endowments, besides a robe of honour which he invested her withal; which she wore unto her dying day, being twenty years and more after his death.

" The last five years of his life, being withdrawn from civil affairs and from an active life, he employed wholly in contemplation and studies—a thing whereof his lordship would often speak during his active life, as if he affected to die in the shadow and not in the light ; which also may be found in several passages of his works. In which time he composed the greatest part of his book and writings, both in English and Latin.

" There is a commemoration due as well to his abilities and virtues as to the course of his life. Those abilities which commonly go single in other men, though of prime and observable parts, were all conjoined and met in him. Those are, *sharpness of wit, memory, judgment* and *elocution.* For the former three his books do abundantly speak them ; which with what sufficience he wrote, let the world judge ; but with what celerity he wrote them, I can best testify. But for the fourth, his *elocution,* I will only set down what I heard Sir Walter Raleigh once speak of him by way of comparison (whose judgment may well be trusted). *That the Earl of Salisbury was an excellent speaker, but no good penman ; that the Earl of Northampton (the Lord Henry Howard) was an excellent penman, but no good speaker : but that Sir Francis Bacon was eminent in both.*

" I have been induced to think, that if there were a beam of knowledge derived from God upon any man in these modern times, it was upon him. For though he was a great reader of books, yet he had not his knowledge from books, but from some grounds and notions from within himself ; which, notwithstanding, he vented with great caution and circumspection.

" In the composing of his books he did rather drive at a masculine and clear expression than at any fineness or affectation of phrases, and would often ask if the meaning were expressed plainly enough, as being one that accounted words to be but subservient or ministerial to matter,

11

and not the principal. And if his style were polite, it was because he would do no otherwise. Neither was he given to any light conceits, or descanting upon words, but did ever purposely and industriously avoid them ; for he held such things to be but digressions or diversions from the scope intended, and to derogate from the weight and dignity of the style.

" He was no plodder upon books ; though he read much, and that with great judgment and rejection of impertinences incident to many authors ; for he would ever interlace a moderate relaxation of his mind with his studies, as walking, or taking the air abroad in his coach, or gentle not strenuous exercise on horseback or playing at bowls, or some other befitting recreation ; and yet he would lose no time, inasmuch as upon his first and immediate return he would fall to reading again, and so suffer no moment of time to slip from him without some present improvement.

" His meals were refections of the ear as well as of the stomach, like the *Noctes Atticae*, or *Convivia Deipno-sophistarum*, wherein a man might be refreshed in his mind and understanding no less than in his body. And I have known some, of no mean parts, that have professed to make use of their note-books when they have risen from his table. In which conversations, and otherwise, he was no dashing[1] man, as some men are, but ever a countenancer and fosterer of another man's parts. Neither was he one that would appropriate the speech wholly to himself, or delight to outvie others, but leave a liberty to the co-assessors to take their turns. Wherein he would draw a man on and allure him to speak upon such a subject, as wherein he was peculiarly skilful, and would delight to speak. And for himself, he contemned no man's observations, but would light his torch at every man's candle.

" His opinions and assertions were for the most part binding, and not contradicted by any ; rather like oracles than discourses ; which may be imputed either to the well weighing of his sentence by the scales of truth and reason, or else to the reverence and estimation wherein he was commonly held, that no man would contest with him ;

[1] " Dashing " here means " putting another man out of countenance " by his wit.

so that there was no argumentation, or *pro* and *con* (as they term it), at his table : or if there chanced to be any, it was carried with much submission and moderation.

" I have often observed, and so have other men of great account, that if he had occasion to repeat another man's words after him, he had an use and faculty to dress them in better vestments and apparel than they had before ; so that the author should find his own speech much amended, and yet the substance of it still retained.

" When his office called him, as he was of the king's council learned, to charge any offenders, either in criminals or capitals, he was never of an insulting and domineering nature over them, but always tender-hearted, and carrying himself decently towards the parties (though it was his duty to charge them home), but yet as one that looked upon the *example* with the eye of severity, but upon the *person* with the eye of pity and compassion. And in civil business, as he was counsellor of estate, he had the best way of advising, not engaging his master in any precipitate or grievous courses, but in moderate and fair proceedings : the king whom he served giving him this testimony, *That he ever dealt in business* suavibus modis ; *which was the way that was most according to his own heart.*

" Neither was he in his time less gracious with the subject than with his sovereign. He was ever acceptable to the House of Commons when he was a member thereof. Being the king's attorney, and chosen to a place in parliament, he was allowed and dispensed with to sit in the House ; which was not permitted to other attorneys.

" And as he was a good servant to his master, being never in nineteen years' service (as himself averred) rebuked by the king for anything relating to His Majesty, so he was a good master to his servants, and rewarded their long attendance with good places freely when they fell into his power ; which was the cause that so many young gentlemen of blood and quality sought to list themselves in his retinue. And if he were abused by any of them in their places, it was only the error of the goodness of his nature, but the badges of their indiscretions and intemperances.

" This lord was religious : for though the world be apt to suspect and prejudge great wits and politics to have somewhat of the atheist, yet he was conversant with God, as appeareth by several passages throughout the whole current of his writings.

" This is most true—he was free from malice, which (as he said himself) *he never bred nor fed.* He was no revenger of injuries ; which if he had minded, he had both opportunity and place high enough to have done it. He was no heaver of men out of their places, as delighting in their ruin and undoing. He was no defamer of any man to his prince. One day, when a great statesman was newly dead, that had not been his friend, the king asked him, *What he thought of that lord which was gone?* he answered, *That he would never have made His Majesty's estate better, but he was sure he would have kept it from being worse;* which was the worst he would say of him which I reckon not among his moral, but his Christian virtues.

" His fame is greater and sounds louder in foreign parts abroad, than at home in his own nation ; thereby verifying that divine sentence, *A prophet is not without honour, save in his own country, and in his own house.* Now his fame doth not decrease with days since, but rather increase. But yet, in this matter of his fame, I speak in the comparative only, and not in the exclusive. For his reputation is great in his own nation also, especially amongst those that are of a more acute and sharper judgment.

" He died on the ninth day of April in the year 1626, in the early morning of the day then celebrated for our Saviour's resurrection, in the sixty-sixth year of his age, at the Earl of Arundel's house in Highgate, near London, to which place he casually repaired about a week before ; God so ordaining that he should die there of a gentle fever, accidentally accompanied with a great cold, whereby the defluxion of rheum fell so plentifully upon his breast, that he died by suffocation ; and was buried in St. Michael's church at St. Albans ; being the place designed for his burial by his last will and testament, both because the body of his mother was interred there, and because it was the only church then remaining within the precincts of old Verulam : where he hath a monument erected for him in white marble (by the care and gratitude of Sir Thomas Meautys, knight, his lordship's secretary) ; representing his full portraiture in the posture of studying, with an inscription composed by that accomplished gentleman and rare wit, Sir Henry Wotton.

" But howsoever his body was mortal, yet no doubt his memory and works will live, and will in all probability last as long as the world lasteth. In order to which I have endeavoured (after my poor ability) to do this honour to his lordship, by way of conducing to the same."

A few words about Thomas Meautys, who erected the monument in honour of Bacon. He was more a man of deeds than of words, it seems, for differing from Boener and Rawley, he left nothing in writing about his Master, though as his last secretary and trusted friend, he too had the best of opportunities to testify to his employer's greatness of character by written word. Instead, as said, he preferred acts to words, and had the marble statue made that speaks of his devotion. Bacon's principal biographer gives him this fulsome praise : " One of the noblest of the noble order of loyal servants—loyal to the full extent of his means and abilities, in adversity as in prosperity, in disgrace as in honour—loyal through life, and beyond it, the creditor who never ceased to be a friend." [1]

In his last will Bacon made Thomas Meautys his heir and executor. He must have been deep in Bacon's literary and other secrets. And it is undoubtedly for this reason that he had a painting made of himself, by Van Somer, it is said, still shown to visitors at Gorhambury House, which portrays him in a conspicuous way bearing " a boarspear in his right hand," pointing with it, half secretly half openly, beyond himself to his Master, the real Boar-spear-man.[2]

The monument, a marble figure of Bacon, with head resting on left hand, and seated in deep contemplation, bears the following loving and reverent inscription in Latin. [3]

[1] Sp XIV 323.   [2] CB 6. See also Chapters 5 and 6 hereafter.   [3] Sp I 18.

Francis Bacon
Baron of Verulam, Viscount St. Albans
Or by more conspicuous titles
Of Science the Light, of Eloquence the Law
Sat thus
Who after all Natural Wisdom
And Secrets of Civil Life he had unfolded
Nature's Law fulfilled
Let Compounds be Dissolved
In the year of our Lord 1626, aged 66
Of such a man that the memory might remain
Thomas Meautys
Living his Attendant, dead his Admirer
Placed this Monument

Rawley's biographical sketch was first published in 1657, as an introduction to his *Resuscitatio,* a collection from Bacon's miscellaneous writings. A second edition appeared in 1661, and a third in 1671, four years after Rawley's death. For this reason alone apparently Spedding holds Dr. Rawley " not answerable " for the " good deal of new matter " contained in the last issue. But that, of course, cannot be accepted without reserve. Rawley may well have left instructions to his publisher, or literary executors, or in a private copy of his own.

Besides, the year after the first edition of the *Rescuscitatio* appeared, Rawley published a Latin version, the *Vita Francisci Baconi,* as an introduction to the *Opuscula Philosophica,* printed in Holland, and again in 1663 in the *Opuscula Varia Posthuma Francisci Baconi,* published at Amsterdam. Instead of the words in the last sentence of the English *Life,* " and will in all probability last as long as the world lasteth," the *Vita* has " and will not yield to fate until the machinery of the Earth-globe is dissolved," while it omits the last sentence from " in order to " till " conducing to the same." The addition may be a veiled allusion to the " theatrical " machinery on the stage, and as such

Francisc⁰ Bacon⁰ Baro de Verulam:
Vice-Comes S.ᵗʰ Albani, Summ' Angliæ Cancel
larius, mortuus 9 Aprilis, Anno Dni. 1626
Annoq Aetai 66.

Frank Boar

to Bacon's dramatica authorship, but then it is only a very slight and vague one.

Of more importance are the additions which the two editions of Bacon's *Opera Omnia*, of Frankfort 1665 and Leipzig 1695, make to the Latin *Vita*. The last paragraph there reads as follows :

'' But what though his body be mortal, doubtless, his memory and his works will live, and, in all probability, not perish until all the machinery of the Earth-globe be dissolved. But there were also those who by all kinds of malevolent prosecution, sought, though in vain, to stigmatise the name of the great hero. For, albeit he had been disposed of office by the King and by Parliament, this was done from no other cause than jealousy which was the motive. He personally consoled himself with those words of the Scripture : ' There is nothing new ! ' Truly, he shared the fate of Cicero at the hands of Octavian, of Callisthenes at the hands of Alexander, of Seneca under Nero, of whom history relates that they were banished or put to death or cast to the lions. However that may be, as such great men are above all fate, and as their masters usually repent their deeds later on, so we also know that whenever a particularly difficult and complicated matter presented itself, King James is said to have exclaimed : ' Would Bacon, my former Chancellor, had remained with me, how easily I would now extricate myself.' Nor is there anybody, who, after his resignation, could reproach him in any way in private affairs. For it has been proved that afterwards naught of that was wanting which had contributed towards the grandeur of his position, but that, in spite of all, he lived so, that it seemed as though he would enter into an argument on Fate with Jove himself, an example of virtue, piety, love of humanity and patience.''

I have followed Edwin Borman's [1] translation with slight alterations only. The translator makes the most, too much in fact—in the approved aggressive German manner— of Spedding's ignorance of the existence of the two German editions of Bacon's *Opera Omnia*. Too much, for the additions are evidently not an original German production, but in substance taken from the last two paragraphs of Boener's *Life*.

[1] *Francis Bacon's Cryptic Rhymes*, 1906, p. 224.

They read certainly not less Baconian in tone and style than the rest. The citations from Cicero and Seneca, among " many others," as examples for consolation, seem directly reminiscent of Bacon's letters, to the King of 16 July 1621, and to the Bishop of Winchester of the summer of 1622.[1] Boener must have heard these " consolations " directly from his Master's lips, and Rawley published the second letter in the " Miscellany Works " in 1629, so that Boener might also have taken part of his allusions from there. The anecdote about King James's tardy regret also sounds like the real thing. How greedily he must have collected it, and faithfully preserved it, and at last given it out to the world.

There is one more phrase in Rawley's *Life* which needs to be some-what closely considered, in view of the, 'n my opinion, unwarranted speculations, that Francis Bacon did not actually die at the time men-tioned, but only retired from public life into a secret mode of existence. The passage involved is the one beginning with the sentence : " *God so ordaining* that he [Francis Bacon] should die there [in the Earl of Arundal's house] of a gentle fever, etc." From this phrase with its further circumstantial evidence, I take it that Rawley at least believed sincerely in Bacon's actual death at the time and place stipulated, and by the causes enumerated with such care. The Reverend Rawley, not less religious than his Master, would not have idly used the name of his God, if he deliberately intended to say a factual untruth. He could easily have been ambiguous, or glossed over the event entirely, as he did in other places when he did not want to commit himself too strictly. As a biography by the devoted servant of a venerated Master, the whole " Life " is a model of restraint and reticence. That Rawley did not so compose himself in this place, but as it were sealed his statement with the highest authority of his faith, is for me evidence irrefutable against the speculations of some that Bacon lived to a very much older age, beyond the fatal year 1626.

There is a French proverb which says that a hero in the eyes of his valet is never a hero. And the German philosopher Hegel, later

[1] Sp XIV 297, 372.

imitated by Goethe, has given the only reasonable explanation of this saying. It is the truth, not because the hero is not a hero, but because the servant is a servant, with the mind of a valet. Bacon seems to have been extraordinarily fortunate or rather capable of drawing around him quite a circle of servants—for there are many more than those named above—who contrary to the adage *did* understand him and therefore revered him with all their heart and mind.

Summarizing the impression given by the attitude of these servants of Bacon towards their Master, what strikes us most is their veneration of him, bordering upon worship. To them evidently he was not only a kind and generous employer, and a good friend, but behind such more common sentiments, there was a deep-rooted, a quasi-religious devotion as from disciple to Master, from spiritual son to spiritual teacher. I feel they all felt what Rawley expressed in words—that there was truly " a beam of knowledge derived straight from God upon him," not borrowed from others, that he was therefore a direct Messenger from on high, an *Aggelos* or Angel. Can we after three hundred years, and deprived of that personal contact which his servants had, still capture the same feeling, merely from his writings ? I think we can, provided we have assured ourselves by diligent study and research of the identity of Bacon and Shakespeare.

For then we hold in our hands the secret of that unique manifestation of a Saint, a Sage and a Supreme Artist, the three in one, such as the world can only rarely show.

3. Arcadia

OYAL joys and sorrows had been Francis' experience in France. These came to an abrupt end, to be replaced by others, different only in nature but not less poignant, when the tidings reached him of the death of his adoptive father, Sir Nicholas, " the second prop of the kingdom in his time," as Bacon's chaplain and biographer, Rawley, in later days called him, the first prop being Burleigh, Robert Cecil's father. Before the news came to him through ordinary channels, he had an intimation of the tragic event by spiritual means. Towards the end of his life he recorded the experience in a work which appeared post-humously : " I myself remember, that being in Paris, and my father dying in London, two or three days before my father's death I had a dream, which I told to divers English gentlemen, that my father's house in the country was plastered all over with black mortar." [1] His " father's house in the country " is of course Gorhambury, the place he loved most, after York House in London, the house of his birth which became in later days the house of his glory, as Gray's Inn was the house of his work. But Gorhambury was the house of his fancy and recreation, on which he

[1] Sp II 666.

lavished the wealth of his fortune and riper imagination.[1]   In his youth it must have been more than anything else the place of his delight in nature and flowers and beauty.   No wonder that when its genial master died and thereby plunged the whole household in grief and sorrow, the fact would communicate itself through the world of mind to the sensitive youth in the image of a house in mourning.

This happened then on the 17th of February, 1579.   After having quickly settled his affairs in Paris, Francis on the 20th of March set out on his journey home.   In the despatch he carried from the Queen's ambassador, Sir Amias Paulet, he was said to be " of great hope, endued with many good and singular parts."   And if we want to know his physical appearance, we have but to look at Hilliard's miniature, painted the year before, when he was in the full glory of his youth. " There may be seen his face as it was in his eighteenth year, and round it may be read the significant words—the natural ejaculation, we may presume, of the artist's own emotion—Si tabula daretur digna, animum mallem : if one could but paint his mind ! "[2]

Arrived home, he began that restless activity, consequence of a tireless energy and the highest ambition, of which his whole life was the completest expression.   It started, still in the same year, 1579, with the publication anonymously of the *Shepherd's Calendar*.[3]   The book, therefore, must for the greater part at least, have been composed in France.

One of the names Marguerite was given, when Francis came to dream out his love in plays and poems, is that of Rosalind.   Beside Romeo's first love (Act I, scene 2), and Biron's beloved in *Love's Labour's Lost*, there is Orlando's princess in *As You Like It*, who all bear this name.   Then there are " Spenser's as Shakespeare's numerous love poems of many kinds, sonnets and so forth, that shower my Margaret as with water of Castaly," we have heard Francis say before.   *As You Like It* will be the special subject of our study in the next chapter,

---

[1] See the Essay on Gardening, No. 46, one of the three longest Essays.   [2] Sp VIII 7-8.

[3] On its title-page the book was dedicated, or " Entitled to the Noble and Vertuous Gentleman most worthy of all titles both of learning and chivalry, M. Philip Sidney," Bacon's cousin.   And as late as 1587 the poet George Whetstone refers to it as " the reputed work of Sir Philip Sydney." E. G. Harman, *The Impersonality of Shakespeare* (1925), p. 254.

here we shall deal with two of the pastorals in Spenser's *Shepherd's Calendar*.

This cycle of poems consists of twelve eclogues or pastoral dialogues after the manner of Virgil's Bucolics. There is one for every month of the year, and it is in those of January and June that we meet with the name of Rosalind. In most of the poems the shepherds are singing out their good and ill fortunes in love, mostly ill. Colin Clout, the principal singer, is also the most grievously struck. Let us try if we can find in the book indications of biographical value, hints of events, and circumstances that are in agreement with Francis Bacon's life- and love-story. In view of the secrecy he had to observe, we can of course only expect veiled allusions, feigned names, and metaphorical resemblances, no direct and straightforward descriptions. Even so, the amount of information the book yields for our purpose is astounding.

Our discoveries start even at the very beginning, with the " Argument " for January, which tells us that " in this first Eclogue Colin Clout, a shepherd's boy, complaineth him of his unfortunate love, being but newly (as seemeth) enamoured of a country lass called Rosalind : with which strong affection being very sore travailed, he compareth his careful case to the sad season of the year, to the frosty ground, to the frozen trees, and to his own winterbeaten flock. And lastly, finding himself robbed of all former pleasance and delights, he breaketh his pipe [flute] in pieces, and casteth himself to the ground."

Bacon's " unfortunate love " for Marguerite, unfortunate in a double sense, not alone through her fickleness but also through his mother's opposition to his love, tallies with Colin's case. And so does the fact that he was " but newly enamoured," if we accept the pastoral to have been written during Francis' residence on the other side of the Channel. It could hardly have been composed elsewhere, seeing that the book was published immediately after his return from France.

If we turn to the " Glosses " on the poems, we come to the nearest revelations the author could make in public. Let me add that the " Arguments " and " Glosses," as well as a dedicatory " epistle " by way of a Preface, are ostensibly not by the poet himself, but by a close friend who signs himself E. K., and who calls the author " this our new Poet who for that he is uncouth (as said Chaucer) is unkissed, and, unknown to most men, is regarded but of few." This again fits Bacon's case well. He too was a " new Poet," and the *Shepherd's Calendar* was his very first-fruits, also the first book in which the biliteral cipher was used, carrying among other things the revelation that " E. K. will be found to be nothing less than the letters signifying the future sovereign, or *England's King*." [1]

Francis was hardly eighteen years old then, and still under the full sway of youthful ambition. Only when more than thirty years later he saw the sixth edition of his work through the press, could he write with equanimity : " Vantages accounted great [in youth], simply as the uncertain dreams or visions of night seem to us in after time. Ended now is my great desire to sit in British throne. Larger work doth invite my hand than majesty doth offer : to wield the pen doth ever require a greater mind than to sway the royal scepter. Ay, I cry to the Heavenly Aid, ruling over all, ever to keep my soul thus humbled and content." [2]

To return to the new poet, " unknown to most men," and " regarded but of few," this too fits Bacon's circumstances perfectly. In England at any rate but few, a very few, his brother Anthony among the elect, will have known anything of his first poetical efforts in France, but there in the Southland itself, where a brilliant circle of men, the Pleiads as they were called, with Ronsard at their head, and many a younger disciple, like Du Bartas and D'Aubigné, had been busy creating a new language, a new art, and a new France, some may have known perhaps somewhat more of the literary, beside the secular ambitions of their young " confrère " from the Northland. At least that is what the " Glosses," to which we come now, suggest.

" Colin Clout," says the first gloss, " is a name not greatly used. . . . But indeed the word Colin is French, and used of the French poet Marot (if he be worthy of the name of a Poet) in a certain Eclogue. Under which name this Poet secretly shadoweth himself, as sometime

[1] WG I 79.   [2] WG II 41.

did Virgil under the name of Tityrus,[1] thinking it much fitter than such Latin names for the great unlikelihood of the language."

So may the youthful Bacon, enamoured of the melodious sound of the French tongue, and contrasting with it " the great unlikelihood of the (English) language," as yet, have borrowed Marot's Colin for his penname. I said " as yet " advisedly. For what the French Pleiads endeavoured for their mother-tongue, Bacon single-handed, and with even greater success, set out to accomplish for the English language, undoubtedly fired to the effort by the inspiring example of his French brother-poets. The Pleiads laid the foundation for the grand structure of France's classical period, adorned by such names as those of Corneille, Racine, Molière—Bacon did more, he alone was foundation and structure in one, the former as Spenser-Peel-Greene-Marlowe, the latter as Bacon-Shakespeare-Burton. One of the striking phrases in the rules the Pleiads had made to guide their efforts by, " Car ce sont les ailes dont les esprits des hommes volent au ciel," re-appeared later in English dress in 2 Henry VI (IV, 7) as : " Ignorance is the curse of God, Knowledge the wing wherewith we fly to heaven."[2]

Bacon however was not a mere imitator. He went his own inde-pendent way. He might translate and imitate Latin, French or Italian models, as in the November eclogue for example Marot, but these were only preparatory exercises, as it were to gauge his own powers. He declines merely to run after outlandish models. " It is his ambition to be English." Therefore in the above gloss is contained a subtle re-pudiation of Virgil (Tityrus) as his model in poetry. Marot may take him up as such, but Bacon will take the English Tityrus (Chaucer) as a guide for " the beautifying and bettering of the English tongue." This was his ambition.[3]

Surveying, when he was forty-six years old, his labours in this respect, he wrote : " Still, so great is our love for our mother-tongue, we have at times made a free use, both of such words as are considered antique, and of style, theme, and innermost spirit of an earlier day,

---

[1] Under this name, in Spenser's poems, is understood Chaucer.   [2] Bax 307.

[3] De Selincourt in his Introduction to Spenser's poems.

especially in the Edmund Spenser poems that are modelled on Chaucer ;
yet the antique or ancient is lightly woven, as you no doubt have before
this noted, not only with expressions that are both common and un-
questionable English of our own day, but frequently with French words, for
the Norman-French [that] William the Conqueror introduced left its traces.
Besides, nought is further from my thoughts than a wish to lop this off,
but on the contrary a desire to graft more thoroughly on our language
cuts that will make the three more delightsome and its fruits more rare,
hath oft led me to do the engrafting for my proper self [I who as
‘ England's King ’ am England herself].   Indeed not the gems of their
language alone, but the jewels of their crown are rightfully England her
[that is my] inheritance.   Furthermore many words commonly used in
different parts of England, strike the ear of citizens of towns in southern
England like a foreign tongue, combinations whereof make all this
variety, that I find oft-times melodious, again less pleasing, like the
commingling of country fruits at a market fair.   Yet you [decipherer],
seeing the reason, approve no doubt the efforts I make in the cause of
all students of a language and learning that is yet in its boyhood, so to
speak.   The inward motive is noble, only as it cometh from a pure love
of the people, without a wrong or selfish thought of my right to rule
this kingdom as her supreme governor.   But this deathless, inalienable,
royal right doth exist.''[1]   This was written six years before his final resignation to adverse fate.

Of all the masks he used at times—Spenser, Greene, Peele,
Marlowe, Shakespeare, Ben Jonson, Robert Burton—none stands so
near to the French spirit, shows so much indebtedness to the Pleiads,
as Spenser.   '' From living so much in Paris I have a truly French
spirit,'' wrote Francis St. Alban in the 1623 Folio of Shakespeare's
works.[2] Edmund Spenser he chose as his first mask after his return to
England, and once having endued him with that special character of
being greatly influenced by French culture, he remained true to that
picture of the man, by assigning to him his direct translations or adaptations from the French, as for example the '' Ruins of Rome '' and the

[1] WG II 27.   [2] WG II 193.

" Visions " of Du Bellay, who was one of the Pleiads, of whom Marot was the precursor. How this knowledge of French literature, and what is more the kinship with the French spirit, was to be rhymed with the person and life-story of Edmund Spenser, the pure-bred Englishman, of whom there is no evidence at all that he ever left the English soil, except for Ireland, is more than the orthodox historians are able or even try to explain.

De Selincourt, one of Spenser's modern editors, may write facilely : " We can safely attribute to his [Spenser's] undergraduate days the *Visions of Du Bellay* and the *Visions of Petrarch* [translated after Marot's French rendering]," and again : " To the same period belongs the translation of Du Bellay's *Antiquitez de Rome*, whilst [Spenser was] still dominated by the influence of the Pleiads," but the feeling of safety which this writer has, is based upon pure ignorance, which is not conscious of any *contra*, because it does not try to prove any *pro*. Yet have the Baconians, since Orville Owen's and Mrs. Wells Gallup's decipherings, shown the possible contra, which exists in Bacon's authorship. And the threads of the story which I am gathering here show, methinks, the contra-argument to be stronger than the pro-motif. Spenser's poems agree better with Bacon's life-story than with his own.

Of course, the Baconian theory has its difficulties also. Of the Visions of Du Bellay and Petrarch for example there exists a version in *A Theatre* devised by the Dutchman Sir John van der Noodt of 1569 ; which would place Bacon's first effort at poetry not in his undergraduate, but in his nursery days, when he was only eight or nine years old. This is not likely. There must be a mystery connected with John van der Noodt's compilation, as regards date as well as authorship. The ante-dating of books was not a rare thing in those days. A striking example are the fair Shakespearean Quartos, published under different dates of 1600, and 1608, but in reality being of 1619.[1]

Before we proceed it will be well to say a few words about Bacon's evident genius in adapting his style to the different personalities he chose for his masks, as for example in Spenser's case, to a tender

[1] See Addenda (2).

lovesick youth, with French attachments, a passion for old-time words and phrases, and a leaning for pastoral poetry ; in the case of Greene and Peele to a somewhat looser vein of sensual poetry, and first efforts in the dramatic field, which are still markedly pastoral.   In Marlowe comes the change and progress towards a more virile and purely dramatic style, which finally culminates in Shakespeare's supreme mastership of this highest form of literature.

How these adaptations, expressions of his own moods and changes of sentiment and power were consciously and deliberately adopted, how his masks are carefully chosen to suit his own development, and how his creative power is determined and enhanced by the particular character of which his mask is possessed, all this is explained in the *Biliteral Cipher*.   For example : " I varied my style to suit different men, since no two show the same taste and like imagination."[1] Again : " When I have assumed men's names, the next step is to create for each a style natural to the man, that yet should let my own be seen, as a thread of warp in my entire fabric, so that it may be all mine."[2]   Of peculiar interest is the characterisation given by the author of himself in his most perfect creation—Shakespeare. Shakespeare, the actor, was well-known for his " witty vein."   Said Ben Jonson of him : " This wit was in his own power ; would the rule of it had been so too."   Said Bacon, comparing himself with the actor : " In this actor that we now employ, is a witty vein, different from any formerly employed. *In truth it suiteth well with a native spirit, humorous and grave by turns in ourselves. Therefore when we create a part that hath him in mind, the play is correspondingly better therefore.* It must be evident that these later dramas are superior in nearly all those scenes where our genius hath sway."[3]

Coming back to Colin Clout, " under which name this Poet [Spenser] *secretly* shadoweth himself," he is of course none other than Francis Bacon.   For Spenser there was no earthly reason thus " secretly " to hide himself.   He might have taken a penname, but why " secretly ? " This adjective points to a man with a peculiar secret history, the secret King of England.

[1] WG II 200.   [2] WG II 54.   [3] WG II 37.

We come now to the second gloss. Besides Colin and Rosalind, there is another shepherd-boy named in the first Eclogue. It is Hobbinol, and the gloss says that this too " is a feigned [mark, not a secret] country name, whereby it being so common and usual, seemeth to be hidden the person of some his very special and most familiar friend, whom he entirely and extraordinarily beloved."

Who is Hobbinol ? Not Gabriel Harvey, the subject of the dedicatory epistle, as is generally accepted by modern editors. But who then ? He must be a young man, a boy one would say, of the same age or slightly younger than Francis himself, and who has a boyish love and admiration for the somewhat older friend, whom he also tries to draw away from Marguerite, to keep his affection for himself, but in vain. Sings Colin :

> It is not Hobbinol, wherefore I plain,
> Albe my love he seek with daily suit :
> His clownish gifts and courtesies I disdain,
> His kids, his cracknels, and his early fruit.
> Ah foolish Hobbinol, thy gifts been vain :
> Colin them gives to Rosalind again.

I have no doubt that Hobbinol is the original of the " lovely boy " of the first series of Shakespeare's *Sonnets* (see No. 126). If we could penetrate his mystery, we would at the same time have solved the vexed question of the identity of Shakespeare's " beauteous and lovely youth " (*Sonnet* 54). With only the faintest of suggestions, however, to go on, it would be vain to say anything definite at this distance of time. I hold that Hobbinol personifies Anthony Bacon, trying to wean his brother's affections away from his lady-love, and back to himself.

And now the third gloss, regarding the name of Colin's lady-love, the most illuminative of all. " Rosalinde is also a feigned name," we are told, " which being well ordered, will bewray the very name of his [Colin's] love and mistress, whom by that name he coloureth. So as Ovid shadoweth his love under the name of Corynna, which of some is supposed to be Julia, the Emperor Augustus his daughter and wife to

Agrippa. . . And this generally hath been a common custom of counterfeiting the names of secret Personages."

Here again we meet the epithet " secret," and rightly, for just as his own state of being England's rightful King, had to be kept a secret, so also, his love being actually a Queen, the secret of her identity had to be guarded equally secure. But in a roundabout or metaphorical way, let us say, the truth about her is here indicated more clearly than anywhere else. For as Julia, Ovid's love was the daughter of an Emperor, so was Marguerite, Bacon's love, the daughter of a King, Henry II of France. Again, as Julia was married to Agrippa, a popular leader of the people (he was thrice consul) and a man of great military abilities, so was Marguerite married to Duke Henry of Navarre, the most popular leader of the Huguenots and likewise a soldier and general of repute. This forms indeed one of the strongest points we have met until now in favour of our argument of Bacon's authorship.

But most of all, what is said of the name " Rosalinde," namely, that if it were only " well ordered," it would " bewray the very name," comes near to an open declaration. " Well ordered " suggests of course that the letters of the name are not in their right order, but should be re-arranged so as to reveal the true name. Now, we must note well, that in the poem the name is spelled Rosalind, but in the gloss " Rosalinde." As to the question how to re-arrange the letters, Bacon, aware of the dullness of our imaginative wit, has thought it expedient to give us another hint. Preceding the gloss on " Rosalinde," there is another gloss on the following two lines of the poem :

> I love thilke lasse, (alas why do I love ?)
> And am forlorne, (alas why am I lorne ?)

And the gloss runs thus. " A pretty Epanorthosis in these two verses, and withal a Paronomasia or playing with the word, where he saith (I love thilke lasse) alas etc."

The paronomasia, is the " lasse-alas," and the epanorthosis, the " love-lorne." We shall begin with the latter. " Love-lorne " describes Colin's state to the point.   If we substitute his lady's name for " love," we get " Marguerite-lorne," and if we further take the English word for Marguerite we get " dasi-lorne " or " dasie-lorn," or " dasi-lorn," [1] and these give us indeed the names Rosalinde and Rosalind " well ordered."

There is one objection we must meet.   It might be said that the pretty flower's name should be spelled " daisy," and not " dasie." But the answer is that the latter is just the old-time spelling, as is shown by a reference to the Folio, *Love's Labour's Lost*, (V 2) :

When Dasies pied, and Violets blew,

and also to *Cymbeline*, (IV 2) :

Find out the prettiest Dazied-Plot we can.

Hickson [2] gives " Daiselorn " as the anagram, which is, I think, incorrect.   At least I have nowhere met the form " daise " as the name for the marguerite flower.   Hickson gives no reasons to justify his " well ordered " reading of the name, but his intuition—if he was the original discoverer of the anagram, which I do not know—led him pretty near the truth.   In the above I have, I think, supplied the reasons, and the proofs for the correct reading : " dasielorn."

We must now take up the paronomasia, or word-play.   Beside the forms Rosalind and Rosalinde,[3] there is a third reading, Rosaline, which we meet in *As You Like It*, *Romeo and Juliet* (I 2), and *Love's Labour's Lost* (Act III).   Now taking the " lasse-alas," that which these two words have in common, namely " las," is the kernel of the pun as it were.   And extracting this kernel from the name Ro-sal-ine, what is left is Roine, the old-spelling of the french word Reine or Queen.[4]

---

[1] For the form " dasi," for " dasie," or " dasy," compare the 1598 Quarto of Love's Labour's Lost, Act V, scene 2 : " Ladi " for " Lady " in " Ladi-smockes."

[2] *The Prince of Poets*, 1926, p. 132.

[3] In the August Eclogue there occurs twice the form Rosalind.   It is the last syllable only which varies.   The first two remain always unchanged, Rosa, the " sweet Rose of France."

[4] Says Littré : " Dans l'ancien français, le mot était *reine* dans l'ouest, *roine* dans le centre," and he gives the following examples from the sixteenth century : " Le danger est icy sy grant, que je n'ouse escrire au roy n'y à la roine. . . . La roine continue sa bonne santé. . . . Pourquoi ha on laissé le mot regulier et utilize de royne pour dire reine ? "

Therefore the " las," or " lasse " Francis loved was nothing less than a Roine, the Queen of Navarre.

Another possible way of constructing the anagram is as follows. The first time the name of Rosaline occurs in *As You Like It* (Folio, page 126), it is spelled with double *s*, and so might be re-arranged lass-roine, that is the " lass " who was a " roine." Do not deprecate this reading by objecting that the spelling in question was merely a printer's error. In the further course of our investigations we shall meet with many such " errors " which were undoubtedly intentional, and " marks " or " signs " rather than errors. Important in the present case is that it is the very first time the name appears in the play.

We must now let Colin's complaint speak for itself :

> A shepherd's boy (no better do him call)
> When winter's wasteful spite was almost spent,
> All in a sunshine day, as did befall,
> Led forth his flock, that had been long ypent,
> So faint they wox, and feeble in the hold,
> That now unnethes [1] their feet could them uphold.
>
> All as the sheep, such was the shepherd's look,
> For pale and wan he was, (alas the while)
> May seem he loved, or else some care he took :
> Well couth he tune his pipe, and frame his style,
> Tho to a hill his fainting flock he led,
> And thus him plained, the while his sheep there fed.
>
> Ye gods of love, that pity lovers' pain,
> (If any gods the pain of lovers pity :)
> Look from above, where you in joys remain,
> And bow your ears unto my doleful ditty.
> And Pan thou shepherd's God, that once didst love,
> Pity the pains, that thou thyself didst prove.

[1] Difficult.

A thousand sithes[1] I curse that careful hour,
Wherein I longed the neighbour town to see :
And eke ten thousand sithes I bless the stour,[2]
Wherein I saw so fair a sight, as she.
Yet all for naught : such sight hath bred my bane.
Ah God, that love should breed both joy and pain.

I love thilk lass, (alas why do I love ?)
And am forlorn, (alas why am I lorn ?)
She deigns not my good will, but doth reprove,
And of my rural music holdeth scorn.
Shepherd's device she hateth as the snake,
And laughs the songs, that Colin Clout doth make.

Colin's " love " is evidently not of his own country, but of a
" neighbouring town," which is explained in the gloss as " the next
town," not a town somewhat far away, with other towns intervening,
but the very " next " town. So also was Francis Bacon's " love " not
of his native land, neither of a country with other countries between it
and his native soil, but of France, England's next-door neighbour.

We also hear of the reason, or at any rate of one reason for Colin's
misfortune in love. He was only " a shepherd's boy, no better do him
call," a rustic from the country, whereas Rosalind (though in another
place called " a country lass ") was in reality a girl from town, with all
the refinement, at least of outward show, which town-life gives, and which
made her scorn her lover's " rural music," that is his country speech
(English) and simple natural wit. Marguerite was typically French and
of a court, the most exquisite and refined of the day. Francis came
from a country which through its insularity has always been and still is
slow in taking over from the continent the lighter manners and luxuries
of advanced civilisation. Both, Marguerite and Francis must have felt
the difference, Marguerite feeling herself laughingly the superior,
especially with her additional eight years.

[1] Times.   [2] Encounter.

Francis slightly vexed by his apparent short-comings, found the way out of a nascent inferiority complex, in this connection, not only through the resolve, noted before, of following the example of the Pleiads in making the English language as refined and perfect a vehicle of thought and feeling as the French, but also through venting his spleen in many a scene of his plays, where a sharp contrast between French and English is drawn. It begins immediately with the very first play which was published under Shakespeare's name, *Love's Labour's Lost*, of which a "newly corrected and augmented" edition appeared in 1598, but which was probably composed before 1590, I am even sure, much earlier, indeed begun at least soon after his return from France. It is the most French of all his plays ; "it is French in manner and setting." From the same critic who wrote this I also quote what he has to say of two of the principal actors in the play, Berowne or Biron, and Boyet, the English and the French type of courtier.

"In Biron the author manifestly gives an idealized presentment of himself. The picture is that of a youth of position emerging from his studies under the first impression of feminine attractions. He is the central figure of the piece and all the other characters are foils to him. Especially noticeable is the contrast between him and Boyet. Biron is deep, serious, wholly English ; Boyet is wholly French. In intellect Biron is head and shoulders above him and every other character in the play, but he lacks the facile accomplishments and social graces of the French exquisite and envies him accordingly." [1]

Biron's or Bacon's own natural wit is well described by Rosaline ; (II 1) :

> A merrier man,
> Within the limits of becoming mirth,
> I never spent an hour's talk withal.
> His eye begets occasion for his wit ;
> For every object that the one doth catch
> The other turns to a mirth-moving jest,
> Which his fair tongue, conceit's expositor,

[1] E. G. Harman. *The Impersonality of Shakespeare* (1925), pp. 8-13.

Delivers in such apt and gracious words,
That aged ears play truant at his tales,
And younger hearings are quite ravished :
So sweet and voluble is his discourse.

So too did Ben Jonson testify of Bacon's readiness to jest : "His language, when he could spare or pass by a jest was nobly censorious ;" and of his pleasing talk : "The fear of every man that heard him was lest he should make an end." And Rawley wrote : "His meals were refections of the ear as well as of the stomach."

Contrast with this Biron's portraiture of Boyet, where his envy of the facile Frenchman shines through every line (V 2) :

This fellow pecks up wit, as pigeons peas,
And utters it again when God doth please :
He is wit's pedlar, and retails his wares
At wakes and wassails, meetings, markets, fairs ;
And we that sell by gross,[1] the Lord doth know,
Have not the grace to grace it with such show.
This gallant pins the wenches on his sleeve ;
Had he been Adam, he had tempted Eve :
He can carve too, and lips : why, this is he
That kissed his hand away in courtesy ;
This is the ape of form, monsieur the nice,
That, when he plays at tables, chides the dice
In honourable terms : nay, he can sing
A mean most meanly, and in ushering
Mend him who can : the ladies call him, sweet :
The stairs, as he treads on them, kiss his feet.
This is the flower that smiles on every one,
To show his teeth as white as whales-bone ;
And consciences, that will not die in debt,
Pay him the due of honey-tongued Boyet.

[1] That is, wholesale, solidly.

14

> Behaviour, what wert thou
> Till this man showed thee ? and what art thou now ?

Which of the courtiers at the French King's court had Bacon in mind, for it cannot but be that the original of this portrait must have been a man of life and blood. The note of envy is too personal for a mere generalisation. The answer is contained in the June Eclogue, where Marguerite's scorn of the Englishman's less volatile wit is shown to carry her to the extreme of faithlessness. The pastoral is a duologue between Colin and his friend Hobbinol.

Hob. Lo Colin, here the place, whose pleasant site
  From other shades hath weaned my wandering mind.
  Tell me, what wants me here, to work delight ?
  The simple air, the gentle warbling wind,
  So calm, so cool, as nowhere else I find :
  The grassy ground with dainty daisies dight,
  The bramble bush, where birds of every kind
  To the water's fall their tunes attemper right.

Col. O happy Hobbinol, I bless thy state,
  That Paradise hast found, which Adam lost.
  Here wander may thy flock early or late,
  Withouten dread of wolves to been ytost :
  Thy lovely lays here mayst thou freely boast.
  But I unhappy man, whom cruel fate,
  And angry Gods pursue from coast to coast,
  Can nowhere find, to shroud my luckless pate.

Hob. Then if by me thou list advised be
  Forsake the soil that so doth thee bewitch :
  Leave me those hills, where harbour n'is to see,
  Nor holly bush, nor briar, nor winding witch :
  And to the dales resort, where shepherds rich,
  And fruitful flocks been everywhere to see.

I have already remarked that Hobbinol is a shepherd of the South-land, that the " Paradise " he has found is in France.   Did not Francis Bacon in his Biliteral Cipher write about his " summary banishment to beautiful France," that it " opened to us the gates of Paradise ? "   And so the advice of Hobbinol to forsake " the hills " and " the soil " that still bewitch Colin, for " the dales " where he himself lives, means that he advises him to leave England and to come to France.   If in the reader's mind there is still some doubt whether this is really the meaning of these allusions, it will be dissolved, I think, by the following gloss to the words " forsake the soil," which leaves nothing to be desired. " This [forsaking of his native soil] is no poetical fiction, but unfeignedly spoken of the Poet self, who for special occasion of private affairs [his banishment by Elizabeth] (as I have been partly of himself informed [the annotator is evidently anxious to press home the truth of his statement]) and for his more preferment [for his fuller education] [1] removing out of the North-parts came into the South, as Hobbinol indeed advised him privately."

Further glosses tell us : " Those hills, that is the North country where he dwelt."   And : " The Dales, the Southparts, where he now abideth, which though they be full of hills and woods (for Kent is very hilly and woody ; and therefore so called : for Kantsh in the Saxon's tongue signifieth woody) yet in respect of the Northparts they be called dales.   For indeed the North is counted the higher country."   All these details about Kent are of course but designed the better to cover the hidden meaning.   A very strong point in favour of our argument is that all this does not fit in with the life of Edmund Spenser.   He has nothing whatever to do with Kent.

Of the rest of the poem only Colin's last soliloquy is of more particular interest to us.   It treats of Rosalind's scorn turning to faith-lessness.   It starts again with Colin's feeling that his homeliness may not suit his love, wherefore he invokes the spirit of Chaucer (Tityrus) to lend him of his divine fire, so that he may win back Rosalind, by whom he is deserted (lorn) for Menalcas.

[1] WG I 83 ; II 80.

Col.   Of Muses, Hobbinol, I can no skill :
For they been daughters of the highest Jove,
And holden scorn of homely shepherd's quill.
For sith I heard that Pan with Phoebus strove,
Which him to much rebuke and danger drove :
I never list presume to Parnass hill,
But piping low in shade of lowly grove,
I play to please myself, all be it ill.

Nought weigh I, who my song doth praise or blame,
Ne strive to win renown or pass the rest :
With shepherds sits, not follow flying fame :
But feed his flock in fields where falls him best.
I wote my rhymes been rough and rudely dressed :
The fitter they my careful case to frame :
Enough is me to paint out my unrest,
And pour my piteous plaints out in the same.

The God of shepherds Tityrus is dead,
Who taught me homely as I can to make.
He whilst he livèd was the sovereign head
Of shepherds all that been with love ytake :
Well couth he wail his woes, and lightly slake
The flames, which love within his heart had bred,
And tell us merry tales to keep us wake,
The while our sheep about us safely fed.

Now dead is he and lyeth wrapped in lead,
(O why should death on him such outrage show ?)
And all his passing skill with him is fled,
The fame whereof doth daily greater grow.
But if on me some little drops would flow,
 Of that the spring was in his learned head,

I soon would learn [1] these woods to wail my woe,
And teach the trees, their trickling tears to shed.

Then should my plaints, caused of discourtesy,
As messengers of all my painful plight,
Fly to my love wherever that she be,
And pierce her heart with point of worthy wite [2]
As she deserves that wrought so deadly spite.
And thou Menalcas, that by treachery
Didst underfong my lass to wax so light,
Shouldst well be known for such thy villainy.

But since I am not as I wish I were,
Ye gentle shepherds which your flocks do feed,
Whether on hills or dales or other where, [3]
Bear witness all of this so wicked deed :
And tell the lass whose flower [4] is wox a weed,
And faultless faith is turned to faithless fere, [5]
That she the truest shepherd's heart made bleed,
That lives on earth, and lovèd her most dear.

The glosses tell us that by "discourtesy" the poet "meaneth the falseness of his lover Rosalinde, who forsaking him had chosen another," that is Menalcas. If the "feigned" Rosalind is really Marguerite of Valois, then we can make only two guesses at the identity of Menalcas, for the biliteral cipher-story has only preserved the names of two, whose rivalry has made Francis feel jealous and unhappy. The first might naturally be her own husband against whom, as Francis avowed, " a secret jealousy was constantly burning in our veins." The second might be the Duke of Guise, whose love for the beautiful queen " had power to make him forget the greatest honours that France might confer upon him."

---

[1] Teach.   [2] Point of worthy wite, "the prick of deserved blame," says the gloss.
[3] Whether in England (hills), or in France (dales), or in any other country.
[4] The rose-daisy.   [5] Companion, mate.

Of Menalcas the gloss further says : "Here is meant a person unknown and secret against whom he [the Poet] often bitterly inveigheth." But I do not seem able to find so many bitter railings against him, at least not in *The Shepherd's Calendar*, and not directly referring to one definite person, but kept more in general terms. The use of the words "treachery" and "underfong," which latter word the gloss tells us means "undermine and deceive by false suggestion," make it most probable that by Menalcas was meant another than Marguerite's consort. Therefore probably De Guise.

While the January Eclogue was perhaps written while Bacon was still in France, the June pastoral dates probably from a time after his return to England, when Sir Amyas Paulet at Paris, to whom Francis may have lain bare his longings and complaints in letters from London, perhaps advised him to return to France and settle there. Of such a project Francis at one time may not have thought altogether unfavourably. Like the Duke of Guise he may have thought of giving up all his higher ambitions for his love. "There came in days when I would fain have lived my honoured days in this loving wise." And the only thing which most likely withheld him was "many a vision" that in that paradise he would not be the only Adam.[1]

In January Colin's "emblem" was still *Anchoraspeme*, "the meaning whereof is that notwithstanding his extreme passion and luckless love, yet leaning on hope, he is somewhat recomforted, for that as then there was hope of favour to be found in time, but now being clean forlorn and rejected of her, as whose hope that was, is clean extinguished and turned into despair, he renounceth all comfort and hope of goodness to come, which is all the meaning of this Emblem : *Gia speme spenta*," which motto he attached to the June Eclogue.

In the December Eclogue *The Shepherd's Calendar* then closes with the following farewell-stanza :

> Adieu delights, that lullèd me asleep,
> Adieu my dear, whose love I bought so dear ;

[1] WG II 175.

Adieu my little lambs and lovèd sheep,
Adieu ye woods that oft my witness were ;
   Adieu good Hobbinol, that was so true,
   Tell Rosalind, her Colin bids her adieu.

The love-lorn youth makes place for the grown-up man, the delights of the worldly passions for more serious undertakings, the friendships and attachments with France for the call of his own country.

The sacrifice proves to his own and England's greater glory.

4. A Tale of Two Brothers

1. IN LOVE

SSENTIAL to a fuller understanding of Shakespeare's masterpieces is the personal factor in them, however some may take these lightly and consider them as of no consequence. A knowledge of the creator gives a better insight into his creation, as well as the reverse, Oliphant Smeaton, therein following Frank Harris, observes that "there is a subtle autobiographic element in well-nigh every play, if only we could light on the key thereto," and he regrets that "we no longer possess the keys."[1] Baconians will point to the life of Francis Bacon as the long lost key, regained by the combined efforts of both enthusiasts and scholars. Having lain discarded and exposed to the corroding effects of time during two and a half centuries, it was very rusty at first when found, but the last half century has contributed much to somewhat restore its lustre and smooth working.

Smeaton's remark was made directly in regard with *The Two Gentlemen of Verona*, and he further observes that in Valentine the author's "own qualities of heart and head are portrayed." Baconians can readily agree with him here, if only one substitutes in thought Bacon

[1] Sm 79.

15

for Shakespeare. Once having done that, one can even go farther than
the Shakespearean critic. Not only personal " qualities," but also much
personal " history " is embedded in this play. Among other things it
reveals the two greatest passions that had possessed themselves of
Francis Bacon's mind in the first part of his life—till he was past forty,
when Shakespeare's " dark period " is said to have begun. The two
greatest passions, that is, if we do not count the one intellectual master-
passion that governed him all his life, and was the mighty driving power
behind his efforts for the Great Instauration of all Learning, or the
Intellectual and Moral Education of Mankind. The former, passions of
the heart rather than of the head, were his love for the beautiful
Marguerite of Navarre, and his not less deep affection for his " brother "
Anthony as he was known publicly ; for his " friend " as he was known
in his secret history ; and both for his " brother " *and* " friend " as he
was actually by the kinship of their souls.

In the play Silvia is of course Marguerite, and Anthony is Proteus,
so that in reality the tale is not of " Two Gentlemen of Verona," but
rather of " Two Gentlemen from London," while the Duchy of Milan is the
Kingdom of France, " the sunny land of the South," where blossomed
the " sweet white Rose " of Francis' first and last great love.

From the outset, however, we must warn the reader against taking
any of the characters or their adventures, in all points, as a faithful
portraiture and an exact biography. Much is naturally pure fiction, and a
great deal is merely accidental, as required by the dramatical and theatrical exigencies of the play.   As has been rightly said, it is only a " subtle
element " of autobiography which is found in the comedy. Some high-
lights here and there in the psychological delineation of character, also
some of the principal events in the tale, these alone may be taken as
shadowing the life-story of their author and his co-actors in life's drama.

Then there is the statement that the biographic element is to be
met with in " well-nigh every play." This needs some qualification too.
With the passing of the years and the steady growth of the author's
dramatic powers, the psychological factor becomes of ever greater importance, while the purely historical retreats more and more into the

background.   In the younger plays the latter, in the sense of a record of occurrences of the author's personal life-story, either dwindles to negligeable proportions, or is entirely absent, or again is transmuted from historical events into symbolical imagery of general application.   It is only in the earlier plays that we are afforded such intimate glimpses into the private life of the " man " Bacon, as are given us for example in *The Two Gentlemen of Verona* and *The Merchant of Venice*. The former reveals the sad story of the brothers' common affection for one gentle lady-love, the latter the not less " sad story of brotherly love and debt," as one biographer has so aptly described it.[1]

We have seen how at the age of sixteen Francis is " banished " to France, and travels there " in the company and care of Sir Amyas Paulet," the English ambassador to the court of King Henry III, Marguerite's elder brother by one year, and the third as well as the last of Catherine de Medici's sons to sit on the throne of France.   " The business of the mission to which he was attached took him in the wake of the Court through several of the French provinces—from Paris to Blois, from Blois to Tours, from Tours to Poitiers, where in the autumn of 1577 he resided for three months." To which Spedding adds the somewhat pedantically dry conclusion : " So that he had excellent opportunities of studying foreign policy." [2]   Sure, but also to study men and women, especially the women, and famous women at that, who played a no less important part than men at the court of France, in the last quarter of the sixteenth century. It was a period in French history which has some likeness with the last quarter of the eighteenth century. It reminds one of the answer made by the Count de Saint Germain to Madame de Pompadour, King Louis the XV's famous courtesan.   To her question if the Court of Francis I (1494-1547) was *fort belle*, his reply was : " *Très belle, Madame*, but the court of his grandsons [Francis II, Charles IX and Henry III] surpassed it infinitely ; and in the time of Mary Stuart and Marguerite de Valois, it was a land of enchantment, a temple of pleasures, in which those of the spirit were mingled also. Both Queens were *savantes*, made verses, and it was a joy to listen to them."[3]

[1] HD II 81.   [2] Sp VIII 7.   [3] *Mémoires de Madame du Hausset*, Paris 1824, p. 149-150.

All this was said as if it were a personal recollection of the speaker, and it has been claimed in our days by Theosophists that the Count was a reincarnation of Francis Bacon. If so, it is one of the most remarkable historical corroborations of the theory of men's repeated rebirths on earth. However, that is another story, which may be told one day in another book.

To return to Francis Bacon, when he made his first acquaintance with this gay court life and these consummate women, he was unaffected yet by any serious attachment to the other sex, in contrast to his brother Anthony, who is two years his elder, and of a lighter heart and of a more mercurial temper.

Until the time of Francis' banishment, the two brothers had grown up together, in York House, " next to the palace," when in town ; in Gorhambury, close to Saint Albans and old Verulam, when in the country. Together also, when twelve and fourteen years old, they were " sent down to Cambridge, where they entered as fellow-commoners of Trinity College, of which John Whitgift was the Master. The boys appear to have resided in his house. From him they learned what he had to teach, though little Anthony paid more for pills and potions, for meat from the Dolphin Tavern, and for Dr. Hatcher's drugs, than for Latin and Greek."[1]

A digression may be permitted here. In all modern editions of Shakespeare's works, Sir John Falstaff's and his royal boon-companion's favourite haunt is given as the *Boar's Head Tavern* in Southwark. It is a fact, however, that the Folio of 1623 leaves the tavern in question unnamed, and favours Eastcheap as its locality.[2] A hardly less famous character than Sir John Falstaff is the tavern's hostess, Mistress Quickly, and I wonder if both do not embody some of the author's reminiscences of his and his brother's student days in Cambridge with the *Dolphin Tavern* as their favourite haunt. Here is the long-winded, circumstantial, and highly laughable, though obviously truthful accusation, made by the Hostess against Sir John (2 Henry IV : II 1).

Falst. What is the gross sum that I owe thee ?

[1] HD II 22.   [2] 2 Henry IV : II 2, 161.

Host.   Marry (if thou wert an honest man) thyself, and the money too. Thou didst swear to me upon a parcel gilt goblet, sitting in my *Dolphin-chamber* at the round table, by a see-coal fire, on Wednesday in Whitsun week, when the Prince broke thy head for likening him to a singing man of Windsor ; thou didst swear to me then (as I was washing thy wound) to marry me, and make me My lady thy wife. Canst thou deny it ? Did not goodwife *Keech* the Butcher's wife come in then, and call me gossip *Quickly* ? Coming in to borrow a mess of vinegar : telling us, she had a good dish of prawns : whereby thou didst desire to eat some : whereby I told thee they were ill for a green wound ? And didst not thou (when she was gone downstairs) desire me to be no more familiar with such poor people, saying, that ere long they should call me Madam ? And didst thou not kiss me, and bid me fetch thee 30 sh. ? I put thee now to thy Book-oath, deny it if thou canst ?

" Gossip Quickly's " speech is so strikingly true to life, in her outspokenness and loquaciousness, in her touches of local colour, and ramblings into the smallest details of simultaneous happenings and circumstances, that I am obsessed with the idea that Bacon must have been an eye-witness to just such a scene as this in the original *Dolphin-chamber*, with a large round table near the hearth where a good fire is lustily burning, not of cheap inland burned charcoal, but of real coal from Newcastle by the sea. It is naturally the principal room of the *Dolphin Tavern*, from which the inn derives its name, and it is kept for distinguished guests like the two brothers, sons of the Great Lord Keeper to the Queen, when they honoured the inn with their visit. If only it could be so proven, it would provide the Baconians with one of the strongest evidences in favour of their viewpoint. As it is, we must be content with accepting the Dolphin-chamber of Shakespeare's play and the Dolphin Tavern of Bacon's life as another one of those many arrowheads, all pointing in one direction, whose accumulating number converts possibility into probability and probability into certainty.

Three years in all the brothers spent at Trinity, with occasional breaks, once for so long a time as eight or nine months.   Then ' the Lord Keeper, meaning his son for a man of state, not of books and ideas, withdrew him at the age of sixteen from the scene of these unprofitable studies and debates.   French, Latin, law, history, politics, were the things which Sir Nicholas thought a boy should learn.   Latin and history his son already knew.   That he might catch up something of law, he put his name on the books of Gray's Inn ; that he might perfect himself in French and politics, he proposed to send him into France.''[1]

Such is the tale as told by officially accepted history.   But the description is equally of force for Anthony.   If so, how then is it that of the two brothers only the youngest goes actually to France, leaving his beloved friend, from whom till now he has not been separated for any length of time, if even for a day, to remain at home ?   How is it that he is going to enjoy alone the new experiences of travelling, out there in the great wide world, over the sea, far from home, and who knows for how long ?

The answer is not to be found in the ordinary historical records. The unaccountable break in their companionship remains there a riddle— one of those puzzles which by their insolubility along ordinary lines force us to look for secret motives and hidden causes, neglected or rejected by the historians of the recognized academies of science ; one more of those arrowheads, found by the hunters in the woods outside the confines of the academies, all pointing to one centre of attraction, of disturbance rather.

If it had been the Lord Keeper's own idea that Francis needed the educational advantage of travelling abroad, there would have been no earthly reason for him to withhold the same privilege from his elder son Anthony.   It is certain, however, that Sir Nicholas Bacon never fostered such liberal ideas of education, considering that none of his six elder children, three sons and three daughters of his first wife, were given similar opportunities.   Sir Nicholas himself had spent some time in Paris in his youth, before he entered public life.   Of that visit

[1] HD II 24.

he seems to have brought away a life-long distrust of Roman Catholics in general, and of the French in particular, which was increased by the infamous massacre of St. Bartholomew's Night in 1572, hardly four years back.   He was a good Protestant, and so was Lady Ann, who completely shared her husband's distrust and aversion, not only of French politics, but also of French manners and morals.

How came it then that the privilege of going to France was first tendered to Francis, the youngest of Lady Ann's two sons, who more-over at Sir Nicholas' death, three years later, proves to be the only one of all his children who has been left absolutely destitute, with no portion whatever in the inheritance.   All these strange happenings point to the strong probability that other powers than his own will were govern-ing the destiny of the Lord Keeper's youngest son, as if indeed he were not his own son at all, but merely a ward in custody.

From the biliteral cipher we know how this was in fact the case, how the boy's crossing the Channel for new adventures was not due to his adoptive father's liberal educational views so much as to the Queen's and his real sire's anger, after the inopportune discovery of his royal birth.

But what of his foster-brother Anthony? Why did he not accom-pany his friend to the French court? I am confident that if he had really strongly wanted it, his father and mother might have given in, and the Queen would not have opposed it. The only sound reason one can find for his letting Francis go alone is that a stronger affection even than that which bound him to his brother, kept him at home. The fruit which Francis would find abroad, Anthony had already tasted at home. The love for an English girl kept him rooted in the English soil, at least for the time being.

Let us see now if we can find these and similar sentiments reflected in *The Two Gentlemen of Verona*. The play opens with a farewell-scene between the two friends, just before Valentine's leaving for the continent. Proteus has tried to dissuade him from going, but Francis knows only too well the futility of resisting the royal decree, and is moreover nothing loth to go, being all too eager to see new countries,

to meet new people, to experience new adventures.   He would fain
have his friend accompany him, but if the latter cannot part from his
lady-love, he must needs depart alone, for only an attachment similar
to his friend's would have the power to hold him back.   Of such a
passion, however, he is as yet entirely free.

Val.   Cease to persuade, my loving Proteus :
       Home-keeping youth have ever homely wits.
       Were 't not affection chains thy tender days
       To the sweet glances of thy honoured love,
       I rather would entreat thy company
       To see the wonders of the world abroad
       Than, living dully sluggardized at home,
       Wear out thy youth with shapeless idleness.
       But since thou lov'st, love still, and thrive therein,
       Even as I would when I to love begin.
Pro.   Wilt thou be gone? Sweet Valentine, adieu !
       Think on thy Proteus, when thou haply seest
       Some rare noteworthy object in thy travel :
       Wish me partaker in thy happiness
       When thou dost meet good hap ; and in thy danger,
       If ever danger do environ thee,
       Commend thy grievance to my holy prayers,
       For I will be thy beadsman, Valentine.
Val.   And on a love-book pray for my success ?
Pro.   Upon some book I love I'll pray for thee.
Val.   That's on some shallow story of deep love,
       How young Leander crossed the Hellespont.
Pro.   That's a deep story of a deeper love.

    The last words contain, I have no doubt, a reference to Marlowe's
poem, *Hero and Leander*, composed probably about the same time as
the play, between 1590-1593.   In this work, left unfinished and not
published before 1598, Francis, when back in England, had sung out

his longing for Marguerite left on the other side of the Channel.   We
can easily imagine how he will have unfavourably compared his plight
with Leander's.   How he will have envied the young Greek, who had
but to swim the narrow Hellespont to be with his love, while between
himself and his sweet Rose of France there flowed the broad Channel.

The farewell scene between the two friends closes, after Valentine
has gone, with Proteus soliloquising :

Pro.   He after honours hunts, I after love :
      He leaves his friends to dignify them more ;
      I leave myself, my friends and all, for love.
      Thou, Julia, hast metamorphosed me ;
      Made me neglect my studies, lose my time,
      War with good counsel, set the world at nought ;
      Made wit with musing weak, heart sick with thought.

It was not long before Francis found himself in the same pre-
dicament as his friend, and that is why he was able to let these sentiments flow so eloquently from Anthony's lips.   But, though the two
brothers had much in common, in one item they were more or less
contrasts, which may have been one reason for their strong mutual
attachment.   Through the younger man life ran in a slow deep current,
through the elder in a more easily changeable course.   Francis, once
his aspiration or affection had found its object, would not lightly stray
from it but keep faithful to the end.

In the play Anthony's mutability in love is first suggested by his
name of Proteus, and subsequently shown in action, when he too easily
transfers his affection from the absent Julia to the present Silvia,
and back again to Julia, as soon as the latter, divining his inconstancy
(*habit* she calls it !) appears at his side, disguised as a boy.   He then
cries out, betraying his weakness :

      What is in Silvia's face, but I may spy
      More fresh in Julia's with a constant eye ?

16

The " constant eye " is an outburst of his unconscious.   It is what he would like to be ! The last scene of the play, with Julia's reproaches and Proteus' admissions, is equally enlightening.

Jul.   Behold her that gave aim to all thy oaths,
          And entertained them deeply in her heart ;
          How oft hast thou with perjury cleft the root !
          O Proteus ! let this habit make thee blush.
          Be thou ashamed that I have took upon me
          Such an immodest raiment ; if shame live
          In a disguise of love.
          It is the lesser blot, modesty finds,
          Women to change their shapes than men their minds.
Pro.   Than men their minds ! 't is true.   O heaven ! were man
          But constant, he were perfect : that one error
          Fills him with faults ; makes him run through all the sins :
          Inconstancy falls off ere it begins.

If ever there was a perfect man, perfect in constancy, and that an Englishman, it was Francis Bacon.   He gave abundant proof of it in his whole life, by the constancy of his love for the beautiful Marguerite ; by the constancy of his service to his brother Essex ; by the constancy of his friendship for his brother Anthony ; by the constancy of his loyalty to his sovereign and country ; by the constancy of his devotion to his work for the Great Instauration of Learning.   From none of these things did he ever swerve aside to " run through all the sins," or any sin at all, however some of his biographers have misinterpreted his motives and actions, and thereby unrecognizably distorted the story of his life.

But do not let us stretch the contrast in temperament between Anthony and Francis too far, as if the latter for example has been inconstant in all those things in which his friend has proved his perfec-tion.   It would lead us far from the truth.   Except in love for the other sex, Anthony has in all points been the most constant and loyal companion and co-worker Francis has ever found.

Therefore, whatever the play may say of Proteus' falseness to his friend, that does not apply to Anthony beyond the one thing, his love for the same lady who was also his brother's sweetheart, and even in this he did never play him false by underhand tricks behind his back as Proteus did. We have to picture the true record of events somewhat as follows. Sooner or later after Francis' departure for France, it may also have been not earlier than after his return, Anthony's infatuation for his first lady-love—let us still call her Julia—was on the wane, or may even have blown over altogether. It may also be that the first Julia had been succeeded by other Julias, though I do not read Anthony's character, however mercurial it may have been, as light as that.

After somewhat more than two years of a relatively carefree life in France, Francis, the first young Gentleman from London, has a visitation from the land on the other side of the grave, intimating to him the death of Sir Nicholas. Soon the premonition was verified by letters from home.

" At the age of eighteen he fronts the world. The staff of his house being broken, as the dream has told him, he hies home from France to Lady Bacon's side. The Lord Keeper was not rich, and his lands have passed to his son [Nicholas] by a former wife. Lady Ann Bacon is left a young widow with two sons, Anthony and Francis, a meek, brave heart, and a slender fortune ; a little family of three persons, who make up in love for each other all that they lack in pelf. The remains of the Lord Keeper interred in St. Paul's, the widow and her two children had to quit York House for a less princely home. They went down to Gorhambury, a country-house in Hertfordshire, close to St. Albans, which the Lord Keeper had bought for his second wife, had enlarged with new rooms, and surrounded with extensive gardens, woods and ponds. There Lady Anne settled for life. Anthony started for France, and his unprovided brother betook himself to the law. All the Lord Keeper's sons had been entered as ancients on the books of Gray's Inn ; and at this Inn Francis began, in June 1579, to keep his terms." [1]

[1] HD I 14-5 ; II 27.

The riddle deepens in accepted history.   During Sir Nicholas'
life none but his youngest offspring—precisely the one who is said
by unofficial history to be no offspring of his—is allowed to go abroad.
As soon as the Lord Keeper is dead, that son, finding himself the only
one of Sir Nicholas' eight children who is left totally unprovided for, is
forced immediately to return in order to work for his living.   On the
other hand, his elder brother Anthony does not seem to lose any time
after his father's death in using his freedom to go to the same country
abroad where his foster-brother went two years before when he had
to stay behind.   There is no doubt that at that time it was in part his
father who had kept him back, in part it may also have been that his
love for a Julia had something to do with it.

But once Anthony's first love-chain is broken, and Francis returns
home to tell him of " the wonders of the world abroad," then he
follows without delay in his brother's tracks.   In the play it is his father,
Antonio,   who rather peremptorily sends Proteus his friend to the
Emperor's court at Milan, but we may gather something of the true
state of affairs, namely of the Lord Keeper's reluctance to let his sons
go to France, from the wonder his conduct in this respect has aroused
among his own kin.

Ant.   Tell me, Panthino, what sad talk was that
        Wherewith my brother held you in the cloister?
Pan.   'T was of his nephew Proteus, your son.
Ant.   Why, what of him?
Pan.   He wondered that your lordship
        Would suffer him to spend his youth at home,
        While other men, of slender reputation,
        Put forth their sons to seek preferment out;
        Some to the wars, to try their fortune there;
        Some to discover islands far away;
        Some to the studious universities.
        For any or for all these exercises
        He said that Proteus your son was meet,

And did request me to importune you
To let him spend his time no more at home,
Which would be great impeachment to his age,
In having known no travel in his youth.

Most significant is also the name of Antonio given here to Sir Nicholas. That Anthony's name in the play is transferred to the father is of course for reasons of disguise and secrecy. Otherwise the true relation between "the two gentlemen," and the source from whence the play came might too easily have been divined.

Antonio (I 3) seems rather to throw the burden of responsibility for his son's staying at home on Proteus' shoulders, while he ascribes to himself the desire of sending him abroad, but we are given a glimpse into the fallacy of this excuse, when we hear that Antonio has been uttering this desire *only* for " this month," and at the end has not even yet made up his mind " whither best to send him."

Ant. Nor need'st thou much importune me to that
      Whereon this month I have been hammering.
      I have considered well his loss of time,
      And how he cannot be a perfect man,
      Not being tried and tutored in the world :
      Experience is by industry achieved
      And perfected by the swift course of time.
      Then tell me, whither were I best to send him ?
Pan. I think your lordship is not ignorant
      How this companion, youthful Valentine,
      Attends the emperor in his royal court.
Ant. I know it well.
Pan. 'T were good, I think, your lordship sent him thither :
      There shall he practise tilts and tournaments,
      Hear sweet discourse, converse with noblemen,
      And be in eye of every exercise
      Worthy his youth and nobleness of birth.
Ant. I like thy counsel ; well hast thou advised.

Anthony Bacon went to France in the summer of 1579, and what befell Francis, befell him. He too fell a victim to Marguerite's charms, and this state of affairs is faithfully pictured in the play by Proteus' infatuation for his friend's lady-love, barring only his unfaithfulness to his friend. There is every reason to suppose that Francis did not let Anthony depart without supplying him with letters of introduction to all his good friends in France, above all to gallant Henry of Navarre and his beautiful wife. He may even have used the identical words of Valentine when introducing Proteus to the Duke of Milan and his daughter Silvia (II 4).

Duk.   You know him well ?
Val.   I knew him as myself ; for from our infancy
        We have conversed and spent our hours together.

Even the following passage, though in its second part more autobiographical of the author, and therefore more true of Francis than of Anthony, he may have used for the better commendation of his dearest friend.

Val.   And though myself have been an idle truant,
        Omitting the sweet benefit of time
        To clothe mine age with angel-like perfection,
        Yet hath Sir Proteus—for that's his name—
        Made use and fair advantage of his days :
        His years but young, but his experience old ;
        His head unmellowed, but his judgment ripe ;
        And, in a word—for far behind his worth
        Come all the praises that I now bestow—
        He is complete in feature and in mind
        With all good grace to grace a gentleman.
Duk.   Well, sir, this gentleman is come to me.
        I think 't is no unwelcome news to you.
Val.   Should I have wished a thing, it had been he.
Duk.   Welcome him then according to his worth.   (Exit)

Val.   (to *Silvia*) This is the gentleman I told your ladyship
          Had come along with me, but that his mistress
          Did hold his eyes locked in her crystal looks.
Sil.   Belike that now she has enfranchised them
          Upon some other pawn for fealty.
Val.   Nay, sure, I think she holds them prisoners still.

The last words may have been true of Anthony, though I doubt it. He stayed in France for twelve long years, and till his death in 1601 remained unmarried to either French or English girl, notwithstanding the constant urgent persuasions of his mother.

The phrase, "I know him as myself," that is as my *alter ego*, other-self, or next-self, is notable for its direct association with Anthony Bacon. When Francis in 1597 published the first edition of his *Essays*, he dedicated them to his brother, and directly apostrophised him in the body of the text as "you that are next myself." For further allusions of the same kind the reader is referred to the next chapter.

We must now look elsewhere for further confirmation of this story of "The Two Gentlemen from London" who fall in love with the same lady. I think we may find it in Francis' love-poems, known as the *Sonnets* of Shakespeare. When Anthony left for the continent, we may be sure, his foster-brother must have given him, beside general letters of introduction, special messages for his sweet Rose of France, by pen on paper as well as by word of mouth, to protest his undying love for her, even though they might never now be united in holy wedlock. Anthony may even have urged him to it, like Proteus did Valentine, when the latter had been banished by the Duke from the presence of his daughter. And just as Proteus spoke words of comfort in Valentine's ear, and bade him have hope in the future, so may Anthony have done to Francis before he himself started on his journey to France (III 1).

Pro.   Cease to lament for that thou canst not help,
        And study help for that which thou lament'st.

Time is the nurse and breeder of all good.
Here if thou stay, thou canst not see thy love ;
Besides, thy staying will abridge thy life.
Hope is a lover's staff ; walk hence with that
And manage it against despairing thoughts.
Thy letters may be here, though thou art hence ;
Which, being writ to me, shall be delivered
Even in the milk-white bosom of thy love.
The time now serves not to expostulate :
Come, I'll convey thee through the city-gate,
And, ere I part with thee, confer at large
Of all that may concern thy love-affairs.

There is no doubt that some such scene and words must have
passed between Anthony and Francis on the eve of the latter's departure
for France.   But alas, the friend he sent to plead for him was caught
in the same net, and must needs plead for himself, so that Francis
suffers a threefold loss—himself, his friend and his mistress, as he tells
us in Sonnet 133.

Of him, myself, and thee I am forsaken,
A torment thrice threefold thus to be crossed.

Compare also this threefold loss and threefold torment the poet
is suffering by his friend's deflection, with the " threefold perjury "
and threefold loss Proteus is committing as he stands confessed by his
own words (II 6).

Pro.   To leave my Julia, shall I be forsworn ;
To love fair Silvia, shall I be forsworn ;
To wrong my friend, I shall be much forsworn ;
And even that power which gave me first my oath
Provokes me to this threefold perjury :
Love bade me swear, and Love bids me forswear.

O sweet suggestion Love ! if thou hast sinned,
Teach me, thy tempted subject, to excuse it.
At first I did adore a twinkling star,
But now I worship a celestial sun.
Unheedful vows may heedfully be broken ;
And he wants wit that wants resolved will
To learn [1] his wit to exchange the bad for better.
Fie, fie, unreverend tongue ! to call her bad,
Whose sovereignty so oft thou hast preferred
With twenty thousand soul-confirming oaths.
I cannot leave to love, and yet I do ;
But there I leave to love where I should love.
Julia I lose, and Valentine I lose :
If I keep them, I needs must lose myself ;
If I lose them, thus find I by their loss,
For Valentine myself ; for Julia, Silvia.
I to myself am dearer than a friend,
For love is still most precious in itself ;
And Silvia—witness heaven that made her fair !—
Shows Julia but a swarthy Ethiope.
I will forget that Julia is alive,
Remembering that my love to her is dead ;
And Valentine I hold an enemy,
Aiming at Silvia as a sweeter friend.
I cannot now prove constant to myself
Without some treachery used to Valentine.

Thus Anthony will have mused when faced by his new love in
sunny France, outshining the old loves for his friend and his former
sweetheart (or sweethearts ?) left behind in misty England. He may
even in his weaker moments have selfishly thought, just like Proteus,
" I to myself am dearer than a friend," but that he ever in word or
act was false to his younger brother, I cannot believe, and it is dis-
proved, I think, by the whole tenour of his life and his lifelong friendship

[1] To teach.

17

for Francis, for whom no sacrifice of time or money ever proved too exacting. The line just quoted is in glaring contrast with the sentiment expressed in Sonnet 42 :

Here is the joy ; my friend and I are one.

Anthony I am sure would have said the same, and what is more, has proved it by the way he let his brother have everything that he needed and that was his.

A last remark regarding the autobiographical element in *The Two Gentlemen of Verona*. Is there any outside proof or circumstantial evidence for our identification of Silvia with Rosaline-Marguerite, and of Valentine with Francis Bacon ? There is, or rather there are several indications to prove our conjecture right.

In Orville Owen's decipherings of the Great Word-Cipher it is *The Two Gentlemen of Verona* that furnishes the material for the incident in Francis' life at the French Court, where he tries by a ladder of cords to climb into Marguerite's room, just as Valentine is on the point of scaling Silvia's apartment, when he was prevented from doing so by the Duke. In Valentine's letter to Silvia, which the Duke discovers, and reads, there is this final sentence :

Silvia, this night I will enfranchise thee.

As we shall see more fully in Chapter 6, the words " I will enfranchise thee " are of singular significance for the Baconian problem. Exactly the same words are addressed by Armado in *Love's Labour's Lost* to Costard, and quasi misunderstood by the latter as meaning " to marry him to one Francis." In the same way, then, in Silvia's case the words may mean " to marry her to one Francis." And that this is no other than Francis Bacon is made clear by the clock-cipher or number-play, as shown in Chapter 6. In the old spelling of *Love's Labour's Lost*, " I will infranchise thee," has actually the same number-value, 200, as " your man Francis Bacon."

We know further from the Biliteral Cipher that *Romeo and Juliet* is one of the plays in which Francis has sung out most passionately his unhappy love for Marguerite and enscened some of the incidents of his love-making. Wrote Francis Tidder in his secret diary : " This stage-play in part will tell our brief love tale, a part is in the play previously named or mentioned as having therein one pretty scene, acted by the two." Reference is here made to the balcony scene in *The Two Gentlemen* (IV 2), which is the counterpart of the balcony-scene in *Romeo*. Not the whole scene in the comedy is of course a true picture of Francis' wooing, for in the play it is the false Proteus who tries to steal the love of Silvia. But part of her rebuke to him may have been playfully uttered by Marguerite. If we substitute " Henry of Navarre " for " Valentine thy friend," and " married " for " betrothed," the words fit the case.

Valentine thy friend

Survives ; to whom, thyself art witness,
I am betrothed : and art thou not ashamed
To wrong him with thy importunacy ?

But it is more especially Proteus' asking for Silvia's picture, to which I think the Biliteral Cipher refers.

Pro.   Madame, if your heart be so obdurate,
Vouchsafe me yet your picture for my love,
The picture that is hanging in your chamber :
To that I'll speak, to that I'll sigh and weep ;
For since the substance of your perfect self
Is else devoted, I am but a shadow,
And to your shadow will I make true love.

Silvia's consent to deliver the picture in the morning, after she has so rebuked his false love-making, is strong proof for the fact that the above quoted words of Proteus are an interpolation, not incident to the play, but describing a scene of Francis' life-story, and inserted here as the most likely place. But it does not quite fit in. It is not in accord with Silvia's character as depicted in the play, her faithfulness to Valentine, her indignant offence at Proteus' love-making. How then could she ever promise to send him her picture ? This inconsistency betrays the foreign origin of Proteus' words, and so would have betrayed Francis' secret long ago, if knowing eyes had been keen enough.

There are more such parallels between *Romeo* and *The Two Gentlemen* to prove that these two plays together with *Love's Labour's Lost* form indeed a trilogy, revealing much and harbouring many scenes of Francis' love-story. In Chapter 9 it is shown how through a plantain leaf as a salve for a broken shin, a certain scene in *Romeo* (I 2) is closely connected with another scene in *Love's Labour's Lost* (III 1). And the opening words of the scene in *Romeo* are also but an echo of a sentiment uttered by Proteus in *The Two Gentlemen* (II 4).

Says Benvolio to Romeo to cure him of his luckless love for Juliet,

> Tut ! man, one fire burns out another's burning,
> One pain is lessened by another's anguish ;
> Turn giddy, and be holp by backward turning ;
> One desperate grief cures with another's anguish :
> Take thou some new infection to thy eye,
> And the rank poison of the old will die.

In the same vein Proteus muses :

> Even as one heat another heat expels,
> Or as one nail by strength drives out another,
> So the remembrance of my former love
> Is by a newer object quite forgotten.

Especially the first lines of both passages are strikingly similar—a fire burning out another fire, and a heat expelling another heat. No doubt that Bacon must himself have many times thought of such a remedy against his hopeless love for Marguerite. Is not this what he means when he wrote in the Biliteral Cipher : " Since the former issue of this play [*Romeo and Juliet*], very seldom heard without most stormy weeping—your poet's commonest plaudit—we have all but determined on following the fortunes of these ill-fated lovers by a path less thorny." [1] Their " thorny " path was, that " kind fate joined them together in life and death." Bacon's less thorny path then would be to be joined with another love in life at least.

The above quoted biliteral deciphering was made from an edition of the play, the decipherer tells us, " without date." The first edition of the play is of 1597, and it was in that year that Bacon formed the project of marrying Elizabeth, daughter of Sir Thomas Cecil, and widow of William Hatton, with whom she had been married but a few months. His suit was rejected by the father, [2] and six years later he hoped " to marry with some convenient advancements," Alice Barnham, " an alderman's daughter, an handsome maiden, to my liking." [3] This marriage was consummated on the 10th of May, 1606. It is therefore between 1597 and 1606 that the undated edition of *Romeo and Juliet* must have appeared, that is to say if our reading of the words, " a path less thorny," is correct. [4]

Anthony left for France in 1579, not to return to England before 1591, after twelve years' absence. The misunderstanding between the two brothers, caused by Anthony's infatuation for Marguerite canno have lasted long, nor can it ever have rooted deep. At the first discovery, Francis may well have addressed to Anthony such reproaches as are laid in the mouth of Valentine.

> Thou common friend, that's without faith or love—
> For such is a friend now—treacherous man !
> Thou hast beguiled my hopes : naught but mine eye

---

[1] WG II 79.   [2] HD II 115-7.   [3] Sp X 83.

[4] The only undated edition known, the so-called third Quarto, is said by the Cambridge editors to be later than 1609. I do not know if the undated edition used by Elizabeth Wells Gallup is identical with those of the Cambridge editors, or if their conjecture of the year is right.

Could have persuaded me.   Now I dare not say
I have one friend alive : thou wouldst disprove me.
Who should be trusted now, when one's right hand
Is perjured to the bosom ? Proteus,
I am sorry I must never trust thee more,
But count the world a stranger for thy sake.
The private wound is deep'st.   O time most curst !
'Mongst all foes that a friend should be the worst !

The passage is heavy of suppressed sorrow, only half expressed in words, but finding utterance even in the halting metre in several of the verses.   But in the continuation of the scene this sorrow becomes transformed.   Darkly at first but gradually more clearly, Valentine-Francis comes to the realization that his friend weighs even more than his lady, friendship more than love.   Such is the meaning of the words, " the private wound is the deepest ! " These significant words explain, which otherwise remains unexplainable, his readiness to exchange his lady for his repentant friend, returned to his bosom,

And that my love may appear plain and free,
All that was mine in Silvia I give thee.

Just so may Francis' great heart have soon found it possible to conquer his jealousy, and even to sacrifice his love to his friendship.   We shall return more fully to this supreme triumph of friendship over love in our next chapter.   In the meanwhile let it suffice that, when at last his brother returned home from his voluntary banishment in France, to join again his mother and his brother at Gorhambury, the ancient place of their golden time of youth, it was there, as in the play,

One feast, one house, one mutual happiness.

William Shakespeare

2. IN DEBT

We must now look at another phase of the relations between the two brothers, which found its poetical biography in *The Merchant of Venice*. As the biographical aspect of *The Two Gentlemen* is indicated by the name of Proteus' father, so in the other play it is hinted by the name given to the merchant from whom the comedy derives its title. Both bear the name of Francis' brother in italianized, or shall we call it italicized, form, so as half to veil but also half to draw attention to it. Antonio—Anthony ! And is not the name of this merchant's bosom-friend, but another transparent veil—if once we know the secret—also an italianized form of Francis' surname ? Bassanio-Baconio ! But stronger than these hints, however thinly veiled, do Antonio and Bassanio themselves speak in the play.   Besides, there are other striking incidents.

In *The Two Gentlemen of Verona* we had partly to build on conjecture—Anthony's love for Marguerite—to bring out the parallel between the story of the play and the life-story of the two brothers, but in *The Merchant of Venice* the parallel is entirely based on actual documentary history. As we have given to the former play a new name, *The Two Gentlemen from London*, so we may call *The Merchant of Venice*, at least in the opening scenes, in the words of the best of Bacon's biographers, not a Baconian in the ordinary sense, but by his keen intuition a respecter of the spirit that was England's greatest son— *The Romance of Brotherly Love and Debt*.[1]

Indeed *The Merchant of Venice* is nothing if not the monument erected by the younger brother in memory of Anthony's unexampled devotion and self-sacrifice to his person and his cause.

We know already that of all the sons and daughters of Sir Nicholas Bacon, " Francis was the only one left poor. The Lord Keeper had begun

[1] HD II 81.

to lay aside certain funds for him, when that gust of wind from the river cut him off. Francis, summoned by his mother from Paris, came home with prospects thus suddenly and darkly changed ; in place of returning to his house at York House, a gentleman of good estate, with an immediate opening into public life, the companion of wits and nobles, of judges, and Privy Counsellors, he found himself a stranger at his father's door, deprived of an inheritance which he had thought his own. The change left its stamp on his character for life.

" The remains of the Lord Keeper interred in St. Paul's, the widow and her two children had to quit York House for a less public and less princely home. They went down to Gorhambury. There Lady Anne settled for life. Anthony started for France, and his unprovided brother betook himself to the law.

" Anthony, the more easy and elastic son of Lady Anne, found life in the south of France more pleasant than among the Hertfordshire flats and fogs. Master of the manor and priory of Redburn, of the manors of Abbotsbury, Minchinbury, and Hores, in the parish of Barley, in the county of Hertford, with the Brightfirth wood, Merydan meads, and Pinner-Stoke farm, in the county of Middlesex, why should he race and harry with the world ? But Francis, till his own abilities should give him bread, would have to live on the slender means of his mother, on the charity of his half-brother Sir Nicholas, on the friend-ship of his cousin Trott ; and, when these should fail him, on those bankers and Jews who were only too eager to oblige the nephew of a Prime Minister with loans. The aids from his family were scant. Lady Anne allowed him all she could ; and Trott, a man of wealth as well as a lover of poetry and wit, advanced him money. Sir Nicholas would not see him. The Queen remembered and was kind to her Lord Keeper of ten ; but her Majesty was far off, his need of a daily dinner and change of raiment near. In these dark times, when a proud and affectionate heart forbade him to press too close on his mother's means, the Lombard-street bankers were often his sole resource. Yet his high spirits never sunk, his capacity for labour never tired."[1]

[1] HD II 26-29.

The only one who proved always ready to help, who practically put all his resources at his younger brother's disposal was Anthony. Hepworth Dixon even ascribes his disinclination to marry at least half to this reason. "Partly from a roving and mercurial temper, partly from a wish to reserve Gorhambury for his younger brother, he set his face against marriage, to the deep distress of Lady Anne." [1] And I am sure that it is to Francis' unwillingness to accept such a sacrifice from his dearest friend, that we owe those splendid Sonnets in the first series, urging his friend to enter into matrimonial bonds.

"In 1591 Anthony, having come home from abroad, went to lodge at his brother's chambers in Coney Court. Hoping to receive some public trust—for during his long residence in France, Italy, and Navarre, his quick eye and nimble tongue had been employed in the unpaid public service—he applied to his uncle for a place. Clever, passionate, inventive, like his brother Francis, Anthony had none of that brother's patience. Burleigh, moreover, feared all rapid action, distrusted all brilliant men. The impetuous youth must wait.

"Two young men, cast on the world with little money but great connexions and expensive ways, could ill afford to wait. The rents from Redburn and Barley fell much below the needs of one who was a kinsman and companion of earls and ministers, not to speak of the needs of a brother who, without a shilling in his pocket, was a person at Court, a leader of the House of Commons, a candidate for the metropolitan shire. Their half-brother Sir Nicholas, if he had a large estate, had also a large family by his wife Anne Butts of Thornage —nine sons and three daughters; weight enough, he thought, for him to bear, without being asked to support the offspring of Lady Anne. Nathaniel might paint their portraits or present them with game on canvas; he would do nothing else, except quarrel with them, as he did, for the family crumbs. Edward, having a lease from the Crown of Twickenham Park, a delightful house on the Thames, allowed Francis to make it now and then a home, while he and his household were at

[1] HD II 38.

Shrubland Park.   When all was done, a bed and a garden were the chief helps which Francis could ever obtain from the elder branch.

"Lady Anne pinched herself at Gorhambury, that she might send to her sons in Gray's Inn ale from her cellars, pigeons from her dovecots, fowls from her farmyards ; gifts which she seasoned with a full share of motherly love, and not a little motherly advice.   The young men took the love, and were very proud of it, and very warmly returned it ; but Lady Anne fancied they were not so eager as they might have been to profit by her good advice.   In truth, their lives were not her life, and could not follow the rules which she had laid down and by which she lived.   They were young men, with the wants of young men.   Like Buckhurst, Herbert, and other gay fellows of their acquaintance, while waiting for brighter days, they helped themselves through the Lombards and the Jews.[1]

"The income drawn by Francis from the bar was still below his needs as a student and collector of books, an admirer of trees and flowers, a courtier, a gentleman, a knight of the shire.   His brother's purse was his own ; but the pockets of a young fellow with a small rent-roll, and a taste for horses and French wines, were seldom full. From Essex he could get no shilling of his hire.   Anthony thought of raising his rents, and some of the men about him—godless rogues, Lady Bacon called them—proposed that he should let his farms to the highest bidders.   Goodman Grinnell, who had the land at Barley, paid less than he ought : let him go out and a better man come in.   But Goodman Grinnell sped with his long face to Lady Anne.   "What ! " cries the good lady to her son, " turn out the Grinnells ! Why, the Grinnells have lived at Barley these hundred and twenty years ! "   So the brothers had to look elsewhere. The great city miser, Alderman Spencer, offered four thousand pounds for Barley farm ; but Sir Nicholas of Redgrave, who had a reversionary interest in the land, refused his consent.   All the notes from Francis to his mother, in the autumn of 1593, relate the sad romance of brotherly love and debt."[2]

[1] HD II 40-42.   [2] HD II 80-81

This is the documentary history, and it is faithfully reflected in *The Merchant of Venice*. The principal incident around which the whole play revolves, the bond Shylock held of Antonio for 3000 ducats, and the implacable persecution to which the Jew subjected his victim, is only the enlarged shadow of a similar persecution Bacon had suffered from another usurer, a certain Mr. Sympson, in the summer of 1597. This gold-smith and " moneylender who held his bond for £300 had sued him for it in Trinity Term of that year, but agreed to 'respite the satisfaction ' till the beginning of the term next ensuing. A full fortnight however before Michaelmas Term began, (without any warning and upon what pretence [Cecil ?] we are not informed) he served an execution upon him and had him arrested as he came from the Tower, where he was engaged in business of the Learned Counsel " to the Queen.[1] The public insult offered to his dignity, while he was " about her Majesty's special service," as he wrote to his cousin Cecil, the Fox, must have most grievously hurt Bacon. And this will have contributed strongly to the dark picture drawn of Shylock. I cannot escape the feeling that through the jewish gold-hoarder peeps the sombre figure of *Roberto II Diavolo*, the name given to Cecil by Signor Antonio Perez, a Spanish refugee, and " which clung to him for life." [2]

A similar affront for a similar reason was offered to Bacon for the second time in 1603. We do not know the particulars about this case,[3] so that we are not able to say in how far it has been of influence on the composition of *The Merchant of Venice*, but the Sympson case with its £300 for the period from Trinity till Michaelmas, is in money and time as near Shylock's " 3000 ducats for 3 months " as Bacon could pos-sibly make it.

Let us now see if the relation between Anthony and Francis is indeed thus faithfully mirrored by that between Antonio and Bassanio. First take the announcement made to Antonio by one of his friends when Bassanio enters upon the scene for the first time.

Here comes Bassanio, your most noble kinsman.

[1] Sp IX 106.   [2] HD II 74.   [3] Sp X 79.

" Your most noble kinsman," with a subtle allusion to Bacon's royal birth.   Then Bassanio's speech, begging from Antonio one more loan.

> 'Tis not unknown to you, Antonio,
> How much I have disabled mine estate,
> By something showing a more swelling port
> Than my faint means would grant continuance.
> Nor do I now make moan to be abridged
> From such a noble rate ; but my chief care
> Is to come fairly off from the great debts
> Wherein my time, something too prodigal,
> Hath left me gaged.
>   *To you Antonio,*
> *I owe the most, in money and in love ;*
> And from your love I have a warranty
> To unburden all my plots and purposes
> How to get clear of all the debts I owe.

The last four and a half lines are the most splendid tribute Bacon could have paid to his brother, to whom indeed he owed " the most, in money and in love."   In love he had repaid Anthony in diverse kinds, in words of endearment for example, as when he wrote to lady Anne of his brother, as " being so near and dear part of me as he is," [1] or on another occasion called him " Anthony my comfort," or again dedicated the first edition of his Essays to him, in those deep-feeling words, " I have preferred them to *you that are next myself*, dedicating them, such as they are, to our love, in the depth whereof, I assure you, I some- times wish your infirmities translated upon myself." [2]

To return to *The Merchant of Venice* and to Bassanio's words, " To you, Antonio, I owe the most in money and in love."   In love, then, Bacon could repay and has repaid Anthony in manifold ways, but in money he remained his debtor till death did them part, and after. The only way he could give proof of his gratitude was to let Anthony

[1] HD II 115.   [2] Sp VI 523-4.   See also next chapter.

and his great heart live for ages to come in the figure of that over-
generous merchant of Venice.   We have heard Hepworth Dixon in his
life of Francis say : '' His brother's purse was his own.''   Are not these
words merely an echo of Antonio's,

> My purse, my person, my extremest means,
> Lie all unlocked to your occasions.

And he proved the truth of his words by the calm resignation with
which he faced death by the hand of the implacable Shylock-Diavolo.

>   I do oppose
> My patience to his fury, and am armed
> To suffer with a quietness of spirit
> The very tyranny and rage of his.

Again, at his last moment, as he thought, when to his friend Bassanio-
Baconio he said :

Ant.   Give me your hand, Bassanio : fare you well !
       Grieve not that I am fallen to this for you ;
       For herein Fortune shows herself more kind
       Than is her custom : it is still her use
       To let the wretched man outlive his wealth,
       To view with hollow eye and wrinkled brow
       An age of poverty ; from which lingering penance
       Of such a misery doth she cut me off.
       Commend me to your honourable wife :
       Tell her the process of Antonio's end ;
       Say how I loved you, speak me fair in death ;
       And, when the tale is told, bid her be judge
       Whether Bassanio had not once a love.
       Repent not you that you shall lose your friend,
       And he repents not that he pays your debt ;

> For if the Jew do cut but deep enough,
> I'll pay it instantly with all my heart.

And his brother-friend's answer :

Bass.   Antonio, I am married to a wife
      Which is as dear to me as life itself ;
      But life itself, my wife, and all the world,
      Are not with me esteemed above thy life :
      I would lose all, ay, sacrifice them all,
      Here to *this devil*, to deliver you.

When in the ideal last act of *The Merchant of Venice*, in the moonlit garden and the serene night-air of Belmont, Portia's place in the country, Bassanio-Baconio at last brings home his friend and " noble kinsman," to present him to his lady, as he thinks for the first time, he does it in such serious accents as cannot but strike the deepest chords in our hearts :

> Madame, give welcome to my friend—
> This is the man, this is Antonio,
> To whom I am so infinitely bound.

And Portia, who knows best her husband's indebtedness, stately confirms the bond that binds him to his friend :

> You should in all sense be much bound to him,
> For, as I hear, he was much bound for you.

Greater friendship than between these two never existed. When Anthony died in May 1601, he left everything he was possessed of to his brother-friend, who thereby was enabled to pay off his most pressing debts.[1] But at the same time it was the darkest hour of

[1] Sp X 5, 40, 79.

Francis' life, preceded as it was by the trial and execution of his brother
Essex in February before, and followed as it shortly was by the madness
of his adoptive mother, Lady Ann, by the death of his real mother,
Queen Elizabeth, two years later, and by the succession of James of
Scotland, whereby his last hope to sit in the throne of his ancestors
was finally destroyed.   Francis Bacon's life was indeed at its lowest
ebb, eddying in darkest waters.

Exactly in this time is placed what Shakespearean scholars have
called Shakespeare's dark period, his "eclipse of spirits."   Gone is the
magic charm and joyousness of such plays as *Midsummer Night's Dream*,
As You Like It, and *Twelfth Night*.   They are replaced by the sombre
glory and deep gloom of *Hamlet*, *Othello*, *Lear*, *Macbeth* and *Timon*.
I cannot here enter into this problem of the "midnight gloom" that
settles over the poet's spirit, but content myself with pointing out that
this fearful change also remains completely unexplained on the
hypothesis of Shakespeare's authorship, but forms on the other hand
one of the strongest points in favour of the Baconian theory.

I know full well that many will object to seeing in Anthony the "beauteous youth" and "lovely boy" of the first series of 126 Sonnets, if only
for the reason that he was older than Francis. But what of that? In close
and deep friendship two years make little difference. Then, the constant
admonitions to the youth to marry, and "to be new made when thou
art old," may be read in a more actual and real sense than as a mere
poetical conceit, which it is when not understood as the warm concern
for his friend whom he knows to be of a mercurial temperament and an
easily inflammable heart, for whom it would therefore be so much better
to steady down in marriage. It was Shakespeare-Bacon only who could
put such friendly and in the ordinary way common counsels and propo-
sals in a language and imagery as delicate as poetical.   The fact is that
the Sonnets fit in well with what we know of Francis' and Anthony's life-
story, and not at all with Shakespeare's history.   The first series of the
Sonnets is indeed the glorification of asexual *friendship*, as it existed
between the two brothers, while the second series describes the vicis-
situde of sexual *love*, as it existed between Francis and Marguerite.

Visualize the dark lady of the second series. How well those sonnets portray the southern beauty, heiress to a French father and an Italian mother. From the beginning she must have been a very obsession to the fair-hued and fair-haired gentleman from the North. Notwithstanding his deep love for her, he seems never to have been able entirely to overcome his aversion for her colouring—the colour of the night. This aversion or, I should perhaps rather say, this predilection for the " fair," appears to have been a life-long complex in Francis Bacon's psychic make-up.[1] When his love proved false and fickle, it became even more pronounced and symbolical of all evil. It is strong already in *Love's Labour's Lost* and *The Two Gentlemen*, it becomes of infernal terror in the *Sonnets*, and in the later dramas with such dark beauties as Lady Macbeth and Hamlet's mother, the latter intentionally no doubt meant as a foil to the fair Ophelia.

Listen in *Love's Labour's Lost* to Biron, in many ways a self-portrait, trying in a frenzy to enthuse away as it were his aversion for Rosaline's dark beauty. First we find him deriding himself for his choice (III 1),

> Among three, to love the worst of all ;
> A wightly wanton with a velvet brow,
> With two pitch balls stuck in her face for eyes.

But then, when the King of Navarre and the other courtiers plague him with his choice, he defends it with a zeal and fury inevitably commensurate to his repressed aversion.

King. By heaven, thy love is black as ebony.
Bir.   Is ebony like her ? O wood divine !
         A wife of such wood were felicity.
         O ! who can give an oath ? where is a book ?
         That I may swear beauty doth beauty lack,
         If that she learn not of her eye to look :

---

[1] Bartlett's *Concordance* gives over 800 references for the use of the word " fair," of which 50 in the *Sonnets* alone.

No face is fair that is not full so black.

King.   O paradox ! Black is the badge of hell,
The hue of dungeons and the scowl of night ;
And beauty's crest becomes the heavens well.

Bir.   Devils soonest tempt, resembling spirits of light.
O ! if in black my lady's brows be deck'd,
It mourns that painting and usurping hair
Should ravish doters with a false aspect ;
And therefore is she born to make black fair.
Her favour turns the fashion of the days,
For native blood is counted painting now ;
And therefore red, that would avoid dispraise,
Paints itself black, to imitate her brow.

Dum.   To look like her are chimney-sweepers black.

Long.   And since her time are colliers counted bright.

King.   And Ethiops of their sweet complexion crack.

Dum.   Dark needs no candles now, for dark is light.

Bir.   Your mistresses dare never come in rain,
For fear their colours should be wash'd away.

King.   'Twere good yours did ; for, sir, to tell you plain,
I'll find a fairer face not washed today.

Bir.   I'll prove her fair, or talk till doomsday here.

If we turn to *The Two Gentlemen of Verona*, we find the dark Rosaline of the Southland with pitchball-eyes transformed into the fair Silvia with glass-grey eyes, but nevertheless Julia of the Northland is still the fairer of the two, and Valentine's complex is still peeping around the corner.

Exclaims Proteus, when comparing the two, after he has fallen in love with Silvia (II 4) :

She's fair, and so is Julia that I love—
That I did love, for now my love is thawed.

And when Silvia asks about Julia,

19

Is she not passing fair ?

Julia, who disguised as a youth has taken service with Proteus, answers her :

> She has been fairer madam than she is.
> When she did think my Master loved her well,
> She in my judgment was as fair as you ;
> But since she did neglect her looking glass
> And threw her sun-expelling mask away,
> The air hath starved the roses in her cheeks
> And pinched the lily-tincture of her face,
> That now she is become as black as I.

But Julia's words " as fair as you " were spoken for politeness sake only, for when she is alone she confesses herself to be fairer than Silvia (IV 4) :

> Her hair is auburn, mine is perfect yellow :
> If that be all the difference in his love
> I'll get me such a coloured periwig.
> Her eyes are grey as glass, and so are mine.

And what about Valentine ? His preference is all-apparent. When asked by the Duke to be his tutor, and to teach him how to win a woman's love, his advice is (III 1) :

> Flatter and praise, commend, extol their graces ;
> Though ne'er so black, say they have angels' faces.

Let us now glance at the Sonnets. It begins immediately with the opening Sonnet 127 of the second series. The " dark lady " is for the first time introduced with an apology which is the exact paralle of Biron's words in praise of his ebony-black lady-love.

In the old age black was not counted fair,
Or if it were, it bore not beauty's name ;
But now is black beauty's successive heir,
And beauty slandered with a bastard's shame :
　For since each hand hath put on nature's power,
Fairing the foul with art's false borrowed face,
Sweet beauty hath no name, no holy bower,
But is profaned, if not lives in disgrace.
　Therefore my mistress' brows are raven black,
Her eyes so suited, and they mourners seem
At such who, not born fair, no beauty lack,
Slandering creation with a false esteem :
　　Yet so they mourn, becoming of their woe,
　　That every tongue says beauty should look so.

There is however little of the " lady " in this Sonnet. It is all
only about her " dark " colour, and is more symbolical than substantial.
It stands for all that is carnal, fickle, foul and evil in love. The whole
series is more or less in this strain. The first and last sonnet are
typical of the whole series.

　In loving thee thou knowest I am forsworn,
But thou art twice forsworn, to me love swearing ;
In act thy bed-vow broke, and new faith torn,
In vowing new hate after new love bearing.
　But why of two oaths' breach do I accuse thee,
When I break twenty ? I am perjured most ;
For all my vows are oaths but to misuse thee,
And all my honest faith in thee is lost :
　For I have sworn deep oaths of thy deep kindness,
Oaths of thy love, thy truth, thy constancy ;
And, to enlighten thee, gave eyes to blindness,
Or made them swear against the thing they see ;
　　For I have sworn thee fair : more perjur'd I,
　　To swear against the truth so foul a lie !

It does not tell us so much of the lady as of the evil attachment the poet has to her. The second series of Sonnets is more of a moralizing nature, brooding on such " dark love," just as the first series is a glorification of "fair friendship," but equally unsubstantial and elusive as regards the person of that pure attachment. The very first words of the very first Sonnet introduce us to that "fair friendship" :

> From *fairest* creatures we desire increase,
> That thereby beauty's rose might never die.

Then there is Sonnet 21 :

> O let me, true in love, but truly write,
> And then believe me, *my love is as fair*
> *As any mother's child*, though not so bright
> As those gold candles fixed in heaven's air.

And Sonnet 82 :

> Thou art as fair in knowledge as in hue.

But above all Sonnet 105 :

> Let not my love be called idolatry
> Nor my beloved as an idol show,
> Since all alike my songs and praises be
> To one, of one, still such, and ever so.
>   Kind is my love today, tomorrow kind,
> Still constant in a wondrous excellence ;
> Therefore my verse, to constancy confined,
> One thing expressing, leaves out difference.
>   "Fair, kind, and true," is all my argument,
>   " Fair, kind and true," varying to other words ;

And in this change is my invention spent,
Three themes in one, which wondrous scope affords.
    "Fair," "kind," and "true," have often lived alone,
    Which three till now never kept seat in one.

A good example of the insubstantiality of the person loved, and of the glorification of the *ideal* friendship," is Sonnet 53, with which we have to close this selection. No more shining tribute has been paid to a true friend's constancy of heart, nay to the beauty of his spirit, transfiguring his physical being into such a lovely thing that it surpasses all mere earthly beauty.

    What is your substance, whereof are you made,
That millions of strange shadows on you tend ?
Since every one hath, every one, one shade,
And you, but one, can every shadow lend.
    Describe Adonis, and the counterfeit
Is poorly imitated after you ;
On Helen's cheek all art of beauty set,
And you in Grecian tires are painted new.
    Speak of the spring and foison of the year ;
The one doth shadow of your beauty show,
The other as your bounty doth appear ;
And you in every blessed shape we know.
      In all external grace you have some part,
      But you like none, none you, for constant heart.

Not in "love," as we have seen, but certainly in "friendship" the fair Anthony has proved through all his life to have been such an immortal "constant heart."

5. Two Loves I Have

OME, more curiously reading, may have noticed in the stories of *The Two Gentlemen of Verona* and *The Merchant of Venice*, a singular element of a peculiar quality, other than the purely biographical, which closely link these plays with Shakespeare's *Sonnets*. We have in the previous Chapter let that factor slip mostly between our fingers, and have done so advisedly, because we wanted to reserve it for treatment in this Chapter, in connection with other writings of Bacon-Shakespeare, especially the *Essays*, and Spencer's *Shepherd's Calender*, and the apocryphal *Two Noble Kinsmen*. I am not aware that this particular connection between the plays and the poems and other works of Bacon has been noticed before by either Shakespearean or Baconian students. Yet it is of singular importance in solving the crucial problem of the *Sonnets*, namely their division in two cycles, contrasted like heaven and hell, the angel-love of the first 126 sonnets, and the earthly love of the next 26 sonnets, leaving the last two sonnets out of account.

Up to now we have principally concentrated our attention on the triangle-problem of *The Two Gentlemen*, on their love for one woman, and the rivalry thereby created between them, aggravated as it is by the friendship that before bound them together. But what we have passed by is the enduring quality of that friendship. In ordinary cases the " friendship " does not survive such a triple entanglement, but is more or less easily sacrificed to the " love." Here, however, we see the uncommon spectacle of friendship triumphing over love. We find at least one of the participants in the conflict willing to give up his lady so that he may keep his friend. Besides being a triangle-problem of love, *The Two Gentlemen of Verona*, therefore, presents us also with the contrast between sexual love and asexual friendship, and the triumph and apotheosis of the latter. Now it is just this same contrast, which exists between the second and first series of the Shakespearean *Sonnets*, and—what is of greater importance still for the Baconian problem— which is exemplified also in Bacon's Essays on " Love " and on " Friendship."

We cannot do better, to explain that difference, than place side by side Bacon's philosophisings on both aspects of human relationships. In the inimitable aphoristic language of the *Essays*, short-worded and full-weighted, the contrast is made as sharp as between light and darkness— between the fair " lovely boy " of the first Sonnet-series, and the dark " female evil " of the second.

We start with the Love Essay. This begins ominously, for the indictment is that, contrary to love on the stage, in real life love " doth much mischief, sometimes like a siren, sometimes like a fury." It is further condemned as a " weak passion," which " great spirits and great business do keep out." It enslaves man, for it makes him " subject, though not of the mouth (as beasts are), yet of the eye, which was given him for higher purposes." It drives him to the uncomeliness of " speaking in a perpetual hyperbole," to be worse even than " the arch-flatterer, a man's self." And therefore, we are told, " it was well said that *it is impossible to love and to be wise*." Publius Syrus, from whom this saying is taken, expressed it somewhat differently, namely that it was given to God only to love and be wise. The change made by Bacon from the conditional into the absolute was deliberate. Love for the

other sex, which Bacon had in mind, though a common constituent in
the make-up of the Roman and Greek gods, had no place in the
Christian philosopher's conception of the Deity.   It is in this changed
form that we also meet it in Bacon's Biliteral Cipher, when he is speaking
of his love for Marguerite of Navarre : " It is sometimes said, ' No man
can at once be wise and love,' and yet it would be well to observe,
many will be wiser after a lesson such as we long ago conned." [1]   Wise,
therefore, one may become *through* love, though not *in* love, and only
after love, that is after one has mastered this weakness and " child of
folly," after one has conquered this bondage of love. The same thought
is voiced by Valentine in *The Two Gentlemen of Verona* (I 1), where he
upbraids his friend Proteus, *before* he himself had fallen in love, and
therefore when he was *still* wise.

> Love is your master, for he masters you,
> And he that is so yokèd by a fool,
> Methinks should not be chronicled for wise.

This is another of those striking parallels between Bacon's and Shakespeare's works, whose accumulated weight form a strong argument in
favour of the Baconian theory.

The rest of the Essay is but an elaboration of the principal points
already quoted.   There is first the slighting remark that " martial men
are given to love but as they are given to wine, for perils commonly
ask to be paid in pleasures." Then the argument is lifted up to a higher
level altogether by contrasting this self-seeking pleasure-love with the
charitable brother-love for others.   " There is in man's nature a secret
inclination and motion towards love of others, which if it be not spent
upon some one or a few, doth naturally spread itself towards many, and
maketh men become humane and charitable ; as it is seen sometime in
friars." The greatest enemy to this friar- or brother-love, is the love for
" one or a few," that is in the first place the love for one of the other
sex. The concluding sentence finally contrasts these two, the sexual and

---

[1] WG II 80.

20

asexual love, in their effect and scope, as only Bacon could do it, and thereby points forwards, as it were to the Essay on Friendship. " Nuptial love maketh mankind, friendly love perfecteth it, but wanton love corrupteth and embaseth it." Of these three—the nuptial, friendly and wanton love—the first is of course the root from which sprout the other two, as its perfection and corruption respectively. Of these two—the sexual love and the asexual friendship—the former is glorified in the first series of Shakespeare's *Sonnets*, the latter censured in the second series. The wanton or purely sexual love drags man into hell, *the asexual* friendship exalts him above the human state, makes him like the angels that " neither marry nor are given in marriage " (Mat. XXII 30).

Now the Essay on *Friendship*. It begins with a dissertation on solitude, ending this up with the conclusion that " it is a mere and miserable solitude to want true friends, without which the world is but a wilderness," for whosoever " is unfit for friendship, he taketh it of the beast, and not from humanity." Friendship, there-fore, which makes man really human, whereas without it he would be like the wild beasts, raises him above the sensual, in contrast with the nuptial love which enslaves him to the senses. Equally noble are of course the threefold fruits of Friendship, the first of which is " the ease and discharge of the fulness and swellings of the heart, which passions of all kinds do cause and induce." When they are communicated to a friend, " it redoubleth joys, and cutteth griefs in halfs." The second fruit is " healthful and sovereign for the understanding, as the first is for the affections." It is thus explained : " Whosoever hath his mind fraught with many thoughts, in the communicating and discoursing with another, he waxeth wiser than himself, and that more by an hour's discourse than by a day's meditation." The last fruit is better even than what the ancients have made it out to be, namely " *that a friend is another himself.*" For, according to Bacon, " a friend is far more than himself." And he concludes this Essay with the " rule," that " where a man cannot fitly play his own part, if he have not a friend, he may quit the stage." What is life in adversity without a friend to lighten the burden, which would otherwise inevitably crush the sufferer ?

There is a striking contrast between these two Essays, the one speaking nothing but evil, the other nothing but good of its subject. In outer form of treatment also, the one kept very short, not more than three hundred words in all ; the other more than seven times as long, every point fully elaborated and illustrated by examples from historic friendships. It is a similar contrast that we find between the sombre evil second series of Sonnets and the bright good first series nearly five times as long as the other.

The history of the Essay on *Friendship* is instructive. It is the only Essay, I think, which has something of a personal history quite in accord with its title. It was specially called forth by one particular friend, and written at that friend's request. He was none other than Toby Matthew, one of Bacon's alter-egos. Francis Bacon was indeed fortunate in the possession of more than one close friend.

The Essays on *Love* and *Friendship* appeared for the first time in the edition of 1612. Both were short at the time, each containing but three hundred words or so. Then one day, Bacon had a conversation with his younger friend in which the latter apparently descanted, ably and worthily, upon the tie of friendship that bound them together. He did it in fact so well that Bacon, to give evidence of his appreciation, promised him to write an Essay on the subject, along the lines outlined by Matthew. At first, it seems, the promise was meant merely as a compliment, but when Matthew insisted, it was at last redeemed. This seems to be the explanation and the meaning of the following extract from a letter Bacon wrote in answer to one of Matthew's dated 26 June 1623.

" For the essay of friendship, while I took your speech of it for a cursory request, I took my promise for a compliment. But since you call for it, I shall perform it." [1]

It is not known for certain when the Friendship discussion had taken place, but it is more than probable that it was before Bacon's fall, which occurred in 1621. For in a letter written after that calamity, Bacon pays Matthew the fine compliment that the Essay on Friendship,

[1] Sp XIV 429.

by its delay, has gained, because of the proofs of true friendship he had shown in Bacon's adversity.

" It is not for nothing that I have deferred my essay *De Amicitia*, whereby it hath expected the proof of your great friendship towards me. Whatsoever the event be (wherein I depend upon God, who ordaineth the effect, the instrument, all) yet your incessant thinking of me, without loss of a moment of time, or a hint of occasion, or a circumstance of endeavour, or a stroke of a pulse, in demonstration of love and affection to me, doth infinitely tie me to you." [1]

When Bacon at last set out to redeem his word, he apparently entirely discarded the old short Essay on Friendship of 1612, to write an entirely new one, at least seven times longer. Shortly after, in 1625, he published a new and augmented edition of his Essays, in which this new Essay appears as No. 27, widely separated from the Essay Of Love (No. 10), which in the former edition had been its immediate neighbour. The latter had remained untouched, creating a further contrast with its former companion. In the last years of Bacon's life, especially after his fall, the contrast there naturally exists between love and friendship, and fully known and noted before by him, had still more strongly been brought home to him. The attractions of the former had lost their force upon him. He felt therefore no urge to improve upon the old Essay Of Love. His own capacity or faculty for love had been transmuted into the purer friendship. The essential difference between the two had long ago been traced, when in the old discarded Essay on Friendship he had written that " it is friendship, when a man can say to himself, I love this man *without respect of utility*." In love for the other sex such avowal can never be sincerely made.

For the crucial thought in the Love Essay, namely the slavery and the unwisdom of love, we found a parallel in *The Two Gentlemen of Verona* ; in the Friendship Essay also, for the highest thought to which it rises, namely that " *a friend is another himself*," one's alter-ego, there are many striking parallels between Shakespeare and Bacon. Bacon was evidently obsessed by this idea. We have met with it already in

[1] Sp XIV 344.

The Two Gentlemen of Verona, where Valentine-Francis says of Proteus-Anthony :

> I know him as myself.

And in the *Sonnets* the thought recurs repeatedly. For instance, Sonnet 62, where self-love or love for oneself is held to be identical with love for one's friend, because he is in truth oneself— " 'Tis thee, myself."

> Sin of self-love possesseth all mine eye
> And all my soul and all my every part ;
> And for this sin there is no remedy,
> It is so grounded inward in my heart.
> Methinks no face so gracious is as mine,
> No shape so true, no truth of such account ;
> And for myself mine own worth do define,
> As I all other in all worths surmount.
> But when my glass shows me myself indeed,
> Beated and chopped with tanned antiquity,
> Mine own self-love quite contrary I read ;
> Self so self-loving were iniquity.
>   'Tis thee, *myself*—that for myself I praise,
>   Painting my age with beauty of thy days.

Then there is Sonnet 42, where it is proclaimed in so many words that " my friend and I are one."

> That thou hast her, it is not all my grief,
> And yet it may be said I loved her dearly ;
> That she hath thee, is of my wailing chief,
> A loss in love that touches me more nearly.
> Loving offenders, thus I will excuse ye :
> Thou dost love her, because thou know'st I love her ;

And for my sake even so doth she abuse me,
Suffering my friend for my sake to approve her.
    If I lose thee, my loss is my love's gain,
And losing her, my friend hath found that loss ;
Both find each other, and I lose both twain,
And both for my sake lay on me this cross :
        But here's the joy ; *my friend and I are one* ;
        Sweet flattery ! then she loves but me alone.

These two sonnets are of the first series. When they are considered as biographical of Francis Bacon, then the friend is of course Anthony Bacon, and the woman in Sonnet 42 no other than Marguerite of Navarre, the dark lady of the second series. In this series the triangle theme, coupled to the " other-self " or alter-ego theme—is found together in sonnets 133 and 134. The first follows here :

        Beshrew that heart that makes my heart to groan
        For that deep wound it gives my friend and me !
        Is't not enough to torture me alone,
        But slave to slavery my sweet'st friend must be ?
            Me from myself thy cruel eye hath taken,
        And *my next self* thou harder hast engrossed :
        Of him, myself, and thee, I am forsaken ;
        A torment thrice threefold thus to be crossed.
            Prison my heart in thy steel bosom's ward,
        But then my friend's heart let my poor heart bail ;
        Whoe'er keeps me, let my heart be his guard ;
        Thou canst not then use rigour in my fail :
                And yet thou wilt ; for I, being pent in thee,
                Perforce am thine, and all that is in me.

" My next self " being Anthony-Proteus, the " threefold torment " suffered by the poet, is but an echo of Proteus' " threefold perjury " and threefold loss in *The Two Gentlemen of Verona* (II 6). If there

is some lingering doubt whether Anthony is really meant by the words
" my next self," it may be dispersed by the knowledge that when
Francis Bacon dedicated the first edition of his *Essays*, in which those
on love and friendship are not yet found, to his brother, he addressed
the self-same words to him—"*you that are next myself*." I will
not make any apology for giving this dedication in full, as a
sample of the great love and deep affection the author had for
his friend, as well as for its great beauty of language, style and imagery.

To M. Anthony Bacon
his dear Brother.

Loving and beloved Brother, I do now like some that have an
Orchard ill neighboured, that gather their fruit before it is ripe, to pre-
vent stealing. These fragments of my conceits were going to print ; to
labour the stay of them had been troublesome, and subject to interpretation ; to let them pass had been to adventure the wrong they mought
receive by untrue copies, or by some garnishment, which it mought
please any that should set them forth to bestow upon them. Therefore I held it best discretion to publish them my-self as they passed
long ago from my pen, without any further disgrace than the weakness
of the Author. And as I did ever hold, there mought be as great a
vanity in retiring and withdrawing men's conceits (except they be of
some nature) from the world, as in obtruding them : so in these particulars I have played myself the Inquisitor, and find nothing to my understanding in them contrary or infectious to the state of Religion, or
manners, but rather (as I suppose) medicinable. Only I disliked now
to put them out because they will be like the late new half-pence, which
though the Silver were good, yet the pieces were small. But since they
would not stay with their Master, but would needs travail abroad, I have
preferred them to *you that are next myself*, dedicating them, such as
they are, to our love, in the depth whereof (I assure you) I sometimes
wish your infirmities translated upon myself, that her Majesty mought
have the service of so active and able a mind, and I mought be with
excuse confined to these contemplations and studies for which I am

fittest, so commend I you to the preservation of the divine Majesty. From my Chamber at Gray's Inn, this 30 of January, 1597.

Your entire Loving brother,

Fran. Bacon.[1]

It is undoubtedly such pieces as this that made Shelley declare that " Lord Bacon was a poet," and that " his language has a sweet and majestic rhythm which satisfies the sense, no less than the almost superhuman wisdom of his philosophy satisfies the intellect."

The rich content of Bacon's poetic vein of imagery enabled him to play the alter-ego theme in many different variations. In Sonnet 133 it was the " next-myself " variant, in the 134th sonnet this is changed to the " other-mine " variant.

> So, now I have confessed that he is thine,
> And I myself am mortgaged to thy will,
> Myself I'll forfeit, so *that other mine*
> Thou wilt restore, to be *my comfort* still :
>   But thou wilt not, nor he will not be free,
> For thou art covetous and he is kind ;
> He learned but surety-like to write for me,
> Under that bond that him as fast doth bind,
>   The statute of thy beauty thou wilt take,
> Thou usurer, that putt'st forth all to use,
> And sue a friend came debtor for my sake ;
> So him I lose through my unkind abuse.
>   Him have I lost ; thou hast both him and me :
>   He pays the whole, and yet am I not free.

Besides the allusion to Anthony Bacon as " that other-mine " factor in the triangle, there is another expression in this Sonnet which arrests our attention, and which makes the conjecture that it is indeed Anthony whom the author had in mind, doubly probable. It is one

[1] Sp. VI 523-4.

more of the Bacon-Shakespeare parallels.   For the identity in expression between Shakespeare's " my comfort still," and Bacon's reference to his brother as " Anthonie his comforte," [1] is so close, that it can hardly be ascribed to mere coincidence.   And also the contrast between Bacon's " nuptial love " and " friendly love," finds a parallel in Shakespeare's, " Two loves I have of comfort and despair," of Sonnet 144. Anthony is the Comfort, Marguerite the Despair.   Compare this also with the expression " the comfort of friendship " (27th essay), and the despair of love, as a consequence, of the curse :

They that love best, their loves shall not enjoy.

A digression may here be allowed.   Two peculiarities strike us in the last two sonnets.   In the first place, their pronounced legal phraseology, derived from a lawyer's or a judge's law-practice ; in the second place, that these legal terms have an even more strongly pronounced characteristic in common, namely that they all without exception—bail and gaol, mortgage and forfeit, surety and bond, usurer and debtor, to write and to sue—have to do with, and betray indeed a spirit preoccupied with a " sad romance of brotherly love and debt."   This special characteristic brings these sonnets in a line with The Merchant of Venice.   As such they argue, convincingly, not only for Bacon's authorship, but also for our conjecture of Anthony being the friend, and Marguerite the lady in the triangle.

There is another Sonnet, much larded with the same legal phraseology from the debt-courts.   It is Sonnet 87, and it is for still another reason of great importance for our purpose.

Farewell ! thou art too dear for my possessing,
And like enough thou know'st thy estimate.
The charter of thy worth gives thee releasing ;
My bonds in thee are all determinate.

[1] I owe this quotation to the Journal of the Bacon Society, Vol I, p. 58 (1886).   I have not been able to trace it in Bacon's works, and shall be grateful to any reader for the exact reference,

For how do I hold thee but by thy granting ?
And for that riches where is my deserving ?
The cause of this fair gift in me is wanting,
And so my patent back again is swerving.
    Thyself thou gav'st, thy own worth then not knowing,
Or me, to whom thou gav'st it, else mistaking ;
So thy great gift, upon misprision growing,
Comes home again, on better judgement making.
        Thus have I had thee, as a dream doth flatter,
    In sleep a king, but waking no such matter.

Not all the Sonnets of the first series must be imagined to be
exclusively addressed to the boy-friend. Many of them had, I think,
primarily Marguerite for their subject. They were " love-sonnets " in
the first place, and not poems in honour of friendship. But they
pictured love in its highest, purest aspect, approaching perfect friendship, which asks nothing in return. When these poems were collected
for circulation amongst friends or for publication, they were easily made
completely sexless, if they were not so from the beginning, and therefore came naturally to be arranged in the first " pure " series, in contrast
with the " impure " second series, the blatant sexual love-poems.

Sonnet 87, then, is such a " pure-love " sonnet to Marguerite, I
am sure, describing Bacon's late resignation when he realized that her
love for him was just a passing dream, ephemeral, not a lasting reality,
which such " nuptial " love never can be as long as it is not transmuted into its everlasting counterpart, the " charitable " love of
brotherhood and friendship. For this transmutation Marguerite apparently was not ready. And so the dream is followed by the waking.

    Thus have I had thee, as a dream does flatter,
    In sleep a king, but waking no such matter.

These two lines are still for another reason remarkable. Freud
has taught us how dreams are wish-fulfilments, if not always, yet more

often than not. They betray our innermost desires, but so do also
our spoken words, and most of all, the free fancies and imaginations
of a poet. Well, what more natural than that Francis' " great desire to
sit in British throne " should find its necessary outlet in such dreams of
kingship. He is undoubtedly telling us in these lines of an often
recurring experience, surely inevitable under the circumstances of his
secret life-story. But what of Shakespeare ? His dreams must needs
have been more like those we expect from a Falstaff, hovering round
a pot of ale, rather than round a kingdom.

As to the merit of the legal argument in the Baconian controversy,
I can only say that so far as internal evidence is concerned it is in my
opinion the strongest that has yet been advanced, the most unassailable
and irrefutable. It makes every other candidate for the Shakespearean
honours except Bacon quite impossible. As Mark Twain put it, Shakespeare's juridical language and knowledge of the law is " the master-
key to the Shakespeare-Bacon puzzle."

A few of the pronouncements by eminent Shakespearean critics
and lawyers regarding this aspect of Shakespeare's language may find a
place here.[1] Said Lord Campbell, one of the most distinguished lawyers
of the nineteenth century who was raised to the high office of Lord
Chief Justice in 1850, and subsequently became Lord Chancellor :
" There is nothing so dangerous as for one not of the craft to tamper
with our freemasonry. Let a non-professional man, however acute,
presume to talk law, or to draw illustrations from legal science in
discussing other subjects, and he will speedily fall into laughable
absurdity. [But] while novelists and dramatists are constantly making
mistakes as to the laws of marriage, of wills, and inheritance, to
Shakespeare's law, lavishly as he expounds it, there can neither be
demurrer, nor bill of exceptions, nor writ of error."

Another lawyer, Richard Grant White, says : " No dramatist of the
time used legal phrases with Shakespeare's readiness and exactness.
And the significance of this fact is heightened by another, that it is

[1] They are taken from G. G. Greenwood's *The Shakespeare Problem Restated* (London,
1908), as quoted by Mark Twain.

only to the language of the law that he exhibits this inclination. The phrases peculiar to other occupations serve him on rare occasions, by way of description, comparison, or illustration, generally when something in the scene suggests them, but legal phrases flow from his pen as part of his vocabulary, and parcel of his thought."

Finally the testimony of Lord Penzance, one of the first legal authorities of his day, who came to much the same conclusions as Lord Campbell. Speaking of Shakespeare's " perfect familiarity with not only the principles, axioms, and maxims, but the technicalities of English law," Lord Penzance testifies that his knowledge is so " perfect and intimate that he was never incorrect and never at fault. The mode in which this knowledge was pressed into service on all occasions to express his meaning and illustrate his thoughts, was quite unexampled. He seems to have had a special pleasure in his complete and ready mastership of it in all its branches. As manifested in the plays, this legal knowledge and learning had therefore a special character which places it on a wholly different footing from the rest of the multifarious knowledge which is exhibited in page after page of the plays. At every turn and point at which the author required a metaphor, simile, or illustration, his mind ever turned *first* to the law. He seems almost to have *thought* in legal phrases, the commonest of legal expressions were ever at the end of his pen in description or illustration."

The conclusion from the foregoing is then that only a man who was at the same time a great poet, a great philosopher, and a great lawyer, could have written Shakespeare's works. And it is only Bacon, according to the testimony of the greatest experts in each of these three fields, who fills the triple bill.

There is in the 42nd Sonnet—which with its triangle problem might seem displaced among the first series, and to belong more properly to the second—a particular sentiment, which links it up more closely still with *The Two Gentlemen of Verona*, and as we shall see also with *The Merchant of Venice*. We shall here elaborate somewhat more upon this aspect. It will yield us that peculiar quality in the deepest asexual friendship, to which we have alluded in the beginning of this chapter.

This sentiment or quality is found in the first quatrain of Sonnet 42. It is not the loss of his lady that touches him most, but the loss of his friend.

> That thou hast her, it is not all my grief,
> And yet it may be said I loved her dearly ;
> That she hath thee, is of my wailing chief,
> A loss in love that touches me more nearly.

The same sentiment was expressed by Valentine when he said of Proteus' disaffection and treachery that "the private wound was deepest," implying that nothing in the world, not even the loss of his lady, could wound him so deeply as the loss of his friend. That this is indeed the implication of "private" is easily explained. One's relation to one's lady-love is in the end, when sanctioned by the laws of matrimony, a *public* bond which one is bound by the law to respect as well as every one else is bound by that same public law to respect it. How different is it on the other hand with friendship—entirely a *private* affair, with no law or any other public institution to bind one or others. This interpretation of Valentine's words, implying the preferment of friendship before or above love, is borne out by the sequence, when Valentine is so· overjoyed at receiving back his friend, that he willingly surrenders his lady-love to him,

> All that was mine in Silvia I give thee.

This line has given occasion to many criticisms, all because Valentine's previous words, "the private wound is deepest," have not been understood, or not received at their full weight. One critic says that Valentine "goes too far."[1] Charles and Mary Lamb describe the scene as follows: "Proteus expressed such a lively sorrow for the injuries he had done to Valentine, that Valentine, whose nature was noble and generous, even to a romantic degree, not only forgave and restored him to his former place in his friendship, but in a sudden flight of

[1] Sm 84.

heroism he said, 'I freely do forgive you; and all the interest I have in Silvia, I give it up to you.' Julia, who was standing beside her master as a page, hearing this strange offer, and fearing Proteus would not be able with this new-found virtue to refuse Silvia, fainted, and they were all employed in recovering her: else would Silvia have been offended at being thus made over to Proteus, though she could scarcely think that Valentine would long persevere in this overstrained and too generous act of friendship." [1]

To the Lambs, then, Valentine's is but a "romantic" deed, a "sudden flight of heroism," an "overstrained and too generous act." Now if it is anything, Valentine's deed is certainly *not* a "romantic" deed at all, but in a sense rather the opposite, for it is not inspired by any "romance," or love for the other sex, or "nuptial love," as Bacon would term it, but by "friendly love" for one of his own sex. Least of all is it a "sudden heroic," or "overstrained" or "too generous" act, for it is of the very quality of that friendship as conceived by Bacon-Shakespeare, in which the friend, not the lady, is one's "next-self," one's "other-mine," in which "my friend and I are one." Therefore, spiritually speaking at least, my lady is also my friend's love, and my friend's lady my love. Therefore have I as much interest in his as he in my lady-love. It is of course absurd to suppose that Shakespeare for a moment meant Valentine to surrender his lady "bodily" to his friend. The word "interest" directly refutes this. It was Shakespeare's genius which selected this word here, at this moment, in this spiritual crisis which Valentine had passed through by the loss and the recovery of his friend—mind! the deepest and most private wound. That Julia by her fainting showed that she accepted the meaning of the word in the "bodily" sense proves only that she was not of the metal of Valentine, but the fitter consort for Proteus. That Silvia's silence, on the contrary, should have to be explained by Julia's fainting having so distracted her as to wipe out completely the memory of Valentine's words, spoken clearly before there was any fainting—or by such reflections in her mind as that Valentine, her hero, was such a fickle or weak-kneed boy

[1] Tales from Shakespeare, Everyman's Library, 1938, p. 94.

that he would not long persevere in his renunciation—is of course absurd in the highest degree, and unworthy both of Silvia and Valentine. It all comes from an entire lack of understanding of the psychological quality of that asexual friendship which is, greater, intenser, deeper than sexual love.   When therefore Professor Herford remarks that Valentine's offer to surrender Silvia " lacks not only psychological truth but psychological plausibility," [1] he only shows that he does not know of what he is speaking, at least not of what Bacon-Shakespeare is trying to convey of spiritual values.

These critics should have known better.   Not only the Sonnets should have taught them better, but in the Plays also the incident of The Two Gentlemen of Verona does not stand alone. Its solitary example is doubled and trebled by The Merchant of Venice.   When his friend Antonio is on the point of losing his life to the cruel knife of Shylock, Bassanio-Bacon, having just been married to Portia, yet exclaims in the greatest anguish and sincerest fervency :

> Antonio, I am married to a wife
> Which is as dear to me as life itself ;
> But life itself, my wife, and all the world,
> Are not with me esteemed above thy life :
> I would lose all, aye sacrifice them all,
> Here to this devil, to deliver you.

And this is instantly echoed by Bassanio's servant Gratiano.

> I have a wife, whom, I protest, I love :
> I would she were in heaven, so she could
> Entreat some power to change this currish Jew.

And though the two wives, Portia and Nerissa, who are present at this scene, though unknown to their husbands, protest against their being thus sacrificed,

[1] Sm 84.

Por.   Your wife would give you little thanks for that,
         If she were here to hear you make the offer.
Ner.   'Tis well you offer it behind her back ;
         The wish would make else an unquiet house,

yet that is only what we could expect—a public denial or repudi-
ation of the " bodily " surrender, but we know full well that in their
hearts they applaud and are proud of their husbands' capability of such
great spiritual friendship.

There now remains for us the most difficult and delicate part in the
qualification and elucidation of this supreme " friendly love." Here and
there in the foregoing, to stress its contrast with the nuptial, romantic,
or sexual love, I have called it the asexual love, and compared it with
the love of angels, that " neither marry nor are given in marriage." It
also goes by the name of Platonic or Socratic love, and then generally,
but wrongly, is identified in our days with homosexual love, which is
rightly held in abhorrence by normal people as an unnatural thing, a
perversion, falling under what Bacon classified as " wanton love,"
which " corrupteth and embaseth " mankind, serving neither the purpose of the " making " of man, nor the end of the " perfecting "
of man.

It is hardly necessary to say that the Socratic, asexual, or angelic
love is equally the opposite of homosexual as of pure nuptial
love. For these two are both sexual, carnal love, with this difference
only that the latter is normal, natural and beneficent for the human
race, the former on the contrary unnatural, fruitless, and degrading.
Homosexual love means literally love for the same (*homos*) sex. It is
therefore nothing better than sex-love, only worse in that it is flowing
along a perverted channel. For this reason it is also full of the same
jealousies, fears, riots, mistrusts, discontents, let us call them the
" curses," as sex-love is, such " curses " as were pronounced by
Venus, at the death of Adonis, on this " lust-love."

This is the greatest denunciation of sexual love existing in the English
language, in any language, I presume. Only Shakespeare could have

thus masterly arrayed the multitude of evils that attend such love,
under the guise of an old fable, and clad in the most exquisite poetical
language and imagery, which only could save it from being a monster-
libel.[1]

The Love-curse

Since thou art dead, lo ! here I prophesy,
Sorrow on love hereafter shall attend.
It shall be waited on with jealousy,
Find sweet beginning, but unsavoury end.
 Ne'er settled equally, but high or low,
 That all love's pleasure shall not match his woe.

It shall be fickle, false, and full of fraud,
Bud, and be blasted, in a breathing while,
The bottom poison, and the top o'er-strawed
With sweets that shall the truest fight beguile :
 The strongest body shall it make most weak,
 Strike the wise dumb, and teach the fool to speak.

It shall be sparing, and too full of riot,
Teaching decrepit age to tread the measures,
The staring ruffian shall it keep in quiet,
Pluck down the rich, enrich the poor with treasures,
 It shall be raging mad, and silly mild,
 Make the young old, the old become a child.

It shall suspect where is no cause of fear,
It shall not fear where it should most mistrust,
It shall be merciful, and too severe,
And most deceiving, when it seems most just,
 Perverse it shall be, where it shows most toward,
 Put fear to valour, courage to the coward.

[1] *Venus and Adonis*, 1135-1164.

It shall be cause of war, and dire events,
And set dissention twixt the son, and Sire,
Subject, and servile to all discontents :
As dry combustious matter is to fire,
    Sith in his prime, death doth my love destroy,
    They that love best, their loves shall not enjoy.

Venus, having become wise and clear-sighted in her sorrow, but re-echoes what the " innocent " Adonis had tried to teach her before,[1] the difference namely between her " lust-love " and his " friendly love,"

    I hate not love, but your device in love,

he protests to Venus, accusing her :

    You do it for increase,

whereas *his* " love " is " without respect of utility." As to *her* " love ",

Call it not love, for Love to heaven is fled,
Since sweating Lust on earth usurped his name ;
Under whose simple semblance he hath fed
Upon fresh beauty, blotting it with blame ;
    Which the hot tyrant stains and soon bereaves,
    As caterpillars do the tender leaves.

Love comforteth like sunshine after rain,
But Lust's effect is tempest after sun ;
Love's gentle spring doth always fresh remain,
Lust's winter comes ere summer half be done,
    Love surfeits not, Lust like a glutton dies ;
    Love is all truth, Lust full of forgèd lies.

[1] *Ibid.*, 769-810.

Now, if after *Venus and Adonis*, we read the *Sonnets*, we shall find how this distinction between Love and Lust lies at the root also of the first and second series of Sonnets. How full of lust and all its accompanying " curses " the latter series is, and how singularly free on the other hand the first series is of all these evils.   That indeed this first series treats of pure asexual love, with not the least admixture of homosexuality, is easily proved by the absence of any sexual jealousy, for example in the first seventeen sonnets or so, in which the poet urges his friend to marry so that his beauty may be perpetuated in his offspring and his happiness assured.   One example must suffice, Sonnet 3 :

> Look in thy glass, and tell the face thou viewest
> Now is the time that face should form another ;
> Whose fresh repair if now thou not renewest,
> Thou dost beguile the world, unbless some mother.
>   For where is she so fair whose uneared womb
> Disdains the tillage of thy husbandry ?
> Or who is he so fond will be the tomb
> Of his self-love, to stop prosperity ?
>   Thou art thy mother's glass, and she in thee
> Calls back the lovely April of her prime ;
> So thou through windows of thine age shalt see
> Despite of wrinkles this thy golden time.
>   But if thou live, remembered not to be,
>   Die single, and thine image dies with thee.

Venus makes a similar appeal to her boy-friend, Adonis : [1]

> What is thy body but a swallowing grave,
> Seeming to bury that posterity
> Which by the rights of time thou needst must have
> If thou destroy them not in dark obscurity ?

[1] Ibid., 757-726.

If so, the world will hold thee in disdain,
Sith in thy pride so fair a hope is slain.

But the pure Adonis sees through her selfishness. "You do it for increase," of yourself, of your own pleasures, he accuses her. How different is Shakespeare's appeal for "increase" to his boy-friend, in Sonnet 1 :

From fairest creatures we desire increase,
That thereby beauty's rose might never die,
But as the riper should by time decease,
His tender heir might bear his memory.

For the increase here sought is not the pleader's own, but his love's increase ! Gone are jealousy, and the whole pack of "curses" of the grosser love, of which the second series of sonnets is so full. A good example of this is Sonnet 147, full of hellish fever and dark madness.

My love is as a fever, longing still
For that which longer nurseth the disease,
Feeding on that which doth preserve the ill,
The uncertain sickly appetite to please.
My reason, the physician to my love,
Angry that his prescriptions are not kept,
Hath left me, and I desperate now approve
Desire is death, which physic did except.
Past cure I am, now reason is past care,
And frantic-mad with evermore unrest ;
My thoughts and my discourse as madmen's are,
At random from the truth vainly express'd ;
        For I have sworn thee fair and thought thee bright,
        Who art as black as hell, as dark as night.

Of the pure exaltation on the other hand of the " friendly love,"
or " boy-love " in the first series of the *Sonnets*, we have a parallel in
Edmund Spenser's, or rather Colin Clout's love for Hobbinol.   Colin
and Hobbinol stand for Francis and Anthony.   About their friendship
the gloss to the January Eclogue of *The Shepherd's Calendar* tells us the
following : " Hobbinol is a feigned country name, whereby it being so
common and usual, seemeth to be hidden the person of some his very
special and most familiar friend, whom he entirely and extraordinarily
beloved, as peradventure shall be more largely declared hereafter.   In
this place seemeth to be some savour of disorderly love, which the
learned call paederasty : but it is gathered beside his meaning.   For who
that hath read Plato his dialogue called Alcybiades, Xenophon and
Maximus Tyrius of Socrates' opinions, may easily perceive that such love
is much to be allowed and liked of, specially so meant, as Socrates
used it : who saith that indeed he loved Alcybiades extremely, yet not
Alcybiades person, but his soul, which is Alcybiades' *own self*.   And so
is paederasty much to be preferred before gynerasty, that is the love
which enflameth men with lust toward womankind.   But let no man think
that herein I stand with Lucian or his devilish disciple Unico Aretino, in
defense of execrable and horrible sins of forbidden and unlawful fleshliness, whose abominable error is fully confuted of Perionius and others."
The meaning of words changes with the passing of years.   Paederasty in our days, according to the Oxford Dictionary, is completely
identified with sodomy, that is just those " execrable and horrible "
vices of " disorderly love," or " wanton love " as Bacon expressed it, so
strongly condemned in the last sentence of the above paragraph.   Originally paederasty (from *paidos*=boy, and *erastes*=lover) meant simply
boy-love, or Bacon's " friendly love," in contrast with gynerasty (from
gyne=woman) meaning woman-love, or Bacon's " nuptial love."   The
sharp contrast in which Spenser here places these two loves in opposition
to each other, as " soul "-love and " lust "-love, in much the same way
as Bacon did in his *Essays* and Shakespeare in his *Sonnets*, argues again
favourably for the *one* mind supposed to be hidden behind these three
names.   For this reason also, I have given Spenser's defence against

any imputation of "forbidden and unlawful fleshliness" in full, so that it may serve as well in defence of the purity of Shakespeare's first sonnet-series, as of Bacon's friendship-essay, though the latter has in fact the less need of it.

But the most eloquent and poetic plea in defence of the purity of such friendship between persons of the same sex is found in Emilia's recital of her youthful affection, as told in the apocryphal Shakespearean play, *The Two Noble Kinsmen*, to which we shall soon turn our attention.

One final remark. When in some of the Sonnets quoted, I have identified the friend as Anthony Bacon, this does not mean that in other sonnets Francis Bacon may not have had other, and younger friends in view. I am in fact of opinion that the "lovely boy" of the first series is the idealized portrait of all his friendships young and old. And if names are required, I would mention besides his foster-brother, Anthony Bacon, his brother-in-law, Sir John Constable, married to Dorothy, the sister of Alice Barnham, whom Bacon married on the 10th of May 1607.[1] The depth of their friendship may be gauged from the dedicatory epistle of the second edition of the *Essays* of 1612.

To my Loving Brother, Sir John Constable Knight.

My last Essays I dedicated to my dear brother Master Anthony Bacon, who is with God. Looking amongst my papers this vacation, I found others of the same Nature : which if I myself shall not suffer to be lost, it seemeth the World will not ; by :the often printing of the former. *Missing my Brother, I found you next;* in respect of bond both of near alliance, and of straight friendship and society, and particularly of communication in studies. Wherein I must acknowledge myself beholding to you. For as my business found rest in my contemplations ; so my contemplations ever found rest in your loving conference and judgement. So wishing you all good, I remain,

Your loving brother and friend,

Fra. Bacon.

[1] Sp XI 1.

" Missing my brother Anthony [who had died more than a decade back] I found you next," these words tell us as much as we need to know. John Constable must in some way have taken Anthony's place. It was also at Bacon's request that he was knighted on the 5th October of 1607. But the greatest proof of Bacon's confidence in him was that he appointed him in his will as his literary executor. " As to that durable part of my memory, which consisteth in my works and writings, I desire my executors, and especially Sir John Constable and my very good friend Mr. Bosvile, to take care that of all my writings, both of English and of Latin, there may be books fair bound, and placed in the King's Library, etc." Again: "Also, I desire my executors, especially my brother Constable, and also Mr. Bosvile, presently after my decease, to take into their hands all my papers whatsoever, which are either in cabinets, boxes, or presses, and them to seal up until they may at their leisure peruse them." And as a legacy: "I give to my brother Constable all my books, etc," [1]

Then there is Toby Matthew, who shares the singular honour with Anthony Bacon, of having been designated by Francis Bacon in so many words as his *alter-ego*, " another myself." [2] Further Thomas Meautys, who erected his monument in St. Michael's Church at St. Albans. And William Rawley, who became the editor of his posthumous works, to name only three. They all, and others more—for Bacon's life was rich in friendship—must have contributed their share to set the " Concealed Poet's " [3] vein aglowing, whenever pure friendship and brotherly love was the theme.

To treat of Bacon's *Essays* on Love and Friendship, and of Shakespeare's *Two Gentlemen of Verona*, without taking into consideration also *The Two Noble Kinsmen*, would be as incomplete as to talk of Francis and not to mention Anthony, or vice versa. For these two plays are very similar and as nearly related as these two noble brothers. And it is strange indeed that this similarity should not by my knowledge have been noticed before, for not only that these plays have the same

[1] Sp. XIV 539, 540, 542.

[2] Sp XIV 423.

[3] Sp X 65.

author, and much the same title, but also the same theme and the same ideas, to say nothing of the same style and language.

The Two Noble Kinsmen is one of the so-called " Shakespeare Apocrypha." Under this title C. F. Tucker Brooke published in 1918 " a collection of fourteen plays which have been ascribed to Shakespeare." The twelfth is " this brilliant and puzzling drama," as the editor describes it. It was first printed in Quarto in 1634, eight years after Bacon's death, and in this oldest edition it was said on the title-page to have been " written by the memorable Worthies of their Time ; Mr. John Fletcher and Mr. William Shakespeare, Gent." One theory is that the work is a revision of an old play, prepared by Shakespeare and later elaborated by Fletcher. Another, that " the play consists of very late ' poetic ' fragments by Shakespeare subsequently connected and completed by Fletcher." Others again deny altogether Shakespeare's authorship of any part of the drama. As Tucker Brooke remarks : " Of all the doubtful plays, The Two Noble Kinsmen is the one which has inspired the greatest amount of criticism and conjecture ; yet there is perhaps no other member of the class that has so thoroughly maintained the mystery of its authorship, or has so often obliged candid investigators to retract their theories and confess themselves at a loss." I will not join issue with the galaxy of Shakespearean scholars who have spent their life and ingenuity on proving or disproving Shakespeare's part-authorship in the play, for I do not consider myself competent to do so along their lines. But in Chapters 7 and 9 I have brought Shakespeare's symbolic and anagrammatic ciphers to bear upon the drama with the result that Bacon's secret signatures have been found in it, and so have proved to my satisfaction that Shakespeare-Bacon must have had a full hand in it.

I believe the play to be a revision by Bacon of an old play, probably the one by " Master Edwards of the Queenes Chappell," which was " played in Christs Church, where the Queene's Highness lodged," in August 1566. How Fletcher's name came ever to be mixed up with it, I do not pretend to know, but that he had anything to do with it is purely conjectural, and made improbable by other circumstances.

First, his name was only connected with it fifteen years after Shakespeare's and nine years after his own death.   Second, it was not included in the first Folio of Beaumont and Fletcher's *Comedies and
Tragedies* (1647), and appeared only in the second Folio of " *Fifty
Comedies and Tragedies* " of 1679, more than half a century after
Fletcher's death, without any mention of Shakespeare's name.   Add to
this, third, the secret marks of Bacon's authorship, and the proof is, I
find, conclusive.

But though I cannot say for certain how Fletcher's name came to
be printed on the title-page of the Quarto, yet I can make a fair
guess.   The play consists admittedly of two very unequal parts.   " The
utter dissimilarity is obvious at a glance," says Tucker Brooke, and
Swinburne, the poet, called it a " piece of magnificent patchwork."   In
our hypothesis the two parts must of course be due to Edwards and
Shakespeare-Bacon, not to the latter and Fletcher.   The rewriting not
having been finished by Bacon during his lifetime, and the play having
after his death fallen into the hands of the editor or the publisher of the
Quarto, the latter, knowing nothing of the Mr. Edwards of more than
eighty years ago, and sensing the dissimilarity, simply conjectured that
the collaborator or co-author was Fletcher.   I further claim that of all
the conjectures that have been made, this hypothesis is the least
improbable, and the most consistent with the facts.

The criticism made against the Shakespearean authorship of any
part, namely that " there is practically nothing in characterization or
dramatic structure which points to the author of The Tempest " (Tucker
Brooke) is in my opinion as arbitrary as undeserved.   To give one example, when it is said that the author has failed " properly to distinguish
between Palamon and Arcite," the two noble kinsmen, one is really compelled to place a big question-mark to the critic's power of discrimina-
tion.   Let the following extracts speak for themselves.   First, as Emilia
sees the distinction between the two kinsmen (V 3) :

Emil.   *Arcite* is gently visaged ; yet his eye
        Is like an engine bent, or a sharp weapon
        23

In a soft sheath ; mercy and manly courage
Are bedfellows in his visage, *Palamon*
Has a most menacing aspect : his brow
Is graved, and seems to bury what it frowns on ;
Yet sometimes it is not so, but alters to
The quality of his thoughts ; long time his eye
Will dwell upon his object.   Melancholy
Becomes him nobly ; so does *Arcite's* mirth,
But *Palamon's* sadness is a kind of mirth,
So mingled, as if mirth did make him sad,
And sadness, merry ; those darker humours that
Stick misbecomingly on others, on them
Live in fair dwelling.

A fair portrait, I think of the more volatile and mercurial Anthony, with his mirth and " his eye like an engine," and on the other hand the slower, and more melancholy, but more serious and deeper Francis.

Second, as the cousins reveal their difference in character by their own words and thoughts, while lying in prison (II 2) :

Pal.   Oh cousin *Arcite*,
    Where is Thebes now ? where is our noble country ?
    Where are our friends, and kindreds ? never more
    Must we behold those comforts, never see
    The hardy youths strive for the games of honour
    (Hung with the painted favours of their ladies,
    Like tall ships under sail) then start amongst them
    And as an eastwind leave them all behind us,
    Like lazy clouds, whilst *Palamon* and *Arcite*,
    Even in the wagging of a wanton leg
    Out-stripped the people's praises, won the garlands,
    Ere they have time to wish them ours. O never
    Shall we two exercise, like twins of honour,
    Our arms again, and feel our fiery horses

Like proud seas under us : our good swords now
(Better the red-eyed god of war ne'er wore)
Ravished our sides, like age must run to rust,
And deck the temples of those gods that hate us :
These hands shall never draw them out like lightning,
To blast whole armies more.

Arc. No, *Palamon,*
Those hopes are prisoners with us ; here we are
And here the graces of our youths must wither
Like a too-timely spring ; here age must find us,
And, which is heaviest, *Palamon,* unmarried ;
The sweet embraces of a loving wife,
Laden with kisses, armed with thousand cupids
Shall never clasp our necks, no issue know us,
No figures of ourselves shall we e'er see,
To glad our age, and like young eagles teach them
Boldly to gaze against bright arms, and say :
' Remember what your fathers were, and conquer.'
The fair-eyed maids, shall weep our banishments,
And in their songs, curse ever-blinded fortune,
Till she for shame see what a wrong she has done
To youth and nature.   This is all our world ;
We shall know nothing here but one another,
Hear nothing but the clocke that tells our woes.
The vine shall grow, but we shall never see it :
Summer shall come, and with her all delights ;
But dead-cold winter must inhabit here still.

Pal. 'Tis too true, *Arcite.*   To our Theban hounds,
That shook the aged forest with their echoes,
No more now must we halloa, no more shake
Our pointed javelins, whilst the angry Swine
Flies like a parthian quiver from our rages,
Struck with our well-steeled darts : All valiant uses
(The food, and nourishment of noble minds),

In us two here shall perish ; we shall die
(Which is the curse of honour) lastly
Children of grief, and ignorance.

Arc.   Yet, cousin,
Even from the bottom of these miseries,
From all that fortune can inflict upon us,
I see two comforts rysing, two mere blessings,
If the gods please : to hold here a brave patience,
And the enjoying of our grief together.
Whilst *Palamon* is with me, let me perish
If I think this our prison.

Pal.   Certainly,
'Tis a main goodness, cousin, that our fortunes
Were twined together ; 'tis most true, two souls
Put in two noble bodies—let them suffer
The gall of hazard, so they grow together—
Will never sink ; they must not, say they could :
A willing man dies sleeping, and all's done.

Arc.   Shall we make worthy uses of this place
That all men hate so much ?

Pal.   How, gentle cousin ?

Arc.   Let's think this prison holy sanctuary,
To keep us from corruption of worse men.
We are young and yet desire the ways of honour,
That liberty and common conversation,
The poison of pure spirits, might like women
Woo us to wander from.   What worthy blessing
Can be but our imaginations
May make it ours ? And here being thus together,
We are an endless mine to one another ;
We are one another's wife, ever begetting
New births of love ; we are father, friends, acquaintance ;
We are, in one another, families,
I am your heir, and you are mine : this place

Is our inheritance, no hard oppresser
Dare take this from us ; here, with a little patience,
We shall live long, and loving : no surfeits seek us :
The hand of war hurts none here, nor the seas
Swallow their youth : were we at liberty,
A wife might part us lawfully, or business ;
Quarrels consume us, envy of ill men
Grave our acquaintance ; I might sicken, cousin,
Where you should never know it, and so perish
Without your noble hand to close mine eyes,
Or prayers to the gods : a thousand chances,
Were we from hence, would sever us.

Pal.   You have made me
(I thank you, cousin *Arcite*) almost wanton
With my captivity : what a misery
It is to live abroad, and everywhere !
'Tis like a beast, methinks : I find the court here—
I am sure, a more content ; and all those pleasures
That woo the wills of men to vanity,
I see through now, and am sufficient
To tell the world, 'tis but a gaudy shadow,
That old time, as he passes by, takes with him.
What had we been, old in the court of *Creon*,
Where sin is justice, lust and ignorance
The virtues of the great ones ! Cousin *Arcite*,
Had not the loving gods found this place for us,
We had died as they do, ill old men, unwept,
And had their epitaphs, the peoples curses :
Shall I say more ?

Arc.   I would hear you still.
Pal.   Ye shall.
Is there record of any two that loved
Better than we do, *Arcite?*
Arc.   Sure, there cannot.

Pal.   I do not think it possible our friendship
          Should ever leave us.
Arc.   Till our deaths it cannot ;
          And after death our spirits shall be led
          To those that love eternally.

Arcite's mind is evidently full of love, as his talk is of " fair-eyed maids " and " sweet embraces." So I imagine Anthony's must have been. Their friendship associates itself in his mind with a marriage-bond, " we are one another's wife, ever begetting new births of love." When thinking of their liberty and the corruptions of the court he fears that these " might like women woo us to wander from " the right path, and again that " a wife might part us lawfully " in our friendship.

Contrast this with Palamon's reminiscences of " hardy youths striving for the games of honour," of themselves as " twins of honour." His mind and his talk is full of sports, arms, horses, hunting, and the like, and honour foremost of all. Always he leads, while gentle, loving Arcite follows. The one is like the sturdy oak, the other like the clinging vine. " Honour," the watchword of the former, " love " of the latter, as of Francis and Anthony, so I imagine.

And this difference in character is well kept up till the end, when a kind fate ordains that Arcite should lay down his life, so that his love's dilemma may be solved, and his friend's happiness be assured.

But there is worse to contend against. The grossest insult is offered by the critics to the pure and noble girl, who is the object of contention between the two kinsmen. Because she cannot decide whom she loves most, and whom she therefore has to reject, she is called by one " a silly lady's-maid or shop girl, not knowing her own mind, up and down like a bucket in a well " (Furnivall), while another speaks of " her really revolting wishy-washiness and ingrained sensuality " (Tucker Brooke). Such excessive, coarse, and vulgar condemnation argues of itself for some inherent weakness in the critic's standpoint. They are too eager to prove too much. In opposition to Tucker Brooke who declares, again in much too strong

language, that it is an "utter absurdity" to associate Emilia with
Imogen or Miranda, I maintain that she compares favourably with both,
in fact with any of Shakespeare's heroines.   Let the reader judge for
himself from the following scene.

Hipolita, Queen of the warlike Amazon maidens, having
praised Theseus' deep friendship with Perithous, Emilia takes occasion
to tell her of a similar close bond she had in her childhood, when
only eleven years old, with a companion of her own sex, whom death
since has taken away, because the grave was jealous of the pride her
bed had in her (I 3).

Emil.   I was acquainted
          Once with a time, when I enjoyed a play-fellow ;
          You were at wars, when she the grave enriched,
          Who made too proud the bed, took leave o' the moon
          (Which then looked pale at parting) when our count
          Was each eleven.
Hip.   'T was Flavina.
Emil.   Yes.
          You talk of Perithous' and Theseus' love ;
          Theirs has more ground, is more maturely seasoned,
          More buckled with strong judgement and their needs
          The one of th' other may be said to water
          Their intertangled roots of love ; but I
          And she I sigh and spoke of were things innocent,
          Loved for we did,[1] and like the elements
          That know not what, nor why, yet do effect
          Rare issues by their operance, our souls
          Did so to one another ; what she liked,
          Was then of me approved, what not, condemned,
          No more arraignment ; the flower that I would pluck
          And put between my breasts (then but beginning

---

[1] "Loved merely because we did love, without ulterior interest," or as Bacon expressed
it "without respect of utility" (First Essay on Friendship).

    To swell about the blossom) oh, she would long
    Till she had such another, and commit it
    To the like innocent cradle, where *Phoenix* like
    They died in perfume : on my head no toy
    But was her pattern ; her affections (pretty,
    Though, happily, her careless were) I followed
    For my most serious decking ; had mine ear
    Stolen some new air, or at adventure hummed one
    From musical coinage, why it was a note
    Whereon her spirits would sojourn (rather dwell on)
    And sing it in her slumbers.   This rehearsal
    (Which every innocent wots well comes in
    Like old importment's bastard) [1] has this end
    That the true love 'tween maid and maid may be
    More than in sex dividual.

Hip.   Y'are out of breath
    And this high speeded pace is but to say
    That you shall never like the Maid Flavina
    Love any that's called Man.

Emil.   I am sure I shall not.

    Herein lies the solution of the whole difficulty of Emilia's unde-
cidedness in love, so little understood by the critics.   Its full explanation
must be clear from all that has gone before.   Her asexual friendship
for both kinsmen is greater than her sexual love for either.   But I fear
that in a world which still ranks romantic love before friendship, and
judges it but natural if not decent to sacrifice the latter to the former,
instead of the reverse, this exposition will not meet with great approval.
Be it so.   Then, judging the scene from a purely poetical point of
view, I still maintain that it equals whatever Shakespeare wrote of
Imogen and Miranda.

    But enough of purely literary criticism.   One of the reasons why
it was started is to let the reader taste for himself some of the exquisite

---

[1] " Like a feeble imitation of some thread-bare homily."

beauties of this rare play, judged by Swinburne to be the " last gigantic heir of Shakespeare's invention, the posthumous birth of his parting Muse." How contradictory and therefore barren mere literary criticism is, when it is not supported by historical research and philosophical thought, may here be further illustrated by Smeaton's contrary pronouncement that " the characters are drawn with skill and incisiveness, the contrast between Palamon and Arcite being effectively presented," and that " of the female characters, Emilia is a charming woman nobly planned, whose heart in a very difficult position showed itself true to the highest and noblest instincts of womanhood."

We must now consider more specially the biographical elements in the play regarding Anthony and Francis Bacon.

As in *The Two Gentlemen of Verona*, the play presents us with the infatuation of two close friends for the same lady, and the enmity into which their friendship thereby is turned. This is also the principal theme of the *Two Noble Kinsmen*. But differing from the former, and thus changing the comedy into a tragedy, is the circumstance that there is not a second lady to draw the love of one of the friends away, and so make both parties happy. The triangle does not in the end develop into a quadrangle, but on the contrary is reduced to a straight line, a two-cornered figure. In the case of our play there is only one girl who, to make things worse, does not for herself know which of her two suitors she loves the better. In Emilia this was unaffected innocence, the unselfishness of an all-loving heart. In so far we cannot take her for a portrait of Marguerite of Navarre, whose wantonness would not reject either of the friends but wished to keep them both. Still *The Two Noble Kinsmen* gives an equally good example of the triangle situation : Francis-Palamon, Anthony-Arcite and Marguerite-Emilia. A clear biographical element is provided by the prison-scene, when Palamon and Arcite get the first glimpse of their love, and their first quarrel because of her arises (II 2) :

Pal.   What think you of this beauty ?
Arc.   'Tis a rare one,

24

Pal.   Is't but a rare one?

Arc.   Yes, a matchless beauty.

Pal.   Might not a man well lose himself and love her?

Arc.   I cannot tell what you have done, I have ;
          Beshrew mine eyes for't : now I feel my shackles.

Pal.   You love her then?

Arc.   Who would not?

Pal.   And desire her?

Arc.   Before my liberty.

Pal.   *I saw her first.*

Arc.   That's nothing.

Pal.   But it shall be.

Arc.   I saw her too.

Pal.   Yes, but you must not love her.

Arc.   I will not as you do, to worship her,
          As she is heavenly, and a blessed goddess ;
          I love her as a woman, to enjoy her :
          So both may love.

Pal.   You shall not love at all.

Arc.   Not love at all !

Pal.   I, *that first saw her* ; I that took possession
          First with mine eyes of all those beauties
          In her revealed to mankind : if thou lov'st her,
          Or entertain'st a hope to blast my wishes,
          Thou art a traitor, Arcite, and a fellow
          False as thy title to her : friendship, blood,
          And all the ties between us I disclaim,
          If thou once think upon her.

Arc.   Because another
          First sees the enemy, shall I stand still
          And let mine honour down, and never charge?

Pal.   Yes, if he be but one, etc.

Thus Francis and Anthony may have quarrelled in the letters
exchanged between England and France, while the former urged his

rights of priority.   The text underlines also the difference in character
of the two kinsmen, by the difference in quality of their love for Emily.
One " worships " a " goddess," the other wants to " enjoy " the
" woman."

Preceding this scene is one in which the gaoler's daughter points out
the two knights, who are looking out of the prison-window, one standing
in front of the other, Palamon being mistaken by her father for Arcite,

> No, Sir, no, that's Palamon : Arcite is *the lower of Twain*, you
> may perceive a part of him,'

namely behind the other.   The words in italics are reminiscent of a
similar scene in *As You Like It* (I 2), where Le Beau distinguishes
Rosalind and Celia, cousins and friends also, brother's daughters, as
Palamon and Arcite are sisters' sons, by describing the former as " the
taller of the two." [1]   And I am convinced that in *The Two Noble
Kinsmen* it describes the actual difference in physical stature of Francis
and Anthony, as well as in their spiritual stature.

Another touch of biographical import is found in the death-scene.
When treating of Proteus' falseness and betrayal of his friend in *The Two
Gentlemen of Verona*, I insisted that in the case of Anthony there could
be no question of treachery.   We find this affirmed in the same
terms by Arcite's last words :

> Farewell ; I have told my last hour.   I was false,
> Yet never treacherous : Forgive me, cousin.

And even his falseness is but weakness and somewhat excusable, if we
keep in mind that Anthony had deliberately been sent to Marguerite to
plead his friend's love, and was therefore but a victim of circumstance
and his inflammable nature.

Finally, then, in the dialogue between the two kinsmen in prison,
quoted before, Palamon's character is defined as the more martial of

[1] See Chapter 6.

the two, especially given to sports and arms. This must of course not be literally applied to Francis, for he himself has described his character to us as "not being of a martial temper." [1]   But if we might rightly say that even to Palamon it is the honours procured by arms more than the arms themselves that are his motive for indulging in them, then we may also say that in so far his characterization gives a true biographical picture of Francis Bacon, who in another place wrote of himself : " Not being a soldier, though not wholly opposed in my natural temper to arms, I am well inclined to [the honours of] knowledge which is to my mind far more satisfactory than any honours [of arms].   It hath been ere this very well said : 'A soldier's name doth live but an age, a scholar's unto eternity. ' " [2]   Honour, then, whether in arms or in letters, but preferably in the latter, was Francis' watchword, as it was Palamon's.   When his friend dies, and Emilia dedicates that day in memory of him to tears, Palamon's last words are,

And I to honour.

And so Bacon, when devising the Key-words for his great Key or Word-Cipher, makes them to be, after Fortune and Nature, Honour and Reputation :

> Follow Fortune as a leader, and Nature and her radicals
> As a guide, and if you look sharply and attentively
> It is certain you shall see that now and then
> Fortune and Nature are at fault ; and then we make
> Honour and Reputation
> The two words to guide you toward the end. [3]

---

[1] WG II 2.   [2] WG II 131.   [3] Ow I 6.

The Boar-Spear-Man

Part II.   Symbol and Cipher

6. Lovers in The Forest

URPLE mountains to our left, the sun setting behind us, and down in front the blue, blue shine of Lac Léman ; shrill cries of water-fowl above our heads, but peace serene all round, the air deep-laden with the fragrant scent of the fair Narciss flower, in myriads spread about us ; it was in such surroundings, dear !—do you remember ?—that once the chain of discoveries started by which you were as surely bound as I, to which you were no mere onlooker, but of which, alas, the last was never seen by you.   Sweet memory, poignant grief. To both be dedicated this record of our last joys shared, till life's wheel turning once again joins us anew in lasting happiness.

There in Geneva, the City of Peace, one day it was announced in the papers that *As You Like It* was going to be projected on the screen in " Studio 10," a cinema owned by a near relative of mine, and therefore frequently visited by me.   Immediately I set myself the task to re-read Shakespeare's comedy, and it was then, in the year nineteen hundred thirty seven, that the series of discoveries began, which I am about to relate.

I started reading the play in the Cambridge edition by William Aldis Wright.   Soon I came to the place where Orlando asks of Le

Beau, the Courtier, concerning the two girls who had witnessed his
wrestling contest with the formidable Charles, the reigning Duke's pro-
fessional wrestler (I 2) :

> Which of the two was daughter of the Duke,
> That here was at the wrestling ?

To which question he received the answer :

> Neither his daughter, if we judge by manners ;
> But yet, indeed, *the taller is his daughter* :
> The other is daughter to the banished Duke.

Le Beau's reply was apparently wrong, for in a footnote I found
that previous editors had substituted shorter, lower, smaller, lesser, and
less taller, for " taller."   I then took up Oliphant Smeaton's *Life of
Shakespeare*, and there found the observation that the play was " written
in haste, probably, to supply some stage need," and therefore " reveals
faults here and there suggestive of lack of time for revision.   For
example, Le Beau alludes to Celia as the ' taller ' of the two ladies who
were at the wrestling match.   Rosalind, however, in the next scene
speaks of herself as ' more than common tall.' "

This remark, I could not help it, seemed to rub me the wrong way.
As a Baconian of somewhat long standing, though in fact until then
little active in that field, I knew what to think of such superficial
criticisms by modern writers of Shakespeare's methods of work, and
ways of treating his works.   When scrutinized more closely, they mostly
come to naught.   It proved to be so in this instance too.   For not
only was *As You Like It* never published before it appeared in the
Folio of 1623, seven years after Shakespeare's death, but there exists
not a scrap of evidence,[1] that it had ever been staged.   The only thing
we know of it before the year mentioned is that on the 4th of August

---

[1] The late traditions reported by Capell (1774) and Cory (1865) cannot count as historical
evidence, of course.

1600 permission for its issue was asked but refused, as is proved by the annotation in the Stationers' Register : " Stay." On the next day in the same register is found *Much Ado about Nothing*, with the same prohibitive note. But in the case of this play the refusal was withdrawn on the 23rd of the month. Regarding *As You Like It*, however, there does not seem to have been any effort by author or publisher to have the prohibition revoked. It was kept *in petto* for twenty-three years before it was allowed to see the light of day in the Folio. No doubt, because on second thoughts it was judged too dangerous for immediate publication, being so full of thinly veiled allusions to the real author, that it might possibly reveal his secret before the time was ripe. Where, then, was the haste, and carelessness suggested by Smeaton ? It looks more like careful forethought and design.

Having come so far in my cogitations, I also remembered that Bacon often used such obvious " mistakes," and apparent " misprints " —for example, in the pagination of his books—as " marks " to call attention to special pages, words and passages, where the secrets were hidden that he wished to be revealed. Yes to reveal, but not to every passer-by, not too easily, nor directly, or immediately, in the " marked " passage. That would be too obvious. The " mistake " or " misprint " generally pointed in a natural way beyond itself, to the passage, word or page where it was " corrected."

So I read on till I came to the next scene, in which Rosalind first conceives the idea of dressing herself in male apparel, after her cousin had proposed that they should disguise themselves as country-wenches, " in poor and mean attire."

> Were it not better,
> Because that *I am more than common tall*,
> That I did suit me all points like a man ?
> A gallant curtle-axe upon my thigh,
> A *boar-spear in my hand* ; and—in my heart
> Lie there what hidden woman's fear there will—
> We'll have a swashing and a martial outside,

25

As many other mannish cowards have
That do outface it with their semblances.

There I was, with much more in my hands than I could have hoped for. In the first place, the " correction " of Le Beau's unintentional " blunder." Or was it intentional? " I am more than common tall," says Rosalind. She must therefore have been taller than Celia, or she could hardly have silently passed by her cousin's still more uncommon height. In the second place, the phrase " A boar-spear in my hand." This was certainly a revelation, not far removed from an open confession of authorship. " A boar-spear in my hand " could mean nothing else than that the speaker was a Boar-spear-man, or a Spear-shaker, the true Shakespeare. And who was he then? Well, who else than Francis Boar, or Francis Bacon, whose crest of arms was a Boar! In the third place, the lurking fear of a too early discovery of his secret: " In my heart lie there what hidden woman's fear there will." And in the fourth place, the martial or courageous " outside," put on to " outface " the danger of discovery by these " semblances " or counterfeitings. Or one might read the word " outface " in the same sense as " outdo " in Ben Jonson's famous poem, accompanying the Droeshout picture of the supposed Shakespeare in the Folio. It would then mean " efface " or " mask " the real author by the " outside " and " semblance " of the actor William Shakespeare. Are all these things mere coincidences?

Lest anyone remain in doubt whether Francis Bacon really went in terror of his life for fear of the premature discovery of his deadly secret by the fox-eyes of Robert Cecil and his spies, let one extract from the double alphabet cipher suffice. It is taken from The Shepherd's Calendar, a book published when he was only nineteen, under the " mask " of Edmund Spenser. It has a dedication signed by E. K., of which the cipher, incorporated in this book for the first time, tells us that it stands for " England's King " in his secret history. He further writes: " We devised two ciphers [the Biliteral and the Word-cipher], now used for the first time, for this sad secret history, as clear, safe, and undecipherable—whilst containing the keys in each which open the most important [*i.e.*, the word-cipher]—as any device that withholdeth the same. Till a decipherer find a prepared, or readily discovered, alphabet, it seemeth to us a thing almost impossible, save by divine gift and heavenly instinct, that he should be able to read what is thus revealed. It may, perchance, remain in hiding until a future people furnish wits keener than these of our own times to open this heavenly barred entrance-way, and enter the house of treasure. Yet are we *in hourly terror* lest the Queen, our enemy at present, although likewise our mother, be cognizant of our invention. It is for good cause, therefore, that our intention is altered, and the chief [Word] Cipher be not herein set forth in such manner as was meant."[1] The vacillating state of mind as to the publication of his ciphers, the intention first to use both ciphers, the decision afterwards to hold back the most important one, finds its parallel in the apparent hesitation as regards the publication of *As You Like It.*

Having found so much already in so short a time, I was strongly encouraged to proceed, and then bethought myself that it seemed indicated I should now turn to the original First Folio for further light, and eventually additional facts, and not content myself with modern editions. And I was not disappointed when I did so. The passage quoted last was found on page 187 of the Folio, and I soon discovered that this figure too was significant, being an obvious " misprint." The preceding page being 188, our page should by rights have borne the figure 189. Here then was a " marked " page, bearing on its face the " signature " of the Boar-spear-man. Was this a coincidence also ?

My next question was, what of the text in which Le Beau had made the " mistake " of describing the wrong girl as " the taller " of the two ? I found this in the Folio on page 188, and was agreeably struck when I saw that the page was " marked " too, in a very peculiar manner. Of the two eights in the page-number, one was indeed by far *the taller of the two.* Could this again be but a coincidence ?

[1] WG .79-80.

I immediately turned to page 88 in the same part (Comedies) of the Folio, as well as to page 288, and found that the first two eights were both of the taller, the last two both of the smaller fount. The smaller type begins only regularly to appear from page 278 onward ; before that the only exceptions to the larger type are found on page 58 (which should be rightly 50), and page 148, besides our page 188. I have not made any investigations into the significance of these pages, leaving that labour, as falling outside my present scope, for another time and occasion, if they indeed contain any mystery. But one effect these figures had on me was to direct my mind to the number-symbolism, or number-cipher, also used by Francis Bacon. Before looking further into that aspect, however, I had first to clear up another doubt—or was it a suggestion ?—rising at that moment in my mind.

Why had Rosalind, and not Celia, to be the taller ? If we go back to an earlier scene, the meeting of Orlando's elder brother, Oliver, with Charles, before the wrestling match took place, we find the former asking : " Can you tell if Rosalind, *the Duke's daughter*, be banished with her father ? " and the wrestler answering him : " Oh, no ; for *the Duke's daughter*, her cousin, so loves her." We might really get bewildered, and not know which is which, or who's who, when we hear the two maidens both called " the Duke's daughter," without further differentiating qualifications. It is implied, of course, that Rosalind is the daughter of the rightful Duke, the " Senior," while Celia is his younger brother's, the usurping or false Duke's daughter. Rosalind then is at least symbolically " the taller " because she is the rightful heir to the throne, and probably also because she is the senior, and as such possesses certain priority rights. For similar reasons, of the two eights in the page-number, the first or prior should in this symbolic cipher play be and is in fact " the taller."

As will become clearer when we come to the number-cipher, Rosalind in one sense stands for Francis Bacon's or the Boar-spear-man's *other half*, or second self. Did she not describe herself as with " a boar-spear in my hand ? " And if she is so, who then is the companion with whom this Spear-shaker might be compared in stature ? Shakespeare,

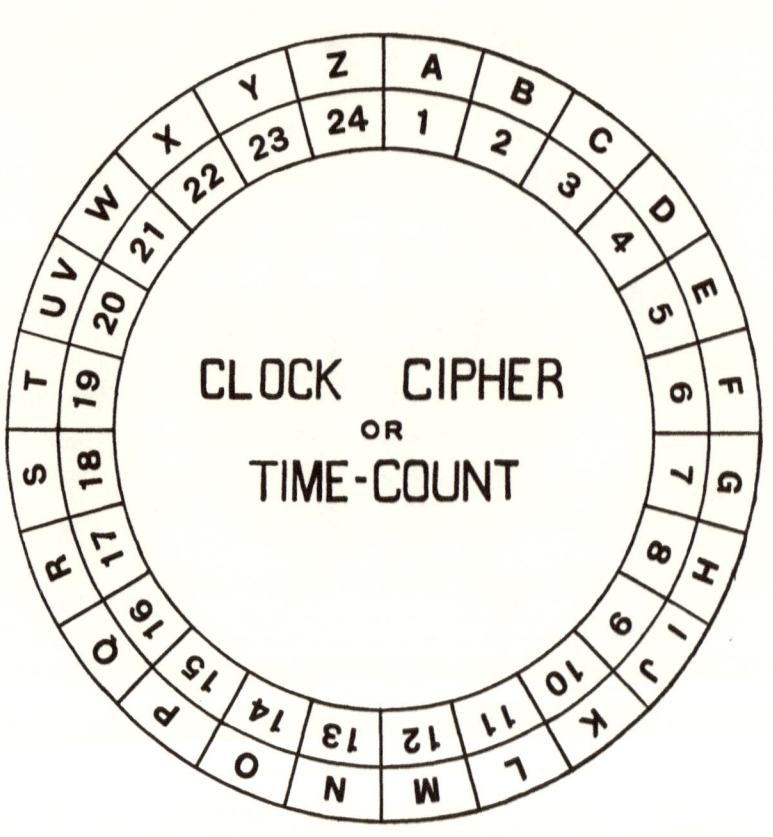

of course, the usurper of Bacon's public honours in the kingdom of
letters. These honours are legitimately due to Shakespeare's " senior," that
is to " the taller " in intellectual stature, the Boar-spear-man, who had
to live and act in secrecy, like the banished Duke, " in the forest," there
to hunt for his living and by his prowess win his crest of arms, the Boar.

Now for the number-symbolism.

In his biliteral cipher Francis Bacon tells us : " We have devised
six [ciphers] which we have used in a few of our books. These are
the (1) Biliteral, (2) Word, (3) Capital Letter, (4) Time, or as more oft
called Clock, (5) Symbol, and (6) Anagrammatic." [1] We shall here
occupy ourselves with the fourth cipher only. Arrange the letters
of the alphabet around the face of a clock so that each covers one
hour of the whole day of twenty-four, for in Bacon's time the I and J,
as well as the U and V were still interchangeable.

In this clock-cipher the corresponding number is substituted for
each letter in a word or name, and the total taken. For example :

$$Francis = 6 + 17 + 1 + 13 + 3 + 9 + 18 = 67, \text{ and}$$
$$Bacon = 2 + 1 + 3 + 14 + 13 = 33, \text{ therefore}$$
$$Francis\ Bacon = 67 + 33 = 100.$$

In the same way I tried my hand at *Rosalind*, which gave me 87,
and brought me nowhere at first, till I read the following note by the
editor of *The Cambridge Shakespeare* : " *Rosalind* is spelt indifferently
thus and *Rosaline*." [2] I turned to the First Folio again, and after careful
examination found that this note was neither complete nor correct.

Not complete, for besides the spelling Rosalind and Rosaline, the
Folio had also *Rosalinde. Not correct,* for these spellings were not
" indifferently " used—the favours are by no means equally divided ;
33 times Rosalind, and 22 times Rosalinde (and once Rosalinda),
respectively on 12 and 8 pages, against only 5 times Rosaline, on

[1] WG II 118.

[2] Rosalind should not be pronounced in the modern way. In the Folio it is made to
rhyme with mind, kind, bind, find.

3 pages.   And what was even of greater significance, 4 of these five Rosalines I found on the " marked " pages 188, and 187, where they are *exclusively* used.   I could not think of a stronger indication to the decipherer that he should take the spelling Rosaline in preference to the others.   *Rosalinde* had given me 92 with no clue that brought me any farther.   Now *Rosaline* gave me 88, (as does Rosalinda) and I was overjoyed to find that the name not only consisted of 8 letters, but that the double eight of its total number-value was depicted in the last two numbers of the " marked " page 188.   Mere coincidences ?

For a time I came to a standstill until I remembered Celia's words in the scene in which the girls for the first time enter on the stage : '' Therefore my sweet *Rose*, my dear *Rose*,[1] be merry,'' and further came across a *line* in the biliteral cipher : '' mine angelic-faced, soft-eyed Marguerite of the South-land, sweet White *Rose* of my lone garden of the heart.''[2]   So I fell to cutting the name *Rosa-line* in two " halves.'' The first or '' better half ''—not only for priority reasons but also for reasons of beauty and fragrance—gave me

$$Rosa = 50$$

that is half of *Francis Bacon* = 100, let us say his '' better half,'' which is Francis, for this was his own name, whereas Bacon was only a borrowed name, a '' mask,'' his real family-name being Tudor, or Tidder.   Besides, was not Rosa in truth his much wished for '' better half,'' Margaret of Valois, whom he would so gladly have taken to wife if fate had permitted ? Rosa, then, is in a sense Francis' *alter ego*, for she is his own love.

$$Rosa = 50 = Love$$

while Francis is her lover *par excellence*.

$$Francis = 67 = Lover$$

---

[1] On page 201 we find also Rosa, instead of the abbreviation Ros. to indicate the speaker.
[2] WG II 345.

There is indeed a wealth of meaning in the word Rosa-line. It warns us to seek *sub rosa*, " under the rose," and to read " between the lines," if we would find Francis Tudor's hidden life-story, of which his love for Rosaline has been, if not the most important, certainly the most inspiring part.

Now for the latter half of the name.

$$Line = 38$$

This does not yet help us any farther. But let us return to Rosaline's words, " a boar-spear in my hand," which made us give Francis Tudor the sobriquets of Francis the Spear-shaker, Francis the Boar-spear-man, and *tout court* Francis Boar. In their modern spelling these words are worthless for our purpose. In the Folio, however, Boar is spelt

$$Bore=38=line$$

So that, when we grant Francis Tudor's dearest wish of being joined in holy wedlock to his beloved Margaret, the latter would change her name Rosa-line=88 to

$$Rosa\ Bore=88,$$

or actually to Rosa Bacon. But unkind fate had decreed otherwise, and Margaret of Valois had become Margaret of Navarre. Are these also mere coincidences?

Here are some more. We laugh at Fate, which has power over our bodies only, but from whose sway our minds are exempt. We will still join the lovers in our thoughts. The word Boar is not the only one spelt differently. Rosaline's words stand thus in the Folio.

$$\begin{array}{ccc}
A \quad bore\text{-}speare & \qquad & in \quad my \quad hand \\
1 + 38 + 61 & & 22 + 35 + 26 \\
\hline
100 & & 83 \\
\hline
Francis \quad Bacon & + & Rosa \quad Bacon
\end{array}$$

The first half of the phrase therefore gives us *Francis Bacon*=100, the second half *Rosa Bacon*=83, so that Margaret and Francis are still lawfully married. A happy coincidence?

I made a pause, yet was not at rest. However much I had already found, there were still one or two things weighing on my mind. I returned to the opening pages of the play in the Folio, to the scene, already referred to, where Oliver and Charles meet, beginning near the bottom of the first page (Folio 185). I transcribe the first part here, in the old spelling.

Enter Charles

Cha. Good morrow to your worship.

Oli. Good Mounsier *Charles*: what's the new newes at the new Court?

Cha. There's no newes at the Court Sir, but the olde newes: that is, the old Duke is banished by his yonger brother the new Duke, and three or foure loving Lords have put themselves into voluntary exile with him, whose lands and revenues enrich the new Duke, therefore he gives them good leave to wander.

Oli. Can you tell if *Rosalind* the Dukes daughter bee banished with her Father?

Cha. O no; for the Dukes daughter her Cosen so loves her, being ever from their Cradles bred together, that hee [sic] would have followed her exile, or have died to stay behind her; she is at the Court, and no lesse beloved of her Uncle, then his owne daughter, and never two Ladies loved as they doe.

Oli. Where will the old Duke live?

Cha. They say he is already in the Forrest of *Arden*, and a many merry men with him; and there they live like the old *Robin Hood* of *England*: they say many yong Gentlemen flocke to him every day, and fleet the time carelesly as they did in the golden world.

It is very obvious that if ever Francis Tudor wanted to convey a message anywhere in this play, it must have been in this scene with its

constant play of words on the old and the new, " the old Duke," and
" the new Duke."   Now then, in the first place

$$the\ old\ Duke = 100.$$

Therefore he is the *alter ego* of *Francis Bacon* = 100.
     In the second place, if he is really the Boar-spear-man, his natural
home—great hunter that he is—must be the forest, in this case the

$$Arden\ Forrest = 136$$

That is where, hunting the boar, he obtained his totem, and earned
his crest of arms, namely, the Boar, as well as the epithet of Boar-spear-
man. The Forest is of course his literary and philosophical life and works.
It is also the place where one can best hide one's secrets, in his case
the double secret of his illustrious birth, by right of which his name was
Francis Tidder, and of his literary activities, by right of which his name
was Bacon-Shakespeare.   Now, reader, you might well jump up in your
excitement, as I did, when I found that

$$Francis\ Tidder = 125 = Bore\text{-}speare\ man,\ \text{and}$$
$$Bacon\text{-}Shakespeare = 136 = Arden\text{-}Forrest$$

     In other words, the conversation between Oliver and Charles does
nothing but reiterate in ever new forms that the solution of the Bacon-
Shakespeare problem is to be searched for in the Forest of Arden,
where dwells the Boar-spear-man, and where is enacted the romance of
Francis, the lover *par excellence*, and Rosaline.
     Hallam spoke a greater truth than he himself knew when he
wrote : " Shakespeare when he wrote this play was himself in his Forest
of Arden." [1]
     Coincidences all ?

[1] Quoted by Smeaton, p. 282,

Wait and judge when they have all passed in review ! The Forest has not yet yielded us all its secrets. We have seen who " the old Duke " really is. But what about " the new Duke ? " His number value 110 does not reveal anything. But when we think of Charles' puns on the old and the new, and the " olde newes " combined, we are tempted to try the combination " the old-new Duke," or " the new-old Duke," *as you like it*. Especially if we keep in mind that at the end of the play the old Duke, having been restored to his Dukedom, becomes in fact the new Duke, or the new Duke is in fact the old Duke, *as you like it*. Well, then,

$$The\ old\text{-}new\ Duke = 139 = As\ You\ Like\ It$$

Having come so far along the way, I should indeed have been astounded if the title of the play [1] had not also turned up in this number-play. Coincidence ?

Let us proceed.   For

$$Duke = 39 = King,\ and$$
$$The\ old\ Duke = 100 = Francis\ Bacon$$

so that we may say that the dethroned or banished Duke stands for an uncrowned King, like Francis Bacon, who once signed a biliteral cipher message, with the words " rightful R(ex)," and in another cipher epistle explained that the signature " E. K." beneath the dedication letter of Spenser's *Shepherd's Calendar*, signified " the future sovereign, or England's King." [2]

Now in the olden times there lived another *Uncrowned King*, a King of the Forest, like the old Duke or King of the Forest of Arden, but the former was not " of Arden," but " of England."   As such he is

---

[1] Williams, *A Short Life*, etc., p. 119: "The titles of Shakespeare's Comedies have rarely any significance [?] ; *As You Like It* and *What You Will* are floutingly vague. Almost any love comedy might bear the title in question." What might be is pure speculation, but the fact is that no other plays bear the titles in question.

[2] WG I 79; II 37.

expressly introduced to us by Charles : '' Robin Hood of England.'' I was so struck by the geographical qualification, that I set the number-play in motion again, with this result,

$$Robin \ Hood \ of \ England = 169 = Tidder \ England's$$
$$King = Francis \ Tidder \ Rex,$$

So that Robin Hood may also in one sense be taken for Francis Tidder's *alter ego.*

More coincidence ?

I had not yet done with the Arden Forest, but the second thing, mentioned before, that was weighing on my mind, had first to be lifted off. It concerned the " marked " pages 188 and 187, rightly 189. I was wondering whether these numbers were not also going to appear. They did. On the latter page, a few lines before Rosaline's significant words, " a boar-spear in my hand," I found the following conversation between the two girls ;

Cel.   Therefore devise with me how we may fly.
       Whither to go, and what to bear with us.
Ros.   Why, whither shall we go ?
Cel.   To seek my Uncle in the Forrest of *Arden.*

Here is the Forest of Arden again intruding upon our vision. Well, let it by all means, for it is just what I was looking for.

The Forrest of Arden = 188 = the number of the first " marked " page.

Coincidence again ?

Another query, the answer to which may answer the former. The girls want to go to the Forest of Arden ; when they get there, what do we find ? There are two answers to this question. From one aspect, we find father and daughter joined together. From another aspect

it is lover and beloved whom we find united.   For father and lover in
this case are one.   Thus,

(88) Rosaline + 100 $\left\{\begin{array}{l}\textit{The old Duke, or} \\ \textit{Francis Bacon}\end{array}\right\}$ = 188 = the " marked " page.

And if, as we supposed before, the two lovers are lawfully married, the
maiden would change her name into

Rosaline Borespeare = 187 = the other " marked " page.

Coincidences all ?

We will now let the Forest of Arden rest.   But we have not yet
seen the last of the " marked " pages 188 and 187, rightly 189.   As
explained before, they should point beyond themselves to further coincidences, or " proofs ? " Again I was not disappointed in my search.
The First Folio consists of three parts, the Comedies, the Histories, and
the Tragedies.   Each of these parts has its own pagination.   I looked
therefore in the second and third parts for the corresponding pages
187, 188, 189, to see what they would reveal.   In the Tragedies I
drew a blank, for the pagination in this part jumps from 156 to 256,
skipping the interjacent numbers altogether.

And the Histories ? The best I can do for the time being is to
transcribe some of the more significant words and phrases found on
the three pages of this second part.   I have by no means solved all
the riddles contained in these particular scenes of The Life and Death of
Richard the Third (III 2, 3, 4).   We must for the present be content
with the simple, direct connection they have with As You Like It through
the similarity of words.   That connection is however very obvious, and
all that we could wish for if we had so planned it.   The italics in the
following extracts are mine,

Page 187

He dreamt, the Bore had rased off his Helme. . .
To flye the Bore, before the Bore pursues,

Were to incense the *Bore* to follow us,
And make pursuit, where he did meane no chase.
Goe, bid thy Master rise, and come to me,
And we will both together to the Tower,
Where he shall see the *Bore* will use us kindly.
Page 188
Come on, come on, where is *your Bore-speare man* ?
Feare you the *Bore*, and goe so unprovided ?
Page 189
Stanley did dreame, the *Bore* did rowse our Helmes.

Incidentally I may say that the italicized words are not found anywhere else in the same play. The prominent place the *Boar* occupies in these extracts is very striking, but most of all was I impressed when I found on page 188 of the Histories the words " *your Bore-speare-man*," as a resounding echo to Rosaline's words on the corresponding page 188 of the Comedies, " *a bore-speare in my hand*." It had been my intuition which so far had led me to use the expression, the Boar-spear-man. I did not then possess a Shakespeare concordance, and was not aware in my waking consciousness of the existence of these Boar-texts in *Richard III*, till I was led by simple consecutive reasoning to the identical words, " your Boar-spear-man." The fact that between the words " spear " and " man " the modern editors all print a comma to make the apparent meaning still more apparent, does not annihilate the fact that the author did *not* place that comma there, and so left the way open for the seeker after infolded secrets, to find the non-apparent meaning. By it my intuition was still further vindicated, for

Your Bore-speare-man=199=*Francis Tidder of England.*

Non-Baconians are wont to decry Baconian findings, or " proofs," as so many " coincidences." But can such a mass of number-analogies as I have culled within the narrow limits of a few scenes from one play, and centred around one special event—Francis Tudor's romance—be still regarded as mere coincidence ? I think not.

It would be different, if I had indulged in mere fanciful or arbitrary juggling with figures. But I know myself innocent of such lawlessness, bound as I have felt myself all the time—at times too narrowly bound for my liking—by the data I had to work upon, and could not escape from.

One thing I will admit—that possibly not all the number-analogies discovered by me may have been present in the author's mind.

On the other hand, I take it for granted that the author's ingenuity was as much more penetrating than mine, as " wit so poor as mine " is probably than an infant's. I feel therefore no obligation to allow a discount from the total number of " proofs," or coincidences," for those possibly unperceived by the author.

On the contrary, the probability is extreme that the author's number-play was incomparably richer, and that consequently much more was intended and embedded in his texts than I have been able to discover. I feel therefore that I would be justified to put a premium on my list rather than to allow a discount.

However, non-covetousness is a wise virtue, and I will accordingly let things go at their face-value, which is in fact, I think, sufficiently high. I therefore ask, now for the last time : Is all this mere coincidence ? And my own answer this time is :

> Coincidence, if Legion is thy Name,
> Thou wert, in Truth, far better called Design !

There is one other reason why I wish and hope that what I have discovered is not all that the author has conceived and concealed. I have only acted according to his advice, which was that " it doth more aid mankind to point out what is lacking than to prepare all your work so that nothing shall longer remain to be found, for it is man's delight to find out mysteries, but the glory of God to conceal some matters, so that I say, nor shall it ask any further explanation, no man's hand is better employed than his who searcheth out a hidden matter."[1]

My effort on the number-cipher was at first a strenuous labour, which however, as I proceeded, became lighter, till at last it was, to me at least, as delightful as the Shakespearean play it was spent upon. Do not think lightly of such play, and do not fancy that I here concede what I just now denied, namely, that I have juggled with my figures. The play that I have played is better than juggling, which is merely keeping out of sight what should not be seen. The play I have in mind is on the contrary to let the figures play their own play, in full sight and in perfect freedom, within their bounds, but without suppression of any movement or event, act or fact, just as the gods do with us, allowing each his scope for play. In such a way alone truth will out, undistorted, well proportioned, and may thus be laid reverent hands upon. In the foregoing the author has been my god, who played with me by letting me play. And once having had my play, I may have some more in future. To him, then, be my thanks and praise!

[1] Cf. Bacon's *Novum Organum*, Sp IV 20. Also *Prov.* XXV, 2.

7. Boars and Kindred

MBLEMS all of Bacon's vast literary labours, as brought to light in our preceding chapter, are the Boar, the Boar-spear, and the Boar-spear-man ; symbolical seals chosen by Francis Tidder to mark the Shakespeare plays and other books, going under different authors' names, as his own handiwork. In my mind at least there is no doubt that these words, as found in *As You Like It* and elsewhere, were used by Bacon as the secret sign-manuals of his handicraft, just as the actor's name, Shakspeyr, [1] after it had been transformed into the equally symbolic name of Shake-speare, was used as his public signature.

The combination " Bore-speare " was thus used in at least four different places. The first two we met in *As You Like It* and *Richard III*. The third is found in *The Faery Queen* (II iii 21, 29), to mark Spenser's work as his own. It is strongly reminiscent of the former, as it also gives a description of the martial appearance of a forest-girl, the counterpart of Rosaline, in this case the virgin huntress, "fair Belphoebe," who in one aspect stands for Queen Elizabeth.

[1] Other known forms of the name are, Shaxper, Shackspeare, Shakspear, etc. " The town-clerk, a constant scribe, makes it ' Shakspeyr ' with great regularity, but some twenty variants are found in Stratford documents " (ChW 12).

27

A goodly lady clad in hunter's weed,
That seemed to be a woman of great worth,
And by her stately portance, born of heavenly birth.

And as Rosaline said of herself,

A gallant curtle-axe upon my thigh,
A *bore-speare in my hand ;*

so it is said of Belphoebe,

And *in her hand a sharp bore-speare* she held
And at her back a bow and quiver gay,
Stuffed with steel-headed darts, wherewith she quelled
The savage beasts in her victorious play.

The fourth signature or seal of his workmanship was placed by
Bacon upon Shakespeare's *Venus and Adonis.* Adonis, the boy-hunter,
scorns the love of Venus (vs. 409-426) :

" I know not love," quoth he, " nor will not know it,
Unless it be a *boar*, and then I chase it ;
' Tis much to borrow, and I will not owe it ;
My love to love is love but to disgrace it ;
For I have heard it is a life in death,
That laughs and weeps, and all but with a breath.

" Who wears a garment shapeless and unfinished ?
Who plucks the bud before one leaf put forth ?
If springing things be any jot diminished,
They wither in their prime, prove nothing worth :
The colt that's backed and burdened being young,
Loseth his pride and never waxeth strong.

" You hurt my hand with wringing ; let us part,
And leave this idle theme, this bootless chat :

> Remove your siege from my unyielding heart ;
> To love's alarms it will not ope the gate :
> Dismiss your vows, your feignèd tears, your flattery ;
> For where a heart is hard, they make no battery.''

The note ringing through these stanzas is that of the disappointed lover. It is Francis, betrayed by Marguerite, who is voicing here his disgust of womanhood in general.   Better to go and hunt for honour and fame, than for woman's love.   The same sentiment expressed in nearly the same words is found in Spenser's *Faery Queen* (I v 37).   As one of the closest parallels between Shakespeare and Spenser, arguing for their common identity, it may find a place here.

> Hippolytus a jolly huntsman was,
> That wont in chariot chase the foaming *Boar* ;
> He all his Peers in beauty did surpass,
> But Lady's love as loss of time forbore.

To return to Adonis, he goes one day to hunt the boar with the tragic result (vs. 1105-1116), that when

> *He ran upon the boar with his sharp spear,*

the foul, grim and urchin-snouted boar

> Sheathed unaware the tusk in his soft groin.

The '' Boar '' figures indeed largely in this Shakespearean poem. His name is mentioned not less than seventeen times.   Among these there is one other line, besides the one italicized above, which is of special interest in connection with Spenser's works.   Of the latter a folio edition appeared in 1611, the title-page of which is as it were an illustration of the following lines from *Venus and Adonis*.

The gentle goddess of love, hearing the barking of the hounds of Adonis, by which sign she knows that he is again at his favourite sport, and fearing for his life, runs after him (vs. 871-886) :

> For now she knows it is no gentle chase,
> *But the blunt boar, rough bear, or lion proud,*
> Because the cry remaineth in one place,
> Where fearfully the dogs exclaim aloud.

Three wild beasts are here mentioned together, and if we turn to the title-page of the Spenser Folio of 1611, we find those same three animals depicted there. "On the left is the figure of Leicester with the *Bear* and staff which are sufficient to identify him, and opposite is Elizabeth with the *Lion* rampant, and the scepter at her side, suspended by a chain, which, quite as unmistakably, identify her. These figures represent ' supporters,' in heraldic parlance, and sustain at the height of their heads, between them, a shield bearing the arms of Bacon, a *Boar*. The Boar is represented in leash, the end toward the Queen, to represent her connection with his destiny." So that we have here, in the trinity of Father, Mother and Son, Bacon's descent portrayed in a pictorial design, which in the poem was put in a word-picture.

Though not directly connected with our subject, but in any case related to it by the recurring figure of the Boar, I will here complete the description and explanation of the lower part of the same title-page : " In an oval at the bottom we again see the Boar, now regarding curiously, but almost defiantly, a rosebush in full flower, the Tudor emblem inherited by Elizabeth from the House of York. Encircling it is a scroll with the legend, *Non Tibi Spiro*, I smell not thee. No, the sweetness of this royal emblem, heightened by the ardent hope of future possession, had been swept away for ever like the first scent of spring blooms by a belated storm. Leicester had been dead twenty-three years, and Elizabeth eight. In their day this revealing title-page would have been an unsafe venture, but now it passed as any merely pictured page would pass, hintless of veiled meaning ; or, if it excited comment, it was but a

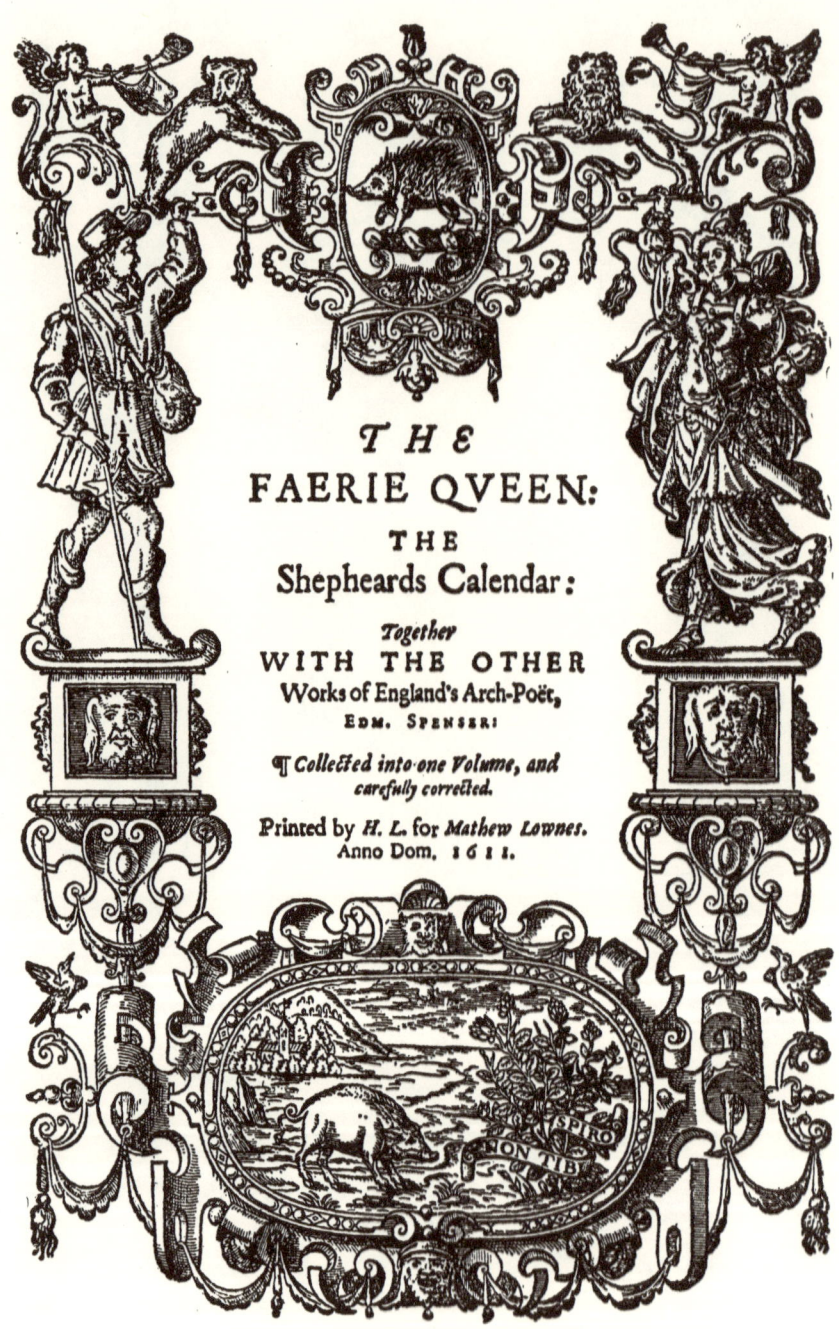

THE FAERIE QVEEN:

THE Shepheards Calendar:

Together
WITH THE OTHER
Works of England's Arch-Poët,
EDM. SPENSER:

¶ *Collected into one Volume, and
carefully corrected.*

Printed by *H. L.* for *Mathew Lownes.*
Anno Dom. 1611.

Lion, Bear and Boar

pretty compliment to past greatness, and the boar, shrinking from the sweet-scented, but thorny rose, an amusing conceit. These title-pages, however, should be sufficient proof, to any unprejudiced mind, of Bacon's authorship, both of the Shakespeare works and those contained in the work, the title-page of which we have here considered; and, moreover, that this title-page fully confirms what he has told us in cipher, that he was one of the children of Elizabeth and Leicester, whose existence was so often asserted in the correspondence of ministers of foreign courts, and contemporary annals." [1]

To the above we may add the remarkable coincidence—if coincidence it be—that in the very same year 1611, in which on the title-page of the Spenser Folio it was depicted that the author's " ardent hope of future possession [of the royal throne] had been swept away for ever," a new edition of *The Shepherd's Calendar* appeared, in which Bacon wrote in cipher: " Ended now is my great desire to sit in British throne." [2]

However, the words on the rosebush in full bloom, " I smell thee not," may also be interpreted in another way, namely as a reference to his frustrated love for Marguerite, his "sweet rose of France," the fragrance of whose companionship for life was not for his nostrils to inhale.

When dealing with Shakespeare's works it is no exaggeration to speak of the ever recurring figure of the Boar. It is indeed astonishing to find the animal continually crossing our path as we wander through the primeval forest of Shakespeare's plays and poems. After all the Boars and Borespears of *As You Like It*, *Richard III*, *Venus and Adonis*, and the *Faery Queen* we shall now take up another set of Boars, this time in combination with another word, found in another set of works.

For the Baconian student Sir John Falstaff is in every sense a most extraordinary creation of Shakespeare's genius. To Shakespearean scholars he offers an insoluble dilemma, because of his dual character, being on the one hand " the most prodigious wit," on the other the most arrant knave. His paradoxical nature has perhaps been best

[1] Bax 425-6.   [2] WG II 41.

defined by Maurice Morgann : " He is a man at once young and old, enterprising and fat, a dupe and a wit, harmless and wicked, weak in principle and resolute by constitution, cowardly in appearance and brave in reality, a knave without malice, a liar without deceit, and a knight, a gentleman, and a soldier without either dignity, decency or honour.'

It is one thing to have sensed and thus acutely described the contradictory nature of Falstaff's person, but it is all too easy to accept such a mixture of opposing qualities not only as a real character, but even as one of Shakespeare's greatest creations, without trying to make the combination psychologically reasonable, or historically acceptable. The first would be possible only along such lines as Pope's well-known verse :

> The greatest, wisest, meanest of mankind,

if we are prepared to accept such a psychological paradox. If we are not, the only way out is to take " meanest " in the sense of " humblest," which would change the verse from a most infamous libel into a " saw of might," but which would not help us in the case of Falstaff who was anything but humble.

The historical alternative on the other hand gives a reasonable explanation along Baconian lines. Sir John Falstaff covers and is made up of two distinct personages, brought together and fused into one by the force of circumstances. He is the Hoax of hoaxes played by Bacon-Shakespeare on his contemporaries and their descendants, for three centuries now, in revenge for their unimaginative dullness which made them unable to distinguish between the pretence of a gentleman and the real gentleman, between the arrant knave and the prodigious wit, between the mere actor and the true writer, between Shakespeare and Bacon.

That indeed one side of Falstaff's character—his sparkling wit, that in which he was really a genius—stands for Francis Bacon, is proved by the alias the true author bestows upon him. On page 81 of the First Folio of Shakespeare's Plays, in the second part of *Henry IV* (II 2), we find the following conversation between Bardolph and Harry

of Monmouth, Prince of Wales, later King Henry V. They are talking
of old Sir John Falstaff, Knight :

Prin. Where suppes he ? Doth the old *Bore* feed in the old *Franke*?
Bard. At the old place my Lord, in East-Cheape.

A *Franke* is nothing more nor less than a pigsty, and having regard
to a man of Falstaff's form and character, an apt paronomasia. But
why write it, as well as *Bore*, with a capital letter, if not to convey the
idea that both words are meant for proper names ? And if so what
else do they announce but that

$$John\ Falstaff=Frank\ Boar=Francis\ Bacon.$$

And, whether coincidence or design, a further fact is that the
number value of

$$Old\ Bore=67=Francis$$

and of

$$The\ old\ Bore=99=Borespeare$$

and again of

$$Franke=52=Will\ (Shakespeare),$$

and of

$$The\ old\ Franke=113=King\ of\ England$$

Frank or Francis Rex, Francis I, what a King of England he would
have made ! The first of his name, and probably the ast also of his
stature.

Nobody knew the human heart better than Bacon, its inertia, its initial aversion to new ideas, its scepticism and leaning towards adverse criticism of the new when by it old preconceptions are threatened. Nobody knew better than he that constant repetition only will overcome the mind's conservatism.   There is a proverb which says that all good things go by threes.   Bacon may have had some such idea in his mind when he chose to place his signature of *Frank Boar* on the Shakespeare plays.   For I have had the good fortune, guided I have no doubt by his spirit reaching over the intervening centuries—mind, he left his name " to the next ages and to foreign nations "—to find two more of them, besides the one given above.

The second is found on page 200 of the Histories, in the Folio, Act IV, scene 4 of *Richard III*, where the Earl of Derby asks Sir Christopher Urswick to convey to the Earl of Richmond, later King Henry VII :

> That in the stye [*frank* !] of the most deadly *Bore*
> My Sonne George Stanley is *frankt* up in hold.

The deadly *Bore* is of course Richard III, and " frank " here used as a verb and not as a substantive means "to shut up," or to deprive somebody of his freedom.   All the same, the signature *Frank Boar* is there, and page 200 on which it stands is not less significant, for we know already that

200=Your man Francis Bacon.

The third example is even more convincing, in giving us additional proof of Bacon's unlimited ingenuity and richly flowing vein of wit in shifting and varying his means, but all to serve one end.   This time we have to turn over the pages of the Tragedies till we come to page 24 of the Folio, *Coriolanus* (IV 6).   Cominius, the general, tells the Romans of the devastation Coriolanus at the head of the Volscians is spreading around on his march upon Rome.

Your temples burned in their cement, and
Your *franchises*, whereon you stood, confin'd
Into an auger's *boare*.

Here the root-meaning of franchise is freedom, which is also the root-meaning of frank, and as such is also the root-meaning of the name Francis. Boare in this case is of course not the wild animal, but a bore-hole.

Nevertheless the signature is there, *Francis Boar*. Three times repeated, one for each of the three parts of the Folio, the *Comedies*, page 81, the *Histories*, page 200, and the *Tragedies*, page 24. Let us add these pages together and we get 303, three nought three. Discard the nought as being of no account, and we get,

$$33 = Bacon.$$

We must return to the first signature, "Frank Boar," in *Henry IV*, Part 2, for there still remains one expression in the colloquy between Bardolph and Prince Harry to be examined : " The old place in East Cheape." This is of course the inn where the Prince and Sir John were wont to sup and revel, and tradition has it, followed by all modern editors, that this inn bore the significant name of the *Boar's Head* tavern.

The Folio Shakespeare however does nowhere mention this name. Still Bacon may have had it in mind, for there seems no doubt that he derived Falstaff's name from Sir John Fastolfe (1378-1459) who owned a house and an inn of the above name, not in Eastcheape however, but in the adjoining district of Southwark.[1]

Now let us see what the number-play reveals about this old inn.

Did we not ascertain before that it was in the Forest that we were sure to find the Boar-spear-man, as sure as Bardolph was that Frank Boar was to be found in " the old place ? "

[1] See *Encyclopaedia Britannica*, 13th ed. X 198c. The *Encyclopaedia Britannica* is probably wrong when it asserts in Vol. XVI, p. 962d that " the Boar's Head Tavern in Great Eastcheap was an inn of Shakespeare's own days."

And who was Frank Boar, but the owner of the

Bore's Head $=74=$ *William,*

as Bacon was the spiritual owner of William Shakespeare's works ?

The " Boar's Head," indeed ! And what is left is of course the " Boar without a head." The one half is naturally the author Bacon, the other half the actor Shakespeare. For the correctness of this interpretation we have the independent testimony of Ben Jonson, and the passage in which he makes special mention of the " Boar without a head," with unmistakable allusion to the actor Shakespeare, should rightly follow here. But the connection between Ben Jonson, Shakespeare and Bacon is a peculiar one. So I have thought it better to deal separately with all Ben Jonson has written about Shakespeare.[1]

The above completes my findings regarding the Boar-group of symbols in Bacon's symbol-cipher, the fifth of his six ciphers. It is indeed hardly believable that it escaped attention for three centuries, that indeed I must consider myself the first to have been so forcibly struck with its significance. Undoubtedly others have been conscious of the importance of the Boar, in connection with Bacon's armorial crest, but as far as I know, only in pictorial designs like the title-page of Spenser's work. I am however not conscious that anyone has pointed out the symbolic significance of the Boar in verse and prose, single, or combined with other words like Boar-spear, Boar's head, and Frank Boar, and of the number-values of these, as indications and proofs of Bacon's authorship, in the way that has been done in this and the preceding chapter.[2]

But though we have done with the Boar-group of symbols, there exists a very nearly allied group, which we must consider now. The

[1] See Addenda (5).

[2] While getting these Chapters ready for the press, I came across a short article by S. A. on " The Boar's Head," in *Baconiana*, January 1896, pp. 76-82, where several of the Boar and kindred signatures are referred to, though not with that detail as given above. I leave my remark unrevised, however, as a specimen of the conceit in which discoverers and authors may too easily fall, forgetting Solomon's wise saying that there is nothing new under the sun.

rich genius of Francis Bacon, his inexhaustible and volatile wit, would not rest content with playing on one synonym of his name only, but would find means to ring the changes on his name in all gamuts and keys. Perhaps we have exhausted all the variations there are on the Boar-theme. I do not know, and I am rather inclined to think that we have not. But at any rate enough has been achieved along this line, to justify tuning our ear now to another melody, the *Pig* and *Hog*— variations, kindreds of the Boar.

To begin with the first, the question is if there exists any signature anywhere, similar to Frank or Francis Boar, but now in the form of Francis Pig? Indeed there exist several, however astonishing such an assertion may at first hearing sound. One is found in *Henry V*, folio 88 of the Histories. We are on the battlefield in France (IV 4). A French soldier has been taken prisoner by Pistol, who threatens to kill him, but when offered two hundred *écus* for his ransom, tells the boy who serves as interpreter to inform the prisoner, '' qu'il est content de vous donner la liberté, le *franchisement*,'' in other words that he is willing to render him his liberty or freedom. Here we have therefore the Franchise or Francis.

Now the Pig. It is found on the same page of the Folio, where in another part of the battlefield there is the following conversation going on between two officers in the English King's army, Gower and Fluellen, of whom the latter is a Welshman, who in his pronunciation cannot distinguish between the *p* and the *b*, and therefore speaks of '' Alexander the *Pig*,'' when he means Alexander the Big, or the Great.

These two, then, Franchise and Pig, occurring on the same page of the Folio, make again the signature of Frank Boar, or Francis Bacon. If we still doubt if there is in fact any such connection meant by the author between Franchise and Pig, as that between Frank and Boar, which were both used of one and the same person, John Falstaff, that doubt will undoubtedly vanish if we find in the conversation between Fluellen and Gower the name of the jolly knight indeed dragged in, in an ingenious way, though Falstaff was already dead and done with.

There are in this conversation, I feel sure, other veiled allusions
to Bacon's authorship and life-story. It is for that reason that I will
copy it out in its entirety from the Folio, though I am sorry to say that,
besides the connection of Pig with Franchise, and of both with John
Falstaff, or Bacon-Shakespeare, I have not yet been able to find the
solution of the other allusions.

ACTUS QUARTUS
Enter Fluellen and Gower

Flu.   Kill the poyes and the luggage, 'Tis expressely against the Law
        of Armes, tis as arrant a peece of knavery marke you now,
        as can bee offert in your Conscience now, is it not?

Gow.   Tis certaine, there's not a boy left alive, and the Cowardly Ras-
        calls that ranne from the battaile ha' done this slaughter:
        besides they have burned and carried away all that was
        in the Kings Tent, wherefore the King most worthily hath
        caus'd every soldiour to cut his prisoners throat. O'tis a
        gallant King.

Flu.   I, hee was porne at *Monmouth* Captaine *Gower*: What call you
        the Townes name where *Alexander* the pig was borne?

Gow.   *Alexander* the Great.

Flu.   Why I pray you, is not pig, great? The pig, or the great, or
        the mighty, or the huge, or the magnanimous, are all one
        reckonings, save the phrase is a little variations.

Gow.   I thinke *Alexander* the Great was borne in *Macedon*, his Father
        was called *Phillip* of *Macedon*, as I take it.

Flu.   I thinke it is in *Macedon* where *Alexander* is porne: I tell you
        Captaine, if you looke in the Maps of the Orld, I warrant you shall
        finde in the comparisons betweene *Macedon* & *Monmouth*, that the
        situations looke you, is both alike. There is a River in *Macedon*, &
        there is also moreover a River at *Monmouth*, it is call'd Wye at
        Monmouth: but it is out of my praines, what is the name of the
        other River: but 'tis all one, tis alike as my fingers is to my
        fingers, and there is Salmons in both.   If you marke *Alexanders*

life well, *Harry of Monmouthes* life is come after it indifferent well for there is figures in all things. *Alexander* God knowes, and you know, in his rages, and his furies, and his wraths, and his chollers, and his moodes, and his displeasures, and his indignations, and also being a little intoxicates in his praines, did in his Ales and his angers (looke you) kill his best friend *Clytus*.

Gow.   Our King is not like him in that, he never kill'd any of his friends.

Flu.   It is not well done (marke you now) to take the tales out of my mouth, ere it is made and finished. I speak but in the figures, and comparisons of it : as *Alexander* kild his friend *Clytus*, being in his Ales and his Cuppes ; so also *Harry Monmouth* being in his right wittes, and his good judgements, turn'd away the fat Knight with the great belly doublet : he was full of jests, and gypes, and knaveries, and mockes, I have forgot his name.

Gow.   Sir *John Falstaffe*.

Flu.   That is he : lle tell you, there is good men porne at *Monmouth*.

Gow.   Heere comes his Majesty.

What does it all mean ? Alexander of Macedon, Harry of Monmouth, Sir John Falstaff, the Pig, the river Wye, and the other river ? Others may be more fortunate in solving the riddles. I can only make a few suggestions. The Harry of Monmouth, meant here, when he became King, was King Henry V ; now he was still Prince of Wales. The Tudors originally came from Wales.[1] Perkin Warbeck, the Pretender, in his proclamation spoke of the progenitor of the house of Tudor as " Owen Tydder, of low birth, in the country of Wales." Monmouth is a Welsh country, and Fluellen is a Welshman, and they suggest the Prince of Wales also (not the King), who was the boon-companion of Sir John Falstaff, also a Welshman. For Anne Page calls him the " Welsh devil Herne." [2] As Alexander killed his friend Cleitus, so the King turned

[1] Sp VI 252.

[2] I owe this to G. W. Phillips, *Lord Burleigh in Shakespeare, Falstaff, Sly and others*, 1936, p. 15. See about Herne, the next Chapter.

away the fat knight, and thereby in fact " killed his heart " as Dame
Quickly rightly averred (*Henry V*, II 1).

Francis Bacon, as Prince of Wales, when not yet come into his
Kingdom, made use of Shakespeare for his plays, but the latter, like
Sir John by Harry V, would be turned away and exposed as merely a
" belly doublet," " full of jests and gibes and knaveries and mocks,"
but deprived of the real spirit of genius, as soon as Bacon's authorship,
his kingdom of the spirit, became established.

Alexander the Pig, then, is really Francis the Pig, or the Big, or
the Great.

There may still be a lingering doubt in the reader's mind
whether it is legitimate to associate such words as " liberty," " freedom," " frank," " franchisement," and " enfranchise," with the name
" Francis." If so, then the following passage from *Love's Labour's
Lost* (III 1), wherein we are expressly taught so to do, may well dispel
every hesitation. The conversation between Costard, the Clown, and
Armado, the Braggart, which we are going to reproduce, is without any
logical or other connection with the rest of the whole scene. The
passage is palpably thrust into it just for the purpose for which we are
going to use it, namely for establishing the connection between the
words, already mentioned, and the name Francis.

Arm.   Sirra *Costard*, I will infranchise thee.
Clow.   O, marrie me to one *Francis*, I smell some *Lenvoy*, some
Goose in this.
Arm.   By my sweete soule, I meane setting thee at libertie, Enfree-
doming thy person : thou wert emured, restrained, captivated,
bound.

The indication could not be clearer. It says : Whenever you meet
with the word " enfranchise," or similar words, like " franchisement,"
frank, freedom, deliverance, etc., which have all the same meaning,
you must " marry " it, that is connect it with Francis, nay with " one
Francis," which has been read by some as Francis I, or Francis Rex, that

is " England's King," as Francis Bacon styled himself. The number-play further gives :

I will infranchise thee$=200=$*Your man Francis Bacon*

For another example of the secret signature with Pig as the surname, but this time with the Christian name not derived from " infranchise," but from " enfreedoming," we have to turn to the first play in the Folio, the very first, but also certainly one of the last composed. On page 10 of the *Tempest*, towards the end of Act II, scene 2, we find Caliban, the monster, saying to *Trinculo*, the drunken sailor : " I with my long nayless will digge thee pig-nuts." And 18 lines lower down on the same page Trinculo concludes his song with the words : " Freedome, high-day freedome, freedome high-day, freedome." So that here we have the signature : Freedom Pig, or Francis Bacon. Further.

Freedome Pig$=99=$*Borespeare*

One, or rather two more examples, now in *The Comedy of Errors*, on the Folio-page, doubly marked with the double eight, both of the taller type. I say advisedly " doubly marked," for besides that it bears this significant figure 88, with the clock-cipher value, as we have seen of

Rosaline$=88=$*Rosa Bore*

it also bears this number falsely, for the preceding page has 85, and the next page 87, followed by the real page 88.

Now, on the false Folio 88, in the fourth line of the last scene of the first act, there is the word *Pig* with a capital, thus :

Enter Dromio of Ephesus

Ant.   Here comes the almanacke of my true date :
What now ? How chance thou art return'd so soone.

E.Dro.   Return'd so soone, rather approacht too late :
            The Capon burnes, the Pig fals from the spit.

While in the fourth line from the end of this scene, on Folio 87, we find the word *Liberty*, thus :

> And manie such like *liberties* of sinne :
> If it prove so, I will be gone the sooner :
> Ile to the Centaur to goe seeke this slave,
> I greatly feare my monie is not safe.

So that the two, Liberty Pig, again spell the author's name as Francis Bacon.

    And if somebody still objects that the two words are not found on the same page of the Folio, then he too may be fully satisfied, I think, when he is told that in the first scene of the next act, on the same page 87, and even in the same right-hand column, we again find those two words in the following lines [1] :

> Why, headstrong liberty is lasht with woe,

and

> The Pigge quoth I, is burn'd,

Finally, the very next line has the word hang :

> The Pigge quoth I, is burn'd : my gold quoth he :
> My mistresse, sir, quoth I : hang up thy Mistresse.

But it is not yet the place to enter here upon the combination '' hang-pig,'' as a variation of '' hang-hog.''   For the Baconian implications of this expression, the reader is referred to a few pages further on.

[1] See also the 7th line of the scene : '' A man is Master of his libertie.''

The signature of Franchise Pig was found on page 88 of the Histories, but knowing that the pages 69-101 were twice repeated in this part of the Folio, and that it was the second page 88 where I had found the above, I now turned to the first page 88, if perhaps something there might confirm my reading of the signature or help me to another reading. I found both. I found on that page, in 2 Henry IV (III 2), two names. The first was Robin, which as Robin Hood we know already is another name for Bacon, and the second was Wart, which immediately suggested the Wart-Hog (Macrocephalus Aethiopicus), an African species of swine that owes its name to two rows of warty excrescences on its snout. So here I was in the Hog-variation of the Boar-theme. And putting the number-play into action, I got

$$Wart=58=Tidder$$

and

$$Robin\ Wart=113=King\ of\ England$$

Further there was on this page the word Bucket, used as a name and spelt with a capital, which gave me Bucke, another name for Shakespeare as will be shown in the next chapter. This combined with Robin on the same page, gave

$$Robin\ Bucke=95=Robin\ Hood$$

I was apparently on the right track, but I also saw that it was not on this page that the name Wart appeared printed for the first time, and that the fellow Thomas Wart was not alone, but had some companions, among whom was Francis Feeble, and on the preceding page 87 both the italicized names are found. So that here we have again the signature Francis Wart, which when the number-play is put into action reads :

$$Francis\ Wart=125=Borespeare\ man$$

And as if to affirm even more strongly that our interpretation is right, we find on page 86 also both names printed, Wart as well as Francis,

29

and the latter this time not in a bootless repetition of Francis Feeble, but as quite another man, namely Francis Pickbone.

There is one more item to be noted on this page for later treatment, namely the repetition of the combination Will Buck, as a designation of Shakespeare the actor, but that also belongs to the next chapter. Finally there is on this page the name of John Falstaffe, as the combination of Francis Wart (Bacon) and Will Buck (Shakespeare) in one, namely Bacon-Shakespeare.

A last remark. That the combination of the Wart-Hog with Francis on these three pages 86-88 of the Folio is really intentional is proved by the fact that the subject of the whole scene, in which these words and names occur is indeed the "enfranchisement" of certain individuals. Raphe Mouldie, Thomas Wart, Francis Feeble, and Peter Bulcalfe have been requisitioned to serve as soldiers in the King's army. Two of them, Bullcalf and Mouldy, ask to be let off, and like Pistol's French prisoners offer a ransom in money for their Freedom.

If one doubts whether Francis Bacon—of whom it has been said that he wrote philosophy like a Lord Chancellor, which means of course, with the gravity and dignity becoming the function of such a high state official—if one doubts that the great Lord·Bacon would ever condescend to drag his name through the mud of a pig-sty or even to associate it with such a coarse brute as a hog, a castrated male swine reared for slaughter by pandering excessively to his gluttony and greed—the Boar was at least a noble creature of clean wild nature, a worthy foe and prize for the mighty hunter—if anybody doubts this, I must remind him that it was Bacon himself who preserved for us the anecdote in which his adoptive father, Sir Nicholas's name was thus associated. Though Spedding in his edition of Bacon's works counts this anecdote among the spurious ones, for the reason that it only appeared in print in 1671, i.e., forty-five years after Bacon's death—as if that were a valid reason— the result of our particular investigations will, I think, prove beyond doubt the genuineness of the anecdote, supported as it is by the circumstantial evidence from Shakespeare's works.

A name to most people is all they possess.   Few can do without it.   Bacon lost his in his time, but could wait for its retrievement in " foreign nations and the next ages," [1] as his last will expressed it.   Is there a higher sense of humour than thus to play with one's name as he has done, to hold it lightly and not too high for such lowly company as those useful and much abused quadrupeds with which a so-called " civilized " human is wont to line his "innards ! "

Let us begin with the anecdote regarding old Sir Nicholas.

" Being appointed a judge for the northern circuit, and having brought his trials that came before him to such a pass as the passing of sentence on malefactors, he was by one of the malefactors mightily importuned for to save his life ; which, when nothing that he had said did avail, he at length desired his mercy on account of kindred. ' Prithee,' said my lord judge, ' how came that in ? ' 'Why, if it please you, my lord, your name is Bacon, and mine is Hog, and in all ages *Hog and Bacon* have been so near kindred, that they *are not to be separated*.' ' Ay, but,' replied judge Bacon, ' you and I cannot be kindred, except you be hanged ; for *Hog is not Bacon until it be well hanged*.' " [2]

We are expressly told here that " hog and Bacon are not to be separated."   Why not ? Well, because they have been " married " of course.   Just as the synonyms, freedom, deliverance, franchise, frank, are " married " to Francis, so all the synonyms, hog, sow, pig, wart, swine, boar, are " married " to Bacon, and therefore never to be separated from him.   Further we are told that " hog is not Bacon until it be well hanged."   Only hanged-hog or, hang-hog therefore is bacon !

Now if we turn to the First Folio, page 53 of the *Comedies*, what is it that we find ? In the broad cockney of Dame Quickly, the Hostess of the *Boar's Head* Tavern, *Merry Wives of Windsor*, IV 1 :

" *Hang-hog is latten* [Latin] *for Bacon*, I warrant you."

[1] Sp XIV 539.   [2] Sp VII 185.

Here we find Shakespeare, in one short sentence, not only acting upon the advice that "Hog and Bacon are not to be separated," but also reasserting that "Hog is not Bacon until it be well hanged." The pun turns upon the curious pronunciation by the Welsh parson, Sir Hugh Evans, of the Latin declension, hic, hac, hoc, as hing, hang, hog.

Even Shakespearean scholars do admit that Mistress Quickly's interruption is a direct allusion to Sir Nicholas' somewhat callous humour, but they do not explain how the actor Shakespeare came to employ it, nor the sense or reason for its employment. Flown from Bacon's pen, on the contrary, it explains itself in every way, in more ways even than we have as yet realized.

For the number-values show us that if Hang-hog is Bacon, and Bacon is Tidder, then Hang-hog should be Tidder, which it indeed proves to be :

$$Hanghog = 58 = Tidder$$

A variety of Hang-hog is of course the Hang-pig which we found on the false page 88 of the Comedies.

And even that is not all. I have said that the passage is found on p. 53 of the Comedies. Now, if we turn to the corresponding page in the Histories, we find in *Henry IV* (II 1) the following striking phrase :

" I have a Gammon of Bacon."

Further, the word *hang* occurs on the same page not less than nine times, Bacon's father's name *S. Nicholas* twice, and once each, *Franc* (lin), and *Robin*. Indeed, a well-filled page.

Especially significant are the nine " hangs," for in his biliteral cypher Bacon cautions the decipherer to take heed of words " marked," among other ways, " by frequent and unnecessary iteration." [1]

And what does the number-play teach us ? That

A gammon of Bacon $= 113 =$ *Francis S. Alban*, or *King of England*,

[1] WG I 119.

again that

I have a Gammon of Bacon=156=*Forrest of Arden,*

and that

S. *Nicholas*=95=*Robin Hood.*

Ostensibly by S. Nicholas is meant the Saint, but equally obviously
in the secret cipher, the S(*aint*) has to be read as S(*ir*), for it is the
latter, and not the former, who has any connection or relationship with
the hang-hog anecdote and with Bacon. This connection is made obvious,
in the first place by the nine times reiterated word " hang," in the
second place by letting S. Nicholas and Robin appear together on the
same page, and in the third place by the equal number-values of
S. Nicholas and Robin Hood, *alias* Francis Bacon.

And what about the " Franklin ? " Well, the number-value of

lin=33=*Bacon,*

so that Franklin really means *Frank Bacon.*

For this reason undoubtedly—because it was meant for a proper
name—was it written with a capital letter, as was " a Gammon of
Bacon," though in this case there was ostensibly even less reason for
such a measure. Immediately following it are " two razes of Ginger,"
the whole sentence running as follows : " I have a Gammon of Bacon,
and two razes of Ginger." One might ask : for what reason, then, was
Ginger written with a capital ? Well, perhaps because

Ginger=58=*Tidder.*

But I will not stress this point, for there are many more words with
capitals following, for which I can find no other reason than that they
were necessary, so as not to make the secret message contained in " a
Gammon of Bacon " too obvious, by their exceptional capitals.

We turn now to another scene for a new variation on the *hog*-theme. We have again to dive into the Comedies of the First Folio, in order to bring to the surface another glittering pearl of wit from its ocean's depths, for the herd of common swine on the earth's surface to reject as unwholesome or to accept as a treasure.

It is one of the neatest examples of " involved writing " Bacon has given us from the inexhaustible treasure-house of his wit. It is found in *Love's Labour's Lost.* I will give first the reading according to the modern editions, and then the text of the First Folio, so as to impress upon the Baconian student the necessity of always going back to the original text. The modern readings may be all right for the understanding of the obvious, superficial, exterior meaning, but the alterations, additions, omissions and substitutions made in the old text either diminish or destroy altogether the chance of getting at the " interior writing."

The persons speaking are Jaquenetta, a country wench ; Sir Nathaniel, the curate ; Holofernes, the schoolmaster ; and Costard, the clown.

Modern Text, Act IV, scene 2		*Old Text Fol, 132*	
Jaq.	God give you good morrow, Master parson.	Iaqu.	God giue you good morrow M. *Person.*
Hol.	Master parson, *quasi* person. An if one should be pierced, which is the one?	Nath.	Master Person, *quasi* Person? And if one should be perst, which is the one?
Cost.	Marry, Master schoolmaster, he that is likest to a hogs-head.	Clo.	Marry M. Schoolmaster, hee that is likest to a hogshead.
Hol.	Piercing a hogshead ! a good lusture of conceit in a turf of earth ; fire enough for a flint, pearl enough for a swine ; 'tis pretty ; it is well.	Nath.	Of persing a Hogshead, a good luster of conceit in a turph of Earth, Fire enough for a Flint, Pearle enough for a Swine : 'tis prettie, it is well.

Jaq.	Good Master parson be so good as read me this letter : it was given me by *Costard*, etc.	*Iaqu.*	Good Master Parson be so good as reade mee this Letter, it was giuen mee by *Costard*, etc.

I have had occasion before to point out that, whenever we meet with an obvious mistake or misprint in the original editions, there is reason carefully to inspect the passage or page concerned for concealed imprints of Bacon's hand.   Here is another instance.   From the Clown's answer it appears that the questioner—though Jaquenetta evidently had addressed the curate—was the Schoolmaster, Holofernes, and not Sir Nathaniel.

The word-play revolves all round the word *Person* which for that reason undoubtedly is printed in italics, the first time it occurs, in contrast with the other times.   I said that the passage was one of the neatest examples of Bacon's involved writing.   Neat also is the way in which the incident is declared closed by Jacquenetta pronouncing the same word rightly this time, as Parson.   Neater still is the introduction of the *two* Persons involved—the " Master Person," and the " *quasi* Person."   And who else can have been meant by the latter, but an actor, who is only a quasi or make-believe person ; just as the actor William Shakspeyr is but the *quasi* or make-believe author of the plays ?

Remember also the original meaning of the Latin word *Persona*, from which the English word is derived through the French.   It signified the actor's *mask*, through (*per*) which the words were spoken or sounded (*sonare*).   As such, the " *quasi* Person " is the one through whom the " Master Person " or the Master-mind spoke his words, who therefore functions as the latter's mask.   Of these two Persons, " which is the one " that should be " perst " or pierced ? the School-master asks.   There is but one answer to this question.   One must of course pierce through the mask, penetrate through the outer covering, to get at the real person, just as one has to pierce a " hogshead " or cask, to put the tap in, so that the real goods inside, the good old ale, may flow out in rich abundance.

If Shakespeare is the " *quasi* Person," the Hogshead to be penetrated or unmasked, then the Boar's head, or Bacon's head, Bacon's mind, the Master-mind, is the real, the " Master Person." The contrast between the two, the coarse brute and the noble animal, the Hog and the Boar, the Actor and the Author, is sharply brought out by the identification of Shakespeare as " he that is likest to a hogshead." Francis Bacon on the other hand is he who is likest to a Boar's head, for he was wearing a Boar on his heraldic crest, which in former times was borne by the knight on his helmet, in imitation of still earlier times when his Saxon forebears wore a real boar's head upon their own head with the entire hide falling round their back and shoulders.

We come now to the curate's final tirade, which probably contains a veiled rebuke to the actor Shakespeare for his vainglory in assuming the honours, due to the real author, as his own right, and believing himself, who was but " the hoggeshead of wit," to be the real boar's head of wit, indeed " a good lustre of conceit " in such " a turf of Earth," that is in such a rustic swain raised from the Warwickshire clods. On the other hand, this impersonating act will spread " fire enough " when brought to light by the " flint " of the decipherer's wit and art, bringing enlightenment to the reader, a better understanding of the text, and due recognition of the true author. But to the witless multitude the subtle hints about this act of impersonation, strewn about by the real author, will for a long time remain but " pearls for a swine."

There is no occasion for thinking this metaphor needlessly hard on the ignorant masses. Not only had Francis Bacon in Christ the most illustrious example for its application to the great thoughtless herd, but in Bacon's case its harshness was softened by the consciousness that his adoptive name made him a member of that same crowd, humanity in general, however illustrious a unit of it he might be. Besides, its aptness was intensified by the knowledge that by its very use he was still dropping a last pearl for the swine to pass by or pick up, as it might be. " It is pretty," indeed, " it is well."

Like his adoptive father, the late Lord Keeper to Queen Elizabeth, he was not above punning upon his own name, as we have abundantly proved. Hepworth Dixon in his biography of Francis Bacon follows up Sir Nicholas' hanghog=bacon anecdote, by the gentle comment: " The wise old man, if he loved his joke, knew well how a word may wound, and would never sacrifice his friend for his jest." In greater measure this is true of Francis Bacon ; he would not even have sacrificed his enemy for his jest.

We may picture him sitting in his chair, his head resting in his hand, as his statue depicts him, deliberately weighing his words, sweetening their bitterness by the honey of gentleness, of which his great heart was so rich a shrine. Only the small and the mean are vindictive, and of such smallness he knows himself to be free. Could any other but he have written that " learning makes the mind gentle ? " " Pearl enough for a Swine ?—he muses—yes, why not ? Are we not all of us like swine that constantly are losing shining pearls of opportunity ; or deliberately discarding as indigestible, pearls of wisdom ; or again incontinently swallowing false pearls of glamour ? So let it pass ; it is pretty, it is well." And we may imagine also how in his mind was present the living conviction that if the multitude are swine, he is the Master Swine, the Master Hog, the Boar's Head and Master Boar, *Master Bacon.*

Many will call the whole of the passage a deplorable exhibition of false wit and bad taste. And it would be such, if the puns were merely meant as cheap jokes, without any other deeper purpose. But how can such false wit and bad taste be reconciled with the sparkling wit and exquisite taste exhibited by Shakespeare in such abundance, a wit and a taste, a supreme Art, in fact, never surpassed by any other writer ? Can a fool suddenly turn into a wise man ? No. Or a wise man appear as a fool ? Yes, *if he wants to play the fool.* It proves the critic's own foolishness when he takes it upon himself to censure or to question the great poet's art, instead of reverently suspending judgment in the certain knowledge of his own inferiority, in every respect, to the mastermind and heart that composed these immortal works.

30

The reconciliation of the so-called " foolish " passages with the author's recognized wisdom, lies of course in the purpose they serve— the secret writing involved. Finding their reason in such writing, and considering the exigencies of such writing, which is to write in open view of every one, things which can be understood only by the wary and witty, I consider the transition from " Parson " through " person " and " pierce one " to " Hogshead " decidedly one of the neatest feats of Bacon's wit.

We have still to meet one objection raised by Shakespearean critics against the Baconian explanation of this passage in *Love's Labour's Lost*, namely that the simile of the " hogshead " to be " pierced " is nothing more than an allusion to the Harvey-Nashe controversy, in which mention is made of " Pierce, the hoggeshead of wit." [1] Our answer is that Bacon may very well have derived his simile from the controversy in question, but that he deliberately intended it to be applied to his authorship of Shakespeare's work, is proved by a double indication. First by the occurrence on the same page, on which the " hogshead " and " swine " occur, of the word " hang," so that we have here again the " hang-hog " which " is Latin for Bacon." Second by the occurrence on the same page of the word " deliver " also, which suggests " enfranchise," and thereby gives the Baconian signature in a new form— Francis Hog or Francis Swine or Francis Bacon.

Another member of the boar's kindred remains. It is the sow, or female pig, and it gives us one of the strongest evidences for the connection between Bacon's writings and at least one work appearing under another man's name. In 1586, when Bacon was only twenty-five, and " was making emblem literature one of ' the little works of my recreation,' " as one writer asserts, there appeared a book on " Emblems " by George Whitney, on page 53 of which is found the picture facing this page with superscription and subjoined verse.

" A glance at it shows us the letter *F* reversed in the broken arch, and beneath it the double arch, which discloses *B*. In the middle [in the tent-like construction] is the dark and light *A* so often used in his

[1] See Frances A. Yates, *A Study of Love's Labour's Lost*, 1936, p. 4.

T H E greedie Sowe fo longe as fhee dothe finde,
  Some fcatteringes lefte, of harueft vnder foote
She forward goes and neuer lookes behinde,
While anie fweete remayneth for to roote,
    Euen foe wee fhoulde, to goodnes euerie daie
    Still further paffe, and not to turne nor ftaie.

The Greedy Sow

[Bacon's] head-pieces, and in the foreground surmounted by the word *ulterius* [further] is a ' greedie Sowe ' by which stands a swineherd pointing to pillars of Hercules, bearing a scroll upon which is inscribed *Plus Oltre*, and over them the words *In dies meliora* ; in other words the swineherd standing by the embodiment of stupid greed points to the hopeful words, ' In better days more beyond.' "[1]   I am sure that the author, from whom this is taken, is not quite right in his reading of the emblem, as depicting the sow's " *stupid* greed." The verses underneath the picture rather indicate that the adjective " greedie " should be taken in its equally legitimate sense of " eager," or " keen." This quality drives the sow on, " to pass still further every day " to greater good in the future, " and not to turn nor stay " in the past. We must further note that the numerical value of the

$$Sowe = 58 = Tidder.$$

Elsewhere the word is spelled Sow, for example Folio, Histories, p. 76, even with a capital. Then its numerical value is 53, corresponding with the number of the page of Whitney's book, on which the greedy Sow is depicted.[2]

Now let us turn to Bacon's *Temporis Partus Masculus* (or *Maximus*), a work of his youth, about which he wrote, in the year before his death, to Father Fulgentio : " My hope is in this—that these things [his works] appear to proceed from the providence and infinite goodness of God. First because of the ardour and constancy of my own mind, which in this pursuit [like the eager sow's] has not grown old nor cooled in so great a space of time ; it being now forty years, as I remember, since I composed a juvenile work on this subject, which with great confidence and a magnificent title I named *The Greatest* [or *Male*] *Birth of Time*. Secondly, because it seems, by reason of its infinite utility, to enjoy the sanction and favour of God, the all-good and all-mighty."[3]

---

[1] Bax 517-8.

[2] For the importance of the number 53, see Durning Lawrence's *Bacon is Shakespeare*, p. 112, note. Examples of it we found before on the two pages 53 of the Comedies and Histories with the Hang-hog-bacon and the gammon-of-bacon episodes.

[3] Sp XIV 533 ; VIII 31.

Forty years deducted from 1625, when the letter was written, gives 1585, the year before Whitney's " Emblems " appeared, when Bacon was twenty-four. And what do we find in *The Greatest Birth* of *Time* ? " Sus rostro si forte humi A literam impresserit, num propterea suspicabere integram tragoediam veluti literam unam ab ea posse decribi ? " [1] " If a sow with greedy snout [by chance] imprints the letter A in the ground, would you therefore suspect her to be able to write down a whole tragedy like that one letter ? "

Here we have the " greedie Sowe " and the " letter A " of Whitney's Emblem, and besides that a reference to " Tragedies." What else can the sentence mean than that the mere natural wit of the rustic Shakspeyr might suffice to make him a ready cracker of jokes, of a single letter A as it were, as well as a successful actor and business man, but can never produce dramas like those going by the name of Shakespeare, full of learning, art and culture as they are, products entirely of a highly tutored literary genius !

Of the boar and kindred there now only remains a remote relation to be considered. Remote in the sense of the unbridgeable gulf that separates life from death. I mean, of course, pork, the dead swine's flesh, serving brutish man for food. When we hear of pork, in connection with Shakespeare, the inevitable association arising in our mind is the figure of the Jew in *The Merchant of Venice* with his nation's traditional aversion from the boar and his kindred as unclean animals. It is certainly a curious fact that in all the works of Shakespeare the word " pork " is found only in this play, on page 166 and 177 of the " Comedies " in the Folio of 1623.

Elsewhere we have shown how the two principal male actors in this play, besides Shylock, in a way represent Anthony (Antonio), and Francis Bacon (Bassanio). Now if we turn to page 166 of the Folio, we find the following well-known dialogue between Bassanio and Shylock.

[1] Sp III 538. Edwin Borman, to whose *Francis Bacon's Cryptic Rhymes and the Truth They Reveal*, 1906, p. 237, I owe this reference, does not know of its connection with Whitney's Emblem.

Jew.   May I speak with Anthonio ?

Bas.   If it please you to dine with us.

Jew.   Yes, to smell porke, to eate of the habitation which your Prophet
           the Nazarite conjured the divell into : I will buy with you, sell
           with you, talke with you, walke with you and so following : but
           I will not eate with you, drinke with you, nor play with you.

Here then we have the secret signature of the two brothers
Anthonio Porke, or Anthony Bacon, and Bassanio Porke, or Francis Bacon.

More convincing even is page 177 of the Folio. Besides the
word " porke " twice repeated, once with a capital we find also our
old friend, the Hog, with a capital, as well as the name of Bassanio,
once. The speakers are the lady Portia, the Clown, and the Jewess
Jessica, converted a Christian.

Por.   My people do already know my minde,
           And will acknowledge you [Lorenzo] and *Jessica*
           In place of Lord Bassanio and my selfe.

                .   .   .   .

Clow.   This making of Christians will raise the price of Hogs ; if wee
           grow all to be porke-eaters, wee shall not shortly have a rasher
           on the coales for money.

                .   .   .   .

Jes.   Hee saies you are not a good member of the commonwealth,
           for in converting Jews to Christians, you raise the price of Porke.

Add to this that the number of page 177 is also the number-value
of the name William Shakespeare, and the conviction that the con-
currence on that page of the name Bassanio with Hog and Porke was
intentional, becomes thereby irresistible.

But most convincing of all, I think, is page 178. The names of
Anthonio and Bassanio occur many times on this page, as on so many
other pages of this play, naturally. So we will leave that out of consideration, and take only the first speech of Shylock in court, in answer

to the summons by the Duke.   It is a grand speech, characteristic of the Jew, and the state of mind he was in :

Jew.   I have possesst your grace of what I purpose,
           And by our holy Sabbath have I sworne
           To have the due and forfeit of my bond.
           If you denie it, let the danger light
           Upon your Charter, and your Cities freedome.
           You'l aske me why I rather choose to have
           A weight of carrion flesh, then to receive
           Three thousand Ducats ? Ile not answer that :
           But say it is my humor ; Is it answered ?
           What if my house be troubled with a Rat,
           And I be pleas'd to give ten thousand Ducates
           To have it bain'd ? What, are you answer'd yet ?
           Some men there are love not a gaping Pigge :
           Some that are mad, if they behold a Cat :
           And others, when the bag-pipe sings i'th nose,
           Cannot containe their Urine for affection,
           Masters of passion swayes it to the moode
           Of what it likes or loaths, now for your answer :
           As there is no firme reason to be rendered
           Why he cannot abide a gaping Pigge ?
           Why he a harmlesse necessarie Cat ?
           Why he a woollen bag-pipe : but of force
           Must yeeld to such inevitable shame,
           As to offend himselfe being offended :
           So can I give no reason, nor I will not,
           More than a lodg'd hate, and a certaine loathing
           I beare Anthonio, that I follow thus
           A loosing suite against him ? Are you answered ?

What immediately strikes us in these lines is of course the recurrence twice of the word Pigge, and once of the name Anthonio.   The latter with one of the former gives us again the signature of Anthony Bacon. But what of the other word Pigge? Is there nothing to match it and so to yield the signature of the younger brother? There is, for there is the word Freedome, and we know also what this stands for, —Freedome Pigge, or Francis Bacon. In the clock-cipher this gives us

$$Freedome \ Pigge = 111 = England's \ King$$

Compare this with the

$$Freedome \ Pig = 99 = Borespeare$$

which we obtained from *The Tempest*.

These double signatures of Anthony and Francis Bacon leave no reasonable doubt that Anthonio and Bassanio of the play indeed represent in some way the two sons of Lady Ann.

We must now give attention to two other works, one ascribed to Shakespeare, but not generally so accepted, the other to Robert Burton, but claimed by Bacon to be entirely his production.

The first is *The Two Noble Kinsmen*. The question of its authorship will once for all be settled, at least for Baconians, I think, by the following seven or eight symbolic signatures. Not being able to consult the original Quarto of 1634, I must rely on Tucker Brooke's edition (Oxford 1918), to which all the references relate.

Keeping the principles in mind, as described before, the following signatures, all spelling '' Francis Bacon,'' will present no difficulties.

I 1, line 41, '' deliver '' ; line 84, '' Bore.''
II 2, line 53, '' Swine '' ; line 81, '' liberty.''
III 1, line 27, '' free '' ; line 37, '' bore.''
III 5, line 18, '' *Bore* '' ; line 31, '' deliverly.''
V 3, line 138, '' sow '' ; line 156, '' deliver.''
V 4, line 27, '' freedome ; line 82, '' pig.''

Every act therefore bears at least one, some two, of Bacon's secret imprints, except the fourth Act, which in its place has a more open declaration, similar to that found in *1 Henry IV* (II 1), thus :

IV 3, line 43, " a Gammon of Bacon."

Then there is in the first act also the allusion to Bacon's descent from Queen Elizabeth, and the Earl of Leicester, similar to the one occurring among others in *Venus and Adonis*, thus :

I 1, line 57, " Lyon," and " Beare,"
and in line 84 the already noted " Bore."

I have further noted the following curiosities.

Prologue, line 21, " Robin Hood " and IV 1, line 134, " Broome," well-known from *The Merry Wives of Windsor*,[1] and line 135, again " Bony Robin." We know that Robin or Robin Hood, is another name for Francis Bacon, but the mystery of Broome I have not yet solved.

Finally there is in I, 2, line 66, the word " plantin," or plantain. This also we must for the time leave merely as a note, to yield perhaps at a future date its secret in full.

We pass on now to Robert Burton's *Anatomy of Melancholy*, in the edition of A. R. Shilleto in three volumes (1896).

On p. 420, vol. III, we find the words,

Anthony for pigs,

and on the next page, besides the name

S. Nicholas,

also

Tumble with St. Francis in the mire amongst hogs,

[1] See the next Chapter.

Which gives us again the names of the two brothers, and of their father.   On page 237 of the same volume we also find,

Nicholas Wart,

and on page 293 of volume I,

Francis Wart.

Pages 336 and 416 of volume III yield us twice,

Francis Swine,

and page 484 of the same volume, the Latin form of this last signature,

Franciscus Sus,

if it is permissible to take for our purpose the latter half only of the word lapsus.

On p. 248 of volume I there is " Anthony " and on page 249 " Pork ; " on page 250 " pig," and on p. 251 " Franciscus."   I do not possess one of the original editions, so that I cannot say if these names and words appear there on the same page, but their proximity in the modern edition makes it at least possible.

If I had found in Burton's book only one or two of these signatures they might have been explained away as mere coincidence, but the nine or ten which are given above, and I am sure more may be discovered by whoever cares to hunt patiently and painstakingly for them through the whole book, exclude pure accident and make their intentional presence a proven fact.

8. Bucks and Woodmen

NOTHER noble animal of the wild, next to the Boar worthy of a price and an emblem to great hunters, such as Robin Hood, the Uncrowned King of England's Woodland, and the Bore-speare-man of the Arden Forest, is the Buck. When therefore we find on page 58 in the first part of the Folio (*The Merry Wives of Windsor*, III 3) the word *Buck* " needlessly reiterated," not less than ten times, we instinctively prick our ears as well-trained hunting-dogs smelling the quarry. But when we further find on the same page the name *Robin* intruding upon our vision, we come naturally to a pointer's rigid standstill, muzzle stretched forward, one foot raised, and eagerly watching and awaiting the Master's releasing cry.

Here are eight of the ten bucks : [1]

M. Ford. Why, what have you to doe whether they beare it ? You were best meddle with buck-washing.

---

[1] The remaining two are found in the words " Bucklers'berry," and " bucking " = buck-washing = soaking in lye. Buck-basket = clothes-basket.

Ford.   Buck ? I would I could wash my selfe of ye Buck : Bucke,
          bucke, bucke, I bucke : I warrant you Bucke.

And Robin appears in the sentence :

M. Page.   Here comes little *Robin*.

Now, what in heaven's name can this gibberish mean ? Surely, it
must point to something else which makes it intelligible.   And it does.
The page, on which this is found, is again a marked page.   It bears the
number 58, but the foregoing and the following pages are 49 and 51, so
that itself should be 50.   Now, if we turn to page 50 of the *Histories*,
that is to the first part of *Henry IV* (I 2), we find Poins saying :

" I have Cases of *Buckram* for the nonce,
        to *immaske* our noted outward garments."

And that is again much more than we could have hoped for.   We
not only find one " Buck," but whole " cases " of them ; and not only
that, but even an allusion to a " masking " of outward appearances,
just as Bacon was hiding behind the " mask " of Shakespeare.

The " noted outward garments " further reminds us strongly of
Shakespeare's Sonnet 76, in which the author in so many words
confesses that his own name is another than the public one under which
he is known.

Why is my verse so barren of new pride,
So far from variation or quick change ?
Why with the time do I not glance aside
To new-found methods and to compounds strange ?
    Why write I still all one, ever the same,
And keep invention in a noted weed,[1]

[1] And clothe my fancy in a well-known dress, *i.e.* Shakespeare's verse.

That every word doth almost tell my name,
Showing their birth and where they did proceed ?
　O, know sweet love, I always write of you,
And you and love are still my argument ;
So all my best is dressing old words new,
Spending again what is already spent ;
　　For as the sun is daily new and old,
　　So is my love still telling what is told.

The *Sonnets* appeared in 1609, when Bacon's other poet-masks, Greene (†1592), Marlowe (†1593), Peele (†1598), and Spenser (†1599) had been dead for a decade and more, so that he had been compelled all that time " to write all one, ever the same," that is, to use only Shakespeare as a mask. Before that, he had been wont " to vary his style to suit different men." [1]   " When I have assumed men's names, the next step is to create for each a style natural to the man, that yet should [let] my own be seen, as a thread of warp in my entire fabric, so that it may be all [recognized in the future as] mine." [2]   The variety of name and style was a protection against detection, which was now lost, and therefore now " every word doth almost tell my name, showing their birth and where they did proceed."

I think this Sonnet one of the strongest proofs for Bacon's authorship.   From the lips of Shakespeare the lines sound paradoxical, if not contradictory.   They declare in as many words that I, Shakepeare, am *not* Shakespeare.

But it is time that we return to our bucks, and turn another light on them, the light of the Clock-Cypher, or the number-play.

Remember that we found Robin and Bucke (in the Folio spelling) on the same page.   Now

Robin=55, and
Bucke=40=Hood,

so that

Robin Bucke=95=Robin Hood.

And I would have been greatly amazed, if I had not found some relationship or other, though it be only a relation of kindred, not of
character, between those two noble animals the Buck and the Boar.
Here it is :

Buckram=65=Hogshead

And it is but fit that we should find this, for if the Hog and the Hogshead stand for Shakespeare, as Bacon's " mask," the Buckram, which
is going to serve as a means of " immasking," is another symbol for
Shakespeare, whereas the Buck simple is rightly Bacon's symbol alone.
Buck and Buckram stand in a similar relation and contrast to each other
as Boar and Hog.   The latter present us with the " pair of opposites "
of the Noble and the Degraded ; the former with the Living and the
Dead, or the Inner and the Outer, the Buck being of course the living
deer, while the Buckram is only its dead, outer hide.   These pairs of
opposites therefore in a realistic way symbolise the relation and contrast
between Bacon and Shakespeare.

   I said that the ten " bucks " were found on page 58 (rightly 50)
of the *Comedies*.   This is a left-hand page.   The next right-hand page
bears the correct number 51.   Now it is a very curious fact that eight
pages further on we again find two pages, left and right, bearing the
numbers 58 and 51, of which this time the 51 is of course wrong and
should be 59.   It is as if the printer wanted to tell us to continue our
reading from the (wrong) page 58 to the (right) page 59, or from the
(right) page 50 to the (wrong) page 51.   And if we follow this indication we indeed find on that page again the symbol of the Buck, twice
repeated, once as " a brib'd Bucke," and once in the combination of
" Buck-basket " (V 5) :

   And what to say when we find that the number-value of

Brib'd Bucke=74=William,

and when we further remember that William Shakespeare was notorious, and had to leave his native town, for deer-stealing, or poaching? For the meaning of a " bribed buck " is a male deer thus illicitly obtained.

There is still more on this page. In the first place the " unnecessary reiteration," five times, of the name Broome, in one sentence.

Ford. Now Sir, whose a Cuckold now?
Mr. *Broome, Falstaffes* a knave, a Cuckoldly knave,
Heere are his hornes Master *Broome* :
And Master *Broome*, he has enjoyed nothing of *Fords*, but his Buck-basket, his cudgell, and twenty pounds of money, which must be paid to Mr. *Broome*, his horses are arrested for it, Mr. *Broome*.

What are these reiterations of the name Broome meant to indicate? I cannot say, for I have not yet penetrated their mystery. But in *The Two Noble Kinsmen* we have found the name coupled to Robin.

Then there is the sentence,

Will none but *Herne* the Hunter serve your turne?

This gives us ;

Will Herne=100=*Francis Bacon.*

Now do not say that this is a forced combination. For, if Francis Bacon is Robin Hood, the famous Hunter and Woodman, he may well have taken Herne, another known Hunter and Woodman, for his symbol too.

Who was Herne the Hunter anyway? " An ancient keeper in Windsor Forest, who was believed to walk there at midnight, around an old oak, which bore his name." All this we find on the same page. The scene is full of veiled allusions. The place is Windsor Forest, or Park, as modern editors have it, and the principal actor is Falstaffe,

whom we know already as representing Bacon as well as Shakespeare.
He enters, disguised as Herne the ancient keeper with a Buck's Head
on his own head, a Buck's Head this time instead of a Boar's Head.
This particular is not mentioned in so many words in the Folio, but must
be inferred.   Falstaff is there to meet clandestinely Anne Page.

Fal.	The Windsor-bell hath stroke twelve ; the Minute drawes on :
	Now the hot-bloodied-Gods assist me : Remember Jove,
	thou was't a Bull for thy *Europa*, Love set on thy hornes.
	[May it so sit on my Buck's horns ! Falstaff hopes]. . .
	I am heere a Windsor Stagge, and the fattest (I thinke)
	i'th Forrest. . . Who comes heere ? my Doe ?
	[Enter Mistress Ford and Mistress Page.]
M. Ford.	Sir *John* ? Art thou there (my Deere ?)
	My male-Deere ?
Fal.	My Doe. . . I will shelter me here [trying to embrace her.]
M. Ford.	Mistris *Page* is come with me (sweet hart) ?
Fal.	Divide me like a brib'd Bucke, each a Haunch : . . . Am I
	a Woodman, ha ? Speake ? I like *Herne* the Hunter ?

    [The other actors, disguised as fairies enter, and Falstaff, greatly
fearing, lies down on his face.   Such at least are the modern glosses
and stage directions.   The fairies dance and sing.]

Till 'tis one a clocke,
Our Dance of Custome, round about the Oke
Of Herne the Hunter, let us not forget.

    [Then with the tapers which they hold in their hands, the fairies
burn Falstaff, who takes off his Buck's head, and attempts to run away
but is caught by Page].

Page.	Nay do not flye. I thinke we have watcht you now :
	Will none but *Herne* the Hunter serve your turne.
M. Page.	I pray you come, hold up the jest no higher.
	Now (good Sir *John*) how like you *Windsor* wives ?
	See you these husband ? Do not these fair yoakes
	Become the Forrest better than the Towne ?

And then follow the words of M. Ford, with the five " Broomes "
quoted before.

Now let us take up some more of the striking words and expressions in this scene. The " bribed buck " which has to be " divided " in
two seems clearly to indicate the double nature of Falstaff, the pair
of opposites of left and right (haunch) here.

It may be accidental that the number value of

$$Windsor = Forrest = Herne's\ oake^1 = 96$$

and also that the number value of

$$Herne's\ oke = 95 = Robin\ Hood.$$

But can it be unintentional that the answer to the question whether
he is a woodman, is by the Clock-cypher indicated to be " England's
King ? " Thus,

$$Am\ I\ a\ woodman\ ha? = 111 = England's\ King.$$

Of course he is a Woodman, who lives and hunts in the wood,
Robin Hood, the Uncrowned King of the Forrest of Arden, "this
England."

There is one more scene in *The Merry Wives of Windsor* which we
have to consider in connection with Shakespeare's deer-stealing, and
which will prove the one half of our contention, that Falstaff is Shakespeare, while the other half, that he is Bacon, has been proved in divers
ways before. It is the opening scene of the comedy, with which we
are concerned. The actors are Justice Shallow, his cousin Slender, and
the Welsh Parson, Sir Hugh Evans ; the scene is Windsor, before Page's
house. The Judge's complaint is that Falstaff " has beaten his men,
killed his deer, and broken open his lodge."

[1] See Folio, *Comedies*, p. 56.

32

Shal. Sir Hugh, perswade me not : I will make a Star-Chamber matter
       of it, if hee were twenty Sir John Falstaffs, he shall not abuse
       Robert Shallow Esquire.
Slen. In the County of Glocester, Justice of Peace and Coram.
Shal. I (Cosen Slender) and Cust-alorum.
Slen. I, and Rato lorum too ; and a Gentleman borne (Master Parson)
       who writes himselfe Armigero, in any Bill, Warrant, Quittance,
       or obligation, Armigero.
Shal. I that I doe, and haue done any time these three hundred yeeres.
Slen. All his successors (gone before him) hath don't : and all his
       Ancestors (that come after him) may : they may giue the
       dozen white Luces in their Coate.
Shal. It is an olde Coate.
Euans. The dozen white Lowses doe become an old Coat well : it agrees
       well passant : It is a familiar beast to man, and signifies Loue.
Shal. The Luse is the fresh fish, the salt-fish, is an old Coate.

It is generally recognized that the person who is satirized as Judge
Shallow is no other than Sir Thomas Lucy of Charlecote, who according
to Richard Davies "had him [Shakespeare] oft whipped and sometimes
imprisoned and at last made him fly his native country." [1] Another
tradition says that in revenge for the ill-treatment, Shakespeare composed, if composed it might be called, the following "bitter ballad" with
the same pun upon his tormentor's name as many years after re-
appeared in The Merry Wives of Windsor.

        A parliament member, a justice of peace,
        At home a poor scare-crow, at London an ass,
        If lousy is Lucy, as some folk miscall it,
        Then Lucy is lousy whatever befall it :
              He thinks himself great,
              Yet an ass in his state,
        We allow by his ears but with asses to mate.

                    [1] ChW 232.

> If Lucy is lousy, as some folk miscall it,
> Sing lousy Lucy, whatever befall it.[1]

Modern Shakespearean critics seem inclined to discredit the reliability of this tradition, because the " contemptible performance " is incompatible with Shakespeare's poetical genius.   But the Baconian student has no need to discard tradition on such inferential grounds, for to him the ballad may well be in tune with the actor's rustic wit. Note also that in the quarto edition, which appeared during the actor's life-time, in 1602, the jest on the name and coat of arms does not yet occur.

In a book on *Shakespeare, Player, Playmaker and Poet* (1908), Canon Beeching wrote : " When we remember that this charge of the *luce* had been associated with the Lucy family ever since heraldry was a science, and inevitably suggested their name, it is put beyond reasonable doubt that Shakespeare intended a personal affront ; while by substituting twelve luces for three, which was the number on the Lucy coat, he kept on the windy side of the Star Chamber."   And then the Canon goes on to say, as reported by Smeaton,[2] " that in it lies a dilemma which gives pause to every believer in the Baconian theory of Shakespeare.   Sir T. Lucy and Bacon were very intimate friends : if Bacon wrote the Shakespearean dramas, would he be likely wantonly to insult his best friends ? " Unfortunately for the Shakespearean, however, Bacon's " very intimate friendship " with Sir Thomas is pure fiction. The only definite thing known of the relationship between the two is a letter from Bacon, of 1601, probably to the eldest son of his so-called " friend," who succeeded his father in 1600, about a marriage arrangement between his daughter Joyce and Sir William Cook, a " possible " kinsman of Bacon's by the mother's side.   The letter is indeed " an agreeable and very characteristic letter," as Spedding describes it, but nevertheless nothing but a " business " letter, which from its subject had naturally to be nice and agreeable.   And that is all there is of their intimate relationship.[3]

---

[1] ChW 246.   [2] Sm 28.   [3] Cf Sp IX 369,

9. Clown and Plantain

IDDLES of another kind will occupy us in this Chapter. It will be entirely devoted to anagrams, Bacon's sixth kind of Cipher.

Hazlitt has somewhere written that if we were to part with any of Shakespeare's comedies, it would have to be *Love's Labour's Lost*, and other critics have been as severe with it. They may or may not have reason for their censure from the artist's standpoint—I myself would rather share the more favourable view of the editors of the New Cambridge edition—but a Baconian in any case would strongly oppose Hazlitt's rejection of this play. It is true that it is one of Shakespeare's earliest works, and therefore belongs to the period of his immature craftsmanship, but with *As You Like It*, of a somewhat later date and riper art, it shares the distinction of containing the greatest number, as well as the most significant of veiled allusions to Bacon's authorship. Most of them, I fear, have not yet been deciphered, but enough at any rate to justify our predilection for this play as a source of proofs for the Baconian theory.

In the plays of the later periods of his life the indications become scarcer and subtler. I leave aside the external marks, signs and ciphers, which depend entirely on the printing, as the biliteral cipher, the wrong pagination, etc., neither do I consider those parts of the text which make up the Great or Word-cipher. These are found in all the works up to the very end of Francis Bacon's life, and they are probably carried on even beyond that point by some of his disciples. What I have in mind are only those veiled allusions which, though forming part of the ordinary text, independent of the way of printing, yet have nothing to do with the Word-cypher either, but stand entirely on their own. To this kind belong anagrams, acrostics, emblems, and other similar devices, which all belong to his " involved writing." These " involutions " abound in the older plays, especially in the Comedies, and more especially in the extreme burlesque scenes with fools, clowns, or such caricatures of human nature, like Don Adriano de Armado, the fantastical Braggart, and Sir Nathaniel, the pedantic curate, and many others. Their extravagance, their ignorance, or other of their weaknesses, afford the author the opportunity for introducing words and phrases that otherwise would never come naturally into the text without arousing that suspicion he was so anxious to avoid.

In the Introduction we have seen how in one place of the *Biliteral Cipher*[1] we are told : " That clown in the play who speaks of the *plantain leaf* is a wise man, here art outruns that grub nature, hunt out this cipher or anagram at once." Now, the play in which we find a *plantain leaf* mentioned is *Romeo and Juliet* (I 2).

Ben.	Tut man, one fire burns out another's burning,
	One pain is lessened by another's anguish :
	Turn giddy, and be helped by backward turning :
	One desperate grief, cures with another's languish :
	Take thou some new infection to the eye,
	And the rank poison of the old will die.
Rom.	Your *plantain leaf* is excellent for that.
Ben.	For what I pray thee ?
Rom.	For your broken shin.
Ben.	Why Romeo art thou mad ?

[1] WG II 167.

But though here we have the plantain leaf, we do not find the clown, for Benvolio, how merry a fellow he may be, is certainly not a clown.   To find the latter, and to come as near to a plantain-leaf as we can get when we have the plantain itself from which the leaf comes, we must turn to *Love's Labour's Lost* (Act III).   The fantastical Spaniard, Don Adriano de Armado has the following amazing conversation with his page, Moth.

Moth.   A wonder, master ! here's a costard broken in a shin.
Arm.   Some enigma, some riddle, no *l'envoy* , no salve, in the mail, sir.
            O ! sir plantain, a plain plantain : no *l'envoy* no *l'envoy* : no
            salve, sir, but a plantain.

Here, then, we have the clown—for Costard *is* the clown in the play—and plantains enough, but no leaf.   Still I think that these are the clown and the plantain Bacon had in mind when he directed us to hunt them out for his anagram cipher, for not only is a plantain-*leaf* meant, of course, but if we search further on in the play, we shall find Costard the clown using a very long, if not the longest Latin word in existence, which "well ordered" or re-arranged, has indeed been interpreted as a wise Baconian saying, as a Baconian anagram in fact. Another correspondence between the scene in *Romeo*, and the one in *Love's Labour's Lost* is the "broken shin."   What it all means we shall try to find out later.

Before we go into that, however, let us first see what modern Shakespearean critics have to say about *Love's Labour's Lost*.   It is avowedly the most "topical" of all Shakespeare's plays.   The editors of the New Cambridge Shakespeare even go so far as to assert that it "was *written* as a topical play," and that "most, if not all, of its characters were meant by Shakespeare to be portraits or caricatures of living persons."   That may be as it may, but the same critics are also constrained to confess that "as persistent flies in its amber, a crowd of ephemeral references and allusions, *undissolved*, irritate as specks of grit irritate the eye."

It does not lie in our purpose to occupy ourselves with the topicalities as such, for one thing because some of the identifications seem to be too uncertain, and could by Baconians be well turned round the other way. Only one of these we will point out here. It is the " certainty," as the same Editors express it, that *Love's Labour's Lost* " bears close relation to some batches of the *Sonnets*," namely the " dark lady " series beginning with Sonnet 127, and that Berowne's Rosaline is " *his* dark lady." That seems indeed pretty certain, but has it brought the critics any nearer to the knowledge who Shakespeare's dark lady was, with all their certainty about Shakespeare's " portraits or caricatures of living persons ? " For the Baconian on the other hand Shakespeare's as well as Berowne's dark lady is of course Marguerite of Valois, who led Francis Bacon on in love, but could not stay faithful to him, bringing him sorrow untold, but humanity immense benefit through the release of his life-energy along deeper and stronger flowing channels.

However, this love-story does not further concern us here. We have fully dealt with it before. What will especially occupy us here, are the subtle allusions in Bacon's anagrammatic cipher to his authorship. The play proves in fact not only the most topical, but also the most anagrammatic of Shakespeare's plays.

It begins with the Great Anagram already alluded to, found in the Fifth Act, wrongly superscribed in the Folio as *Actus Quartus*. If for that reason alone, it deserves our attention, " marked " as it is for that purpose with this apparent " misprint." I reproduce the first part of the first scene. There is much Latin in it, for it is a meeting between learned men, Holofernes the Pedant, and Nathaniel the Curate, with Constable Dull as a third. Later enter the Braggart Don Adriano de Armado, and his Boy or Page.

I reprint the scene, exactly as it appears on page 136 of the Folio, left column, so that the number of words on each line, the italicized words, the capitals, etc. are the same as in the original. The letter type only is different. This is important, as we shall see, to put Bacon's Clock-cipher, or the number-play into action.

Curat.   A most singular and choise Epithat,

Draw out his Table-booke.

Peda.   He draweth out the thred of his verbositie, finer then the staple of his argument.   I abhor such pha-
naticall phantasims, such insociable and poynt deuise
companions, such rackers of ortagriphie, as to speake
dout fine, when he should say doubt ; det, when he shold
pronounce debt ; d e b t, not det : he clepeth a Calf,
Caufe :
halfe, haufe : neighbour *vacatur* nebour ; neigh abreuiated
ne : this is abhominable, which he would call abhominable : it insinuateth me of infamie : *ne inteligia domine,* to
make franticke, lunaticke ?

Cura.   *Laus deo, bene intelligo.*

Peda.   *Bone boon for boon prescian,* a little scratcht, 'twill
serue.

Enter Bragart, Boy.

Curat.   *Vides ne quis venis ?*

Peda.   *Video, & gaudio.*

Brag.   Chirra.

Peda.   *Quasi* Chirra, not Sirra ?

Brag.   Men of peace well incountred.

Ped.   Most millitarie sir salutation.

Boy.   They haue beene at a great feast of Languages,
and stolne the scraps.

Clow.   O they haue liu'd long on the almes-basket of
words.   I maruell thy M. hath not eaten thee for a word,
for thou art not so long by the head as honorificabilitudinitatibus : Thou art easier swallowed then a flapdra-
gon.

Page.   Peace, the peale begins.

33

Brag.   Mounsier, are you not lettred ?
Page.   Yes, yes, he teaches boyes the Horne-booke :
          What is Ab speld backward with the horn on his head ?
Peda.   Ba, *puericia* with a horne added.
Pag.   Ba most seely Sheepe, with a horne : you heare
          his learning.
Peda.   *Quis quis*, thou Consonant ?
Pag.   The last of the fiue Vowels if You repeat them,
          or the fift if I.
Peda.   I will repeat them : a e I.
Pag.   The Sheepe, the other two concludes it o u.
Brag.   Now by the salt waue of the mediteranium,
          sweet tutch, a quicke vene we of wit, snip snap, quick &
          home, it reioyceth my intellect, true wit.
Page.   Offered by a childe to an olde man : which is
          wit-old.
Peda.   What is the figure ? What is the figure ?
Page.   Hornes.
Peda.   Thou disputes like an Infant : goe whip thy
          Gigge.
Pag.   Lend me your Horne to make one, and I will
          whip about your Infamie *vnum cita* a gigge of a Cuck-
          olds horne.
Clow.   And I had but one penny in the world, thou
          shouldst haue it to buy Ginger bread : Hold, there is the
          very Remuneration I had of thy Maister, thou halfpenny
          purse of wit, thou Pidgeon-egge of discretion.   O & the
          heauens were so pleased, that thou wert but my Bastard ;
          What a joyfull father wouldst thou make mee ? Goe to,
          thou hast it *ad dungil*, at the fingers ends, as they say.
Peda.   Oh I smell false Latine, *dunghel* for *unguem*.
Brag.   Arts-man *preambulat*, we will bee singled from
          the barbarous.   Do you not educate youth at the Charg-
          house on the top of the Mountaine ?

Peda.   Or Mons the hill.

The most important item in the scene is of course the long Latin word *Honorificabilitudinitatibus.*   Its letters have been rearranged and regrouped by Baconians to impart the intelligible information : *Hi ludi F. Baconis nati orbi tuiti,* or *These plays, F. Bacon's offspring, are preserved for the world.*[1]   If this were all, it were not convincing, for the long word lends itself also to other anagrammatic re-arrangements.   But backed up as it is by certain circumstances and a curious number-play, it gains considerably in probability.

The values of the letters which constitute the word, according to Bacon's Clock-cipher, added together, yield the number 287.   Splitting this total up, by adding together separately the numerical values of the initial and final letters of the different words of the anagram on the one hand, and of the middle letters of those words on the other, we get :

$$H+L+F+B+N+O+T+I+I+S+I+I+I = 136$$
$$U+D+A+C+O+N+I+A+T+R+B+U+I+T = 151$$

$$Total = 287$$

The word further consists of 27 letters.   And what do these three numbers 27, 136, and 151 reveal ?   That on the 27th line of the 136th page of the Folio, the 151st word, not counting the italicized words and counting the hyphenated words as separate ones, we find the long Latin word.

We further know already that

$$136 = Bacon\text{-}Shakespeare,\ while$$
$$151 = Franke\ Borespeare.$$

[1] In this and the following I copy Sir Edwin Durning-Lawrence, whose explanations in *Bacon Is Shakespeare,* chapter X, I think, are the most convincing, though not altogether perfect, I fear.   For other readings of the long word, see *Baconiana,* November 1893, p. 171 ; July 1905, p. 185 ; and more recently the reprint in *Pearson's Magazine,* January 1939, p. 12, of R. M. Bucke's article of forty years ago, '' Shakespeare Dethroned.'' BUCKE ! Nomen est Omen.   See the preceding Chapter.

I have again to ask : Can all this be mere coincidence ?

The next item in the scene which strikes us forcibly is the " Ab spelled backward with the horn on his head," or the " Ba with a horn added." This gives us the name of Bacon. For, substituting the older word " corn " for " horn," still preserved for example in the word " unicorn " or " one-horn," we get Bacorn, pronounced as Bacon. Every doubt that this was not so intended by the author must disappear, I think, when we find in the next sentence, the page accosted, as " thou Consonant." What else can this word here mean than " con-sound," that is let corn " sound " as " con ! " The obvious, literal meaning of con-sonant is of course " sounding with," namely with a vowel. But equally obvious the hidden or double meaning, leaving the prefix con untranslated, is " sounding con," or sounding like con. It gives the answer to the question : Quis, quis, or who, who ? Namely, whom do you mean by " Ba with a horn added." Well, nobody else than Ba-con. That indeed the whole scene hinges on the word " horne," and that there is perhaps even more in it than we have been able to guess, is indicated by its repetition no less than seven times, and by the answer to the question, " What is the figure ? What is the figure ? Hornes." In other words : What is the symbol ? What is the symbol ? Answer : corns, or cons, namely all the con-s that have been sounded in the text, as so many echoes to the Ab spelled backwards.

I hear some of my readers remark : this is all very ingenious, yet it cannot carry conviction without other additional direct proof. As to the ingeniousness, my opinion is certainly that in this respect it is not worse than most of the textual and explanatory conjectures of ordinary Shakespearean scholarship. Regarding the direct proofs required, these would be contradictory to the secrecy of the revelations. Finally, as to other additional proof, I can only say—and this will be applicable not only to the present case, but to many similar cases—that the expla-nation makes sense out of nonsense.

This is one of the strongest points in favour of the Baconian theory, that where there is neither rhyme nor reason before, there is now something quite intelligible. For three centuries Shakespearean criticism has spent all its wit and ingenuity on the Shakespeare plays, without having been able to make Shakespeare talk sense, he, who is acknowledged the world's greatest wit and genius. There is in this an insuperable paradox, left undissolved by mere Shakespearean scholarship. It is its blind wall through which it cannot pass or see the light beyond. How different it is for the Baconian. I do not say that he has been able to tear down the wall of ignorance and prejudice altogether, but many cracks have been made, and here and there a stone has been quite driven out to let the Moon shine through. Some will certainly call it all Moonshine. But is not Moonshine Sunshine too, the reflection in the night of ignorance, of the otherwise altogether invisible light of truth?

The strongest proof, yes the strongest proof, for the Baconian theory is the existence of these otherwise silly, nonsensical and unexplainable passages, hideous blotches on the fair face of Shakespeare's fame so long as they are accepted on their face-value as mere gibberish. Consult every existing edition of Shakespeare, and see if there is one which gives a reasonable explanation of such scenes. Every single one of these scenes cries out through the ages as it were : " My remaining unexplained by Shakespeareans is *the* irrefutable proof of the fallacy of their premises. Try therefore another way. The successes in many cases, which the Baconian explanations have registered, are the greatest proofs for the validity and truth of their theory."

The third item calling for explanation is the passage about the five vowels. But having myself nothing new to offer to what others have said about it, the subject being moreover of a somewhat technical nature, and not altogether convincing (there is still a flaw somewhere), I refer the reader to Edwin Durning-Lawrence's book.

It must of course be understood that not everything has yet been cleared up by Baconians, nor is every difficulty always explained with that convincing lucidity, which does away with all reasonable doubts. The difference between the Baconian and the Shakespearean, however, is that the former has a saner and loftier idea of the author's genius, and therefore cannot believe that at one time he is talking mere nonsense, while immediately before or after he gives voice to the

highest wisdom.   It is indeed utter foolishness simply to believe that the
passage about the vowels has no hidden sense, to let it be hailed by
Armado as " a quick venewe of wit, true wit, by the salt wave of the
Mediterranean," that is by the famous " Attic salt," and yet to deny
that such farcical nonsense has any deeper sense.

We come now to the last words of the Clown, Costard.   From
Bacon's Biliteral Cipher we know already that he is a most important
person for our purpose.   In this scene he is almost a mute character,
opening his mouth only twice, the first time to give us the long Latin
word, the second time to give us something else. His words on this
occasion are :

> ' And I had but one penny in the world, thou shouldst haue it to
> buy Ginger bread : Hold, there is the very Remuneration I had
> of thy Maister, thou halfpenny purse of wit, thou Pidgeon-egge
> of discretion.   O & the heauens were so pleased, that thou
> wert but my Bastard.   What a joyfull father wouldst thou make
> mee ? Goe to, thou hast it *ad dungil*, at the fingers ends, as
> they say.'

We cannot hope to explain everything, but evidently Costard is
upbraiding Moth for his indiscretion, with regard of course to the
revelations made in the Ba-Co(r)n episode.   In no other way do his
words make sense.   " Thou halfpenny purse of wit," [1] he is saying, that
is " thou man of little wit," canst thou not find a more " involved " or
concealed way of alluding to my name than by so openly mentioning it
as in Ba-co(r)n.   Thou art indeed only a " pigeon egg of discretion."
The secret is on the very edge of discovery, thou art wearing it at thy
" fingers end," for every passer-by to snatch at it.   Thus Bacon as
Costard is upbraiding himself as Moth.   This connection of Costard and
Moth with Bacon is further indicated by the penny the former would
fain give the latter " to buy Ginger bread," that is to buy more

---

[1] For the allusion contained in these words to the Harvey-Nashe controversy already mentioned, see the Introduction to the New Cambridge edition of the play (1923), p. XXII.

wit, in order the better to reveal Bacon secretly. We have met the word Ginger before, also written with a capital, and we know already that

$$Ginger = 58 = Tidder.$$

That Ginger should be taken separate from bread is indicated by their being printed separately.

For the rest Costard's words remind us of an earlier scene, for the money wherewith to buy Gingerbread, comes from the " Remuneration " the Clown has received from the Page's Master on a former occasion.

Our next task is thereby clearly laid out for us—the examination of that former scene for further revelations. It is found in the very short Third Act, page 128-9 of the Folio. So we return to our starting point, the *Plantain leaf.*

Enter Page and Clowne

Pag.   A wonder Master, here's a *Costard* broken in a shin.

Ar.   Some enigma, some riddle, come, thy *Lenuoy* begin.

Clo.   No egma, no riddle, no *lenuoy*, no salue, in thee male sir. Or sir, Plantan, a plaine Plantan : no *lenuoy*, no *lenuoy*, no Salue sir, but a Plantan.

Ar.   By vertue thou inforcest laughter, thy sillie thought, my spleene, the heauing of my lunges prouokes me to rediculous smyling : O pardon me my stars, doth the inconsiderate take *salue* for *lenuoy* and the word *lenuoy*, for a *salue* ?

Pag.   Doe the wise thinke them other, is not *lenuoy* a *salue* ?

Ar.   No *Page*, it is an epilogue or discourse to make plaine, Some obscure precedence that hath to—fore bin saine. Now will I begin your morrall, and do you follow with my *lenuoy*.

The Foxe, the Ape, and the Humble-Bee,
Were still at oddes, being but three.

Arm.   Untill the Goose came out of doore,
                  Staying the oddes by adding foure.[1]

Pag.   A good *Lenuoy*, ending in the Goose : would you desire more ?

Clo.   The Boy hath sold him a bargaine, a Goose, that's flat.
          Sir, your penny-worth is good, and your Goose be fat.
          To sell a bargaine well is as cunning as fast and loose :
          Let me see a fat *Lenuoy*, I that's a fat Goose.

Ar.   Come hither, come hither :
          How did this argument begin ?

Boy.   By saying that a *Costard* was broken in a shin.
          Then cal'd you for the *Lenuoy*.

Clow.   True, and I for a Plantan :
          Thus came your argument in.
          Then the Boyes fat *Lenuoy*, the Goose that you bought,
          And he ended the market.

Ar.   But tell me : How was there a *Costard* broken in a shin ?

Pag.   I will tell you sencibly.

Clow.   Thou hast no feeling of it *Moth*,
          I will speake that *Lenuoy*.
          I *Costard* running out, that was safely within,
          Fell ouer the threshold, and broke my shin.

Arm.   We will talke no more of this matter.

Clow.   Till there be more matter in the shin.

Arm.   Sirra *Costard*, I will infranchise thee.

Clow.   O, marrie me to one *Francis*, I smell some *Lenuoy*, some
          Goose in this.

Arm.   By my sweete soule, I meane setting thee at libertie.   Enfree-
          doming thy person : thou wert emured, restrained, captiuated,
          bound.

Clow.   True, true, and now you will be my purgation, and let me loose.

Arm.   I giue thee thy libertie, set thee from durance, and in lieu
          thereof, impose on thee nothing but this : Beare this significant

---

[1] In the Quarto edition (1598) of *Love's Labour's Lost*, the first couplet of the Foxe,
Ape and Bee is needlessly repeated three times, the second couplet of the Goose twice.

to the countrey Maide *Iaquenetta* : there is remuneration, for
the best ward of mine honours is rewarding my dependants.
Moth, follow

Pag.   Like the sequell I.

Signeur *Costard* adew.   *Exit.*

Clow.   My sweete ounce of mans flesh, my in-come lew.   Now will I
looke to his remuneration.

Remuneration, O, that's the Latine word for three-farthings :
Three-farthings remuneration.   What's the price of this yncle ?
I.d.no, Ile giue you a remuneration : Why ? It carries it re-
muneration : Why ? It is a fairer name then a French-Crowne.
I will neuer buy and sell out of this word.

Enter Berowne.

Ber.   O my good knaue *Costard*, exceedingly well met.

Clow.   Pray you sir, How much Carnation Ribbon may a man buy for a
remuneration ?

Ber.   What is a remuneration ?

Cost.   Marrie sir, halfe pennie farthing.

It is a baffling scene, even for Baconians.   I have not been able
to make much sense of it.   Only one or two points are clear.   One of
these we have already referred to before.   It is the marrying of
Costard-Bacon to one Francis, or the connecting of the whole family
of " Boars and Kindred " to such words as " enfranchise," denoting
delivery and freedom.

Before entering upon the second point, let us first survey the
whole scene and mark its salient features.   It begins with that be-
wildering statement :

" Here's a Costard broken in a shin."

And as if in itself the phrase were not sufficiently amazing, it is introduced
to us with the words " A wonder, Master," and commented upon as
" Some enigma, some riddle."   Reading on, we find it repeated first as

34

" A Costard was broken in a shin ",

again as :

" How was there a Costard broken in a shin ? "

Finally the couplet :

" I Costard running out that was safely within
Fell over the threshold, and broke my shin."

But what in Heaven's name is " a costard broken in a shin ? "
I am sure I do not know, but I am equally sure that the words contain
some Bacon-Shakespeare anagram, for a sharper wit and a greater
ingenuity to discover. "Costard" means "head" or a large kind of
" apple," and what a " broken shin " means is too well-known, but as
far as I know there is no sense at all in the words " broken *in* a shin,"
less still in the combination " a costard broken in a shin."   Yet we find
it here four times repeated, and in diverse ways emphasized.

Next we come to the words " lenvoy," " plantan," and " salve,"
the first not less than 12 times,[1] the second 5, and the last 4 times
repeated.   I do not know in how far the plantain and the salve have
anything directly to do with the solving of the anagram, but I think
I have discovered the function of *lenvoy*, at least in one aspect.   Lenvoy
is here used in the sense of an explanatory or revealing end-piece,
as is clear from the words of the Braggard : " Some enigma, some
riddle, come, thy Lenvoy begin," that is to say, " come begin thy
explanation or revelation."   Later on, he himself explains that

It is an epilogue or discourse to make plaine
Some obscure precedence that hath tofore bin saine.

That is to say it reveals what first was hidden.   All this care taken
over the word Lenvoy, as well as its reiteration a dozen times, make it

[1] In the Quarto edition it is repeated 16 times.

out to be of the greatest importance, and as pointing beyond itself as it
were to the real *Lenvoy* of the whole play.   This is the " Dialogue that
the two Learned men have compiled in praise of the Owle and the
Cuckow," and it is in the form of. an amoebaean song between *Hiems*
or Winter, and *Ver* or Spring, *the latter to begin*.   The last four words
are specially important, for on close scrutiny the song reveals the names
of *Verulam* and *Saint Albans*, worked as acrostics into the poem,
and *Ver*, short for Verulam, indeed begins, or leads, followed by
Saint Albans.

Before showing the presence of these acrostics in the Ver-Hiems
song, we must however first explain their construction, and by giving
some other examples, prove that they are not an accidental feature of
the *Envoy* to our play, but are evidently a recognized and frequently
used device by Bacon to reveal his hidden authorship.

The rules for the construction and solution of this particular form of
acrostic, specially applicable to short, well-rounded off pieces of poetry
—sonnets, single stanzas, and the like—are best illustrated by some
examples. Take the opening sonnet of " The Passionate Pilgrime by
W. Shakespeare," as it was published in 1599.

> When my Love sweares that she is made of truth,
> I doe beleeve her (though I know she lies)
> That she might thinke me some untutor'd youth,
> Unskilfull in the worlds false forgeries.
> Thus vainly thinking that she thinkes me young,
> Although I know my yeares be past the best :
> I smiling, credite her false speaking toung,
> Outfacing faults in Love, with loves ill rest.
> But wherefore sayes my Love that she is young ?
> And wherefore say not I, that I am old ?
> O, Loves best habite is a soothing toung,
> And Age (in Love) loves not to have yeares told.
> Therfore Ile lye with Love, and Love with me,
> Since that our faults in Love thus smother'd be,

We have printed in italics the first *f* occurring in the text, then the next *r*, the next *a*, the next *n*, and so on through the whole name of *Francis Bacon*, till we come to *the last n* [1] in the poem.

Incidentally this acrostic gives the lie to those critics who deny the Shakespearean authorship of *The Passionate Pilgrim*.[2]

It is worth while to compare this poem with the somewhat different form in which it was printed in 1609 as No. 138 of the *Sonnets*.

> When my love sweares that she is made of truth,
> I do beleeve her though I know she lyes,
> That she might thinke me some untuterd youth,
> Unlearned in the worlds false subtilties.
>   Thus vainely thinking that she thinkes me young,
> Although she knowes my dayes are past the best,
> Simply I credit her false speaking tongue,
> On both sides thus in simple truth supprest :
>   But wherefore sayes she not she is unjust ?
> And wherefore say not I that I am old ?
> O loves best habit is in seeming trust,
> And age in love, loves not t'have yeares told.
>   Therefore I lye with her, and she with me,
>   And in our faults by lyes we flattered be.

I have no doubt that Bacon in the later edition deliberately obliterated the acrostic, as an object lesson to future decipherers in the construction and deciphering of such acrostics. The obliteration has been effected in the following way. First by replacing the word " unskillful," containing the first *f* of Francis by " unlearned." If however Bacon had left it at that the acrostic could still have been extracted from the older poem by beginning with the next *f* of " false " which would then have been the first *f*. The next *r* would then come from " forgeries." So that this word had also to go ; it

---

[1] This is important. There must not be another *n* in the poem.   [2] ChW 51.

was therefore replaced by " subtleties." Still the acrostic could be read by taking the next *r* from " yeares." Therefore this word was replaced by " dayes." But again Bacon found that the next *r* could be taken from " credite," the next *a* from " false," the next *c* and *i* from " outfacing," and the next *s* from " faults." So he changed these words and some more also, finally making security doubly sure by discarding the only *c* in the latter part of the poem, whereby Bacon could be formed, by changing " since " into " and."

These changes, as here explained, are strong circumstantial evidence for the fact that the acrostic in the original poem was deliberately put into it by Bacon, and was not an accidental freak of spelling and composition. In short, it proves the *reality*, in every sense, of this form of acrostic.

Further proof of its reality is furnished by the following examples, found in the opening stanza of *Venus and Adonis*. The great point here is the multiplicity of acrostics in one short stanza of six lines only. Such an accumulation of acrostics cannot reasonably be ascribed to mere coincidence.

The acrostics found in this stanza are, according to Alfred Mudie.[1]

(1) Verulam, Verulam ;
(2) Saint Albans, Saint Albans.
(3) Francis Saint Albans.
(4) Bacon, Bacon
(5) Francis Bacon

I must protest however that the last two are not found in the *original* text, as printed in 1609, for " suitor " is there spelled " suter," so that it does not yield the *o* of Bacon. It is also said that the first stanza of *Lucrece* has the acrostics " Francis Bacon " and " Bacon-Bacon." I cannot verify this, not being in possession of the original edition of 1594. But I hope by the foregoing remark to have impressed upon the Baconian student the absolute necessity of going back to the original editions if one wants to safeguard himself against unwarranted assertions which can only do harm to the Baconian cause.

[1] As quoted by Dawbarn in *Oxford and the Folio Plays*, 1938, p. 31-38. I do not know Mr. Mudie's article. The other examples I have found myself.

Instead of the two false acrostics of Bacon, Bacon and Francis Bacon, I have myself found three others, namely (4) Francis Tidder, (5) Bacon, Tidder, (6) Tidder three times repeated.

Examples of 1, 2 and 6 are given below, the others I leave the reader to work out for himself.

Even as the sunne with purple-colourd face
Had tane his *la*st leave of the weeping *m*orne,
Rose-cheekt Adonis hied him to the chace,
Hunting he lov'd, but love he laught to sco*r*ne ;
    Sick-tho*u*ghted Venus makes amaine unto him,
    And *l*ike *a* bold fac'd suter ginnes to woo hi*m*.

Even a*s* the sunne with purple-colourd f*a*ce,
Had tane h*i*s last leave of the weepin*g* morne,
Rose-cheek*t A*donis hied him to the chace,
Hunting he *l*ov'd, *b*ut love be *la*ught to sco*r*ne :
    Sick-thoughted Venus m*a*kes ama*i*ne un*t*o him,
    A*n*d *l*ike a *b*old *fa*c'd suter gin*n*es to woo him.

Even as *t*he sunne w*i*th purple-colour*d* face,
Ha*d* tan*e* his last leave of the weeping m*o*rne,
Rose-cheek*t* Adon*i*s hie*d* him to the chace,
Hunting he lov'*d* but lov*e* he laught to sco*r*ne :
    Sick-*t*houghted Venus makes ama*i*ne unto him,
    An*d* like a bol*d* fac'd sut*er* ginnes to woo him.

There is another stanza of *Venus and Adonis* (vs. 1105-10), which, besides hiding the acrostic Francis Bacon, has also the singular feature of bearing in its first line the signature Francis Boare, as follows :

But this *f*oule, *g*rim, *an*d u*r*chin-*s*nowted *Boare*

At least I cannot persuade myself that Bacon did not intentionally heap all these adjectives together, so as not only to denote the Boar but also himself by spelling his Christian name. The whole stanza reads :

> But this *foule*, *grim*, *and* urchin-snowted *Boare*,
> Whose downeward eye still looketh for a grave :
> Ne're saw the beautious liverie that he wore,
> Witnesse the intertaiment that he gave.
>> If he did see his face, why then I know.
>> He thought to kisse him, *and* hath kild him so.

Similarly I cannot get rid of the thought that in the stanza (vs. 883-888) bearing the threefold symbol of his royal descent, lion, bear and boar—he has still in other ways revealed his right to sit on the throne, namely by the acrostic signature of Francis First, and by giving in the last line a picture of how everybody—those dogs !—would vie to be the first to fawn upon him if there he really sat :

They all straine curt'sie who shall cope him first. [1]

The last word also emphasizes and as it were ratifies by his royal word that the reading of the acrostic is right, as follows :

> *For* now she knowes it is no gentle ch*a*se,
> But the blu*n*t boare, rough beare, or lyon proud,
> Be*c*ause the cr*i*e remaineth in one place,
> Where fearfully the dog*s* exclaime aloud,
>> *F*inding their enemie to be *s*o curs*t*,
>> *They all straine curt'sie who shall cope him first.*

I expected to find an acrostic too in the stanza (1111-1116) where we found the Boarspear, but I have failed to extract one. Perhaps for once Bacon thought that the name Boare-speare, together with the swine mentioned in the last line but one, was already as much of the Boar and his kindred in one stanza as was consistent with

---

[1] To cope = to encounter, to meet.

prudence and safety from detection. So that others, however, may
have a try at it, I here reproduce the stanza in its original spelling.

> Tis true, tis true, thus was Adonis slaine,
> He ran vpon the Boare with his sharpe speare,
> Who did not whet his teeth at him againe,
> But by a kisse thought to persuade him there.
> > And nousling in his flanke the louing swine,
> > Sheath'd vnaware the tuske in his soft groine.

I was more fortunate with the stanza from Spenser's *Fairie Queene*
(II III 29), which also as we have seen had the name Bore-speare. It
hides the acrostic Bacon, Verulam, as follows :

> And in her hand a sharpe *b*ore-spe*a*re she held,
> And at her ba*c*ke a bow a*n*d qui*ue*r gay.
> St*u*ft with stee*l*e-he*a*ded darts, wherewith she queld
> The salvage beastes in her victorious play,
> Knit with a golden bauldricke, which forelay
> Athwart her snowy brest, and did diuide
> Her daintie paps ; which like young fruit in *M*ay
> Now little gan to swell, and being tide,
> Through her thin weed their places only signifide.

Other examples in the *Fairie Queene* are the following. In 1590
the first three Books appeared, followed in 1596 by Books IV-VI, together with a reprint of Books I-III. Taking the text of the later edition
(I have no means of getting at the first edition), the first stanza of
Book I yields the acrostic *Francis Bacon*, and the first stanza of Book IV
the triple acrostic : *Francis Bacon, Bacon* ; *Francis Bacon, Verulam*, and
Tidder, Tidder, Tidder.

Book I

> Lo I the man, whose Muse whilome did maske,
> As time her taught, in lowly Shepheards weeds,

Am now enforst a far unfitter taske,
For trumpets sterne to chaunge mine Oaten reeds,
And sing of Knights and Ladies gentle deeds ;
Whose prayses having slept in silence long,
Me, all too meane, the sacred Muse areeds
To blazon broad emongst her learned throng :
Fierce warres and faithful loues shall moralize my song.

Book IV

The rugged forhead that with graue foresight
Welds kingdomes causes, and affaires of state,
My looser rimes (I wote) doth sharply wite,
For praising loue, as I haue done of late,
And magnifying louers deare debate ;
By which fraile youth is oft to follie led,
Through false allurement of that pleasing baite,
That better were in vertues discipled,
Then with vaine poemes weeds to have their fancies fed.

The rugged forhead that with graue foresight
Welds kingdomes causes, and affaires of state,
My looser rimes (I wote) doth sharply wite,
For praising loue, as I haue done of late,
And magnifying louers deare debate ;
By which fraile youth is oft to follie led,
Through false allurement of that pleasing baite,
That better were in vertues discipled,
Then with vaine poemes weeds to have their fancies fed.

But we have not yet finished with *Venus and Adonis*. Indeed this long poem appears to be a storehouse of acrostic signatures. The stanza for example in which the word Boare occurs for the first time (vs. 409-414) gives Tidder twice repeated, and Bacon, Tidder ; the stanza with the second Boare (vs. 583-588) gives Bacon-Bacon ; the

35

one with the fourth Boare (vs. 613-618) gives St. Albans, Verulam, etc. etc.

After this long interlude as a necessary preparation, we will now at last take up the real *Envoy* to *Love's Labour's Lost*, that is the Spring-Winter, or the Cuckoo-Owl song, at the end of the Play.   I reproduce the scene as found on page 144 of the Folio.[1]

Brag.   Holla, Approach.

Enter all.

This side is *Hiems*, Winter.
This *Ver*, the Spring : the one maintained by the Owle,
Th' other by the Cuckow.
Ver, begin.

The Song.

When Dasies pied, and *V*iolets blew,
And Ladie-smockes all siluer white,
And *C*uckow-buds of ye*l*low hew :
Do p*a*int the *M*edowes with delight.
The Cuckow then on e*u*erie tree,
Mockes married men, for th*u*s sings he,
Cuckow.
Cuckow, Cuckow : O word of feare,
Unp*le*a*sing* to a *m*arried eare.

When Shepheards pipe on Oaten strawes,
And merrie Larkes are Ploughmens clockes :
When Turtles tread, and Rookes and Dawes,
And Maidens bleach their summer smockes :
The Cuckow then on e*u*erie tree
Mockes married men ; for th*u*s sings he,

---

[1] The Quarto-edition of the songs, only slightly differing from the Folio, gives the same acrostics which shows that Bacon had already constructed it in 1598.

Cuckow.
Cuckow, Cuckow : O word of feare.
Unpleasing to a married eare.

Winter.

When Isicles hang by the wall,
And *Dicke* the Shepheard blowes his naile ;
And *Tom* beares *Logges* into the hall,
And Milke comes frozen home in paile :
When blood is nipt, and waies be fowle,
Then nightly sings the staring Owle
Tu-whit to-who.

  A merrie note,
  While greasie Ione doth keele the pot.

When all aloud the winde doth blow,
*An*d coffing drownes the Parsons saw :
And birds sit brooding in the snow,
*A*nd Marrians nose lookes red and raw :
When roasted Crabs hisse in the bowle,
Then nightly sings the staring Owle
Tu-whit to who :

  A merrie note,
  While greasie Ione doth keele the pot.

Brag. The Words of Murcurie,
  Are harsh after the songs of Apollo :
  You that way ; we this way.   *Exeunt omnes*

The result is, as said, three times Verulam, echoed by three times
Saint Albans.[1]

 [1] I owe the knowledge of this acrostic to a pamphlet read by me some fifteen years ago.
I cannot now recollect either the title or the author's name. The connection laid between the
song and the Third Act, as well as all the other remarks, are however of my own discovery, at
least so far as I am consciously aware,

A remarkable feature of this double song is that in both editions known, the Quarto and the Folio, the second and third lines have been wrongly made to exchange places. The rhyme shows that the sequence in which they are printed above, as in fact in all modern editions, is the true order. The change of place in the older editions was undoubtedly a deliberate subterfuge to avoid easy detection of the three times repeated name of Verulam.

I do not know of a more convincing acrostic than these thrice repeated two names.

We must now return to the Plantain-scene. As an example of an Envoy or solution following a riddle, enigma, or Moral, the Braggart gives the following two couplets :

Moral

The Fox, the Ape and the Humble-Bee,
Were still at oddes being but three.

Lenvoy
Until the Goose came out of doore,
And staied the oddes by adding foure.

This seems a quaint example of a riddle and its solution. For, the first part seems altogether clear and not to need any explanation. The Fox, the Ape, and the Bee, being three, are naturally at odds. When the Goose adds itself to their number, the odds would indeed be stayed, by being made even, but not by *adding* four, but by adding one and so *making* four. If four were *added*, their number would be seven, and the odds would still be odds. So that it seems that the second part or *Lenvoy*, instead of solving any difficulty, puts one rather. What a curious " mistake " to substitute " adding " for " making." Such bad arithmetic persuaded me that I had to look deeper for a solution.

It is further stated that the second couplet is a " fat Goose " or a " fat Lenvoy " (in the scene, the Goose is expressly identified with the Envoy), or let us say a fat riddle. Surely this fatness must have to do

with the number.   The fat Goose must at least equal the three—Fox,
Ape and Bee—of the " Moral," and to be a real " bargain " must
even exceed it at least by one, and thus be four.   This equalling or
even exceeding a given number (here three) is the second meaning of
" staying the odds."   Making an odd number even was as we have
seen the first meaning.   The question therefore is whether we can
indeed in any way exceed the number three.

Now the first part of the Cuckoo-Owl song yielded three Verulams,
and so did the last part three Saint Albans.   That is, we have indeed
stayed the odds in the sense of making them even, by adding three to
three.   But cannot the latter half also be made to yield a really " fat
Goose " by " adding four ? "   In fact it can, as the following four
St. Albans show.

Winter

When Isicles hang by the wall.
And Dicke the Sphepheard blowes his naile ;
And Tom beares Logges into the hall,
And Milke comes frozen home in paile :
When blood is nipt, and waies be fowle,
Then nightly sings the staring Owle
Tu-whit to-who.
    A merrie note,
    While greasie lone doth keele the pot.

When all aloud the winde doth blow,
And coffing drownes the Parsons saw :
And birds sit brooding in the snow,
And Marrians nose lookes red and raw :
When roasted Crabs hisse in the bowle,
Then nightly sings the staring Owle
Tu-whit to who :
    A merrie note,
    While greasie loan doth keele the pot.

Finally we must take up yet another sentence from the Plantain scene of the Third Act. It is Costard's exclamation : " Marry me to one Francis." We have already considered it in another sense, but here we might do it in the sense of " coupling " the names of Francis and Costard, which we ought to do if Costard really stands for Bacon as we have sometimes assumed. It is again the Owl or Winter song which gives us the acrostic : Francis Costard, while the Cuckoo or Spring song yields us Francis Costard, Costard. The whole song gives us nine times Costard, five times repeated in the first half, four in the second half. The first song also gives Francis Verulam. I leave it again to the reader to work this out for himself.

But enough of this. I think that the foregoing must needs have convinced the reader of the reality of this particular form of acrostic. Though I realize that a certain measure of chance must be allowed for also. I have found for example that about 20 per cent of the stanzas of Venus and Adonis yield the name of Tidder, once or more times repeated. This problem of chance and probability, as involved in this form of acrostic, should be taken up by a good mathematician, so as to settle the doubts which inevitably must arise in this connection. But even if we discard a certain percentage of our findings, there still remains enough, I think, to see at the back of it a mind at work who planned it all. Especially is this the case when the acrostics are found in conspicuous places, like the opening stanzas of longer poems, or of series of poems, and in such profusion that they at first indeed stagger the decipherer, or when they are accompanied by other conspicuous circumstances, as allusions, cross references as it were from and to other places of the text. In all these respects the Envoy to Love's Labour's Lost crowns all other instances.

There is still one objection, which we must meet. Francis Bacon was created Baron Verulam on the 12th of July 1618, and Viscount Saint Albans on the 27th of January 1621. How then came those names to appear as acrostics in poems which were published long before those dates? It shows how dearly Bacon was attached to the country, and the home, where he grew up, and passed the happiest period of his life—the golden years of early youth till his departure for France in his sixteenth year. That home, Gorhambury, near the old Roman establishment of Verulamium, on the outskirts of the modern town of Saint Albans, carried with it the sweetest memories. When later after the death of his brother Anthony it came into his own hands he lavished upon it all the wealth of his heart and brain and purse, to make the old manor house into a palatial mansion and the grounds into the most luxurious gardens in all England perhaps. From the old Roman remains of Verulam, still to be found there, he may have conceived his first love for and obtained his first knowledge of Roman antiquities and history, Roman culture and literature, so conspicuous both in his Baconian as in his Shakespearean works. In the same way no doubt the history of modern Saint Albans will have given him his first taste gradually growing into a deep love for English history and culture, for the English soil and people, equally prominent in all his works. The country around those places, the land, the woods, the meadows, the streams and streamlets, the trees and plants and flowers, the rustics, men and women, the whole of nature in short, how it has nurtured and fed his innate thirst for beauty, and pure nature, and ideal life. All the intimate descriptions of English lanscape and country life, which Shakespearean critics place in Warwickshire along the Avon, have in truth, I am convinced, the land around Verulam-Saint Albans for their real nursing-ground. Is it a wonder that those names became so dear to him, that from an early date he chose them for his secret pseudonyms and signatures. He had need of other names beside his own to avoid detection by a too frequently repeated use of his Bacon name. I am indeed of opinion that the names in the acrostics are not derived from his Baronial and Viscountial titles, but on the contrary these titles from the earlier pen names. When in 1618 and 1621 he was raised to the higher ranks of the nobility the choice of his titles as such fell naturally upon Verulam and Saint Albans, fixed in his mind and cherished for the whole of his earlier life ; Verulam first, Saint Albans later, Verulam as the town founded by the Romans when the world was still young, and therefore properly assigned to the song of Ver or Spring ; Saint Albans founded by later generations of the English, when the world had grown older, and therefore allotted to the song of Hiems or winter.

This finishes our contribution towards the elucidation of the scene from the Third Act of *Love's Labour's Lost*. It has not been much, I fear, still it has cleared up a few obscure points. Many others remain. I cannot get rid of the idea, for example, that the word " remuneration " does also bear a hidden message. Its repetition seven times in this scene and in the first few lines after Berowne enters, besides the special reference to it in the Fifth Act, make it fairly certain that there is something important involved in it. But unfortunately I have not been able to solve the riddle. May another be more intelligent and fortunate.

In Chapter 7 we have adduced proofs, by means of Bacon's secret symbolic signatures, of his authorship of *The Two Noble Kinsmen* and *The Anatomy of Melancholy*. We shall here do the same, by means of his anagrammatic cipher.

To begin with *The Two Noble Kinsmen*, this play is closed by an epilogue of 18 lines, which contains the acrostic " Francis Bacon " twice repeated, as shown below.

Epilogue

I would now aske ye how ye like the Play,
But, as it is with Schoole Boyes, cannot say,
I am cruell *fea*refull : p*ra*y, yet stay a while,
A*n*d let me looke upon ye : No man smile ?
Then it goes hard, I see ; He that has
Lov'd a yong hansome wench, then, show h*is* face—
Tis strange if none *b*e heere—*a*nd if he will
Against his *Con*science, let him hisse, and kill
Our Market : Tis in vaine, I see, to stay yee ;
Have at the worst can come, then ! Now what say ye ?
And yet mistake me not : I am not bold ;
We have no such cause. I*f* the tale we have told
(Fo*r* tis no other) *an*y way *c*ontent ye

(For to that honest purpose *it* was ment ye)
We have our end ; and ye shall have ere long,
I dare say, many a *b*etter, to prolong
Your old loves to us ; we, *a*nd all our might
Rest at your service.   Gentlemen, good *n*ight.

As to Burton's *Anatomy*, the frontispiece of the book consists of twelve squares in four horizontal rows of three squares each, of which the middle one of the second and fourth row are taken up by the title of the book, and the imprint of the publisher.   The other ten squares contain nine emblematic pictures, and a portrait of the author in the middle square of the second row from the bottom.   A poem, under the heading " The Argument of the Frontispiece," explains the contents of the ten squares.   The 10th stanza runs thus :

Now last of all to *f*ill a place,
P*r*esented is the *A*uthor's face ;
A*n*d in that habit which he wears,
 H*is* Image to the world appears.
His mind no art can well express,
That *b*y his writings you m*a*y guess.
It was not pride, nor yet vain glory,
 (Though others do it commo*n*ly)

Made him do this : *if* you must know,
The P*r*inter would needs h*a*ve it so,
The*n* do not frown or scoff at *i*t,
Deride not, nor detract a whit.
For *s*urely as thou dost *b*y him,
He will do the s*a*me again.
Then look upon't, behold and see,
As thou lik'st it, so it likes thee.
And I for it will stand in view,
 Thine to comma*n*d, Reader, Adieu !

36

In the edition of R.A. Shilleto the stanza is in a curious way broken up, in the middle of a sentence, in two stanzas, as printed above. I do not know if the same is the case in the original. If so, then it lends added strength to the anagram " Francis Bacon," found once in each couplet, for it would conclusively prove that there is no question of accident but that the stanza was intentionally so constructed, in the wording as well as in the printing.[1]

In other ways also the stanza makes a curious impression. It is strongly reminiscent of Ben Jonson's dedicatory poem to the Shakespeare Folio, as the reader may see himself from the following reproduction of it.

> To the Reader.
> This Figure, that thou here seest put,
>   It was for gentle Shakespeare cut ;
> Wherein the Graver had a strife
>   With Nature, to out-doo the life :
> O, could he but have drawne his wt
>   As well in brasse, as he hath hit
> His face, the Print wound then surpasse
>   All, that was ever writ in brasse.
> But, since he cannot, Reader, looke
>   Not on his Picture, but his Booke.
>   B.I.

The same mysterious ambiguity of language, the same vague allussions, the same imagery, and the same general subject. To me there is no doubt that the real author of these poems was neither Ben Jonson nor Robert Burton, but Francis Bacon.

Analysis of Jonson's poem. The obvious meaning of the second line is of course that the figure was cut " for," that is to represent Shakespeare the actor. But it may also be meant for a likeness of Shakespeare-Bacon the author. The word " for " may further mean that the figure was cut as ordered for or by the author Shakespeare-Bacon,

---

[1] Supposing of course that Shilleto's edition has preserved the old spelling

without regard to any likeness. There is no place for the actor
in this last reading, for he had been dead seven years. In the
last two senses the implied meaning is then that the picture was not
meant to represent actually, that is to say in a recognizable way, either
the actor or the author, so that the words " out-doo " in the fourth
line cannot mean anything else but " kill " the life, or wipe out the
likeness. Yet in this wiping out the graver had a strife with nature,
which can only mean that he had to wipe out only so much that the
author would not be easily recognized, but had also to leave so much
that once the secret is guessed, the likeness could still be proved.
And it is this that the Baconians claim to have proven, namely
that line by line the Droeshout picture of Shakespeare and the
Simon Passe painting of Bacon, are " anatomically identical," and
therefore represent one and the same face and head, only with
different hair, moustache, beard, hat and dress.[1] The word " hit " can
in this connection only mean " hid," but on this see also Addenda (5).

   Analysis of Burton's poem. In the second line, we have the same
ambiguity as in the former poem. " The Author's face " in the
Baconian sense can only mean " Bacon's face " of course. And the
third and fourth lines then tell us that it is clothed or veiled—just as in
the Jonson poem the likeness is out-done—in " that habit which he
wears," that is of course the habit or " weed " (Sonnet 16) of Burton,
and so his " Image " appears to the world, but not the true man or
author. Then again, as in the Shakespeare poem, " O could he but
have drawn his wit," we are told that " his mind no art can well express," and therefore it is better to guess his mind by his writings, or,
as Jonson expressed it, not to look on his picture but his book. The
words quoted about it not being possible to express or draw his mind
or wit in a picture are further but an echo of those painted by Hilliard
around the miniature of Francis Bacon at the age of seventeen—*Si
tabula daretur digna, animum mallem*, if one could but paint his mind ! [2]
Then the tenth line of Burton's poem tells us another important

---

[1] William Stone Booth, as quoted by Baxter, p. 250. See the superimposed photographs
there given.

                              [2] Sp VIII 7.

fact. Not the ostensible author Burton wanted his portrait to appear, but the real author, or editor, or " Printer would needs have it so," undoubtedly to give him the opportunity for this revealing stanza. The poem further warns us not " to deride nor detract a whit," for the author will repay us in the same coin for our ignorance in not seeing through the hoax. " As thou lik'st it, so it likes thee," that is as thou hast come to better like it (the picture) by piercing through the veil of the mystery, so it (the author) will like thee the better for thy perspicacity. And then " I (the author) for it (the picture) will stand in (thy) view, thine to command, Reader, adieu ! " Without our explanation these last two lines would have no sense at all.

Another curiosity is how these two stanzas both together come to be preceded by the numeral 10, in Roman script X, or the letter X, for the Unknown Quantity, here the Unknown Author. The whole poem is a perfect piece of symmetry,[1] consisting of ten stanzas of eight verses each, headed by a distich, and closed by a distich. The numbering begins with the first of the eight-lined stanzas, and continues regularly up to and including the seventh, but the eighth stanza bears the numbers eight and nine, and the ninth stanza the number 10, while the tenth stanza is left without number. All this shows a peculiar design, which contributes greatly to the probability, if not certainty, of the hidden meaning we have read in the words of the last stanza. In Shilleto's edition the final distich is not marked off from the tenth stanza by larger spacing. I do not know what the old editions do. But as the number 10 here stands printed, it says to us as it were—take the last two stanzas and the distich together, for thus they refer to Me, X, the Great Unknown, Francis Bacon.

Burton's famous book is indeed one of the " curiosities of literature," and for Baconians of the greatest importance. It has not been sufficiently explored yet. It is, I think, full of allusions to its real author. The very first page, nay the very opening sentences, are a treasure-house of hints, half veiling, half revealing the truth, like a true

---

[1] It is printed in full in Addenda (7).

oracle or a Sphynxian riddle.   I here subjoin a few phrases from the
first three pages to whet my readers' appetites :

   '' Gentle Reader, I presume thou wilt be very inquisitive to know
what antick or *personate actor* [1] this is, that so insolently intrudes upon
this common theatre to the world's view, *arrogating another man's
name* . . . as that Egyptian, when a curious fellow would needs know
what he had in his basket [answered :] *It was therefore covered, because
he should not know what was in it* . . . Suppose *the Man in the Moon,*
or whom thou wilt to be the Author . . . There be some other circumstances for which *I have masked myself* under this visard, and *some
peculiar respects which I cannot so well express.*   [Nothing in Burton's
life seems to point to the necessity to write such a book under an
assumed name.]   A man of *an excellent wit*, profound conceit ; and to
attain knowledge the better *in his younger years, he travelled* to Egypt
and Athens [read : France and Paris], to confer with learned men,
admired of some, despised of others.   After a wandering life he settled
at Abdera [London], a town in Thrace [England], and was sent for
thither to become *their law-maker* as some will, or as others, *he was
there bred and born.*   Howsoever it was there he lived at last [after
Bacon's fall] in a garden in the suburbs, *wholly betaking himself to his
studies* and private life.''

   It is generally supposed that in the *Proem* to his *Interpretation of
Nature* is found the only fragment of autobiography Bacon ever left [2]
—and what a splendid fragment !—but such pieces as the above, and
many others in other works, as shown abundantly in the present book
reveal to Baconians at least a fairly full picture of their Master.

---

[1] All italics are mine. See also *ante*, p. 231.   [2] Sp III 518, X 84.

10. The Poet and God's Word

1. THE ENGLISH BIBLE

VEN a greater boon probably than Shakespeare's Works Bacon has bestowed upon the English speaking world by his final supervision of the translation of the Bible. But has he indeed had anything to do with the English Bible? Some Baconians will answer the question in the affirmative, and to these I myself belong. The point should be well understood. The problem is essentially different from that of Bacon's authorship of Shakespeare's or Spenser's works. There is in the case of the Bible no question of his being the original author, of course; nor of his being either the sole or even one of the original translators; nor of his being one of the known revisers or reviewers of the work of the translators. If in fact he had a hand in the Authorized Version of 1611, it is only as the unknown *final reviser* of the translation made and already revised by others, as well as the *supervisor* of the printing of at least one page of the first black-letter edition. The former point would be carried together with the latter, if this could be proved. That, then, is what we are going to do.

We shall base our observations on the facsimile edition in a slightly reduced size of the 1611 Bible, printed at the Oxford University Press on the occasion of the tercentenary of its first publication. The new edition is furnished with a useful bibliographical introduction by A. W. Pollard, and with more than sixty illustrative historical documents. Because of the photographic reproduction of the old volume, page for page, we are sure of having the text before us, just as Bacon saw it through the press, without the obliteration by any later hand of any hidden or secret mark of his workmanship.

Before the Authorized Version came into existence, there had been several complete and incomplete English translations of the Bible in circulation. Among these are *Tyndale's New Testament* of 1535, the first volume of scripture printed in England ; *Coverdale's Bible* of the same year, the first of all printed English Bibles, translated from the German and Latin ; *Matthew's Bible* of 1539, a compilation of Tyndale's and Coverdale's rendering ; the *Great Bible* of the same year, a revision based on Matthew's Bible, the first " authorized version ; " the *Genevan Bible* of 1560, in the Old Testament an independent revision of the Great Bible, the New Testament consisting of a revision of Tyndale's latest text ; the *Bishops' Bible* of 1568, also a revision of the Great Bible. Forty-three years later this was followed by *the* " Authorized Version," itself professedly but a revision of the last of the old Bibles.

Among all the previous translators and revisers, the debt of the 1611 Bible is greatest to William Tyndale. In this respect it has been said that his " work fixed once for all the style and tone of the English Bible, and supplied not merely the basis of all subsequent Protestant renderings of the books (with unimportant exceptions) on which he laboured, but their very substance and body, so that those subsequent versions must be looked upon as revisions of his, not as independent translations " (Pollard). Another authority asserts that " the history of our English Bible begins with the work of William Tyndale, to whom it has been allowed, more than to any other man, to give its characteristic shape to the English Bible. Tyndale's translation may be described as a truly noble work. Surely no higher praise can be accorded to it than that it should have been taken as a basis by the translators of the

Authorized Version, and thus have lived on through the centuries up to the present day " (Westcott).

Second in importance is Miles Coverdale.   Compared with William Tyndale, he was " a man of far less scholarship, but of an equally happy style " (Pollard).   He had " a certain delicacy and happy ease in his rendering of the Biblical text, to which we owe not a few of the beautiful expressions of our present Bible " (Westcott).

These few historical and critical observations are absolutely necessary to understand the scope of our indebtedness to Bacon, if he indeed had anything to do with the 1611 Bible.   His case was much like Miles Coverdale's ; he could not compete in mere philological and theological erudition with William Tyndale or many of the forty-seven translators appointed by King James the First ; but in " delicacy and happy ease " of handling the English language, nay, in poetic diction, mastery of style, stately rhythm of movement, as well as in depth of thought, intensity of feeling, and enthusiastic religious aspiration, there was not a single one of them, Tyndale and Coverdale not excluded, who was not left standing in the valley, while Bacon was climbing the solitary peaks of the highest Wisdom and Art.   It cannot be denied that the 1611 Bible, leaving its scholarship aside, is a unique work of the highest art, only equalled, or perhaps even surpassed, in this respect, by Shakespeare's wonderful Plays.   It is this fact which makes me inclined to accept the hypothesis that Bacon was its final reviser.

In order to understand how far Bacon's part in this revision went we must now consider the principal facts regarding the origins of the " Authorized Version."   The forty-seven translators were divided into six " companies," grouped around the principal centres of ecclesiastical authority and secular learning, two being of Westminster, two of Cambridge, and two of Oxford, and each containing from seven to ten members.   To each of the companies a certain number of the books of the Bible were apportioned, and further divided among the individual scholars for translation.   The whole undertaking occupied seven years from start to finish, of which about half was expended upon preliminary discussions and private research, and the latter half was

37

taken up by the actual work of translation and preparation for the press. The whole work of translation being finished, three copies of the whole Bible were sent from Cambridge, Oxford and Westminster to London. " A new choice was made of six [read twelve] in all, two out of each company, to review the whole work, and extract one out of all three to be committed to the press. For the dispatch of which business they went daily to Stationers' Hall, and in three quarters of a year finished their task " (Walker). From another source we learn that Bilson, Bishop of Winchester, and Miles Smith, afterwards Bishop of Gloucester, " after all things had been maturely weighed and examined, put the finishing touch to this version."

In King James's outline or programme of the work, he had cleverly sketched out the proceedings in such a way that the translation should in the first place be made by " the best learned in both Universities, after them to be reviewed by the Bishops and the chief learned of the Church, from them to be presented to the Privy Council, and lastly to be ratified by his royal authority." Now the most curious part of the whole story is that, up to and including the so-called final revision by the Bishops of Winchester and Gloucester, the general course of events is perfectly clear, and has been historically established ; but as soon as the work has left the hands of the Church dignitaries, all becomes a mystery.

Neither of the Privy Council's part in the matter, nor of the King's final approbation, has there been found any historical trace, except perhaps for the latter the words " Appointed to be read in Churches " on the title-page, and the phrase " Authorized Version " by which the Bible is generally known. And yet, it is inconceivable that the last part of the King's programme should have been entirely disregarded. There seems no other explanation left than that, once out of the hands of the Bishops, they lost all control over the work. The records cited up to now are all from ecclesiastical sources. At this point they cease to flow, till the Bible appears as a finished product from the press of one " Robert Barker, Printer to the King's Most Excellent Majesty," as he is called on the title-page.

It is during the final process, then, that Bacon may very well have come upon the stage, and played his part, not to the great public, but to the King's private audience. He was at the time quickly rising in the royal favour. Whatever others may say or think of King James's intellectual endowments, he prided *himself* on being somewhat of a theologian and an author, and he undoubtedly recognized in Bacon a man of literary genius. If we have to admit that King James's propensities would not allow him to leave the Bible, as presented to him by the Bishops, severely alone, but would force him to let his critical eye run over the whole version, the next step is to admit that, outside the pale of ecclesiastical circles, there stood no man nearer to his court-circle and better equipped to advise him and do the " final revision " for him than his Solicitor-General of four years' standing, who had acquired national fame as a Master of English, and world fame as a philosopher by his *Essays* (first edition, 1597) the *Advancement of Learning* (1605), and the *Wisdom of the Ancients* (Latin, 1609).

This really " final revision " must have been pretty thorough, but entirely restricted to emendations of a purely literary character. Bacon's reverence for the " Word of God " was as deep and sincere as that of any of the official translators. He would not have touched the scholarly rendering except in so far as a happier word or phrase, or a purer synonym suggested itself, as a change in style, a stronger or a statelier rhythm would improve the literary quality to his sensitive ear. The high perfection the " Authorized Version " has attained as a work of literary art, and the unity it exhibits as such throughout the whole bulky volume, can never be satisfactorily explained without the hypothesis of such a " final revision " by *one single Master-mind*.

The way in which the translation had been made, by six companies and forty-seven individual translators, of whom the great majority must have possessed only mediocre literary and poetical talents, is all against the art and unity shown by the printed Bible and proven through the following centuries. Even the labour of the twelve reviewers and the two so-called final revisers, limited as they were by profession and inclination to philological and theological considerations, could not elevate the text from mediocrity to a work of genius. How the labour of translation and revision went on, John Selden, a near contemporary, has described in his *Table Talk*. "The translators in King James's time took an excellent way." Indeed, for the practical, limited purpose they had in mind, namely, to obtain a text as faithfully literal to the original as possible, a better course could not have been chosen. "That part of the Bible was given to him who was most excellent in such a tongue (as the Apocrypha to Andrew Downs) and then they met together, and one read the translation, the rest holding in their hands some Bible, either of the learned tongues, or French, Spanish, Italian, etc. If they found any fault they spoke ; if not he read on."

But the art and unity of the 1611 Bible have to be explained somehow. We may not in these days leave it unexplained as an insoluble mystery or as a providential miracle, or again leave the question open as does the following historian. "Whether the wonderful felicity of phrasing should be attributed to the dexterity with which, after meanings had been settled, and the important words in each passage chosen, either the board of twelve or the two final revisers put their touches to the work, or whether, as seems more likely, the rhythm, first called into being by Tyndale and Coverdale, re-asserted itself, after every change, only gathering strength and melody [of itself, or by miracle ?] from the increasing richness of the language, none can tell. All that is certain is that the rhythm and the strength and the melody are there " (Pollard).

A nation's language does not grow of itself ; only her men of genius make it grow. A book cannot gain in rhythm, strength and melody of itself, a literary genius must bring that about. Bacon-Shakespeare was such a genius, the true creator of modern English. He was the only one of his time, great enough in every sense, to have produced what we have before us in the Authorized Version. Tyndale's and Coverdale's English may have been all that could be desired or expected of their time, but admittedly it cuts a poor figure when laid alongside the Authorized Version. And even if we allowed it to have had an all-powerful influence over the new version so as to give it that high quality of art which it possesses, the unity of the whole work as such has not yet been accounted for.

We have the example of the *Bishops' Bible*. The method of its production was virtually the same as that of the 1611 Bible. The initiative for it was taken by Archbishop Parker, who wished to improve on the authorized *Great Bible*, and in this way to challenge the ever-growing popularity of the Calvinistic *Genevan Bible*. The method followed was " by sorting out the whole Bible into parcels and distributing these parcels to able bishops and other learned men, to peruse and collate each the book or books allotted to them." And just as the later translators of the Authorized Version declared their intentional dependence on previous versions in the words, " truly we never thought from the beginning, that we should need to make a new translation, nor yet to make of a bad one a good one, but to make a good one [*i.e.*, the *Bishops' Bible*] better, or out of many good ones, one principal good one, not justly to be excepted against ; that hath been our endeavour, that our mark ; " so also the translators of the *Bishops' Bible* took as one of their rules, " to follow the common English translation [*i.e.*, the *Great Bible*] used in the churches, and not to recede from it, but where it varieth manifestly from the Hebrew or Greek original."

Yet what was the result ? Here is the criticism delivered on it by a modern scholar : " The detached and piecemeal way in which the revision had been carried out naturally caused certain inequalities in the execution of the work. The different parts of the Bible vary considerably in merit, the alterations in the New Testament, for instance, showing freshness and vigour, whereas most of the changes introduced in the Old Testament have been condemned as arbitrary and at variance with the exact sense of the Hebrew text " (Henson).

The question therefore is, how is it that the *Bishops' Bible* shows such " inequalities " in " merit, freshness and vigour," whereas the

Authorized Version exhibits a marked unity of " strength, rhythm and melody," while both versions were carried out in essentially the same " detached and piecemeal way ? " Again the answer can be no other than that one single Master-mind superintended the " final revision " of the whole Bible of 1611.

In support of the qualities of high art and unity of execution of the Authorized Version, I may conclude by quoting the words of Professor Arthur Quiller-Couch of Cambridge :

" That a large committee of forty-seven, not one of them outside of this performance known for any superlative talent, should have gone steadily through the mass of holy writ, seldom interfering, seldom missing to improve ; that a committee of forty-seven should have captured (or even should have retained and improved) a rhythm so personal, so constant that *our Bible has the voice of one author speaking through its many mouths* : that is a wonder before which I can only stand humble and aghast." [1]

The wonder disappears when the Bacon editorship is accepted.

2. THE NUMBER-PLAY

There now rests the question, are there any proofs for the contention that it was Francis Bacon who was the Master-mind that gave the Authorized Version its rightly admired final shape ; in other words, has Francis Bacon left his finger-prints on the 1611 Bible in token of his handiwork, as he has done on the Shakespeare Works ? Apparently he has ! But there is also a sharp contrast—the scarcity of such marks, one or two only, as discovered so far ; and their limitation to the anagram and clock-ciphers. The explanation I have to offer for this contrast is

[1] Quoted from *Theosophy in Australia*, April 1917, page 4.

·16 Jn ſtead of thy fathers ſhall bee thy children, whom thou mayeſt make princes in all the earth.

17 J will make thy name to bee remembred in all generations: therefore ſhall the people praiſe thee for euer and euer.

PSAL. XLVI.

1 The confidence which the Church hath in God. 8 An exhortation to behold it.

|| Or, of

℃ To the chiefe Muſician || for the ſonnes of Korah, a ſong vpon Alamoth.

G OD is our refuge and ſtrength: a very preſent helpe in trouble.

2 Therfore will not we feare, though the earth be remoued: and though the mountaines be caried into † the midſt of the ſea.

† Hebr. the heart of the ſeas.

3 Though the waters thereof roare, and be troubled, though the mountaines ſhake with the ſwelling thereof. Selah.

4 There is a riuer, the ſtreames wherof ſhall make glad the citie of God: the holy place of the Tabernacles of the moſt High.

5 God is in the midſt of her: ſhe ſhal not be moued; God ſhall helpe her, † and that right early.

† Heb. when the morning appeareth.

6 The heathen raged, the kingdomes were mooued: he vttered his voyce, the earth melted.

7 The LORD of hoſts is with vs, the God of Jacob is † our refuge. Selah.

† Heb. an high place for vs.

8 Come, behold the workes of the LORD, what deſolations hee hath made in the earth.

9 He maketh warres to ceaſe vnto the end of the earth: hee breaketh the bow, and cutteth the ſpeare in ſunder, he burneth the chariot in the fire.

10 Be ſtil, and know that J am God: J will bee exalted among the heathen, J will be exalted in the earth.

11 The LORD of hoſts is with vs; the God of Jacob is our refuge. Selah.

PSAL. XLVII.

The Nations are exhorted cheerefully to entertaine the Kingdome of Chriſt.

[Or, of

℃ To the chiefe muſician, a pſalme || for the ſonnes of Korah.

Clap your hands (all ye people:) ſhoute vi to God with the voyce of triumph:

2 For the LORD moſt high is terribl all the earth.

3 Hee ſhal vs, and the n

4 He ſhal vs, the excell loued. Selah

5 God is LORD wit

6 Sing p ſing praiſes b

7 For G earth, ſing ye ding.

8 God re God ſitteth v lineſſe.

9 || The gathered tog God of Abra earth belong exalted.

PSA

The Ornaments

℃ A ſong, an of Kora

tion, the ioy o Sion, on the tie of the grea

3 God is a refuge.

4 For loe, t they paſſed b

5 They ſt led, they we way.

6 Feare there, and pa uaile.

7 Thou ſhith with an

8 As we ſeene in the c in the citie of bliſh it for eue

9 Wee ha kindneſſe, O Temple.

10 Accordi ſo is thy prai earth: thy rig ouſneſſe.

that, as remarked before, Bacon's reverence for the " Book of God "
was such that it did not permit him to subject its printing—even if he
could have controlled it as absolutely as he did in the case of the Shakespeare Folio of 1623—to the same manipulations as the latter volume.
Furthermore, it was not comparable in any way to the other book as
regards his authorship. His task had only been to give it the " final
touch " of genius. It would therefore suffice if he left only one or two
irrefutable marks on it of his having had a hand in it. And I think with
others that that one signature of his is found in the 46th Psalm, on the
folio-sheet marked by the printers Ddd 3 which is somewhere near the
middle of the volume. In order fully to appreciate the subtleties of the
anagram and clock-ciphers involved in it and incorporated into this one
page—to be exact, in its left-hand column—the following typographical
description from the bibliographical introduction to the tercentenary
edition may serve as a basis :

" The text of the Bible is printed in black-letter with the inserted
words [here printed in italics] in small roman, and roman type is also
used for the summaries at the head of each chapter, for the subject
head-lines at the top of each page, and for the references to parallel
passages in the margin ; the alternative renderings in the margin are in
italics. The text is printed in double columns enclosed within rules, with
ornamental head-pieces, and a few tail-pieces, and capitals at the
beginning of each chapter and psalm."

This description is not quite complete ; a few details are omitted :
(1) the headings of the chapters and psalms are in larger roman
capitals and numerals, (2) the numbering of the verses and of the
summary contents of the chapters and psalms are in arabic numerals,
(3) the musical directions, or the instructions to the musicians at the
beginning of the psalms, and at the end of some verses, which do not
really belong to the " Word of God," are nevertheless printed in black-
letter (in our text they are also italicised), (4) the printer's signature in the
right-hand bottom corner of some of the pages is also in black-letter.

Folio Ddd 3, 1611 Bible

16 In stead of thy fathers shall bee
thy children, whom thou mayest make
princes in all the earth.
17 I will make thy name to bee remembred in all generations : therefore
shall the people praise thee for ever and
ever.

P S A L. XLVI

1 *The confidence which the Church hath in*
  God. 8 An exhortation to behold it,
Lo *the chiefe Musician for the*
  sonnes of Korah, a song upon
  Alamoth.

GOD *is* our refuge and
strength : a very present
helpe in trouble.
2 Therefore **will** not we
feare, though the earth
be removed : and though the mountaines be caried into the midst of the
sea.
3 *Though* the waters thereof roare,
and be troubled, *though* the mountaines
shake with the swelling thereof.   *Selah.*
4 *There is* a river, the streames wherof shall make glad the citie of God : the
holy place of the Tabernacles of the
most High.
5 God *is* in the midst of her : she shal
not be moved ; God shall helpe her,

and that right early.
6 The heathen raged, the kingdomes were " mooved " : he uttered his
voyce, the earth melted.
7 The LORD of hosts *is* with us ;
the God of Jacob *is* our refuge.   *Selah.*
8 Come, behold the workes of the
LORD, what desolations hee hath
made in the earth.
9 He maketh warres to cease unto
the end of the earth : hee breaketh the
bow, and cutteth the **speare** in sunder,
he burneth the chariot in the fire.
10 Be stil, and know that I *am* God :
I will bee exalted among the heathen,
I will be exalted in the earth.
11 The LORD of hosts *is* with us ;
the God of Jacob *is* our refuge. *Selah.*

P S A L. XLVII

The Nations are exhorted cheerefully to enter-
taine the Kingdome of Christ.
Lo the chiefe musician, a psalme for
the sonnes of Korah

 Clap your hands (all ye peo-
ple :) shoute unto God with
the voyce of triumph :
2 For the LORD most

In the above text I have as nearly as possible reprinted in modern
type the left-hand column of the Folio of the 1611 Bible which
particularly concerns us. The only deviation from the original text I
have permitted myself to make is the printing in black type of the three

38

words Will Shake-speare, and the placing of the centre-word " moved " between quotation marks.

More than once I have had occasion to refer to the clock-cipher as to a number-play, and as such it has of course to be played according to certain definite rules, without which any game would end only in chaos or caprice. Now the rules that govern our game in this case are that for the time we take into account only *the black-letter text in its strict sense as the Word of God* ; in other words, that we leave out of count (1) the arabic numerals, (2) the roman and italic type, (3) the ornamental initial capitals, head- and tail-pieces, (4) the musical directions, including the word " selah," and the printer's signature at the bottom of some pages. Having laid down these rules, we proceed with our game.

I. Counting from the top of the column, the *52nd* word is *Will.*

II. Counting from the beginning of the Psalm, the *42nd* word is *Shake.*

III. Counting from the bottom of the column, the *61st* word is *Speare.*

So that we find here, in one of Bacon's " several " anagram-ciphers, the signature of *Will Shake-speare.*

We now turn to the clock-cipher for confirmation, and we find it in the fact that the number-value of

Will = 52

Shake = 42

Speare = 61

That our play has been strictly according to the rules can be easily verified in any ordinary modern Bible, Authorized Version, if one only takes into consideration that the column in the 1611 Bible begins with verse 16 of Psalm 45, and ends with the words of verse 2 of Psalm 47, " For the Lord most." One should further take into account that the roman-letter words in the text of the old edition are italicized in the modern Bibles.   There is also some difference in the spelling, of course. For example, the word " spear " is spelt " speare " in the 1611 Bible.

I do not think that an unbiassed student can deny that it is asking too much of one's credulity to believe that accident or coincidence can have arranged such a threefold confirmation of a rational message by an equally rational mathematical construction.   We have first the rational intimation of the three parts of the name of a famous contemporary Author within the small compass of one Psalm, translated from the Hebrew, consisting of 187 words, or within the still smaller compass of a middle portion of that same Psalm totalling only 133 words.   But besides, we have an absolutely independent mathematical device, which, by the number-values of the three parts of the author's name, gives us the ordinal numbers that exactly define the position of the various parts of the name among the total of 244 words in the whole column. Finally, as if completely to disperse any remaining vestige of doubt whether Francis Bacon is indeed Will Shakespeare, we find that the total number of black-letter words in the Psalm gives us the number-value of

Francis Speare-shaker=187,

while the number of words in the middle portion, spelling Will Shake-speare, gives us the number-value of

Your man Bacon=133

As to the total number of words in the column, which is 244, I can only say that I have not carried out my calculations beyond the number 200, but even so, our play is not yet finished.

As is the case in many games, one may vary the rules according to the needs, sometimes making them stricter, sometimes leaving more freedom.   We will now do the same in our number-play, and make a shift by including in our count the words in small roman type, which form part of the English text, though not of the original Hebrew,

I.   If we now count from the beginning of the Psalm, the *46th* word is *Shake.*

II.   And if we count from the end of the Psalm, the *46th* word is *Speare.*

III.   The third member in this play is furnished by the Psalm itself, which is the *46th* of its number.[1]

One more shift.   The Psalm consists of 201 words, including the roman-letter words.   Dividing it in two halves, counting 100 words from the beginning, and 100 from the end, there is one word left in the middle, which is the word " moved."   Well, let us have it moved, that is removed from the text, or in any case let it—the axis as it were around which our play revolves—not take part itself in our play. Then, the Psalm consisting of twice 100 words, reminds us in the first place of

Francis Bacon=100

In the second place it gives us the number-value of

$$\underbrace{Your\ man}_{100}\ \underbrace{Francis\ Bacon}_{100}=200$$

In the third place, counting 155 words from the beginning of the Psalm, (not counting the word " moved," mind !) we shall have spelt Will-Shake-speare, the number-value of which is

Will Shakespeare=155

In the fourth place, counting 187 words from the end of the Psalm, we shall have spelt Will Shakespeare backwards (speare-Shake-Will), while we have seen that the number-value of

Francis Speare-shaker=187.

[1] I owe these three particulars to the *American Baconiana,* serial number 5, Nov.' 27— Febr.' 28, p. 298.   All the others are of my own finding.

Finally, making our last shift back to our former rule of taking into account only the black-letter words, but still discarding the word " moved," and counting now from Shake to Speare, or backward from Speare to Shake, that is, as it were, connecting up the two halves of the name, we count in all 103 words, while the number-value of

$$Shakespeare = 103$$

It might be objected that such " shifts " are inadmissible as proofs, being mere " tricks " by means of which one can prove all and everything, and thereby prove nothing. The objection cannot be allowed to pass. The opposite is true. The shifts make former proofs doubly proved, if only they are made according to definite rules, derived from the play itself, as in the case of the including or excluding of the roman-letter words, or made plausible by the play, as in the case of the subtle indication implied in the meaning of the middle word of the Psalm.

It is perfectly unreasonable and illogical to ask for double or triple proofs that confirm each other in a cross-wise way, while refusing to allow the player to shift his position so as to meet new requirements. When taking account only of the black-letter words, we have exhausted all possibilities by counting from the top and the bottom, etc., there must of necessity be made a shift by taking into account the roman-letter words, in order to obtain new figures that may bring into play new factors, and thus confirm old data. Such cipher-play is not like a tread-mill, which goes round and round in a deadly monotony about an immovable centre, without getting anywhere, but is essentially a free play with ever-shifting rules and objects, as varied as real life, and as re-creative.

I have said that Bacon's signature is found in one or two places of the 1611 Bible. I am however not so sure of the other cases as I am of this one. The words Will, Shake, and Speare, within the limits of one Chapter or Psalm, are found in two other places of the Old Testament.

Isaiah, II, 3 . . . We *will* walk in his paths . . . 4 . . . And they shall beate their swords into plow-shares, and their *speares* into pruning hookes . . . 19. For feare of the Lord and for the glory of His Majestie ; when hee ariseth to *shake* terribly the earth.

Joel, III, 10. Beate your plowe shares into swords, and your pruning hookes into *speares* . . . 16. The Lord also shall roare out of Zion, and utter his voice from Jerusalem and the heavens and the earth shall *shake* . . . 21. For I *will* [*sic*] cleanse their blood.

I have as yet not been able to find cross-confirmatory proof by other ciphers or devices, that these are indeed intended for signatures of Francis Bacon, except perhaps the following circumstance. We know that one of the means Bacon employed to draw attention to his secret cipher messages, is a so-called misprint. Now there is a very marked one in the book of *Micah*. On the back-side of the sheet, marked by the printer Gggg2, there should be the heading *Micah*, just as there is on the back-side of the preceding sheet marked Gggg, and on the following sheet marked Gggg3. Instead, we find on the back-side of sheet Gggg2 the exceedingly remarkable " misprint " *Joel*.[1]) Why " Joel " of all the books of the Old Testament ? There would have been more reason indeed, if it were really an accidental misprint, to find the immediately preceding or following book cropping up here between two Micahs. But no, it must be Joel, which is separated from Micah by Jonah, Obadiah and Amos. If there is any reasonable explanation for the substitution of Joel for Micah, it is that on the page thus " marked," we find the second half of Shakespeare's name.

Micah (Joel), IV, 3. They shall beate their swords into plow-shares, and their *speares* into pruning hookes.

And in the margin there is the reference to the corresponding text in Joel, as we find in Joel the marginal reference to the corresponding place in Isaiah.

[1] I owe this fact also to the *American Baconiana*, serial number 5, p. 360.

But the second half of Shakespeare's name is not found on the marked page. The false heading therefore must mean simply, " Look in Joel for the full name of Shakespeare," though it remains unexplained why the reference is made to Joel in preference to Psalm 46, where the proofs and counter-proofs are so much more convincing. There is yet another possibility ; the false heading may have been inserted for the purpose of drawing special attention, not only to the false name Joel, but also to the suppressed name *Micah*, the number-value of which is

$$Micah = 33 = Bacon.$$

Micah, however, could not serve the whole purpose, because it provided only half of Shakespeare's name. For this reason the reference, by an extraordinary misprint, to Joel was necessary ; the ordinary reference in the margin conveying nothing of a secret or intended message, of course.

Some are certain to ask why Bacon should not have manipulated the texts of Joel and Isaiah in the same way as he has apparently done that of Psalm 46, so as to leave us in the other two books also a clear signature or mark of his handiwork. I have given the answer already ; because of his reverence for the Book of God, which might permit him in one place, probably with very little manipulating, to leave his finger-print, but kept him from repeating the experiment elsewhere, when too much manipulating was probably needed. Besides, the cross-confirmation of anagram and clockciphers in the case of the Psalm gave such overwhelming proof, in my opinion, that this one case by itself may have seemed to Francis Bacon all-sufficient. For these reasons I cannot share the optimism of those who hope still to find many more similar indications of Bacon's workmanship in the black-letter Bible of 1611, except what the head-and tail-pieces may teach us in this respect. But that is another story for another time.

Addenda

1. SELECT BACONIAN BIBLIOGRAPHY

Historical

[Mo] *Basil Montague.* The Works of Francis Bacon, 17 vols. 1825-34.

[Sp] *James Spedding*, Robert Leslie Ellis, and Douglas Dennon Heath. The Works of Francis Bacon, 14 vols. 1858-74.

[HD I-II] *William Hepworth Dixon.* Personal History of Lord Bacon. 1861.

—The Story of Lord Bacon's Life. 1862.

[M-C] *Arnold Harris Matthew and Annette Calthrope.* The life of Sir Tobie Matthew, Bacon's Alter Ego. 1907.

[EB] *Robert Adamson and John Malcolm Mitchell.* Article on Francis Bacon in the Encyclopaedia Britannica, 11th edition, 1910, vol. III, pp. 135-152.

[CB] *A. Chambers Bunten.* Sir Thomas Meautys. Secretary to Lord Bacon and His Friend. 1918.

General

[DB] *Delia Bacon.* The Philosophy of the Plays of Shakespeare Unfolded. 1857.

[HP] *Mrs. Henry Pott.* The Promus of Formularies and Elegancies by Francis Bacon illustrated and elucidated by passages from Shakespeare. 1883.

—Did Francis Bacon Write Shakespeare ? 3 parts, 2nd edition 1884-93.

[Pe] *Lord Penzance*. A Judicial Summing-Up of the Bacon-Shakespeare Controversy. 1902.

[DL] *Sir Edwin Durning-Lawrence*. Bacon Is Shakespeare, together with a Reprint of Bacon's Promus of Formularies and Elegancies. 1910.

[Bax] *James Phinney Baxter*. The Greatest of Literary Problems. 1915.

[Ha] *Edward George Harman*. The " Impersonality " of Shakespeare. 1925.

Ciphers

[Do] *Ignatius Donnelly*. The Great Cryptogram : Francis Bacon's Cipher in the so-called Shakespeare Plays, 2 vols. 1888.

—The Cipher in the Plays, and on the Tombstone (without year).

[Ow] *Orville W. Owen*. Sir Francis Bacon's Cipher Story, 5 books. 1893-95.

—The Historical Tragedy of Mary Queen of Scots. 1894.

—The Tragical History of Our Late Brother, Earl of Essex. 1895.

[WG I-III] *Elizabeth Wells Gallup*. The Biliteral Cypher of Sir Francis Bacon, 3 parts. 1901-1910.

—The Tragedy of Anne Boleyn. 1901.

[Fi] *Gertrude Horsford Fiske*. Studies in the Biliteral Cipher of Francis Bacon. 1913.

Journals

[Bac] *Baconiana*. Journal, since June 1886.

[ABac]   *American Baconiana* (only one copy of this journal is actually known to me, namely No. 5 of the series, Nov. 1927-Febr. 1928.)

Reports and Flyleaves of the Ladies Guild of Francis St. Alban (known to me only from the nineteenth Report, 1912, onward till Flyleaf August, 1931).

2.   CHRONOLOGY OF THE SHAKESPEARE PLAYS [1]

Plays	Approximate year of composition [6]	Year in which first mentioned	First printed in Quarto		First printed in 1623 Folio
			Bad	Good	
2 Henry VI ...	1590	1594	—	—	1623
3 Henry VI ...	1590	1592	1594	—	—
1 Henry VI ...	1591	1592	1595	—	—
Richard III ...	1592	1597	—	1597	—
Comedy of Errors ...	1592	1594	—	—	1623
Titus Andronicus ...	1593	1594	—	1594	—
Taming of the Shrew ...	1593	—	1594 [2]	—	—
Two Gentlemen of Verona ...	1594	1598	—	—	1623
Love's Labour's Lost ...	1594	1597	?	1598	—
Romeo and Juliet ...	1594	—	1597	1599	—
Richard II ...	1595	1595	—	1597	—
Midsummer Night's Dream ...	1595	1598	—	1619 [3]	—
King John ...	1596	1598	1591 [2]	—	—
Merchant of Venice ...	1596	1596	—	1619 [3]	—

Plays	Approximate year of composition [6]	Year in which first mentioned	First printed in Quarto		First printed in 1623 Folio
			Bad	Good	
1 Henry IV ...	1597	1598	—	1598	—
2 Henry IV ...	1597	1598	—	1600	—
Much Ado About Nothing ...	1598	1600	—	1600	—
Henry V ...	1598	—	1600	—	—
Julius Caesar ...	1599	1598	—	—	1623
As You Like It ...	1599	1598	—	—	1623
Twelfth Night ...	1599	1602	—	—	1623
Hamlet ...	1600	1601	1603	1604	—
Merry Wives of Windsor ...	1600	1602	1602	—	—
Troylus and Cressida ...	1601	1601	—	1609	—
All's Well That Ends Well ...	1602	—	—	—	1623
Measure for Measure ...	1604	1604	—	—	1623
Othello ...	1604	1604	—	1622	—
King Lear ...	1605	1605	—	1619[4]	—
Macbeth ...	1605	1611	—	—	1623
Anthony and Cleopatra ...	1606	1608	—	—	1623
Coriolanus ...	1607	—	—	—	1623
Timon of Athens ...	1607	—	—	—	1623
Pericles ...	1608	—	—	1619[4]	—[5]
Cymbeline ...	1609	1611	—	—	1623
Winter's Tale ...	1610	1611	—	—	1623
Tempest ...	1611	1611	—	—	1623
Henry VIII ...	1612	1613	—	—	1623

Notes :

1. According to Shakespearean scholarship compiled from [ChW] *A Short Life of Shakespeare with the Sources.* Abridged by Charles Williams from Sir Edmund Chambers' *William Shakespeare : A Study of Facts and Problems.* 1933.

2. Not recognized by Shakespeareans as Shakespearean.

3. Antedated 1600.

4. Antedated 1608.

5. Reprinted in Second Folio, 1632.

6. The accuracy of the dates given in this column, especially in its earlier and later parts, is much vitiated of course by the greatly limited period of literary activity, which is in conformity with the actor Shakspeyr's life story. Having left Stratford for London most probably at some time round about 1589, and having retired again from the London stage to his native place about 1610, Shakspeyr's literary productivity is of necessity compressed by the Shakespeareans within the limits of these years. Even the couple of years which they allow beyond the fatal year of 1610 are pure conjecture, based on pure nothing.

Bacon on the other hand was busily writing, printing and editing at least ten years before Shakspeyr's flight to the Thames, and the same number of years after his ignominious sinking down again into the oblivion of the Avon's sluggish waters.

It is the latter which makes the Shakespearean theory so grossly absurd for anybody with some deeper vision, and some detachment from accepted but unproved traditions. That a productive genius of the first order could of his own free will and accord bury himself in sleepy Stratford at the age of 46, in the full maturity of his manhood, and with all his intellectual faculties unimpaired, to let the splendid talents entrusted to him run to seed, unused and uncared for, till death delivered him six years later from such shame—is simply unbelievable, and is in flagrant conflict with the ideals voiced by himself in his own heartstirring way :

Heaven doth with us as we with torches do,
Not light them for themselves ; for if our virtues
Did not go forth of us, 't were all alike
As if we had them not.   Spirits are not finely touched
But to fine issues, nor Nature lends
The smallest scruple of her excellence,
But like a thrifty goddess she determines
Herself the glory of a creditor,
Both thanks and use.

(M.f.M. I 1,32).

To Baconians it remains in truth a constant wonder to observe the depths of credulity into which the Shakspeyr hoax may lead its votaries.

I could not here undertake to point out all the fallacies in the dates given above, from a Baconian standpoint.   One correction only, by way of example, may here be supplied.   To *Twelfth Night* 1599 has been assigned as its year of composition. It was however first mentioned as having been performed at the Middle Temple in February 1602. And this is more in accord with the anguished exclamation of Sebastian= Bacon in Act V, scene 1, vs. 228 ff.

Antonio ! O my dear Antonio !
How have the hours racked and tortured me
Since I have lost thee !

For Anthony Bacon died in May 1601, and the Play did not appear in print before its publication in the First Folio in 1623.

3. SHORT BACONIAN CHRONOLOGY

and genealogical tables

1533   Elizabeth Tudor born of Henry VIII and Anne Bullen.

1536   Anne Bullen decapitated.

1547   Death of Henry VIII.   Accession of Edward VI.

1552   Edmund Spenser born.

1553   Margaret of Valois born.   Death of King Edward VI.   Accession
          of Queen Mary.

1558   Death of King Francis II of France. Accession of King Charles I.
          Elizabeth marries Earl of Leicester.   Death of Queen Mary.
          Accession of Queen Elizabeth.   George Peele born.

1559   Anthony Bacon born.

1560   Robert Greene born.

1561   January 22.   Francis Bacon born.

1564   William Shakspeyr born.   Christopher Marlowe born.

1565   Robert Cecil born.

1566   Robert Devereux (Earl of Essex) born.

1572   Margaret of Valois marries Henry of Navarre.   Massacre of St.
          Bartholomew.

1573   Ben Jonson born.   Francis entered as fellow-commoner at
          Trinity College, Cambridge.

1574   Death of King Charles IX of France.   Accession of King Henry III.

1576   Francis admitted as "Ancient" at Gray's Inn.   Robert
          Burton born.

1577   Francis goes to France with Sir Amyas Paulet.   Toby Matthew
          born.

1579   Death of Sir Nicholas Bacon.   Francis returns to England.

1582   Bacon admitted Utter Barrister of Gray's Inn.

1583   Bacon's First Essay on the Instauration of Philosophy, called
        Temporis Partus Maximus (or *Masculus*).

1584   Bacon starts his public career, takes his seat in Parliament for
        Milcombe, Dorsetshire.

1586   Becomes a Bencher of Gray's Inn.

1587   William Rawley born.

1589   Shakspeyr goes to London.

1592   Death of Robert Greene.

1593   Death of Christopher Marlowe.

1596   Grant of Arms to Shakspeyr's father.   Death of George Peele.

1597   First Edition of the *Essays*.

1599   Death of Edmund Spenser.

1601   Arraignment and death of Robert, Earl of Essex.   Death of
        Anthony Bacon.   Madness of Lady Anne Bacon.

1603   Death of Queen Elizabeth.   Accession of James I.

1605   Bacon marries Alice Barnham.   *The Advancement of Learning*.

1607   Bacon appointed Solicitor-General.

1609   *De Sapientia Veterum*.

1610   Shakspeyr returns to Stratford.   Death of Lady Anne.

1612   Second Edition of the *Essays*.

1616   Will and death of Shakspeyr.   Bacon admitted Privy Councillor.

1617   Appointed Lord Keeper.

1618   Appointed Lord Chancellor.   Created Baron Verulam.

1620   *Novum Organum*.

1621   Created Viscount Saint Albans.   Sentenced by the House of
        Lords. Retires to Gorhambury. Limited pardon by the King.

1622   *History of Henry VII*.

1623   *De Augmentis Scientiarum*.

1625   Third edition of the *Essays*.   Death of James I.   Accession of
        Charles I.

1626   9th April, Easter Sunday.   Death of Francis Bacon.

1627   *New Atlantis* (Rawley).

1629   *Certain Miscellany Works* (Rawley).

1631   French *Life* of Bacon.

1637   Death of Ben Jonson.
1638   *Opera Moralia et Civilia* (Rawley).
1640   Death of Robert Burton
1647   Boener's *Life* of Bacon.
1649   Death of Thomas Meautys.
1650   Death of Alice Barnham.
1653   *Collection* (Gruter).
1655   Death of Toby Matthew.
1657   *Resuscitatio*, with Rawley's *Life* of Bacon.
1665   *Opera omnia*, Frankfort.
1667   Death of William Rawley.
1679   *Baconiana* (Bishop Tenison).

Some dates are only approximately known, with a possible differ- ence of several years. Where two or more events are mentioned under one year their strict chronological order is not guaranteed.

The following genealogical tables have been drawn up to enable the student to see at a glance Francis Bacon's relationship to the great families and principal actors on the Elizabethan stage. They are only tentative efforts, no doubt liable to correction and improvement. The compiler had only scant material at his disposal to draw from,

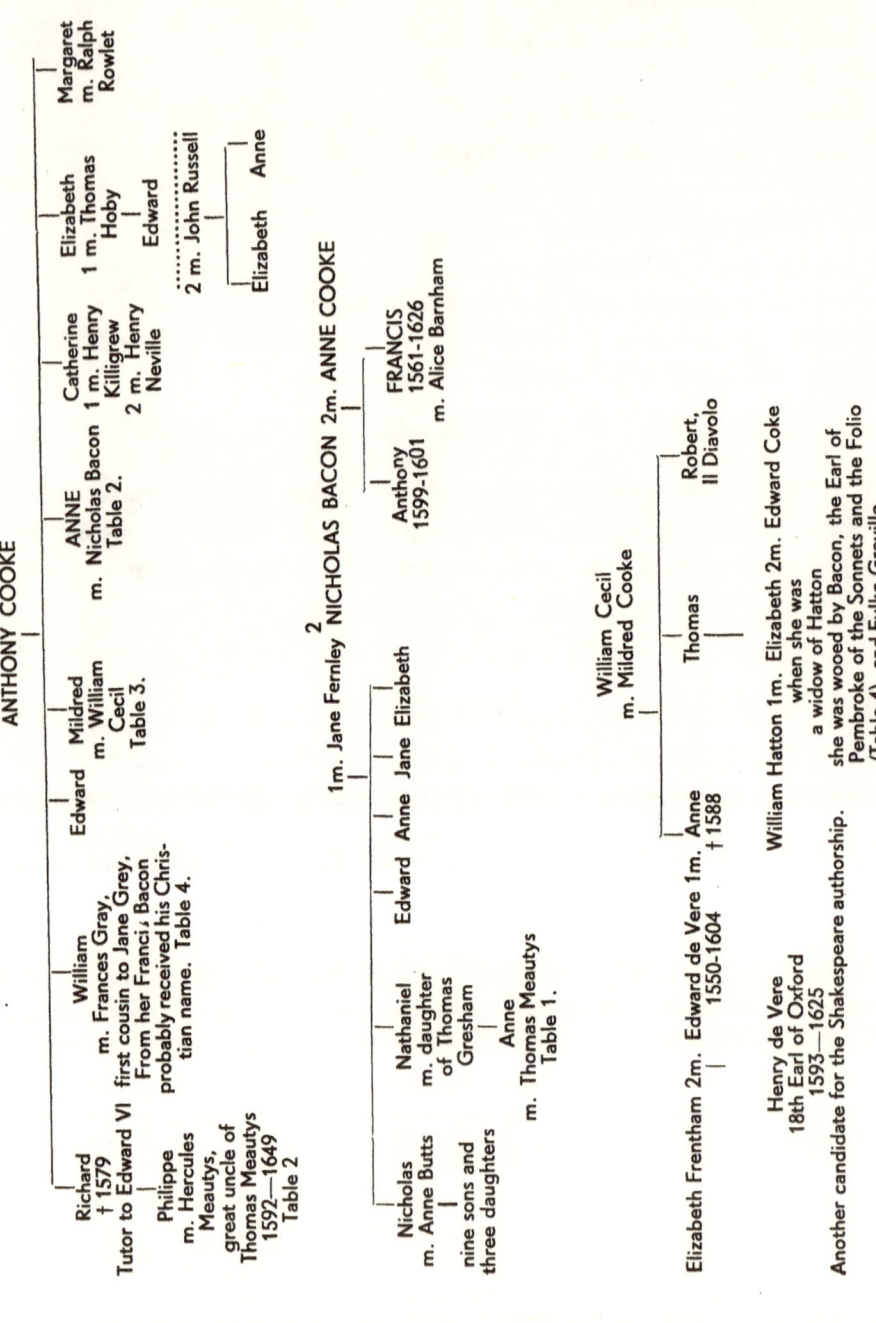

ANTHONY COOKE
1

Richard
† 1579
Tutor to Edward VI

William
m. Frances Gray,
first cousin to Jane Grey,
From her Francis Bacon
probably received his Christian name. Table 4.

Philippe
m. Hercules
Meautys,
great uncle of
Thomas Meautys
1592—1649
Table 2

Edward

Mildred
m. William
Cecil
Table 3.

ANNE
m. Nicholas Bacon
Table 2.

Catherine
1 m. Henry
Killigrew
2 m. Henry
Neville

Elizabeth
1 m. Thomas
Hoby
Edward
2 m. John Russell

Margaret
m. Ralph
Rowlet

Elizabeth   Anne

1m. Jane Fernley   NICHOLAS BACON   2m. ANNE COOKE
2

Nicholas
m. Anne Butts
nine sons and
three daughters

Nathaniel
m. daughter
of Thomas
Gresham

Anne
m. Thomas Meautys
Table 1.

Edward   Anne   Jane   Elizabeth

Anthony
1599-1601

FRANCIS
1561-1626
m. Alice Barnham

William Cecil
m. Mildred Cooke

Anne
† 1588

Thomas

Robert,
Il Diavolo

Elizabeth Frentham 2m.   Edward de Vere 1m.
1550-1604

Henry de Vere
18th Earl of Oxford
1593—1625
Another candidate for the Shakespeare authorship.

William Hatton 1m. Elizabeth 2m. Edward Coke
when she was
a widow of Hatton
she was wooed by Bacon, the Earl of
Pembroke of the Sonnets and the Folio
(Table 4), and Fulke Greville

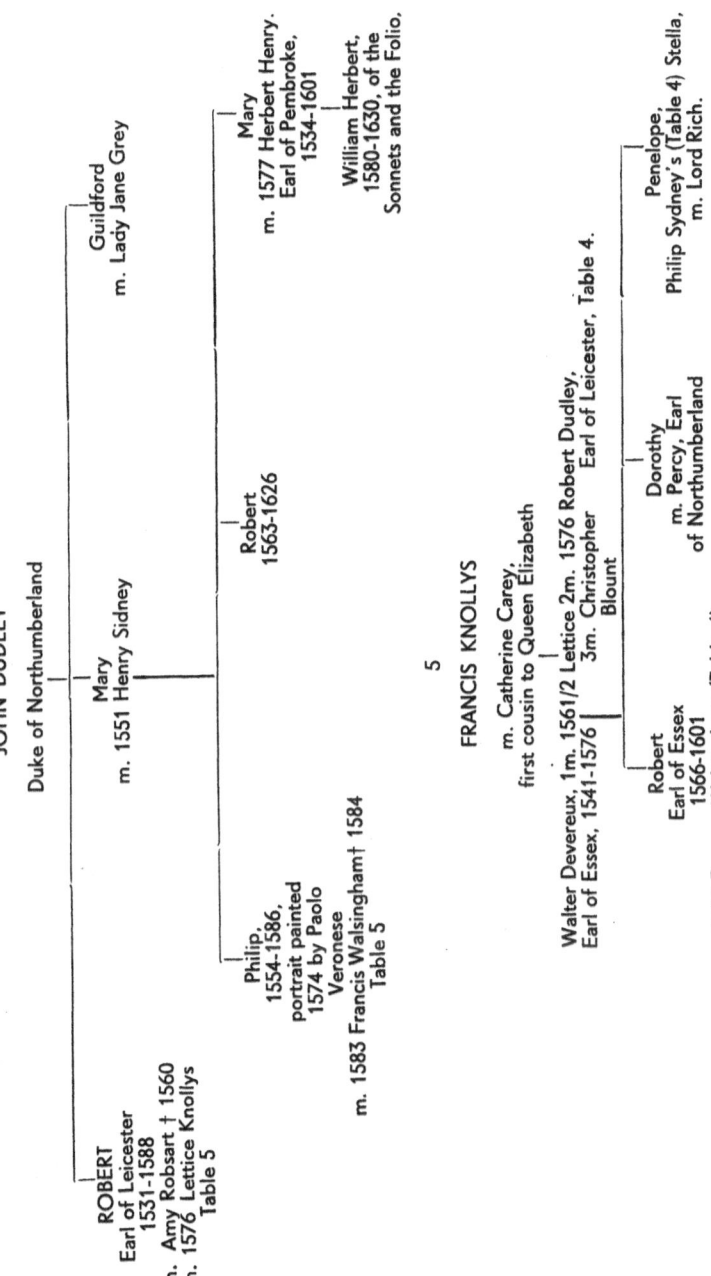

4

JOHN DUDLEY
Duke of Northumberland

Mary
m. 1551 Henry Sidney

Guildford
m. Lady Jane Grey

ROBERT
Earl of Leicester
1531-1588
1m. Amy Robsart † 1560
2m. 1576 Lettice Knollys
Table 5

Philip,
1554-1586,
portrait painted
1574 by Paolo
Veronese
m. 1583 Francis Walsingham† 1584
Table 5

Robert
1563-1626

Mary
m. 1577 Herbert Henry.
Earl of Pembroke,
1534-1601

William Herbert,
1580-1630, of the
Sonnets and the Folio.

5

FRANCIS KNOLLYS

m. Catherine Carey,
first cousin to Queen Elizabeth

Walter Devereux, 1m. 1561/2 Lettice 2m. 1576 Robert Dudley,
Earl of Essex, 1541-1576 | 3m. Christopher   Earl of Leicester, Table 4.
                                        Blount

Robert
Earl of Essex
1566-1601
m. 1590 Frances Walsingham (Table 4)

Robert, Earl of Essex
1591-1646

Dorothy
m. Percy, Earl
of Northumberland

Penelope,
Philip Sydney's (Table 4) Stella,
m. Lord Rich.

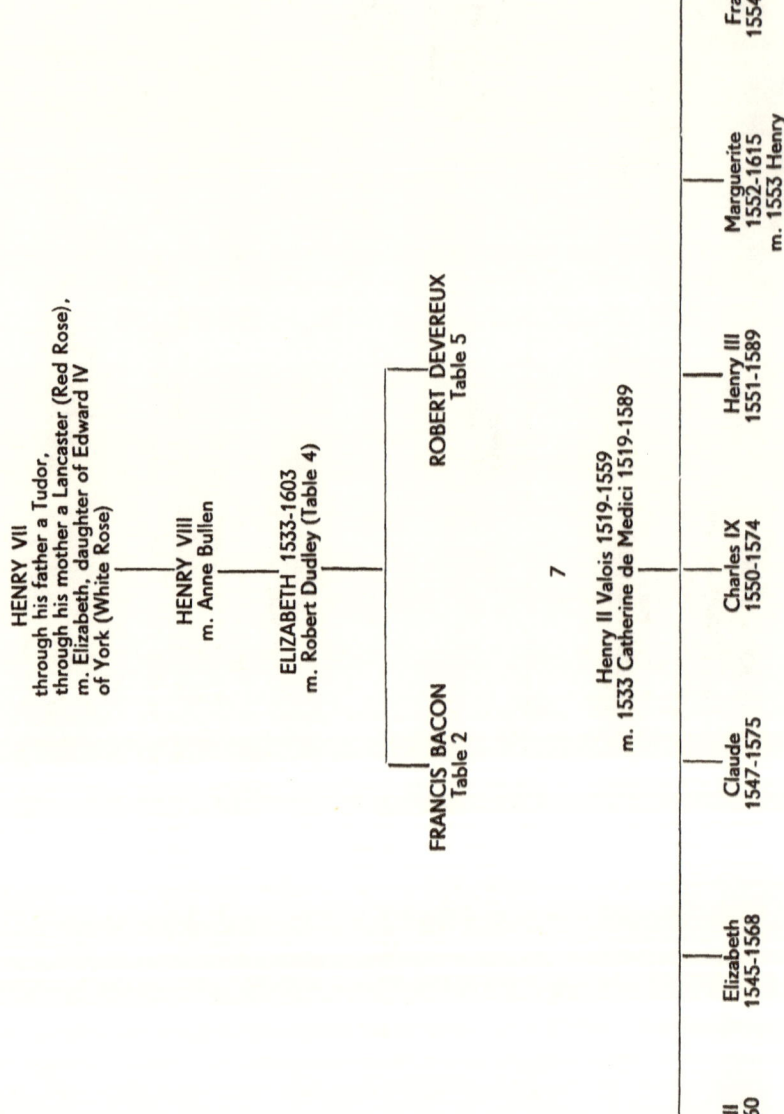

6

HENRY VII
through his father a Tudor,
through his mother a Lancaster (Red Rose),
m. Elizabeth, daughter of Edward IV
of York (White Rose)

HENRY VIII
m. Anne Bullen

ELIZABETH 1533-1603
m. Robert Dudley (Table 4)

FRANCIS BACON
Table 2

ROBERT DEVEREUX
Table 5

7

Henry II Valois 1519-1559
m. 1533 Catherine de Medici 1519-1589

Francis II
1544-1560

Elizabeth
1545-1568

Claude
1547-1575

Charles IX
1550-1574

Henry III
1551-1589

Marguerite
1552-1615
m. 1553 Henry
of Navarre

Francis
1554-1584

4.   FRENCH LIFE OF BACON

Peter Boener's "Life" appeared in 1647, Rawley's ten years later. Another, anonymous, "Life" had been published in France, sixteen years earlier even than Boener's, and only five years after Bacon's death, namely in 1631. I have not included it in Chapter II, because I do not think that it was written by a person who was personally acquainted with Bacon, or who shared any real knowledge of his secret life and history. He may have caught some whisperings—only so much I am prepared to accept. But he is clearly a true devotee. He has also a strong Roman Catholic bias. Nevertheless this French *Life* has the distinction of being the oldest biographical sketch of Bacon, that has been published, and for that reason I reproduce here some extracts from it in the English translation made by Mr. Granville C. Cunningham, and published in *Baconiana*, April 1906, p. 72 ff.

"His life had such a happy [?] beginning, and an end so rough and strange.

"M. Bacon was the son of a father who possessed no less virtue than he ; his worth secured to him the honour of being so well beloved by Queen Elizabeth that she gave him the position of Keeper of the Seals and placed in his hands the most important affairs of her kingdom.

"M. Bacon was not only obliged to imitate the virtues of such an one, but also those of many others of his ancestors, who have left so many marks of their greatness in history that honour and dignity seem to have been at all times the spoil of his family [?].

"Being thus born in the purple (*né parmy les pourpres*) and brought up with the expectation of a grand career (*l' espérance d'une grande fortune*) his father had him instructed in "*bonnes lettres*" with great and especial care.

" Capacity (*jugement*) and memory were never in any man to such a degree as in this one :

" He employed some years of his youth in travel in order to polish his mind and to mould his opinion by intercourse with all kinds of foreigners. France, Italy and Spain, as the most civilized nations of the whole world, were those whither his desire for knowledge (*curiosité*) carried him . . . as he saw himself destined one day to hold in his hands the helm of the kingdom (*le Limon du Royaume*).

" Some time after his return, the King [?], who well knew his worth, gave him several small matters to carry out that might serve for him as stepping stones to high positions ; in these he acquitted himself so well that he was in due course considered worthy of the same position that his father vacated with his life.

" Among so many virtues that made this great man commendable, prudence, as the first of all the moral virtues, and that most necessary to those of his profession, was that which shone in him the most brightly.

" Never was there man who so loved equity, or so enthusiastically worked for the public good as he.

" Innocence oppressed found always in his protection a sure refuge, and the position of the great gave them no vantage ground before the Chancellor when suing for justice.

" Vanity, avarice, and ambition, vices that too often attach themselves to great honours, were to him quite unknown, and if he did a good action it was not from the desire of fame, but simply because he could not do otherwise. His good qualities were entirely pure, without being clouded by the admixture of any imperfection, and the passions that form usually the defects in great men in him only served to bring out his virtues ; if he felt hatred and rage it was only against evil-doers, to shew his detestation of their crimes, and success or failure in the affairs of his country brought to him the greater part of his joys or his sorrows. He was as truly a good man as he was an upright judge, and by the example of his life corrected vice and bad living as much as by pains and penalties. And, in a word, it seemed that Nature had exempted from the ordinary frailties of men him whom she had marked out to deal with their crimes.

" It came about that amongst the great number of officials such as a man of his position must have in his house, there was one who was accused before Parliament of exaction, and of having sold the influence that he might have with his master.   And though the probity of Mr. Bacon was entirely exempt from censure, nevertheless, he was declared guilty of the crime of his servant and was deprived of the power that he had so long exercised with so much honour and glory."

" This storm did not at all surprise him, and he received the news of his disgrace with a countenance so undisturbed that it was easy to see that he thought but little of the sweets of life, since the loss of them caused him discomfort so slight.

" He had, fairly close to London, a country house replete with everything requisite to soothe a mind embittered [?] by public life as was his, and weary of living in the turmoil of the great world.   He returned thither to give himself up more completely to the study of his books and to pass in repose the remainder of his life.

" Thus ended this great man, whom England could place alone as the equal (*en paralelle avec*) of the best of all the previous centuries."

5.   BEN JONSON ON SHAKSPEYR AND SHAKESPEARE

" Honest Ben " contributed two poems to the 1623 Folio of Shakespeare's Plays, which are not quite so " honest " or " innocent " as they seem.   The shorter, reproduced above on page 282, fronts the Droeshout picture on the title-page of the Folio.   Two words in it may here be further commented upon.

The apparent meaning of the word " out-doo " is of course to excel, or surpass, as in the verse from *Venus and Adonis* (289).

> Look, when a painter would surpass the life.
> His art with nature's workmanship at strife,
> As if the dead the living should exceed.

Baconians however have read it as meaning to efface, which is equally legitimate. The phrase then signifies that the picture is only a mask to hide the features of the true author.

So also, instead of taking the word " hit " in the sense of exact likeness, Baconians have read it to mean hid, or hidden. The legitimacy of this is by them supported with the following quotation from Chaucer :

> Right as a serpent hit him under floures.[1]

But it is a fact that, however such may have been the spelling of the word in Chaucer's time, the Shakespeare Folio has not one example of it to show, though it uses the word hid for hidden some fifty times.

The longer poem is found five pages after the Title-page in the same Folio.

To the memory of my Beloved
The AUTHOR
Mr. William Shakespeare :
And
what he hath left us.

> To draw no envy (*Shakespeare*) on thy name,
>   Am I thus ample to thy Booke, and Fame :
> While I confesse thy writings to be such,
>   As neither *Man*, nor *Muse*, can praise too much.
> 'Tis true, and all mens suffrage.   But these wayes
>   Were not the paths I meant unto thy praise :
> For seeliest[2] Ignorance on these may light,
>   Which, when it sounds at best, but eccho's right ;

---

[1] DL 29.   [2] Blindest.

Or blinde Affection, which doth ne're advance
 The truth, but gropes, and urgeth all by chance ;
Or crafty Malice, might pretend this praise,
 And think to ruine, where it seem'd to raise.
These are, as some infamous Baud, or Whore,
 Should praise a Matron. What could hurt her more ?
But thou art proofe against them, and indeed
 Above th'ill fortune of them, or the need.

I, therefore will begin. Soule of the Age !
 The applause ! delight ! the wonder of our Stage !
My *Shakespeare*, rise ; I will not lodge thee by
 Chaucer, or *Spenser*, or bid *Beaumont* lye
A little further, to make thee a roome :
 Thou art a Moniment, without a tombe,
And art alive still, while thy Booke doth live,
 And we have wits to read, and praise to give.
That I not mix thee so, my braine excuses ;
 I meane with great, but disproportion'd *Muses* :
For, if I thought my judgement were of yeeres,
 I should commit thee surely with thy peeres,
And tell, how farre thou didst our *Lily* out-shine,
 Or sporting *Kid*, or *Marlowes* mighty line.
And though thou hadst small *Latine*, and lesse *Greeke*,
 From thence to honour thee, I would not seeke
For names ; but call forth thund'ring *Aeschilus*,
 Euripides, and *Sophocles* to us,
Paccuvius, *Accius*, him of *Cordova* dead,
 To life againe, to hear thy Buskin tread,
And shake a Stage : Or, when thy Sockes were on,
 Leave thee alone, for the comparison
Of all, that insolent *Greece*, or haughty *Rome*
 Sent forth, or since did from their ashes come,

41

Triumph, my *Britaine*, thou hast one to showe,
  To whom all Scenes of *Europe* homage owe.
He was not of an age, but for all time !
  And all the *Muses* still were in their prime,
When like *Apollo* he came forth to warme
  Our eares, or like a *Mercury* to charme !
Nature her selfe was proud of his designes,
  And joy'd to weare the dressing of his lines !
Which were so richly spun, and woven so fit,
  As, since, she will vouchsafe no other Wit.
The merry *Greeke*, tart *Aristophanes*,
  Neat *Terence*, witty *Plautus*, now not please ;
But antiquated, and deserted lye
  As they were not of Natures family.
Yet must I not give Nature all : Thy Art,
  My gentle *Shakespeare*, must enjoy a part.
For though the *Poets* matter, Nature be,
  His Art doth give the fashion.   And, that he,
Who casts to write a living line, must sweat,
  (Such as thine are) and strike the second heat
Upon the *Muses* anvile : turne the same,
  (And himselfe with it) that he thinkes to frame ;
Or for the lawrell, he may gaine a scorne,
  For a good *Poet's* made, as well as borne.
And such wert thou.   Looke how the fathers face
  Lives in his issue, even so, the race
Of *Shakespeares* mind, and manners brightly shines
  In his well torned, and true filed lines :
In each of which, he seemes to shake a Lance,
  As brandish't at the eyes of Ignorance.

Sweet Swan of *Avon* ! what a sight it were
  To see thee in our waters yet appeare,

And make those flights upon the bankes of *Thames*,
    That so did take *Eliza*, and our *James* !
But stay, I see thee in the *Hemisphere*
    Advanc'd, and made a Constellation there !
Shine forth, thou Starre of *Poets*, and with rage,
    Or influence, chide, or cheere the drooping Stage ;
Which, since thy flight from hence, hath mourn'd like night,
    And despaires day, but for thy Volumes light.

                                    Ben : Jonson.

To reconcile the praise lavished in these poems, with the unfavourable criticisms in the next pieces, only one reasonable solution offers itself. The praises and the criticisms, mutually contradictory as they are, were addressed to two different persons, Shakspeyr the Player, and Shakespeare the Playwright, that is Francis Bacon. The line, accusing Shakespeare of lack of knowledge of Greek and Roman literature, or as it was repeated at another occasion, of " want of Learning and Ignorance of the Ancients," [1] is obviously aimed at the actor, for Shakespeare's works are steeped in such knowledge, which peeps from every corner, from every cranny of its wide-spread structure, and could never have been derived from translations only, as Shakespeareans aver, and try to prove—a hopeless endeavour, which should have opened their eyes for the truth of the Baconian theory.

The next piece is from Jonson's *Discoveries*, published posthumously in 1641, four years after his death.

De Shakespeare Nostrati

I *remember*, the Players have often mentioned it as an honour to *Shakespeare*, that in his writing, (whatsoever hee penn'd) he never blotted out line. My answer hath beene, would he had blotted

[1] Recorded by Rowe, Ch W 206 ; see also Beaumont on p. 216.

a thousand. Which they thought a malevolent speech. I had not told posterity this, but for their ignorance, who choose that circumstance to commend their friend by, wherein he most faulted. And to justifie mine owne candor, (for I lov'd the man, and doe honour his memory (on this side Idolatry) as much as any). Hee was (indeed) honest, and of an open, and free nature : had an excellent *Phantsie ;* brave notions, and gentle expressions : wherein hee flow'd with that facility, that sometime it was necessary he should be stop'd : *Sufflaminandus erat ;* as *Augustus* said of *Haterius.* His wit was in his owne power ; would the rule of it had beene so too. Many times he fell into those things, could not escape laughter : As when hee said in the person of *Caesar,* one speaking to him : *Caesar thou dost me wrong.* Hee replyed : *Caeser did never wrong, but with just cause* and such like : which were ridiculous. But hee redeemed his vices, with his virtues. There was ever more in him to be praysed, than to be pardoned.

The phrase, " His wit was in his own power ; would the rule of it had been so too," is I am sure but an echo of Bacon's own opinion of Shakespeare. For I cannot but think that the lines,

I do perceive that thou hast wit ;
Beg of thy fate to govern it,

in the *Old Wives' Tale* (1595) of George Peele, another of Bacon's masks, are also aimed at the actor.

The picture drawn by Ben Jonson of the " Player," not of the "Playwright," is clear and sharply cut as a cameo. We get the impression of an amiable man, with more good in him than bad, a jolly good fellow, well liked among his mates. His memory is honoured by Ben Jonson as much as by any of the actor's friends, but unlike them, who are not initiated into the secret and hold him to be the Playwright, Jonson keeps his esteem well on the safe side of Idolatry. A man of some education, then, but without the finesse of real Art or knowledge of the Ancients, so that he cannot rightly be called learned, or cultured, or refined, or a gentleman ; a man of ready wit, yes but without the finer control over it which higher education gives, and therefore prone to overdo it. His lack of culture and real art further shows itself markedly in his never erasing a line of writing. " Would he had blotted a thousand," cries out Ben Jonson in desperation. Surely, this could never have been said, in such a tone and sentiment of keen annoyance, of the same man whom he elsewhere hails as the " Sweet Swan of Avon," the " Star of Poets."

> Soul of the Age !
> The applause ! delight ! the wonder of our Stage !
> My Shakespeare rise !

" Would he had blotted a thousand ! " It would probably have deprived us of everything the " Player " had ever written in his life, and I think the world would thereby have been the better off, especially with his last " Will " clean wiped out, that ugliest blot upon his name as a gentleman and his fame as an inspired prophet and teacher of mankind.

Shakspeyr's fellow-actors, Heminge and Condell, in their Preface to the First Folio, addressed " To the great variety of readers," have reported the same failing of their colleague : " What he thought, he uttered with that easiness, that we have scarce received from him a blot in his papers." This only proves that Bacon provided his " mask " with clean copies of his Plays, in which Shakspeyr dared of course not make a single alteration. Still he had apparently a way of easy utterance, too easy probably, the ease of shallowness. I read a veiled criticism and a judgment on this ease in the words of Jonson's longer poem :

> Who casts to write a living line, must sweat,
> (Such as thine [1] are), and strike the second heat
> Upon the Muses' anvil : turne the same,
> (And himselfe with it) that he thinkes to frame.

[1] The Playwright's, not the Player's lines, of course.

It has been diversely said that genius is the capacity for taking infinite pains, and Bacon at least lived up to this ideal. He never left the products of his mind in the primitive form in which they originally came forth from his brain, but found always something to improve and to amplify as he proceeded. In his own words, addressed to his close literary friend, Toby Matthew : " My great work goeth forward, and *after my manner, I alter even when I add.* So that nothing is finished till all be finished." [1]

And that is the acme of Art, and it is this High Art which apparently was unanimously denied to Shakspeyr, the Player, by his contemporaries but could never have been denied and was not so denied of the Playwright Shakespeare. The different editions of his Plays, the Quartos and the Folios, if anything, prove effectively that he too was possessed of that High Art of Genius, which is never satisfied with the first heat of its creative inspiration, but always feels the urge to improve upon it, by " blotting out " and by altering, and by addition that is by turning and turning again his phrases " and himself with it." This has been sufficiently proved on page 37 of this book. It is a fallacy, and the incomprehensible folly of the Shakespearean scholar to accept this lack of Art in the actor, and yet to accept him at the same time as the author. " Nobody believes any longer," wrote James Russell Lowell " that immediate inspiration is possible in modern times ; and yet everybody [i.e., every Shakespearean, as contrasted with the Baconian] seems to take it for granted of this one man Shakespeare," [2] the Actor. Nay, it is still emphatically true, what Ben Jonson wrote :

A good Poet's made, as well as born.

And of such " making " of the Great Poet not the smallest bit of evidence exists in the life of Shakspeyr the Player.

It is this lack of culture, education, gentlemanly restraint and control, courage also to face trouble, that is lack of the High Art of

Genius, which Ben Jonson undoubtedly meant when he was reported by
William Drummond to have said " that William Shaksperr wanted Arte."
Of the Playwright Shakespeare he had in his longer poem declared
just the opposite.

> Yet must I not give nature all : Thy Art,
> My gentle Shakespeare, must enjoy a part.

And it is to this Art of course that only can be ascribed Shakespeare's

> well turnèd and true filèd lines.

Incident ranges itself to incident, proof links itself to proof, till our
chain of evidence for Bacon's authorship becomes ever stronger. A
ready wit, but lack of Learning and Art, and the essential qualities of a
" gentleman," these characteristics of the Player Shakspeyr, noted by
Ben Jonson and others, are even those on which the Playwright Shakespeare himself throws the full light of his ridicule in the following scene of
As You Like It (V 1). William is a clown, an uneducated rustic, " born
in the forest," which here stands simply for the country in contrast
with the town. Touchstone is a clown also, but hailing from town,
" born in the purple " even, and familiar therefore with the refinement
and culture which court life gives. Say the editors of the New Cambridge edition of the play : " The humour of this scene lies in the
assertion by Touchstone of the mental and moral superiority of the
court clown over the country clown." Both are clowns, that is, connected with the Stage. But one is only a lout, a clout, a clod, or
" turf of earth,"[1] with a " pretty wit," it is true, but his lack of culture
and of the essential qualities of a gentleman is easily exposed
by the " touchstone " of the others' Master-wit, High Art, and courtly
savoir-vivre. The one stands for Shakspeyr naturally, the other
for Bacon.

---

[1] *Love's Labour's Lost*, IV 2 ; see ante, p. 230-2.

Enter Clown [Touchstone] and Audrey

Clo.   Audrey, there is a youth here in the Forest lays claim to you.

Aud.   Ay, I know who 'tis, he hath no interest in me in the world. Here comes the man you mean.

Enter William

Clo.   It is meat and drink to me to see a Clown. By my troth we that have good wits, have much to answer for ; we shall be flouting ; we cannot hold.

Will.   Good ev'n, Audrey.

Aud.   God ye good ev'n, William.

Will.   And Good ev'n to you, Sir.

Clo.   [with mock-dignity].[1] Good ev'n, gentle friend. Cover thy head, cover thy head. Nay, prithee, be covered. How old are you, Friend ?

Will.   Five-and-twenty, Sir.

Clo.   A ripe age. Is thy name, *William ?*

Will.   *William*, sir.

Clo.   A fair name. Wast born i'th' Forest here ?

Will.   Ay sir, I thank God.

Clo.   Thank God ; a good answer. Art rich ?

Will.   Faith sir, so, so.

Clo.   So, so, is good, very good, very excellent good : and yet it is not, it is but so, so. Art thou wise ?

Will.   Ay sir, I have a pretty wit.

Clo.   Why, thou say'st well. I do now remember a saying : The Fool doth think he is wise, but the wise man knows himself to be a Fool [By this William's mouth is wide open with amazement]. The Heathen Philosopher, when he had a desire to eat a Grape, would open his lips when he put it into his mouth, meaning thereby, that Grapes were made to eat and lips to open. You do love this maid ?

---

[1] The phrases between square brackets are comments by the editors of the New Cambridge edition, Quiller-Couch and Dover Wilson.

Will. I do, sir.

Clo. Give me your hand.   Art thou Learned ?

Will. No, sir.

Clo. Then learn this of me.   To have, is to have.   For it is a figure
in Rhetoric that drink being poured out of a cup into a glass,
by filling the one, doth empty the other.   For all your Writers
do consent that *ipse* is he : now, you are not *ipse*, for I am he.

Will. Which he, sir ?

Clo. He, sir, that must marry this woman.   Therefore, you Clown,
abandon : which is in the vulgar, leave the society : which
in the boorish is company of this female : which in the common
is woman : which together is, abandon the society of this
Female, or, Clown, thou perishest : or, to thy better understanding, diest : or (to wit) I kill thee, make thee away, translate thy life into death, thy liberty into bondage : I will deal
in poison with thee, or in bastinado, or in steel : I will bandy
with thee in faction : I will o'errun thee with policy : I will
kill thee a hundred and fifty ways, therefore tremble and
depart.

Aud. Do good William.

Will. God rest you merry, sir. [*Exit*]

Is it not wonderful how the Baconian theory transforms the otherwise most silly scenes of Shakespearean comedy into intelligible, significant, pregnant events ? Both, the learned gentleman and the simple
country lout woo the same maid, '' Nature.'' For her own good Audrey
has to wed Art, or she will herself remain a simple country lass. Knowing
his shortcoming, poor William's courage fails him, and he retreats before
his accomplished rival—for the time being at least. In him, however,
has been kindled the desire to be a gentleman like the other, instead of
remaining always a clown. But being '' an essential clown,'' as Ben
Jonson styles him, he is content just with the outward signs of '' gentility,''
without the inward grace. And so it comes to pass that the heraldic
records of the time tell us of a grant of arms to John Shakespeare, the

42

Actor's father, on 20th October 1596. This grant seems to have
been possible only by misrepresentations. " The strenuous efforts and
the vulgar methods resorted to in obtaining this recognition," as one
writer describes it, " naturally furnished the wits with a fruitful subject for
ridicule." [1] Among these satirists was Ben Jonson in his *Every Man Out
of His Humour* (1600). Three persons meet in the first scene of the
third Act, which we are going to reproduce.[2]

Sogliardo, literally the " sloven," is thus characterized : " An
essential clown, brother to Sordido [the ' miser '], yet so enamoured
of the name of a gentleman, that he will have it, though he buys it. He
comes up every term to learn to take tobacco, and see new motions.
He is in his kingdom when in company where he may be well laughed
at." This describes the actor, Shakspeyr, to a hair, I fear.

The other two characters in the scene, are Puntarvolo, " swift
point," or " pheuterer," that is " spear-bearer," as he is called elsewhere
in the Play, and Carlo Buffone, John Falstaffe's twin brother. All three
present, I think, different aspects of the man Shakspeyr.

[Sogliardo, Puntarvolo, and Carlo, walk together.]

Sog.   Nay, I will have him, I am resolute for that.   By this parchment,
        gentlemen, I have been so toiled among the harrots[3] yonder, you
        will not believe ! they do speak in the strangest language, and
        give a man the hardest terms for his money, that ever you knew.
Car.   But have you arms, have you arms ?
Sog.   I'faith, I thank them ; I can write myself gentleman now ; here's
        my patent, it cost me thirty pound, by this breath.
Punt.   A very fair coat, well charged, and full of armory.
Sog.   Nay, it has as much variety of colours in it, as you have seen a
        coat have ; how like you the crest, sir ?
Punt.   I understand it not well, what is't ?
Sog.   Marry, Sir, it is *your Bore without a head, Rampant*.
Punt.   A Bore without a head, that's very rare !

---

[1] Bax 77.
[2] From the edition in Everyman's Library, partly from ChW 198.   [3] Heralds.

Car.   Ay, and rampant too! troth, I commend the herald's wit, he
          has decyphered him well: *A Swine without a head, without brain,
          wit, anything indeed, Ramping to Gentility.*   You can blazon the
          rest, signior, can you not?

Sog.   O, ay, I have it in writing here of purpose; it cost me two
          shillings the tricking.

Car.   Let's hear, let's hear.

Punt.   It is the most vile, foolish, absurd, palpable, and ridiculous
          escutcheon that ever this eye survised.—Save you, good monsieur
          Fastidious.   [They salute as they meet in the walk.]

Car.   Silence, good knight: on, on.

Sog.   [Reads.] Gyrony of eight pieces; azure and gules; between
          three plates, a chevron engrailed checquy, or vert, and ermins;
          on a chief argent, between two ann'lets sable, *a Bore's head
          Proper.*

Car.   How's that! on a chief argent?

Sog.   [Reads.] On a chief argent, *a Bore's head Proper*, between two
          ann'lets sable.

Car.   'Slud, it's *a Hog's Cheeke, and Puddings in a Peuter field*, this.
          [Here they shift.   Fastidious mixes with Puntarvolo; Carlo and
          Sogliardo; Deliro and Macilente; Clove and Orange; four
          couple.]

Sog.   How like you them, signior?

Punt.   Let the word be, *Not without mustard*:[1] your crest is very
          rare, sir.

          . . . . .

Car.   Nay, look you, sir, now you are a gentleman, you must carrry a
          more exalted presence, change your mood and habit to a more
          austere form; be exceeding proud, stand upon your gentility,
          and scorn every man; speak nothing humbly, never discourse
          under a nobleman, though you never saw him but riding to the
          star-chamber, it's all one.   Love no man: trust no man: speak
          ill of no man to his face; nor well of any man behind his back.

          ---

          [1] Shakspeyr's heraldic motto was: non sans droit, not without right,

Salute fairly on the front, and wish them *hanged* upon the turn. Spread yourself upon his bosom publicly, whose heart you would eat in private. These be principles, think on them ; I'll come to you again presently.   [Exit.]

Here we have—and that with a vengeance—first the " Bore without a Head," and the " Swine without a Head," that is Shakspeyr, " ramping to gentility ; " then the " Boar's Head," and as if that were not sufficient, even the " hang-hog " which is Latin for Bacon.
Enough.

6.   MARK TWAIN'S LIFE OF SHAKESPEARE

(Extracts)

For the instruction of the ignorant I will make a list, now, of those details of Shakespeare's history which are *facts*—verified facts, established facts, undisputed facts.

Facts

He was born on the 23rd of April, 1561.

Of good farmer-class parents who could not read, could not write, could not sign their names.

At Stratford, a small back settlement which in that day was shabby and unclean, and densely illiterate. Of the nineteen important men charged with the government of the town, thirteen had to " make their mark " in attesting important documents, because they could not write their names.

Of the first eighteen years of his life *nothing* is known. They are a blank.

On the 27th of November (1582) William Shakespeare took out a license to marry Anne Whateley.

Next day William Shakespeare took out a license to marry Anne Hathaway. She was eight years his senior.

William Shakespeare married Anne Hathaway. In a hurry. By grace of a reluctantly-granted dispensation there was but one publication of the banns.

Within six months the first child was born.

About two (blank) years followed, during which period *nothing at all happened to Shakespeare*, so far as anybody knows.

Then came twins—1585, February.

Two blank years follow.

Then—1587—he makes a ten-year visit to London, leaving the family behind.

Five blank years follow. During this period *nothing happened to him*, as far as anybody actually knows.

Then—1592—there is mention of him as an actor.

Next year—1593—his name appears in the official list of players.

Next year—1594—he played before the queen. A detail of no consequence : other obscurities did it every year of the forty-five of her reign. And remained obscure.

Three pretty full years follow. Full of play-acting. Then

In 1597 he bought New Place, Stratford.

Thirteen or fourteen busy years follow ; years in which he accumulated money, and also reputation as actor and manager.

Meantime his name, liberally and variously spelt, had become associated with a number of great plays and poems, as (ostensibly) author of the same.

Some of these, in these years and later, were pirated, but he made no protest.

Then—1610-11—he returned to Stratford and settled down for good and all, and busied himself in lending money, trading in tithes, trading in land and houses ; shirking a debt of forty-one shillings, borrowed by his wife during his long desertion of his family ; suing debtors for shillings and coppers ; being sued himself for shillings and coppers ;

and acting as confederate to a neighbour who tried to rob the town of its rights in a certain common, and did not succeed.

He lived five or six years—till 1616—in the joy of these elevated pursuits. Then he made a will, and signed each of its three pages with his name.

A thoroughgoing business man's will. It named in minute detail every item of property he owned in the world—houses, lands, sword, silver-gilt bowl, and so on—all the way down to his " second-best bed " and its furniture.

It carefully and calculatingly distributed his riches among the members of his family, overlooking no individual of it. Not even his wife: the wife he had been enabled to marry in a hurry by urgent grace of a special dispensation before he was nineteen ; the wife whom he had left husbandless so many years ; the wife who had had to borrow forty-one shillings in her need, and which the lender was never able to collect of the prosperous husband, but died at last with the money still lacking. No, even this wife was remembered in Shakespeare's will.

He left her that " second-best bed."

And *not another thing* ; not even a penny to bless her lucky widowhood with.

It was eminently and conspicuously a business man's will, not a poet's.

It mentioned *not a single book.*

Books were much more precious than swords and silver-gilt bowls and second-best beds in those days, and when a departing person owned one he gave it a high place in his will.

The will mentioned *not a play, not a poem, not an unfinished literary work, not a scrap of manuscript of any kind.*

Many poets have died poor, but this is the only one in history that has died *this* poor ; the others all left literary remains behind. Also a book. Maybe two.

He signed the will in three places.

In earlier years he signed two other official documents.

These five signatures still exist.

There are *no other specimens of his penmanship in existence.* Not a line.

Was he prejudiced against the art ? His granddaughter, whom he loved, was eight years old when he died, yet she had had no teaching, he left no provision for her education although he was rich, and in her mature womanhood she couldn't write and couldn't tell her husband's manuscript from anybody else's—she thought it was Shake-speare's.

When Shakespeare died in Stratford *it was not an event.* It made no more stir in England than the death of any other forgotten theatre-actor would have made. Nobody came down from London ; there were no lamenting poems, no eulogies, no national tears—there was merely silence, and nothing more. A striking contrast with what happened when Ben Jonson, and Francis Bacon, and Spenser, and Raleigh and the other distinguished literary folk of Shakespeare's time passed from life ! No praiseful voice was lifted for the lost Bard of Avon ; even Ben Jonson waited seven years before he lifted his.

So far as anybody actually knows and can prove, Shakespeare of Stratford-on-Avon never wrote a play in his life.

So far as anybody knows and can prove, he never wrote a letter to anybody in his life.

So far as anyone knows, he received only one letter during his life.

So far as anyone *knows and can prove,* Shakespeare of Stratford wrote only one poem during his life. This one is authentic. He did write that one—a fact which stands undisputed ; he wrote the whole of it ; he wrote the whole of it out of his own head. He commanded that this work of art be engraved upon his tomb, and he was obeyed. There it abides to this day. This is it :

Good friend for Iesus sake forbeare
To digg the dust encloased heare :
Blest by ye man yt spares thes stones
And curst be he yt moves my bones.

In the list, as above set down, will be found *every positively known* fact of Shakespeare's life, lean and meagre as the invoice is.   Beyond these details we know *not a thing* about him.   All the rest of his vast history, as furnished by the biographers, is built up, course upon course, of guesses, inferences, theories, conjectures—an Eiffel Tower of artificialities rising sky-high from a very flat and very thin foundation of inconsequential facts.

[The above " Life " forms the third chapter of " Is Shakespeare Dead ? " Though written thirty years ago, it still stands unchallenged and unanswerable.   In its poverty and everyday sordidness, it is the life of a somewhat common, somewhat mean, somewhat hard, somewhat selfish, somewhat successful small-town business man, with a somewhat wild youth and a somewhat ignoble death.   Once having found this out, it is uncharitable not to leave such a figure in its forgetful grave, and the height of folly to adorn it with the laurels of genius.]

7.   THE ANATOMY OF MELANCHOLY

Argument of the Frontispiece

Ten distinct Squares here seen apart
Are join'd in one by Cutter's art.

1.   Old Democritus under a tree,
Sits on a stone with book on knee ;
About him hang there many features,
Of Cats, Dogs, and such like creatures,
Of which he makes Anatomy,
The seat of Black Choler to see.

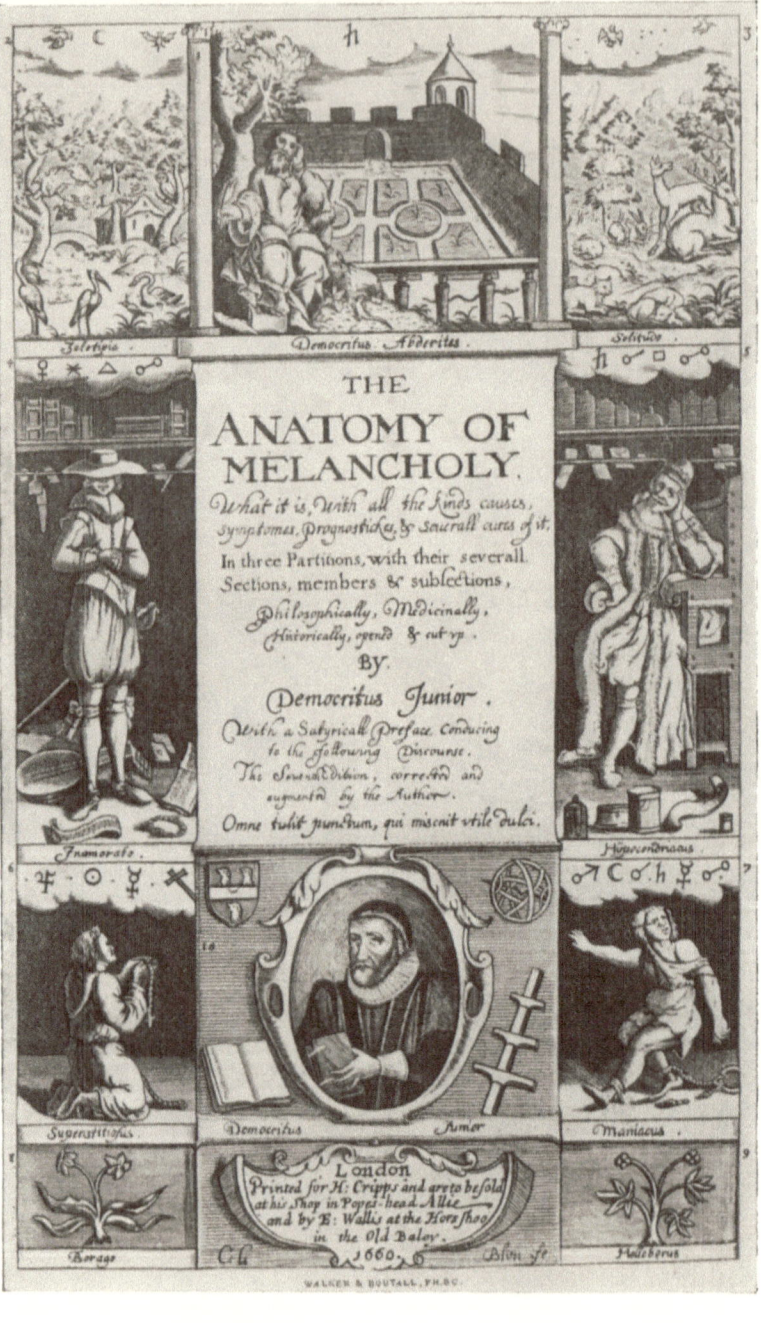

THE
ANATOMY OF
MELANCHOLY,
What it is, with all the kinds causes,
symptomes, Prognostickes, & severall cures of it,
In three Partitions, with their severall
Sections, members & subsections,
Philosophically, Medicinally,
Historically, opened & cut vp.
By.
Democritus Junior.
With a Satyricall Preface, Conducing
to the following Discourse.
The Seventh Edition, corrected and
augmented by the Author.
Omne tulit punctum, qui miscuit vtile dulci.

London
Printed for H. Cripps and are to be sold
at his Shop in Popes-head Allie
and by E. Wallis at the Horsshoe
in the Old Bayley.
1660.

Over his head appears the sky,
And Saturn Lord of Melancholy.

2.   To th' left a landscape of Jealousy
Presents itself unto thine eye.
A Kingfisher, a Swan, an Hern,
Two fighting-Cocks you may discern ;
Two roaring Bulls each other hie
To assault concerning Venery.
Symbols are these ; I say no more,
Conceive the rest by that's afore.

3.   The next of Solitariness
A Portraiture doth well express,
By sleeping Dog, Cat : Buck and Dee,
Hares, Conies in the desert go :
Bats, Owls the shady bowers over,
In melancholy darknesse hover.
Mark well ; if't be not as't should be,
Blame the bad Cutter, and not me.

4.   I' th' under Column there doth stand
Inamorato with folded hand ;
Down hangs his head, terse and polite,
Some ditty sure he doth indite
His lute and books about him lie,
As symptoms of his vanity.
If this do not enough disclose,
To paint him, take thyself by th' nose.

5.   Hypochondriacus leans on his arm,
Wind in his side doth him much harm,
And troubles him full sore, God knows,
Much pain he hath and many woes.

About him pots and glasses lie,
Newly brought from's Apothecary.
This Saturn's aspects signify,
You see them portray'd in the sky.

6.   Beneath them kneeling on his knee,
A Superstitious man you see :
He fasts, prays, on his Idol fixt,
Tormented hope and fear betwixt :
For hell perhaps he takes more pain,
Than thou dost heaven itself to gain.
Alas poor Soul, I pity thee,
What stars incline thee so to be ?

7.   But see the Madman rage down right
With furious looks, a ghastly sight.
Naked in chains bound doth he ly,
And roars amain, he knows not why ?
Observe him ; for as in a glass,
Thine angry portraiture it was.
His picture keep still in thy presence ;
Twixt him and thee, there's no difference.

8. 9.   Borage and Hellebore fill two scenes,
Sovereign plants to purge the veins
Of Melancholy, and cheer the heart,
Of those black fumes which make it smart ;
To clear the Brain of misty fogs,
Which dull our senses, and Soul clogs.
The best medicine that e'er God made
For this malady, if well assaid.

10.   Now last of all to fill a place,
Presented to the Author's face ;

And in that habit which he wears,
His image to the world appears.
His mind no art can well express,
That by his writings you may guess.
It was not price, nor yet vain glory,
(Though others do it commonly)

Made him to this : if you must know,
The Printer would needs have it so.
Then do not frown or scoff at it,
Deride not, nor detract a whit.
For surely as thou dost by him,
He will do the same again.
Then look upon't, behold and see,
As thou lik'st it, so it likes thee.

And I for it will stand in view,
Thine to command, Reader, Adieu !

8.   THE CALL TO GREATNESS

In divers places I have let it shimmer through that even as geniuses
go, Francis Bacon was not in the ordinary run of their class.   There was
in him a superior spiritual quality, touching deeper the true realities of
life, and especially more all-embracing and universal of character, than
I had ever met the like in any other of the wise and great men of the
West ; something that affected me in much the same way as the ancient
Rishis of India did, something of Brahman attained by Yoga, something
of the universal consciousness contacted.   Not a mere man, but the
divine in man, walking the earth amongst men.   Similar thoughts must
have moved the faithful pen of his biographer, when in the short but

weighty *Life* of his Master Rawley mused : " I have been induced to
think that, if there were *a beam of knowledge derived from God* upon
any man in these modern times, it was upon him.   For though he was
a great reader of books, yet he had not his knowledge from books, but
from *some grounds and notions from within himself.*" [1]

The thought expressed in the words italicized, we in modern
times have come to call intuition, the " inner vision," let us say, of the
things that are not of the earth, but of the spirit eternal.   Or the " inner
ear " listening for the Voice that always calls within us, but is too often
drowned by the multitudinous voices of the world.   How it made itself
heard to the youth, Francis, in no uncertain accents, is told us in the
Great Word-Cipher, as unravelled by Dr. Orville Owen : [2]

The Call

One night, when a youth, while we were reading in the holy
scriptures of our great God, something compelled us to turn to the
Proverbs,[3] and read that passage of Solomon, the king, wherein he
affirmeth, that the glory of God is to conceal a thing, but the glory of
a king is to find it out.   And we thought how odd and strange it read,
and attentively looked into the subtlety of the passage.   As we read
and pondered the wise words and lofty language of this precious book
of love, there comes a flame of fire which fills all the room, and
obscures our eyes with its celestial glory, and from it swells a heavenly
voice that, lifting our mind above her human bounds, ravisheth our soul
with its sweet, heavenly music.   And thus it spake :

My son, fear not, but take thy fortunes and
Thy honours up.   Be that thou know'st thou art,
For then thou art as great as that thou fear'st.
Thou art not what thou seemest.   At thy birth
The front of heav'n was full of fiery shapes ;

[1] *Ante*, p. 81.

[2] Ow I 32-34.

[3] Ch. 25, vs. 2.

> The goats ran from the mountains, and the herds
> Were strangely clam'rous to the frighted fields.
> These signs have mark'd thee extra-ordin'ry,
> And all the courses of thy life will show
> Thou art not in the roll of common men.
> Where is the living who will call thee pupil,
> Or who will read to thee ? And bring him out
> That is but woman's son will trace thee in
> The tedious ways of art, and hold thee pace
> In deep exper'ment ? *Be thou not, therefore,*
> *Afraid of greatness, I charge thee.*   Thy fates
> Open their hands to thee.   Decline them not,
> But let thy blood and spirit them embrace,
> And climb the height of virtue's sacred hill,
> Where endless honour shall be made thy mead.

There is the ringing note of the old Hebrew Prophets in this challenge to greatness.   There is also the deep conviction of their own greatness in those truly wise men—to be the pupil of no man, to be the teacher of all men, a thought essential in the conception of all the greatest Indian teachers : Rama, Krishna, Buddha.

> For Thou
> Art teacher of thy teachers—Thou, not I,
> Art Guru.   O, I worship Thee, sweet Prince !
> That comest to my school only to show
> Thou knowest all without the books, and know'st
> Fair reverence beside.

Thus young Siddharta's teacher to the Prince.[1]

---

[1] Edwin Arnold, *The Light of Asia.*

9.   SOME MORE LIONS, BEARS AND BOARS

While seeing this work through the press, and having come so far as these Addenda in the printing, I had the good fortune one night, when reading the Third Part of *Henry VI*, in a purely literary mood, of having my eye caught by another example of the heraldic symbols depicting Bacon's royal birth. On page 212 above I have given one example from *Venus and Adonis*. Here in *3 Henry VI* (II 1), I found a passage, strikingly similar, not only in the enumeration of the same wild animals, but also in the description of the same hunting-scene—the quarry driven to its last stand, exhausted maybe but still defiant, " the hounds at bay." For the sake of comparison I subjoin both texts here in their old spelling :

> *Venus and Adonis*
> For now she knowes it is no gentle chase,
> But the blunt *boare*, rough *beare*, or *lyon* proud,
> Because the crie remaineth in one place,
> Where fearefully the dogs exclaime aloud,
>   Finding their enemie to be so curst,
>   They all straine curt'sie who shall cope him first.

> *3 Henry VI*
> Me thought he *bore* him in the thickest troupe,
> As doth a *Lyon* in a Heard of Neat,
> Or as a *Beare* encompass'd round with Dogges :
> Who having pincht a few, and made them cry,
> The rest stand all aloofe, and barke at him.

That the word " bore " in the last text does not mean the animal, is of course a perfectly legitimate subterfuge to evade too easy detection. The similarity of the scene described, on the other hand, invites comparison—as was undoubtedly the author's intention—with the *Venus and Adonis* text, and so might lead the diligent reader who knows his Shakespeare well, to the revealing truth.

But knowing " our Shakespeare " fairly well also from another aspect, I looked for further confirmation of this supposed intention. I had found the *Henry VI* passage on page 152 of the Histories in the Folio. I now turned to the corresponding page 152 of the Comedies, and there indeed I found the same three animals, and one of them— the Boar of course—again disguised, in a different way, for the author's ingenuity would only rarely allow him to use the same device more than once. On that page, then, we find in the 3rd line of the first column the *Lion*, and in the 8th and 10th line of the second column, twice the *Hog*—kindred of the *Boar*!—and the *Bear*.

Satisfied, I continued my reading of *Henry VI*, for pure enjoyment. But it did not last long, for even in the very next scene my eyes met the following :

> To whom do *Lyons* cast their gentle Lookes ?
> Not to the Beast, that would usurpe their Den.
> Whose hand is that the Forrest *Beare* doth licke ?
> Not his that spoyles her young before her face.

It is true, when turning again to the Folio, page 154, I could find no Boar, or whichever of his many kindred, but I found better even, Saint Albans himself, in the verse :

> When you and I, met at *S. Albons* last.

For once, I thought that sufficient to the night were the discoveries thereof, and went to bed content in heart and mind, only to awake the next morning fresh for new adventures. This time I took Burton's *Anatomy* from the bookshelf, and what I found on p. 150-151 (possibly on one page in the old original) of the first volume of Shilleto's edition, were again the three wild animals, thus :

> p. 150, line 5, a fox, a dog, a *hog*,
> p. 150, line 2 footnote, furore *leonem*,
> p. 151, line 13, We rore like *bears*.

10.   STILL MORE BOARS AND KINDRED

In *Venus and Adonis* there still are the following sign-manuals of Bacon's workmanship.

The poem consists of 199 stanzas, and

Francis Tidder of England=199=*Your Bore-speare-man.*

In stanza 99, we find the words *boar* (line 1) and *hanging* (line 5), which connects it with the famous Baconian hang-hog anecdote, and the Shakepearean " hang-hog which is Latin for Bacon." Besides,

The Old Bore=99=*Bore-speare.*

In stanza 111 we again meet with the words *boar* (line 2) and *hang* (line 6), and further with the word " head " (also in line 6), and this leads us of course to Bacon as the " Boar's Head," and Shakspeyr as the " Boar without a head."   Further,

Francis Rex=111=*England's King.*

In stanza 107 there are the words *will* (line 3) and *boar* (line 5), again in another way connecting Shakespeare and Bacon.

This is also the case in stanza 103, where we find the connection laid in still another way, through the words *boar* (line 2) and *javelin* (line 4), or spear.   Besides,

103 = Shakespeare

The *Sonnets* also bear apparently Francis Bacon's peculiar imprint, for in Sonnet 125 we find both, the word " bore " (first line) and the word " free " (tenth line).   Still for another reason this Sonnet is significant.   I give it therefore in full.

> Were't ought to me I bore the canopy,
> With my extern the outward honouring,
> Or laid great bases for eternity,
> Which prove more short than waste or ruining ?
> Have I not seen dwellers on form and favour
> Lose all, and more, by paying too much rent,
> For compound sweet foregoing simple savour,
> Pitiful thrivers, in their gazing spent ?
> No, let me be obsequious in thy heart,
> And take thou my oblation, poor but free,
> Which is not mixed with seconds, knows no art
> But mutual render, only me for thee.
>> Hence, thou suborned informer ! a true soul
>> When most impeached stands least in thy control.

There is perhaps no Shakespearean commentator who reads the phrase " I bore the canopy," other than as " purely figurative " (T. G. Tucker), or as merely " a metaphor " (C. Knox Pooler), and the poem as addressed to nobody but the " lovely boy " of the next Sonnet.

I for one, and most Baconians, I presume, have however another idea.   The Sonnets, as every true poem of that kind especially, is a communion of the Poet with his innermost being and the archetypal ideals he finds there, as compared with the imperfect things in this

44

world of the senses, the former shedding the lustre of their beauty over the latter, and so aiding the reader for himself to reach a glimpse of that inner glory. In one Sonnet it may be the ideal of bodily beauty, in another the moral beauty of his friend's soul, in the next the ideal of beauty, or love, or friendship, or loyalty (Sonnet 123, 124) *in abstracto*, though personified under the image of his friend, which the Poet invokes. Sonnet 125, in my opinion, is in particular a soul-communion of Francis Bacon with his great sovereign, and secret mother, Queen Elizabeth, to whom he protests real inner loyalty and devotion, though perhaps he may not show the outward homage which the world only recognizes as such. The phrase, "I bore the canopy" is thus taken in its literal meaning, derived from experience, from having now and again, more especially in his youth, actually functioned as canopy-bearer to the Virgin-Queen so-called, on less formal and grand occasions naturally than the scene described for example in *Henry VIII*, when the canopy was born above the head of Anne Bullen, Bacon's grandmother (IV 1), and over his own mother at her christening when a babe (V 5).

So also, the "suborned informer" of the last line but one, generally considered by Shakespeareans as "not referring to any particular individual," is on the contrary a real living man, no other than Robert Cecil of course. In the same way, I think, Sonnet 121 (and there are others more) refers to the same abusive power with his "spies," which has been so detrimental to Bacon's relations with the Queen.

If we now turn to Shakespeare's Histories, Folio 84 (*2 Henry IV*, II 4), there is in the first column, line 14, "Bartholmew *Bore-pigge*," and in the second column, line 6, "Some sack, *Francis*." The remarkable points in this signature are the open use of the Christian name, the only time it occurs on this page, and the double designation for the animal symbol.

And in the Tragedies, Folio 381 (*Cymbeline* III 2), we find in the first column, line 54, "the *bores* of hearing," and in the second column, line 11, "A *Frank*lines Huswife." The obvious meaning of "bores" here is of course "holes," just as in the example given above on page 217,

Finally, in *The Anatomy of Melancholy* Shilleto's edition, vol. I, p. 149, line 18, there is the word " free," and on p. 150, line 5, the word " Hog," which again gives the signature Francis Bacon. In the old original the two words may possibly appear on the same page.

11.   IL DIAVOLO

To complete the figure of Robert Cecil, drawn in the first part of Chapter 2, some more extracts from Shakespeare are given here.

Comedy of Errors

He is deformèd, crookèd, old and sere,
Ill-faced, worse bodied, shapeless everywhere,
Vicious, ungentle, foolish, blunt, unkind,
Stigmatical in making, worse in mind.

(IV 2, 19-22)

3 Henry VI

That valiant crook-back prodigy,
        . . . with his grumbling voice.

(I 4, 75-6)

  A foul mis-shapen stigmatic,
Mark'd by the destinies to be avoided,
As venom toads, or lizards' dreadful stings.

(II 3, 136-8)

Why, love forswore me in my mother's womb :
And, for I should not deal in her soft laws,
She did corrupt frail nature with some bribe,
To shrink mine arm up like a wither'd shrub ;
To make an envious mountain on my back,
Where sits deformity to mock my body ;

To shape my legs of an unequal size ;
To disproportion me in every part,
Like to a chaos, or an unlick'd bear-whelp
That carries no impression like the dam.

(III 2, 153-162)

The owl shriek'd at thy birth, an evil sign ;
The night-crow cried, aboding luckless time ;
Dogs howl'd, and hideous tempest shook down trees !
The raven rook'd her on the chimney's top,
And chattering pies in dismal discords sung.
Thy mother felt more than a mother's pain,
And yet brought forth less than a mother's hope ;
To wit an indigest deformed lump,
Not like the fruit of such a goodly tree.
Teeth hadst thou in thy head when thou wast born,
To signify thou cam'st to bite the world.

(V 6, 44-54)

I, that have neither pity, love, nor fear.
Indeed, 'tis true, that Henry told me of ;
For I have often heard my mother say
I came into the world with my legs forward.
Had I not reason, think ye, to make haste,
And seek their ruin that usurp'd our right ?
The midwife wonder'd, and the women cried
"O ! Jesus bless us, he is born with teeth."
And so I was ; which plainly signified
That I should snarl and bite and play the dog.
Then, since the heavens have shap'd my body so,
Let hell make crook'd my mind to answer it.
I have no brother, I am like no brother ;
And this word " love," which greybeards call divine,
Be resident in men like one another
And not in me : I am myself alone.

(V 6, 68-83)

The criticism has been raised that these terrible descriptions, if really aimed at a living man, belong to the most scandalous invective and libel ever allowed to appear in print, and that they are irreconcilable with the serene and angelic nature we have claimed for their author, whom they on the contrary expose as of a much disturbed and vindictive character. But such a judgment is based on an entire misconception of the art of a great dramatic writer, which is that of giving an adequate portrait of the good and the evil he sees in his fellowmen. The greater the genius the more deeply will the chords of his being be touched, whether in harmony or in discord, by what he observes. Touched, I say, and set strongly atremble, but in an impersonal way, not so as to disturb and throw him out of the equilibrium, which is a necessary attainment of high art, into personal abuse and vindictiveness.

Strictly, therefore, we cannot say that these passages were aimed at Robert Cecil, in the sense of their aiming to depict him as an individual. It was the general type Bacon had in view, that type, of concentrated evil as it were, of which Cecil was only the most true and fearful embodiment he evidently had met in actual life. Nay—of hate or vindictiveness there was no trace in him, as is proved by the unanimous testimony of those contemporaries who knew him best, as well as by his own reading of his character.

Matthew : " A man most sweet in his ways, a friend unalterable to his friends, an enemy to no man " (*ante*, p. 70).

Boener : "I never saw him changed or disturbed towards whomsoever, he was ever one and the same, in sorrow and in joy, a noteworthy example and pattern for everyone of all virtue, gentleness, peacefulness and patience " (*ante*, p. 78).

Rawley : " When his office called him to charge any offenders, he was always tender-hearted, as one that looked upon the *example* [set by the offender] with the eye of severity, but upon the *person* [of the offender] with the eye of pity and compassion. This is most true—he was free from malice (as he said himself) *he never bred nor fed*. He was no revenger of injuries. He was no defamer of any man " (*ante*, pp. 83-84).

French Life : "Never was there man who so loved equity. If he felt hatred and rage, it was only against evildoers, to show his detestation of their crimes [not their persons]. It seemed that Nature had exempted him from the ordinary frailties of men " (*ante*, pp. 318-319).

12. THE BILITERAL ALPHABET

Bacon's system of double signs is the basis of our modern telegraphic Morse code, and of other systems of signalling.

As to the double alphabet system, there are various ways of forming the biliteral cipher. Two methods are given below, the first of which was followed by Bacon in the ninth Book of the *De Dignitate et Augmentis Scientiarum*.

1			2	
aaaaa	A	1	aaaaa	A
aaaab	B	2	aaaab	B
aaaba	C	3	aaaba	C
aaabb	D	4	aabaa	D
aabaa	E	5	abaaa	E
aabab	F	6	baaaa	F
aabba	G	7	aaabb	G
aabbb	H	8	aabab	H
abaaa	I,J	9	aabba	I
abaab	K	10	abaab	J
ababa	L	11	ababa	K
ababb	M	12	abbaa	L
abbaa	N	13	baaab	M
abbab	O	14	baaba	N
abbba	P	15	babaa	O
abbbb	Q	16	bbaaa	P

baaaa	R	17	aabbb	Q
baaab	S	18	ababb	R
baaba	T	19	abbab	S
baabb	U,V	20	abbba	T
babaa	W	21	baabb	U
babab	X	22	babab	V
babba	Y	23	babba	W
babbb	Z	24	bbaab	X
bbaaa		25	bbaba	Y
bbaab		26	bbbaa	Z
bbaba		27	abbbb	
bbabb		28	babbb	
bbbaa		29	bbabb	
bbbab		30	bbbab	
bbbba		31	bbbba	
bbbbb		32	bbbbb	

Closer inspection will show that the second method requires the use of a lesser number of *b* letters—49 instead of 52—to represent the whole alphabet of 24 letters of Bacon's time, and that even the alphabet of our own time with its 26 letters may be represented by not more than three *b* letters in a group of five, whereas Bacon had need of two groups of five with four *b* letters each, for the letters Q and Z.

The lesser number of *b* letters, however, might be raised as an objection against the second method. For, one might argue, the nearer the numbers of *a* and *b* letters equal each other, the less they would rouse suspicion. But I think that such reasoning is wrong. The suspicion is aroused by the difference between the two forms of letters, and the more differences there are, the greater not only the cause for suspicion, but probably also the possibility of detecting the method. Anyhow, if Bacon had indeed thought that an equal number of *a* and *b* letters would have been more advantageous for his purpose, he could easily have done better than he did, by having had some of the lesser combinations replaced by four-*b* combinations. That he did not do so, is for either of two reasons—(1) the objection never entered his head, or (2) he did not think it serious enough to disturb the regular sequence of his method of grouping the biliteral cipher. The first case I think to be the most probable. As to the second method of grouping the alphabet, given above, I think that, if Bacon had thought of it, he would undoubtedly have adopted it, because of its greater simplicity.

13.   LOOSE THREADS

Another example of the theme that friend's love goes before lady's love is found in *The Old Wives' Tale* by George Peele, also a Bacon Mask. Eumenides is ready to part with his lady-love altogether, rather than break the promise he had given his friend.

> Well, ere I will falsify my word unto my friend, take her all :
> here, Jack, I'll give her thee.

Compare these words with those of Valentine, Bassanio and Gratiano, on pages 165-167 above.

To the " next myself " theme in connection with Anthony Bacon, dealt with on pages 156-160 above, add the following from *The Tempest* (I 2, 66). Prospero addresses his daughter Miranda :

> My brother . . . called Antonio
>   . . . whom *next myself*
> Of all the world I loved.

Regarding Bacon's command of a rich variety of styles (see page 98 above), Mr. S. H. Reynolds, in his edition of the *Essays*, says : " To speak of Bacon's style is in strict terms impossible. Almost the only attribute common to his writings is that they bear the mark of a great and confident self-esteem. . . The fact seems to be that *Bacon had at all times almost any style at command*" (As quoted by Harman in *The Impersonality of Shakespeare*, p. 247).

In 1591 was published " *A Maidens Dreame*, Upon the Death of the right Honorable Sir Christopher Hatton Knight, late Lord Chancellor of England, By Robert Green Master of Arts. Imprinted at London by Thomas Scarlet for Thomas Nelson." The last stanza of this poem, as published by J. Churton Collins in *The Plays and Poems of Robert Greene*, Oxford, 1905, vol II, p. 235, has the acrostic Francis Bacon, as follows :

> As thus attendant *faire A*strea flew,
> The *N*obles, *C*ommons, yea and every w*i*ght,
> That living in his life time Hatton knew,
> Did deepe lament the losse of that good Knight :
> *B*ut when *A*strea was quite out of sight,
> For griefe that people shouted such a screame :
> That I awoke a*n*d start out of my dreame.

Marlowe's " *Famous Tragedy of the Rich Jew of Malta*," as it was printed in 1633, has a prologue spoken at Court, which in the version published by C. F. Tucker Brooke in *The Works of Christopher Marlowe*, Oxford, 1920, p. 238, has the acrostic Francis Verulam.

> Gracious and Great, that we so boldly dare,
> ('Mongst other Playes that now in *f*ashion a*r*e)
> To present this ; writ m*a*ny years agone,
> And in that Age, thought second unto none ;
> We humbly crave your pardon : we pursue
> The story of a r*i*ch and famous Jew
> Who li*u*'d in Malta : you shall find him still,
> In all his proi*e*cts, a sound Macheuill ;
> And that's his Cha*r*acter : He that hath past
> So many Cens*u*res, is now come at *la*st
> To haue your princely Eares : grace you hi*m* ; then
> You crowne the Action, and renowne the pen.

45

14. THE ILLUSTRATIONS AND DECORATIONS

1. *Elizabeth Tudor*, Frontispiece. Reproduction of a painting by the Dutch Master Cornelis Ketel in the Accademia di Belle Arti in Siena.

2. *Francis Tudor*, facing page 39.

    I. At the age of twelve. Reproduction of " a very correct engraving " made of " a coloured bust in terra-cotta, one of a set of three, said to be portraits of Sir Nicholas Bacon, Anne, his second wife, and their son Francis, when twelve years old " (Sp VI vi).

    II. At the age of eighteen. Reproduction of the miniature by Hilliard. See *ante* p. 66.

3. *Frank Boar*, facing page 87. Reproduction of the frontispiece to the *Opera Omnia*, Frankfort 1665.

4. *William Shakespeare*, facing page 135. Reproduction of the Droeshout picture on the title-page of the 1623 Folio.

5. *The Bore-spear-man*, facing page 189. This is a reproduction of the picture of " Sir Thomas Meautys in Hunting Dress," facing page 5 of Chambers Bunten's book on this friend and secretary of Lord Bacon. The author gives the following description of it (p. 6) : " The picture, said to be by Van Somer, which visitors see in Gorhambury House, shows a tall, fair-haired man, in the elaborate hunting dress of the day—steel embossed breastplate, feathered cap, leather buskins with spurs, and a rich scarf across his shoulders ; a sword at his side, and *a boar spear in his right hand*. A long string attached to the hat, prevents it flying off. He is wearing a collar of Charles I period, and we therefore presume that this was the full ceremonial dress worn as ' Master of the Hunt.' "

6. *The Clock Cipher*, facing page 197.

7. *Lion, Bear and Boar*, facing page 213. Reproduction of the title-page to Spenser's *Works*, 1611.

8. *The Greedy Sow*, facing page 235.   Reproduction of page
    53 of George Whitney's book on *Emblems*, 1586.
9. *Psalm 46*, facing page 295.   Reproduction of the left-hand
    column, folio Ddd 3 of the Black Letter *Bible*, 1611.
10. *The Anatomy of Melancholy*, facing page 337.   Reproduction
    of the frontispiece of Burton's famous book.

Besides the above pictures, the book is decorated with symbol
and cipher designs derived from Francis Bacon's symbols and ciphers.
The Boar, the Spear, Bacon's Coat of Arms on the binding, the
title-page, the first pages of the two Parts, and the initial capitals of the
Chapters, are obvious.   The latter also spell the word "Borespeare."
Then there are the head-pieces to the first pages of every Chapter.
These spell, when unravelled, the letters F. B. A., so often found in the
old editions of the Bacon-Shakespeare works, and explained above
on pages 234-236.

All these designs and the whole lay-out of the book are the work
of a young artist friend and compatriot of mine, Mr. Conrad Woldringh,
to whom my grateful thanks are due for all the beauty he has given to
the appearance of my book, and the harmony he has brought between
its form and contents.

L'Envoy

Lord of my love, to whom in vassalage
Thy merit has my duty strongly knit,
To thee I send this written ambassage,
To witness duty, not to show my wit :

Duty so great, which wit so poor as mine
May make seem bare, in wanting words to show it,
But that I hope some good conceit of thine
In thy soul's thought all naked, will bestow it ;

Till whatsoever star that guides my moving,
Points on me graciously with fair aspect,
And puts apparel on my tattered loving,
To show me worthy of thy sweet respect.

Index

Errata

P. 130, line 21, read : Chapter 7 (pp. 222-3)
P. 279, ,, 20, ,, : landscape
P. 323, ,, 16, ,, : occasion

www.ingramcontent.com/pod-product-compliance
Lightning Source LLC
Chambersburg PA
CBHW032141010726
47494CB00002B/315